CITY SURGEON, SMALL TOWN MIRACLE

BY
MARION LENNOX

BACHELOR DAD, GIRL NEXT DOOR

BY
SHARON ARCHER

 MILLS & BOON®

Hot-shot City Docs...
Small Town Brides!

These top-notch doctors have left their cosmopolitan city lives behind them and sailed into warm and welcoming small towns!

Here they've found communities that have made them feel at home—and beautiful, independent women who claim their hearts!

It won't be long before wedding bells will be ringing out in these two small Australian towns!

CITY SURGEON, SMALL TOWN MIRACLE
by Marion Lennox

and

BACHELOR DAD, GIRL NEXT DOOR
by Sharon Archer

CITY SURGEON, SMALL TOWN MIRACLE

BY
MARION LENNOX

With thanks to the fabulous Anne Gracie,
whose friendship means the world to me.

First published in Great Britain 2010
Harlequin Mills & Boon Limited,
Eton House, 18-24 Paradise Road, Richmond, Surrey TW9 1SR

© Marion Lennox 2010

ISBN: 978 0 263 87878 3

Harlequin Mills & Boon policy is to use papers that are natural,
renewable and recyclable products and made from wood grown in
sustainable forests. The logging and manufacturing process conform
to the legal environmental regulations of the country of origin.

Printed and bound in Spain
by Litografia Rosés, S.A., Barcelona

Dear Reader

Sometimes reality meshes with the stories in my head. This year, a visit to a friend with a passion for ancient tractors was followed by a holiday to Coogee—one of Sydney's fabulous beaches. While we were there the lights went out. No power! And, what was worse, no breakfast coffee. *Aagh!* So, while the love of my life tried to read his morning paper in a café so dimly lit I could barely see the table, I was forced to sit over cold cereal and think up a story instead.

The couple at the next table were fussing over their sleeping baby. They looked to be older first-time parents, and their love for each other and their joyful adoration of their beautiful daughter shone out despite the gloom. That'll do, I thought, as I sulked over my orange juice. I named them Max and Maggie, and their lovely baby Rose. But there's always an obstacle to a truly great romance, and suddenly those tractors sprang to mind. Sadly, that's where my story stopped. There's only so much a woman can do without caffeine :-(

Luckily the power came back on, and with it came coffee. Hooray, I thought as I headed home to start Chapter One. I've fallen in love with Maggie and Max and Rose and tractors. I hope you do, too.

Happy reading

Marion

Marion Lennox is a country girl, born on an Australian dairy farm. She moved on—mostly because the cows just weren't interested in her stories! Married to a 'very special doctor', Marion writes Medical™ Romances, as well as Mills & Boon® Romances. (She used a different name for each category for a while—if you're looking for her past Mills & Boon® Romances, search for author Trisha David as well.) She's now had 75 romance novels accepted for publication.

In her non-writing life Marion cares for kids, cats, dogs, chooks and goldfish. She travels, she fights her rampant garden (she's losing) and her house dust (she's lost). Having spun in circles for the first part of her life, she's now stepped back from her 'other' career, which was teaching statistics at her local university. Finally she's reprioritised her life, figured out what's important, and discovered the joys of deep baths, romance and chocolate. Preferably all at the same time!

Recent titles by the same author:

A SPECIAL KIND OF FAMILY*
A BRIDE AND CHILD WORTH WAITING FOR**
WANTED: ROYAL WIFE AND MOTHER†
A ROYAL MARRIAGE OF CONVENIENCE†

*Mills & Boon® Medical™ Romance
**_Crocodile Creek_
†Mills & Boon® Romance

CHAPTER ONE

THE road was narrow, with a sheer cliff face on one side and a steep fall-away to the sea on the other. The scenery was fantastic, but Dr Max Ashton was in no mood to enjoy the view. He'd had enough of this bucolic setting. He'd had enough of holiday. All he wanted was to get back to Sydney, to work and to solitude.

Which wasn't happening anytime soon. As he nosed his gorgeous, midnight-blue sports coupé around the fourth blind bend since town, a cattle truck veered around from the opposite direction. The small but ancient truck wasn't travelling at speed, and neither was he, but the road was too narrow to let them both pass.

The truck jerked sideways into the cliff-face and the back of the tray swung out to meet him. Collision was inevitable, and collision was what happened.

He wasn't hurt—his car was too well built for that—but it took moments to react to the shock, to see past his inflated airbags to assess the damage.

Mess, he thought grimly, but no smoke. The cab of the truck didn't look badly damaged, and his own car looked bent but not broken. Hopefully this meant nothing but the hassle of a probably uninsured idiot who didn't know enough to keep rust-buckets off the road.

But the accident wasn't over yet. There was a bang, like a minor explosion, and the back of the truck jerked sideways. A tyre had just decided to burst. As he stared out past his airbags, the steel crate on the rear of the truck lurched in sympathy—and didn't stop. It slewed off the truck and crashed sideways down onto the edge of the road.

It was as if a bucket of legs was suddenly upended. A cluster of calves, a soft toffee colour, with huge eyes, white faces and white feet, was tumbling out onto the road. He couldn't count them for sure. They were too entwined.

The tangle of calves, all legs, tails and wide, scared eyes, was scrambling for collective purchase, failing and pushing itself further toward the edge of the cliff. Before Max could react, the calves disappeared from view, and from the cabin of the truck came a woman's frantic scream.

'No-o-o!'

Shock and the airbags had kept him still for all of thirty seconds, but the scream jolted him out of his stupor. He was out of the car before the scream had ended, heading for the cab.

The truck's passenger side was crumpled into the cliff but the driver's side looked okay. As he reached it, the cab door swung open and a woman staggered out. A blur of black and white flashed past her. A collie?

'Stop them,' she yelled, shoving past him as if he wasn't there. 'Bonnie, go. Fetch them back.'

And the black and white blur was gone.

She was bleeding. All he noticed in that first brief glance was a slight figure in faded jeans, blood streaming down her face, but it was enough.

He grabbed her arm as she headed past, and tugged her

towards him. She wrenched back, fighting to be free, but she was small enough that he could stop her. He reeled her in against him, an armful of distressed woman intent on following her calves over the edge of the cliff.

'Let me go,' she yelled. 'They're Gran's calves. Stop them.'

In answer he held her tighter. No matter how bad his weekend had been up to now, no matter that this woman had just made it worse, he was feeling a certain obligation to stop her self-destructing.

'You're hurt.'

She was. There was blood oozing from a cut on the side of her head, and she was staggering, as if one of her legs wasn't doing what it was supposed to.

She was also pregnant. Seven months or so. Apart from the pregnancy she looked like a kid, scruffy, dressed in worn jeans, a blood-spattered windcheater and ancient leather boots. What else? He was doing a lightning assessment as she struggled. Her carrot-red hair was tied roughly into two bright plaits. She had a cute snub nose, freckles and wide green eyes, currently filled with fear.

She was hurt. There was no way he could let her chase calves.

'Sit,' he said, and tried to propel her to the edge of the road, but she wasn't about to be propelled.

'Gran's calves.' She was practically weeping. 'She has to see them before… Please, let me go!' She made to shove past him again, but he wasn't moving.

'Not until I see how badly you're injured. You've cut your head.'

She swiped blood from her face with her sleeve and glared up at him, and he was astonished at the strength of her glare. 'It's not arterial,' she gasped. 'If I'm bleeding out then I'm not bleeding in so there's nothing to worry about. I'm not about to drop dead from raised intracranial pressure, so let me go.'

Too focussed to note her unexpected knowledge, Max settled for a calm 'No.'

'Yes.' Then before he could react she kicked out. Her boot hit his shin. Hard.

He was so astounded he let her go, and she was over the cliff like the hounds of hell were after her.

Luckily the cliff wasn't sheer. It was a steep incline, sloping sharply twenty feet down to the beach, so the calves—he could count four now they'd disentangled themselves—hadn't fallen. They looked essentially unhurt, and were heading north along the sand, with the collie tearing after them.

The woman was presumably wanting to tear after them as well, and for a fraction of a second he was tempted to let her go.

That wasn't exactly heroic, he thought ruefully. Neither was it possible. She was battered and torn and pregnant, and she was heading off to rescue calves that he'd been in part responsible for releasing. So he groaned and headed down the cliff after her.

He had no trouble catching up to her, but as he reached her she swiped out at him and kept on going. She lurched as she put weight on what presumably was an injured leg. He grabbed her again—and she kicked him again.

Why was he doing this? Her rust-bucket of a truck had caused this mess. She'd kicked him and her boots packed a painful punch. *Women*, he thought bitterly. Since his wife's death he'd carefully constructed a solid and impervious armour, and once again his desire to retreat behind it came to the fore. Why worry? She could head off after her calves and her dog, and he could ring a tow truck and wait for her to come to her senses.

But she was bleeding, and she was pregnant.

Personal choice didn't come into this. Doctors didn't sign the Hippocratic oath anymore, but conscience was insidious. Besides, he wasn't at all sure she was bright enough to stop before she passed out from shock or blood loss, and an unconscious woman would complicate his life so much he didn't want to think about it.

So he groaned and headed off again, and snagged her just as she hit the beach. This time he grabbed her by the back of her jeans. She swung back to face him, already lashing out, but he was ready for her. He reeled her in by the waist and swung her up into his arms, tugging her so close she couldn't struggle.

'Let me go. I'll bleed on you,' she snapped, and she had a point. He'd bought this jacket in Italy and he liked it. Ruining it for a woman who didn't have a grain of sense to bless herself with seemed a waste. But it was unavoidable.

'Go right ahead, I'll send you the cleaning bill.'

'Blood doesn't come out of leather.'

'No, it comes out of torn skin, which is why you have to shut up, keep still and let me put something on your head to stop the bleeding.'

'I can fix it myself—when I've got the calves. Do you have any idea how I'm going to tell Gran where her cows are?'

'You could say, "Gran, they're on the beach,"' he said mildly, ignoring her struggles and starting to climb the cliff again. 'Okay, they're important but your dog seems to have their measure. They look unhurt. The cliff gets steeper in either direction so my guess is that they'll stay on the beach until you can organise a muster, or whatever you do with cows. Meanwhile my car's in the middle of the road on a blind bend, blocking traffic, and I don't want what's left of it squashed.'

She glared up at him. 'That's a bit inequitable,' she said, and suddenly he saw a hint of humour in her wide eyes. 'What about my truck?'

'I'll save your truck too,' he growled. 'If you'll let me.'

'Thank you,' she said meekly, and abruptly subsided.

He climbed back up to the road, suddenly aware that his own knees weren't too steady. The airbags had kept him safe but shock was setting in. Plus he'd been kicked.

Almost as he thought it he felt an answering tremor in her body. She wasn't as feisty as she was making out, he thought. Or she was hurting more than she'd admit.

Or maybe she was feeling guilty.

'I'm sorry I kicked you,' she said, and to his surprise she put her arms around his neck to hang on. It kept them both steadier as they climbed. It felt okay, too. His knees didn't shake as much when she held him. 'It might have been a little inappropriate,' she conceded. 'Especially since I think the accident was my fault.'

'I'm sure it was your fault.'

'That's not very gracious.' She pushed her hair back from her face—her braids were working loose—then looked at her hand in disgust. She shrugged and put it back round his neck. 'Gross. Look, okay, I overreacted. Yes, I'm bleeding, so maybe you could lend me something to make a bandage. But then I need to go back down to the beach so I can take care of the calves. Maybe you could drive to my farm and ask Gran to send Angus?'

'How far's the farm?'

'Five-minute drive.'

'Angus will rescue you?'

'Angus will rescue the calves.'

'Sorry,' he said, setting her down on the verge. 'I don't

know what fairy-tales you've been reading, but in the ones I read heroes don't put calves before fair maidens.'

'I'm not exactly fair,' she retorted. 'I'm red.'

'So I've noticed.' But she was wilting, he thought, and it worried him. 'So let's stop you getting redder.'

Before she could protest he tugged off his bloodstained jacket, grabbed the sleeve of his very classy shirt—bought in Italy at the same time as his jacket—and ripped it from the shoulder. He folded the linen into a pad, placed it over her forehead and applied pressure.

'That was a very nice shirt,' she said, sounding subdued.

'I'll send you a bill.'

'Do heroes say stuff like that?'

'I believe I just did,' he said, and grinned, and she managed a smile back. Whoa.

She was older than he'd thought—and she was a lot more attractive. Compellingly attractive, in fact.

Her smile was just plain gorgeous.

'I can do that,' she said, and put her hands up, grabbed his shirt-pad and pressed.

As well as being attractive, she was also a lot less stupid than he'd first thought, he conceded. She'd talked about raised intracranial pressure. Did she have medical training?

No matter. She was in no state to practise any medicine right now, and he had no time to concentrate on her smile.

Her head was okay for the moment. But he stood and looked down at her and thought, There's more here than scratches. She was trying to make light of her injuries, but he recognised pain when he saw it.

She'd been limping. One knee of her jeans was shredded and bloodstained, though not nearly as dramatically as her face. Still…

He bent, carefully took the torn part of the leg of her jeans in both hands and ripped it to the ankle.

Hell.

How had she managed to climb down the cliff? How had she stood up at all?

She'd cut her knee—it was bleeding sluggishly—but that was only part of it. Already it had swollen to almost twice its size. There was a massive haematoma building behind.

'Yikes,' she whispered, pushing herself up on her elbows to look. 'Why did you do that? It was better when I couldn't see.'

'Let's get it elevated,' he said, and mentally wished his jacket farewell. He folded it then wedged it under her bloodied knee. A spare tyre had spilled from the cattle crate. He put that under her feet, so her legs were raised on an incline as well.

She needed X-rays. Both leg and head, he thought. No matter what she said, he wasn't about to let her die of an intra-cranial bleed just because she was stubborn. And there was also the biggie. The baby might have suffered a blow, and even if it was okay the impact could cause problems with the placenta. She needed an ultrasound, and bed-rest and observation.

Her baby needed attention. That meant he needed to hand her over and get away. Fast.

'We need an ambulance,' he told her, tugging his cell-phone from his pocket. 'You need X-rays.'

'You can give that up as a joke,' she said wearily. 'Even if there was reception out here—which there isn't—you're looking at Yandilagong's only ambulance right here.'

'Sorry?'

'It's not usually the truck. I have a decent-sized estate wagon, only it blew the radiator hose this morning.'

'What are you talking about?'

'My truck's the local ambulance until I can get a new radiator hose,' she said patiently, as if talking to someone who wasn't very bright. 'And there's not one to be had locally for love or money. I'll get one from Gosland tomorrow—if I can leave Gran for that long.'

'There's no ambulance?' He didn't have time for the extra information she was throwing at him. He needed to ignore what wasn't making sense and concentrate on essentials. 'Why not?'

'You try attracting medical staff or funding for decent equipment to a place as remote as this,' she said bitterly. 'This weekend there'll be a couple of first-aiders with the music festival, but that's all the help I have. If I can't get an ambulance from other areas then I use my own vehicle to take patients to Gosland. That's our nearest hospital, about an hour away. There's basic stuff here, like an X-ray machine, but that's in town, and getting through the crush of the festival isn't going to happen. But it doesn't matter,' she said resolutely. 'I'd like to check my baby's heartbeat but I'm sure I'm fine. I just need to get home to Gran. It's Gran who's the emergency and she doesn't need an ambulance. She needs me.'

Was she some kind of volunteer paramedic? This was sounding crazier and crazier.

He turned away and surreptitiously checked his phone. Sure enough, no reception. Okay, he conceded. No ambulance.

'What's your name?' he asked, trying to figure where to start.

'Maggie. We're wasting time.'

'How pregnant are you?'

'Thirty-two weeks.' And all of a sudden there was a quaver in her voice. 'He's okay.'

'Can you feel him?' Even asking that hurt, he thought. Hell, he'd lost his son six years ago. Would he ever get over it?

Luckily she'd only heard his professional question. 'Yes.' But there was still the quaver. 'He's kicking.'

'Good.' Kicking was good. But as Maggie had said, he needed to check the heartbeat. He wanted a stethoscope. Add it to the list, he thought grimly. Ambulance, X-rays, stethoscope, ultrasound, a medical team to take over while he walked away.

It wasn't going to happen. Meanwhile, there was the small problem of the mess blocking the road.

'If someone else comes round this bend…' he said, trying to figure out priorities.

'It's not used much,' she told him. 'But there's the odd out-of-towner stupid enough to try and get to the highway this way.'

'Gee, thanks.'

She winced. 'Sorry. Yes, that was rude. But we do need to clear the road.' She stared across at the mess. 'You'll need help pulling the crate out of the way. Hang on.' And she put her hands onto the ground to push herself up.

'No!' He was down beside her in an instant, taking a shoulder in each hand and pressing back.

And his preconceptions were changing all over the place. At first he'd thought she was little more than a teenager, like the young mothers he saw clustered outside the prenatal clinics near his consulting suite in the hospital he worked in. They were mostly scared kids, forced by pregnancy into growing up too fast, but the more he saw of this woman the more he acknowledged maturity. There were lines etched around her eyes—smile lines that had taken time to grow. And more. Life lines?

She looked like a woman who'd seen a lot, he thought suddenly.

She wasn't beautiful—not in the traditional sense—and yet

the eyes that met his as he pushed her back down onto the verge were clear and bright and almost luminous. They were eyes to make a man take another look.

And then another.

'Hey, let me up,' she ordered, as if sensing the inappropriate direction his thoughts were taking, and he came to with a snap.

'You want that leg to swell so far I have to lance it to take the pressure off?'

Her eyes widened. 'What the…?'

'You're bleeding into the back of your knee,' he said. 'If it gets any worse you'll have circulation problems. I want it X-rayed. And like you, I'm worrying about the baby. You need an ultrasound.'

'You're a doctor?' Her voice was incredulous.

'For my pains,'

'Well, how about that?' she whispered, sounding awed. 'A doctor, and a bossy one at that. A surgeon, I'll bet.'

'Sort of, but—'

'They're the worst. Look, if I promise to sign insurance indemnity, can I get up?'

'No.'

'The crate…'

'I'll move the truck.'

'You and whose army?'

'Just shut up for a minute,' he said, irritated, and there was her smile again.

'Yes, *Doctor*.'

The words were submissive but the smile wasn't. It was a cute smile. Cheeky. Pert. Flashing out despite her fear.

'You're a nurse,' he demanded, suspicious.

'No, Doctor,' she said, still submissive, still smiling,

though there was no way she could completely disguise the look of pain and fear behind her eyes. 'But you need to let me help.'

'In your dreams,' he growled, disarmed by her smile and struggling to keep a hold on the situation. Worst-case scenario—she could go into labour.

Or she could lose the baby.

Another death…

He needed a medical kit. Usually he carried basic first-aid equipment but his friends' luggage had filled the trunk and the back seat. Fiona and Brenda. No medicine this weekend, they'd said, and they'd meant it.

Women. And here was another, causing trouble.

But, actually, Maggie wasn't causing trouble, he conceded, or no more than she could help. She looked like there was no way she'd complain, but he could see the strain in her eyes.

Okay, he told himself. Move. This woman needs help and there's only me to give it.

'I meant what I said about keeping still,' he told her. 'I have work to do and you'll just get in the way. So stay!'

'Yes, sir,' she said meekly, but he didn't believe the meekness for a minute.

There wasn't a lot of choice. In truth, Maggie's leg hurt so much she was feeling dizzy. She lay back on the grass and tried not to think about the consequences of what had just happened and how it might have affected her baby. That was truly terrifying. She tried not to think how Gran would be needing pain relief, and how she'd been away from home for far too long. She thought about how her leg felt like it might drop off, and that she wouldn't mind if it did.

If this guy really was a doctor he might have something in the back of his fancy car that'd help.

He really was a doctor. He had about him an air of authority and intelligence that she knew instinctively was genuine. He was youngish—mid-thirties, she guessed—but if she had to guess further she'd say he was in a position of power in his profession. He'd be past the hands-on stage with patients—to a point in his profession where seniority meant he could move back from the personal.

She wasn't a bad judge of character. This guy seemed competent—and he was also seriously attractive. Yeah, even in pain she'd noticed that, for what woman wouldn't? He was tall, dark and drop-dead gorgeous. But also he seemed instinctively aloof? Why?

But this was hardly the time for personal assessments of good-looking doctors. The pain in her leg stabbed upward and she switched to thinking what the good-looking doctor might have in the back of his car that might help.

What could she take this far along in pregnancy? Her hands automatically clasped her belly and she flinched. No.

'We need to get through this without drugs,' she whispered to her bump. 'Just hang in there.'

There was an answering flutter from inside, and her tension eased slightly. The seat belt had pulled tight across her stomach in the crash. There'd been an initial flutter, but she wanted more. This flutter was stronger, and as she took a deep breath the flutter became a kick.

Great! Maybe her baby hadn't noticed the crash or, if he had, he was kicking in indignation.

'We'll be okay,' she whispered for what must be the thousandth time in her pregnancy. 'Me and you and the world.'

And she had a doctor at hand. A gorgeous one.

But gorgeous or not, doctor or not, the guy had no time for medicine right now, and her training had her agreeing with him. Triage told her that unless her breathing was impaired or she was bleeding to death, the road had to be cleared. Someone could speed around the corner at any minute and a minor accident could become appalling.

But how could he move the crate? It was blocking the road in such a way it stopped both the car and the truck from being moved. He couldn't lift it.

He didn't. As she watched, he put his shoulder against it, shoving harder than she'd thought possible.

The crate was about eight feet long by six feet wide, iron webbing built around a floor of heavy iron. It had been on the back of the truck for the last twenty years. She'd had no idea it could come loose.

Gran hadn't told her that. There were lots of things Gran hadn't told her, she thought grimly, a long litany of deception. In fact, Maggie's decision to have this baby had been based partly on Gran's deceit.

But there was no way she could yell at Gran now. In truth, she was so worried about the old lady she felt sick.

What else? She wanted to cry because her leg was throbbing. She desperately needed to check on her baby's heartbeat.

But instead she was lying still as ordered, her leg stuck up in front of her, watching this bossy surgeon shift her crate.

If she had to have an arrogant surgeon bossing her while he organised her life, at least she'd been sent one whose body was almost enough to distract her from the pain she was feeling.

When she'd first seen him he'd looked smoothly hand-some, expensive. Now his perfectly groomed, jet-black hair was wet with sweat, dark curls clinging to his forehead. A trace of five-o'clock shadow accentuated his strongly boned face, and his dark eyes were keen with the intent of strain.

He also looked gorgeous. It was an entirely inappropriate thought, she decided, but it was there, whether she willed it or not. This man was definite eye-candy.

He had all his weight against the crate now. He was grunting with effort, sweat glistening. One of his arms was bare—courtesy of the pad she was holding above her eye— and his arm was a mass of sinews. As was his chest. The more he sweated, the more his shirt became a damp and transparent nothing, exposing serious muscles.

And the more he sweated the more she was distracted from everything she should be focussed on. This was crazy. She was seven months pregnant. She was injured. She had so many worries her head was about to explode, yet here she was transfixed by the sight of a colleague attempting to move a weight far too big for one man.

Only it wasn't. The crate was moving, an inch at a time and then faster, and then he found rhythm. He was right behind it and he kept on pushing, right up to the verge.

The verge was too narrow to hold it.

She should have been thinking forward to what he intended, but she was caught. Watching him. Fascinated.

'Move!' He gave one last gigantic heave—and it slid onto the verge and further. Before she realised what was happening, the crate was toppling over the side of the cliff, crashing its way down to the beach below. Leaving her stunned.

'So how do you suggest I get the calves home now?' she muttered, awed, but he wasn't listening. He was in her truck already, shoving it into gear, reversing it from the cliff face. It sounded like something disastrous was happening inside the engine, but at least it moved. He drove it further along the road, parked it on a widened section of verge, then jogged back for his car.

She was a passive audience, stunned by his body and by his energy. And by…his car! She'd never seen an Aston Martin up close before. Not bad, she conceded, growing more distracted by the moment. Surgeon in open-topped roadster. Cool.

Or…hot.

Or maybe the blow to her head was making her thinking fuzzy. She should be too caught up with the pain in her knee to react like…well, like she was reacting.

But then, as he turned his fabulous car away from her, suddenly her fuzziness disappeared. It was replaced with a stab of panic so great it took her breath away. He'd backed away from the cliff, turning the car to head north.

North. Toward Sydney.

She was staggering to her feet, her hands out, rushing straight forward so he had to slam his brakes on or she would have run right into him. As it was, he stopped with barely an inch to spare.

She put her hand on the bonnet and tried to regroup. Tried to think of some way to say that this was panic, she hadn't really thought he'd leave.

She was being hysterical. Insulting.

But she had no breath to say it. She could only lean on his car and gasp. And then he was out of the car, taking her hands, tugging her toward him. He looked shocked to the core, as well he might be. Crazy woman runs straight into path of car.

She had to explain. 'I—I can't leave Gran,' she stammered. 'You have to take me home. You must. You can't leave me here.'

She could hardly breathe through fright. He swore and held her, and then as she couldn't stop trembling he held her tighter.

'Hey, Maggie, I'm not leaving,' he said, sounding appalled. 'I swear. I'm not that big a rat. I was just turning the car away from the bend so it's safe for you to get in.' And then as she tried desperately to think how to respond and could only think that her leg hurt and she was close to tears and she could have killed her baby, by running into a car of all things, how could she have been so stupid, he swore again, tugged her even tighter into his arms and held her close.

'It's okay,' he whispered into her hair. 'I won't leave you. You're safe. I'll take you back to Gran, whoever Gran is. I'll do whatever we have to do. We'll do it together.'

His chin was resting on her hair.

He'd assumed she'd realise he was just moving the car; that he had no intention of leaving her. But why would she assume anything? He was a stranger.

Up until now it had been all about him, he thought, savage with himself. Sure, he'd reacted to her injuries, but he'd reacted as if she was a patient in Emergency where he was one of a team; the surgeon doing his job without looking at the whole picture.

But here he had to see the whole picture.

She had no obvious life-threatening wounds, but she was hurt, she was shocked and she was pregnant. Her truck was a write-off, and without a working cellphone she was stranded.

He'd climbed into his fancy car and turned away, probably making it clear by his body language he wanted to be shot of her. Her reaction—that he was about to leave—was so understandable he felt ill.

So he held her close and waited until her racing heartbeat eased, until he felt the rigid terror go out of her. Finally he felt her body soften, mould into his, take comfort from his hold.

It wasn't exactly professional, to hold her like this, but who was worrying? He'd been shocked, too. If it felt good to hold onto this woman, then so be it. He could take comfort as well as give it.

And it felt good.

Different.

He'd hardly touched a woman for six years. He hadn't wanted to. Now slipping into the edges of shock and concern and the need for professional care came something else.

Desire?

Surely not. There was no way he could desire this woman, for she was everything he most wanted to avoid. To feel like this within moments of meeting her was crazy. But there was no escaping the way touching her made him feel. There was no avoiding the way his body was responding.

Her body was soft, yielding against him. Her hair was naturally curly, and her curls were escaping their braids. Her hair was really cute.

Really soft.

Nice.

And then…*pow*!

The thump between them was such a surprise it drove them apart. They stood at arm's length, staring at each other in astonishment. Then staring down.

'I'm s-so…' she stammered. 'I'm so s-sorry.'

'I don't think it's you who needs to apologise for that one,' he growled. The sensation of her baby had slammed the need for sense into his head and he took a step back. Literally as well as emotionally. What the hell had he been thinking?

Caring for a pregnant woman… No and no and no.

Her wide green eyes stared up at him, and then down at her still heaving bump.

'He's got a good kick,' she ventured, cautiously.

'He surely has.' New emotions were surging in now, and his head was scrambling to reassemble his emotional armour. How long since he'd felt a baby's kick? It made him feel...

No. Don't even think about going there.

'Maybe it's to reassure us he's okay,' he managed, feeling lame, dredging up a smile.

'Maybe,' she said and wobbled a smile in return. And then: 'That was unforgivable,' she said. 'Thinking you were leaving.'

'I hadn't told you otherwise. I'm sorry. But consider me kicked. By...'

'Archibald.'

'Really?' He found himself smiling properly this time, caught by her fierce determination to apologise, and her equal determination to insert humour into the situation. This was one brave woman. The sensations he was feeling toward her were inappropriate but clinical approval was fine. 'You've decided on his name already?'

'He knocked my mug of tea over last week,' she said darkly. 'I had to run cold water over my tummy for ten minutes until I stopped stinging. Until then, *she* was going to be Chloe or *he* was going to be William, but that's in the past. Archibald it is.'

'Named for the baby's father, then?' he said, still striving to sound professional. He smiled again, but it was her turn for her smile to fade.

'His father would be William, but Archibald takes precedence.'

He was still holding her, by both hands, but now she made to pull away, as if naming the baby's father had brought her to her senses. Both of them had to come to their senses. 'Look, I am sorry,' she whispered.

'And I'm sorry, too,' he said. 'So let's stop apologising and get things moving. I need to take you to hospital.'

'I'm not going to hospital, but I do need to get back to Gran's. It's not far. If I hadn't hurt my leg, I could walk.'

Yes! Suddenly things seemed simple. This wasn't his problem. He could take her to her family and explain the need for hospital assessment. She'd said Gran was ill, but where there was a gran surely there'd be other relatives. He could hand her over with instructions to take her to the nearest hospital, and his nightmare of a weekend would be over.

'The calves won't go anywhere,' she said, thinking out loud. 'With Bonnie's help Angus can drive them home by foot from here.'

Hooray for Angus, he thought. And William and Gran. A whole family. Better and better.

But she was wilting, and he was wasting time.

'Okay,' he said, and ignoring protests he lifted her across to his car, blessing the fact that the Aston Martin had a rear seat. Once again, though, he was surprised at how little she weighed.

Were things okay? Was this a normal pregnancy?

This was Not His Problem, he reminded himself sharply. He needed to cope with the emergency stuff only. She'd have her own obstetrician. Her family could take her there.

Stay professional and stay clinically detached.

But as he lifted her into the car he smelled a faint citrusy perfume, and he was caught once again in a totally unprofessional moment.

Her luminous green eyes were framed by long, dark lashes, surely unusual in a redhead. Her freckles were amazingly cute. Her flame-coloured curls were still doing their best to break out of their braids, and he had an almost irrational desire to help them escape.

Whoa. What was it with him? He was being dumb and irrational and stupid.

This was his patient. Therefore he could stop thinking dumb thoughts about how she smelled and how she felt against him and how her hair would look unbraided.

So turn professional.

'Let's do formal introductions,' he said, trying to sound like he was about to key it into her patient history. 'Can you tell me your full name?'

'Maggie Maria Croft. You?'

'Maxwell Harvey Ashton.'

'Dr Ashton?'

'Max is fine, we'll forget the Harvey and I'm hoping we don't need the Doctor. But if necessary…' He hesitated but it had to be said. 'If your family can't take you, I'll drive you to the hospital at Gosland—or even to Sydney if you prefer.'

'Thank you,' she said, courteously but firmly. 'But it won't be necessary. If you can just take me back to the farm I can sort this mess out by myself.'

CHAPTER TWO

SO FIVE minutes later he turned into the farm gate—and found himself staring at a graveyard. A tractor graveyard.

The driveway from the road to the house was a long avenue of gumtrees, and underneath their canopies old tractors were lined up like sentinels. There were tractors from every era, looking like they dated from the Dark Ages.

'Wow,' he breathed, and involuntarily slowed to take a better look. Some of the tractors looked like they could be driven right now if he had the right crank and didn't mind using it. Some were a wheel or two short of perfect. Some were simply skeletons, a piece of superstructure, like a body without limbs.

'William likes tractors?' he ventured.

'Gran and Angus like tractors. Gran bought her first one when she was fifteen. I believe she swapped her party dress for it. The tractor didn't work then. It doesn't work now, but she still thinks it was a bargain.

'She sounds a character.'

'You could say that,' she said morosely. 'Or pig stubborn, depending on how you look at it.'

He glanced into the rear-view mirror, and saw a wash of

bleakness cross her face—desolation that could have nothing to do with the accident. And her expression caught something deep within him. For a fraction of a second he had an almost irresistible urge to stop the car so he could touch her; comfort her. It took strength to keep his hands on the steering-wheel, to keep on driving.

He did not do personal involvement, he told himself fiercely, confused by his totally inappropriate reaction. This woman was married and pregnant and he hadn't felt this way about a woman since Alice died. Had he hit his head in the crash? Was he out of his mind?

They'd reached the end of the driveway now, and he pulled up beside an old estate wagon with its bonnet up. The car with the damaged radiator hose. He focussed on that. Something practical and something that didn't make his heart twist.

'So that's your wagon. Is there something else you can use to drive to hospital?'

'What's wrong with tractors?' she demanded, and he caught a glimmer of a rueful smile in the rear-view mirror. Once again, he had that kick of emotional reaction. This lady had courage and humour. And something more.

'I'll be fine,' she told him, seemingly unaware of the effect her smile had on him. 'Thanks for driving me home. I'll give you my licence details, and our insurance companies can take it from here.'

So that was that. He was dismissed. He could retreat back to Sydney. Which was what, until an hour ago, he'd been desperate to do.

It seemed to Max that Yandilagong was about as far from civilisation as it was possible to get without launching himself off the New South Wales coast and swimming for New Zealand. Not for the first time, he wondered what he'd been thinking to let his friends—a cohort of career-oriented medicos—talk him into coming.

'It'll be fun,' they'd told him. 'Music festivals are all the rage and this one has a great line-up.'

Since he'd moved to Australia he'd been asked to many hospital social events, but each time he'd refused. Since Alice's death he'd immersed himself in his work to the exclusion of almost everything else. Now his surgical list was growing to the point where the pressure had become ridiculous. More and more patients were queuing, and his teaching commitments were increasing exponentially.

Last week, working out in the hospital gym in the small hours, trying to get himself so physically tired that sleep would come, he'd realised he was reaching breaking point.

So he'd accepted, but what neither he nor his colleagues had realised was that the festival was a family event. There were mums, dads and kids, young women holding babies, grandmas bossing grandkids, dads teaching kids to dance. His friends, men and women who were truly married to their career paths, were appalled.

'We're so lucky not to be stuck with that,' they'd declared more than once. 'Hicksville. Familyville. Who'd want it?'

He didn't, of course he didn't, so why had it hurt to hear them say it?

Then this afternoon they'd announced they were bored with music and children, so they'd organised a tour of a local winery. He'd spent a couple of hours listening to his friends gravely pontificate about ash and oak and hints of elderberry, and how wonderful it was to be away from the sound of children, and how the advertisers should be sued for not letting ticket buyers know how many children's events there'd be.

And then his anaesthetist had rung from Sydney. A woman was being flown in from outback New South Wales with complications from a hysterectomy. When was he coming back?

His registrar could cope. He knew he could, but the choice was suddenly obvious. He'd left feeling nothing but relief. For six years he'd been alone and that was the way he liked it.

He wanted to be alone now. But instead he was parked in a tractor graveyard while a seven-months-pregnant woman was struggling to get out of his car.

Wishes aside, he couldn't leave her. Not before he'd handed her over to someone responsible.

'Who's here?'

'Gran.'

'But she's ill.'

'Yes.'

'So where's William?' he asked, knowing it was a loaded question but hoping there'd be a solid answer.

'William was my husband,' she said flatly. 'He's dead.'

'Dead.' He felt like he'd been punched. Dead. Hence the bleakness. Hell.

'Not recently. You don't need to say you're sorry.'

Recent enough, he thought, looking at her very pregnant tummy. Alice had been dead for six years yet still...

Well, there was a crazy thing to think. Make this all about you, he told himself. Or not.

'So who's Angus?'

'William's uncle.'

'How old?'

'Sixty.'

This was better. 'He'll look after you?'

'He'll enjoy the challenge of getting the calves up to the

house. Bonnie's his dog. Any minute now he'll be here to demand what I've done with her. So thank you, Dr Ashton. I'll be right from here.'

He was dismissed.

For the last forty-eight hours all he'd wanted to do was get out of Yandilagong. He still did.

But he needed to see how competent this Angus person was, and how forceful. For all Maggie was struggling to pull herself from the car, she was looking paler and paler.

Placental bleeding? The two words had been playing in his head for half an hour now and they weren't going away.

He might not have done anything closely related to obstetrics for six years, but the training was there and he knew what a strain a car crash could put on a placenta.

Archibald had kicked him. That was a good sign but he needed more. He wanted to listen to the baby's heartbeat and then he wanted Maggie in hospital under observation.

And that bleak look on her face was etched into his mind. He couldn't leave her. And even if he could... Still there was that tug he didn't understand.

'You're not walking,' he growled, and before she could resist he'd lifted her up into his arms again. He strode up through a garden that smelled of old-fashioned roses, where honeysuckle and jasmine fought for smell space as well, where tiny honeyeaters flitted from bush to bush and where noisy rosella parrots swooped in random raids to the banksias around the edge.

The garden looked neglected and overgrown but beautiful. The farmhouse itself was looking a bit down at the heel, in want of a good coat of paint and a few nails, but big and welcoming and homely.

Once again there was that wrench of something inside

him. Like coming home. Which was clearly ridiculous. This was like no home he'd ever known.

He'd reached the top of the veranda steps and as he paused she wriggled out of his hold and was on her feet before he realised what she was about.

'Thank you,' she said, breathlessly, sounding…scared? 'I can take it from here.'

Scared? Was she feeling what he was feeling?

He didn't know what he was feeling.

'Not unless there's someone through that door to give you a strong cup of tea, then carry you out to a nice, safe non-tractor-type car and get you to hospital,' he said, making his voice stern. 'Can you tell me that?' Even though she was standing, he was blocking her way through the door.

'I can't,' she admitted. 'But I don't have a choice. Please, I can't leave Gran.'

'Then I can't leave you.' Neither, he realised bluntly, did he want to.

'Maggie, is that you?' The high, querulous voice came from inside, and without waiting for permission Max pushed it open.

The first thing he saw as he opened the door was a vast open fireplace filled with glowing embers, a burgundy, blue and gold carpet, faded but magnificent, great squashy settees and a mantel with two ornate vases loaded with roses from the garden. And jasmine and honeysuckle. The room was an extension of the garden, and the perfume was fabulous. Then, as his eyes became accustomed to the different light, he saw Gran. She was a tiny wizened woman, bundled in blankets on the settee, looking toward the door with obvious anxiety.

'I'm okay, Gran,' Maggie said urgently from behind him, and made to push past, but she stumbled on her bad leg. He caught her and held her against him, and she didn't fight.

But suddenly Gran was lurching to the hearth to grab the poker. She turned toward him, but then fell back on her pillows, waving the poker, fright and feistiness fighting for supremacy.

'Let her go.' Her voice came out as a terrified rasp and he felt Maggie flinch and struggle again to get free.

The two settees in the living room were opposite each other, forming a corridor to the fire. He ignored the poker— there wasn't a lot of threat when Gran didn't seem to be able to stand—and moved to set Maggie down. Gran's head and the poker were at the fire end. He set Maggie the opposite way, so the poker was away from his head.

'He's helping, Gran. Put the poker down,' Maggie muttered, and he felt her tension ease a little. She was back in familiar territory now, even if it was did seem crazy territory. A tractor museum, roses, roses and more roses, and a poker-waving Gran.

'What's he doing here?'

'He's Dr Ashton,' Maggie said, flinching as she moved her leg. 'A doctor. Imagine that. Right when we need him.'

There was a lot to ignore in that statement, too. He released her onto the cushions, aware once again of that weird stab of a sensation he didn't understand. Something that had nothing to do with a doctor/patient relationship.

Something that had to be ignored at all costs.

'You do need a doctor, but not me,' he growled, moving instinctively to load more logs from the wood-box to the fire. Thankfully Gran kept her poker hand to herself. 'Maggie, you need hospital.'

'I don't.'

'Your baby needs to be checked.'

'I can't leave Gran. I'll put my stethoscope on my tummy and lie here and listen to him,' she said. 'That's all I can do.

'You have a stethoscope?' he demanded, while the old lady rubbed her poker longingly, like she might still need it.

'Yes.'

'You're a nurse?'

'I'm a doctor.'

'*A doctor*?'

'They don't all come in white coats,' she said bitterly. 'Or Aston Martins and gorgeous leather jackets.'

'Maggie, tell me what's going on.' Gran was trying again to heave herself to a sitting position, gasping as if breathing hurt, and the fear was still in her voice.

'Dr Ashton crashed into our truck.'

'The calves,' Gran said in horror, but Max was playing triage in his head, and calves were somewhere near the bottom.

Maggie was a doctor. A doctor!

The personal side of him wanted to take that aside and think it through, for all sorts of reasons he didn't fully understand, but the professional side of him had work to do and wasn't giving him time to consider. 'So you're a doctor,' he managed. And you have a stethoscope?'

'The calves are okay, Gran,' Maggie said, seeming to ignore him. 'Bonnie's looking after them.' Then she turned back to him. 'Yes, there's a whole medical kit in the back of the wagon. Enough to cope with anything from typhoid to snakebite.' She winced again and lay back on the cushions, her hands instinctively returning to her belly. 'And, yes, I'd appreciate it if you could get my stethoscope.'

He stared at her and she stared back. Defiance and fear mixed.

'I'll take you both to hospital,' he said.

'Over my dead body,' the old lady said from the other settee.

'Mrs Croft?'

'I'm Betty,' she snapped.

'Betty, then,' he said, and softened his tone. 'I'm not sure what's wrong with you…'

'I'm dying.'

'So are we all,' he said without changing his tone. If she wanted histrionics she wasn't going to get them from him. 'Some faster than others. I gather you're ill and I'm sorry. I also know that your granddaughter—'

'Maggie's my granddaughter-in-law.'

'Your granddaughter-in-law, then,' he said evenly, glancing back at Maggie and knowing he was right. 'Maggie's been in an accident and her baby needs to be checked. If the placenta's damaged, there could be internal bleeding. The only way she can be checked is to have an ultrasound. If she doesn't have that ultrasound the baby could die, and she could be in trouble herself. Betty, I'm sorry that you're ill, but it's true I'm a doctor and I have to sort priorities. Is it right that we risk Maggie's baby's life because you won't go to hospital?'

'We're not risking…' Maggie said, and he turned back to face her. He had to ignore emotion here and speak the truth.

'If you really are a doctor, you know that you really are putting your baby at risk.'

She was torn. He could see it—he saw fear behind her eyes and he knew that she was desperately trying to hide it. Why?

'We don't have time to mess around,' he said. 'I should have insisted at the start.'

'I can do an ultrasound,' she said.

'What, here?'

'Not on myself.' Her voice was suddenly pleading. 'But there's everything we need in my car. I know, it's asking a lot, but if you could help… Gran doesn't want to go to hospital and neither do I. If I must for my baby's safety then of course

I will, but there's Angus as well and he'll be so afraid. So, please, Max, can you do an ultrasound on me here and reassure me that things are okay?'

'Why will Angus be afraid?'

'Angus is my son and he's disabled,' Gran whispered, as Maggie fell silent. 'He has Asperger's syndrome. He's not...he's not able to cope with people. It'd kill Angus to leave the farm. He's the reason I made Maggie come here. She's promised me she'll stay and she won't break that promise. She's a good girl, our Maggie.'

'My baby comes first,' Maggie muttered, looking trapped, and once again he caught that look of utter desolation.

'Yes, but he'll be okay and you'll both look after Angus and the farm,' Gran said. 'I know you won't leave. You'll keep your word. I know you'll stay here for ever.'

CHAPTER THREE

THIS was crazy. Worse than crazy, it was dangerous. No, she wouldn't leave Gran and the unknown Angus, but maybe his responsibility was to pick both women up and take them to hospital regardless.

But he'd have to chain Gran into the car, he thought ruefully. Plus he didn't know what facilities Gosland hospital had, and the long drive to Sydney was the last thing either of them needed.

But caring for an injured, pregnant woman at home…

And for him personally to have to check her baby…

Max was out on the back veranda, supposedly on his way to fetch Maggie's gear from the back of her wagon. He'd taken a moment to phone Anton, his anaesthetist, to tell him that their more-than-competent registrar would be needed for the woman coming in with the hysterectomy complications. Now he was staring down at the river winding down to the sea, taking a second to catch his breath. And his thoughts.

Maggie would agree to hospital if there was a real threat to her baby. He knew it. The moment he'd laid it on the line—that they were risking the baby's death—he could tell that both women would finally agree to go. Only there was such despair in the old lady's eyes, and such a sense of defeat and fear on Maggie's face, that he'd agreed to help them stay.

So all he had to do now was to find Maggie's ultrasound equipment and turn into an obstetrician again.

No. Checking one baby didn't make an obstetrician.

He wasn't even delivering a baby. He was simply checking it was healthy, before heading back to the city to his very successful gynaecological practice—the surgery he was good at and that he could do without the emotional investment every pregnant woman seemed to demand of him.

The need to care.

Not that he didn't care about his patients. He did. He gave excellent service, making the lives of the women who came to him much more comfortable. He was even saving lives.

He just didn't do babies anymore.

Except this one.

This was insane. He should refuse to have anything to do with it.

Yet…the way she looked at him…

It was the craziest of reasons and yet he couldn't let it go. She looked as trapped as he felt. More.

He didn't know what was at stake here. He shouldn't want to know, he reminded himself. Do not get personally involved.

Stay professional, he told himself harshly. Find the ultrasound equipment, make sure things are okay and then leave. An ultrasound was no big deal. It wasn't like she was expecting him to deliver the baby.

That was really when he'd run a mile.

'Is he really a doctor?'

'He says he is and he knows all the right words.'

The open fire was wonderful, the room was warm, but Maggie was still shivering. Reaction, she thought. Nothing more. It couldn't be anything like internal shock—caused by a bleed, say, from a torn placenta.

She had to fight the fear. But what was keeping him?

She had a sudden vision of Max in his beautiful car, heading back to Sydney, and she felt ill. But she wasn't running after him this time. She trusted him.

She had no choice.

'Where are my calves?' Gran said fretfully.

'The crate slid off the back of the truck. The calves ended up on the beach. Bonnie's watching over them.'

'Are you sure they're okay?'

'They're fine.' Hopefully they were.

'How do you know? Of all the irresponsible… You only had to bring four calves less than ten miles.' The old lady's voice was querulous and Maggie looked at her sharply.

'How bad's the pain? Scale of one to ten?'

'Three.'

'Betty…'

'Eight, then,' she said, goaded.

'You have to let me put up a syringe driver.' With a permanent syringe, morphine could be delivered continuously so there wasn't this four-hourly cycle of pain, relief, sleep, pain that Betty was suffering. But so far Betty had resisted. She'd insisted on control at every stage of this illness and she wasn't letting go now.

'I'll take a pill in a few minutes.'

'Take one now. No, take two.'

'When I see our baby's okay,' Betty said roughly. 'Oh, my dear…'

'It'll be fine.' Maggie hauled herself around and stretched

her hand out to her. Betty's hand was thin and cold and it trembled.

Probably hers did, too, Maggie thought. Things were going from bad to worse.

Hurry up the man with the ultrasound. Max. A doctor for her baby.

And more.

Max.

He'd carried her and he'd made her feel cared for. The remembered sensation was insidious—almost treacherous. It undermined her independence. Stupidly it made her want to cry.

Max.

He opened the back of the wagon, expecting to see a basic medical kit—or even no kit at all, because he still hardly believed she was a doctor—but what he saw was amazing. The equipment, carefully stored, sorted and readily accessible, was state of the art.

What had she said back at the crash site? She was the ambulance?

Maybe she was, for in the centre of the shelves of equipment lay a stretcher. It had been fitted to custom-built rails, with wheeled legs folded underneath. It was narrow, but otherwise there was little difference to the stretcher trolleys used at his city teaching hospital.

The ultrasound equipment was impossible to miss for it was in a red case labelled 'Ultrasound'. Useful for a doctor in a crisis, he thought, to be able to say to an onlooker, 'Fetch me the red case with this label.' And the cases were stacked and fastened against the sides in such a way that in a crisis they could be pulled out fast.

He had a sudden vision of an emergency—maybe a child

with breathing problems. With this set-up Maggie could haul out the side cases fast, then have someone else drive while she worked on the patient until they reached help.

Basic but effective. She was efficient, then, this Dr Maggie.

He needed to be as well. He tugged the ultrasound case, grabbed another case labelled 'Pain/Anaesthetic'—and then, thinking of the strain on the old lady's face and the wheeze behind her voice, he grabbed an oxygen canister as well.

Okay. Doctor with equipment.

They dropped their linked hands as he walked back into the room. Up until now he'd seen only an underlying tension, but there was now an obvious tie between the women. Emotional as well as physical?

Was the old lady really dying? He gave himself time to look at her—really look. She was dreadfully gaunt, as though eating had long ceased to be a priority, and her face was taut with pain. And her eyes... He'd seen that look before. Turning inward.

'Betty needs a shot of morphine,' Maggie said before he could say anything. 'Please. Ten milligrams. You'll find everything in my bag.'

'The baby...'

'One injection's not going to take time. Betty needs it badly.'

'Diagnosis?' he said, watching Betty now and talking directly to the elderly woman.

'Bone metastases,' Betty whispered. 'Ovarian cancer ten years back. I knew it'd get me in the end.'

'Is Maggie your treating doctor?'

'Now I'm not in hospital, she is,' Betty said fretfully. 'But look after her. I'm fine.'

But Max was already flipping open the case, drawing up the

injection, aware both women were watching him like two hawks with a mouse between them. Or two mice with a hawk?'

'You agree to this?' he said, watching Betty's face. Feeling Maggie's tension behind him.

'Yes,' Betty whispered. 'Please.'

He injected the morphine, feeling her pulse as he did so. Faint, irregular. If she was forty he'd be roaring for help, he thought, bullying her into hospital, pulling out all stops to help her, but her body language told him she knew exactly what was happening. He placed pressure on the injection site for a moment and her hand lifted to his and held.

'Thank you,' she whispered, and closed her eyes. 'Now Maggie.'

'Now Maggie,' he agreed, and Maggie nodded and pointed to a power plug behind the couch.

'We can do it here.'

'You don't want to be private?'

'I doubt I'll shock Betty by showing a bit of skin,' Maggie said, smiling wryly. 'And it's warm in here.'

She shivered as she said it. He didn't comment, though— she'd know as well as he did that shock would be causing her to shiver.

And internal bleeding?

Please not.

'You've used one of these before?' she asked him.

'Not a portable one.'

'Nothing to it,' she said.

And there wasn't. In moments he had it organised, set up on a side table right by Maggie's abdomen.

She was wearing jeans with an elasticised waist and a sloppy windcheater that could easily be pulled up. He rubbed the stethoscope in his hands to take away the chill, then knelt beside her. As she tugged up her windcheater, he glanced up at her and once again saw the flash of fear. He should take her blood pressure first, he thought, and check her pulse, but he had a feeling they'd be high and racing until he gave her the reassurance she needed. Was she shivering from shock or shivering from fear? Probably the latter.

So he placed the stethoscope over her tummy and listened. And heard.

'What is it?' she whispered, and he glanced up and realised his emotions were showing in his face. How many years since he'd done this? And the last baby he'd heard…

'It's fantastic,' he said, but he said it too fast, and saw doubt remain. Try as he may, he couldn't get his face in order. As an alternative he put an arm around her shoulders, propped her up and handed the stethoscope to her.

She listened, and her face relaxed. As it should. And strangely he found himself relaxing as well, in a way that had nothing to do with the sound of a strong baby's heartbeat. He was holding her, feeling the tension ease, feeling her body relax into his.

Just like…

No.

'You looked like there was something wrong,' Maggie whispered.

'Nothing's wrong.'

'Then why—?'

'No reason. Let's move on with this ultrasound,' he said, more roughly than he'd intended, and she nodded and lay back on her cushions and looked at him directly.

'Do you need me to tell you how to work this?'

'I'm fine.'

'But—'

Okay, truth time. 'Maggie, I'm not a general surgeon,' he

told her. It went against the grain to admit it but he was up to his ears in this mess already—he may as well commit the whole way. 'I'm a gynaecologist.'

'A gynaecologist,' she said, stunned.

'Yes. I'm in charge of surgical gynaecology at Sydney South.' He smiled wryly and glanced across at Betty. 'If Betty's ovarian cancer had been diagnosed now rather than ten years back maybe I'd be able to help her. It's what I'm good at.'

He was searching for gel, laying out what he needed. She was staring at him as if he'd just grown two heads.

'A surgical gynaecologist,' she muttered, awed. And then: 'You don't get to be a gynaecologist in this country without being an obstetrician as well.'

'I'm English. But, yes, that's right. I've done the training.'

'You're a baby doctor?' He'd thought Betty had drifted into sleep as the morphine took effect, but now the old lady's eyes flew open. 'We so need a baby doctor,' she whispered.

'I'm not a baby doctor,' he said, more roughly than he'd intended. 'I work with women with gynaecological problems. Surgical problems.'

But Betty was no longer listening. Instead she was smiling. 'That was the only thing missing,' she said. 'Now we have everything we need. Oh, Maggie…'

'Don't you dare give up,' Maggie said, sounding fearful, and Betty tried a feeble wave but didn't have the strength to pull it off. She closed her eyes.

'You just concentrate on our baby,' she said. 'On William's son.'

'Okay,' Max said, trying not to sound grim as he saw the colour drain from Betty's face. The more he saw what was happening to Betty, the less he liked it, but he needed to focus on Maggie. 'Let's get some gel on you and have a look.'

He rubbed gel on her bulge. Maggie closed her eyes. Yes, she was desperately anxious about the outcome of this ultrasound but she was so tired. If she could just sink into her cushions and sleep for twenty-four hours, that's exactly what she'd do.

There was not a snowball's chance in a bushfire of that happening.

Where was Angus? And how was she going to cope with her patients, with the farm, with Gran, with an injured leg?

She couldn't. She'd hoped she'd have another few weeks to work before the baby was born, but now, with her leg hurting as much as it did, and with Betty dying, and…

And as if on cue the doorbell pealed.

She tried really hard not to groan.

Max was about to place the paddle on her tummy. He paused and looked questioningly at her.

'They'll keep knocking till we answer,' she said, and tried to sit up.

'They?'

'It'll be a patient. The locals know where I live. I need to answer.'

'You're not going anywhere,' he said, sounding appalled she could think such a thing. He placed his hands firmly on her shoulders and pushed her back on the cushions. Which, she had to admit, felt excellent.

This man was taking charge. Even if it was only for a moment, it'd do, she conceded. There were too many worries to fit in her head. He'd carried her, he'd cared for Gran, he was caring for her.

So soak it in.

She could lie back and imagine that this arrogant, bossy doctor could take all her worries away. He'd check her baby, tell her everything was fine, make sure Betty was pain free, reassure Angus, fix whoever was at the door, fix her world…

Yeah, and pigs might fly. But, meanwhile, he'd said she wasn't going anywhere and he meant it. She let herself relax against her cushions. She didn't quite close her eyes but she almost did. If she shut her eyes the world might disappear.

She wasn't quite ready for that, she conceded. Not yet. Disappearing worlds were for Betty.

But she wouldn't mind if ninety per cent of hers went away.

He was wasting time. The ultrasound was becoming urgent. He had to get to the door, tell whoever it was to wait and get back to his patient. To Maggie.

But when he tugged the door wide he found a deputation. Mother, father, a scrawny little boy clinging to the mother's jeans, and a baby.

'The baby's got a cold,' the man said quickly, as if he was worried the door might be slammed in his face. 'We've all had it, but she's been bad all day and then she went limp. She looks okay now but the missus got scared. So I said we'll stick her in the car and bring her here. Can Doc have a look?'

This was a nightmare. He should tell them to go away.

But Maggie had said she was the ambulance. Was she also the only local doctor?

These people looked terrified. For good reason?

He glanced down and saw the tiny child was swaddled in so much wool he could barely see her.

'How long was she limp?' he asked.

'Only for a moment,' the man said. 'Ben here and me were watching telly while Cathy was feeding her in the bedroom. Cathy screamed but by the time I got there she was okay again. But Cathy's *that* scared. Said she looked awful. We wrapped her up and brought her straight to Doc Maggie.'

'Okay, unwrap her,' Max said tersely. 'Fast.' He turned back to the living room, calling to Maggie. 'Where's your bathroom?'

'Shall I come?' Maggie called.

'Stay where you are,' he growled. The last thing Maggie needed was cross-infection, and she had to stay still. 'Bathroom?' he demanded again.

'Door on the right of the hall,' she called, sounding bewildered.

He glanced again at the baby, touched her face lightly with the back of his hand, felt how hot she was and knew he was right. 'You go in there,' he told the frightened parents. 'Strip off all her clothes and pop her into a tepid bath. Tepid. Not cold but not warm either. She's running a fever. I'm guessing she's had a febrile convulsion and she needs to get cool in a hurry. You're to keep her in the bath and keep her cool until I come back. I have an emergency in the other room.'

'But Doc,' the man said. 'We want Doc Maggie.'

'Doc Maggie's the emergency,' he snapped. 'I'm a doctor, too, and I'm all there is. I need to take care of her.'

'How do we know you're a doctor?' the man said, fear and belligerence mixed. 'We want Maggie.'

'Pete,' the woman said, and she'd peered past Max into the living room. Seen what was there. 'Maggie's pregnant. If anything happens to Maggie the whole community's in trouble. Just thank God there's another doctor. Shut up and do what he says.'

Betty was asleep. Maggie was still slumped against the cushions, looking anxious. And exhausted. And pale.

'Febrile convulsion?' she queried.

'I'm assuming so,' he told her. 'But I'll check her when your baby's been checked.' He was worrying in earnest now. She was looking too shocked, too pale. If he'd messed around this long and she was bleeding… 'Lie back and let me see.'

So she did, and in the middle of chaos there was suddenly peace.

There was no way to rush an ultrasound. There could be no urgency about it. He smoothed the gel over her tummy, settled the paddle and started moving it with care.

The screen beside him started showing images.

She was watching, too. He didn't need to explain it to her. He moved his hand in careful, precise rhythm, taking in the whole picture with care.

He'd seen so many. This was just one baby more. There was nothing here to make his heart clench.

Only his chest was certainly tight.

One baby more…

Be professional, he told himself, and there was no choice to be anything but. He was focussing first on the placenta, moving carefully, seeing its position, noting carefully the visuals around it. He was looking for pooled blood. Looking for evidence of damage.

Not finding it.

One tiny heart, beating, beating.

A tiny fist curled close to the wand.

A tiny, perfect hand…

A miracle. Just like…

No. He felt himself blink and thought, hell, he was hardly hiding his emotions. If Maggie was watching him…

Only of course Maggie wasn't watching him. She had eyes only for the screen. He glanced at her and saw tears coursing down her cheeks, and a tremulous smile.

'He's okay,' she whispered, fighting to get the words out.

'Did you think he wouldn't be?'

'I shouldn't think. If I wasn't a doctor I wouldn't think. I wouldn't have even known about torn placentas. I'd have felt him kick and thought he was fine.'

'He is fine.' Involuntarily he flicked a tear from her cheek and it was just as well he was still holding the paddle for he was suddenly aware of an almost overwhelming urge to let it go and gather her into his arms. To take away the look of almost unbearable strain.

This woman was so alone.

'When did your husband die?' he asked gently as he moved the wand on.

'Three years ago.'

His hand paused in mid-stroke. *Three years*.

'World's longest pregnancy,' Maggie whispered, still watching the screen. Then she managed a wavering smile. 'Sorry. William had non-Hodgkin's lymphoma, and we stored sperm before he started chemotherapy. When the chemotherapy didn't work he said if I ever wanted to have his baby he'd be honoured. At first the thought was unbearable but gradually it seemed…right. But it took me this long and Betty's coercion to feel strong enough, and maybe that strength was an illusion anyway.'

She winced and bit her lip, fighting for composure. 'But, hey, it's okay,' she said, and struggled to smile again. 'As long as my baby's fine.'

'He is,' he said. And then he paused.

They were both looking at the screen.

'You know you called him Archibald?' Max ventured cautiously, not sure where to take this conversation with a colleague who was seeing exactly what he was seeing. 'That may cause problems. Not that unusual names aren't all the rage, but…'

'*She*,' she breathed. 'My baby's a girl.'

'You didn't know?'

She was staring at the screen in stunned amazement. 'I had my last ultrasound at three months, but Betty and I always assumed it'd be a boy.'

'Because?'

'Because Betty has a blue crib,' she breathed. 'She's been knitting blue matinee jackets for ever. Someone should alert the share market. It's about to be flooded with blue.' She looked again at the screen, seeing the irrefutable evidence, and she was smiling again, this time like she meant it. 'Don't tell Betty,' she whispered.

'You think she'll be upset?'

'She wants a boy so much, and why tell her?' The smile faded and her voice was suddenly bleak again. 'Do you think Betty will live to see my baby born?'

He glanced across at Betty. She'd collapsed into sleep but it was more than sleep. The amount of morphine he'd given her couldn't explain the look of total lack of consciousness. He shifted slightly so he could reach over and take her wrist. Her skin was parched and dry, her pulse was thready and her fingers were cold to touch.

'She needs fluids,' he said. 'She's dehydrated. And blood tests. Is she hypoxic?'

'I'm assuming so. She hasn't let me do anything but give her pain relief for weeks now. But it's okay. It's what she wants. And now…now I know my baby's okay… If you could just check the other one before you go…'

'The other one?'

'The one you left in the bathroom,' she reminded him.

He knew that. But he was moving past it in his head. Facing the inevitable.

'Okay, here's the plan,' he said softly. 'I stay here. I attend to our bathroom baby. I dress your head and your knee, I keep a check on you tonight to make sure your head injury's not causing trouble, and in the morning I find a way to get you X-rayed. Until those things happen I'm not leaving.'

She stared up at him for a long moment—and then she closed her eyes. For a moment he thought she was going to react with anger. With denial.

Instead she opened her eyes again and the relief he saw there was stunning. Her face looked lighter, younger. Free. As if an unbearable burden had been lifted.

He'd given her a promise of one night. Her eyes said it was much more.

'Thank you,' she whispered softly. 'You have no idea how much I would love you to stay.' And she reached up and took his hand and held it.

He'd finished the ultrasound. He'd sorted Maggie's need for the night. His next priority was the baby in the bathroom. He should move.

Instead he stayed, looking into her eyes while her hand held his. Just looking.

Feeling the touch of Maggie's hand, and knowing it was so much more.

Feeling a web he'd taken years to break free from tighten once more inexorably around his heart.

This woman was pregnant. This woman represented everything he ran from.

Yet still he couldn't disengage his hand.

CHAPTER FOUR

THE tepid bath had worked. When he finally made it to the bathroom he found the little family comforted and happy.

'We need two doctors so much,' the woman said as he saw them to their car a little later, the baby wrapped in light cotton and nothing else. 'We had old Doc Sharrandon, but the minute Maggie arrived he left. Said he'd waited ten years too long for retirement and he wasn't waiting a minute longer. So instead of having one ancient doctor we have one pregnant one. Not that we're complaining. Maggie's lovely, only it's too much for her.'

It was.

He saw them off from the veranda—then as he turned to go inside he paused. There was a dark shape moving down the track, behind the tractors. Or… Several shapes.

He stood watching, waiting for his eyes to become accustomed to the moonlight.

It was a figure in some sort of greatcoat, behind three—no, four—calves. And one dog.

Bonnie and the calves, he thought, and this must be Angus. Until now he hadn't realised it was weighing on him—the thought of calves and dog on the beach alone—but it felt great to see them come. He walked down through the garden to meet them, only to have both man and calves start away from him. Fifty yards away it was clear he wasn't getting closer—indeed, it looked as if only the dog stopped both man and calves from bolting.

He left them, walking slowly back into the house to find Maggie propped up on her cushions, watching the door with anxiety. Was she wondering whether he was true to his word—that he'd come back? More and more the knowledge settled in his mind. He couldn't leave her. The part of him that was fearful of relationships was screaming at him to stay dispassionate but it was being firmly overruled by sensations he wasn't close to understanding.

'What's wrong?' Maggie demanded. Maybe his emotions were showing on his face. Who knew? If he was having trouble quelling them internally, how did he keep his face in order?

'Nothing's wrong,' he told her. 'Angus has the calves. Four calves and Bonnie, walking up the driveway right now.'

'He's brought them here.' For a moment he thought she was about to cry—and once again came that stab of need to comfort. He stayed where he was but it was hard.

'He must have seen you bring me home,' she said, so happily that she was obviously oblivious to what he was feeling. 'He'd have walked back looking for them.' She sighed and managed a wavering smile. 'Thank heaven. Can we wake Gran and tell her?'

Wake Betty? That was the last thing he wanted to do. 'I'm about to clean your head.'

'This is more urgent.'

'Waking Betty?'

'Please,' she said, suddenly passionate. 'It really is. If you knew how Gran's connived for this, you couldn't doubt it. Gran's sole focus for the last year has been to get me and my baby here, to set Angus up with a milking herd again, and keep him safe. She's so close to running out of time and she knows it. I had to get the calves today no matter what, and she's desperate to know they're here. Please.'

'So we wake her up and tell her?'

'No. We wake her up and show her. Can you get me a set of crutches? You'll find some out in the garage. There's three pairs—I reckon I'm the middle.'

'Why do you want crutches?' he demanded, appalled at the sudden change in her. From passive and frightened patient she was suddenly all purpose.

'I'm going with you. And you're carrying Gran over to see Angus's calves.'

'In the morning, maybe.'

'No! Look at her,' she said urgently. 'Can you guarantee there'll be a morning? Max, I know this seems dumb,' she admitted, 'but medicine's not only about drugs and bed care. Betty needs this more than anything in the world and I need to give it to her. This whole night will leave me with a debt I can never repay, but you've said you'll stay and we have to do this. Please can you carry Gran over to see what she's achieved.'

He stared down into her face, saw desperation, saw passion, and more. There was love, he thought. Maggie had spoken of coercion but, whatever was between these two women, her commitment to her now was absolute.

And suddenly he thought, It's not just for Betty. Maggie must be a wonderful doctor. She cared. Where he'd spent the last six years pushing his emotions away, hers were out there, front and centre. Her husband's death hadn't taught her to protect herself. She was way too exposed.

What should he tell her now? 'You're not fit to do anything more tonight. Betty needs to sleep. To do what you ask would be crazy.'

He couldn't. Her passion was shifting his armour, finding a way in.

Tomorrow he'd put this behind him, he thought, but for tonight…he had to do it her way.

He stared down at her and she stared straight back, those luminous eyes meeting his with a directness he found disconcerting. More than disconcerting.

He should run a mile from what he was starting to feel, he thought inconsequentially, and then he thought maybe he was running out of time to run.

Maybe he couldn't run if he tried.

Time out of frame.

He was walking across an unused cow-yard in the moonlight, carrying a dying woman in his arms, with a seven-months-pregnant colleague limping along on crutches beside him.

Gran was still half-asleep. She'd roused when he'd lifted her, but Maggie had simply said, 'The calves are here, Gran. You've got what you want. You need to see them.'

She shouldn't be on crutches. He was walking slowly, worrying about her, but she wasn't complaining. Her whole focus was on what lay ahead.

Ahead was a haystack, dark and forbidding against the night sky. As they neared it Maggie paused and so did he.

'Angus?' she called, and there was no answer, but a soft lowing told them the calves were there.

'Angus, Gran wants to see the calves she's given you,' Maggie called. 'I have the doctor who helped me home from the crash. You'll have seen him. His name's Max and he's carrying Gran because she can't walk. Angus, Gran really wants to see you with the calves.'

Again, there was no response, but Maggie looked up at him and nodded, a tiny, definite nod. 'It's as good as we'll get,' she whispered. 'Let's go.' She limped on.

He stood back and watched her for a moment, knowing how much she must be hurting, knowing how desperately she needed to be in her own bed, but knowing she wasn't going to stop.

She paused and glanced back at him, questioning, and he caught himself, tightened his grip on Gran and kept going. He was rounding the haystack, following a woman he was starting to be in awe of. More. A woman who left him feeling disorientated, as if his world was shifting on its axis and he was having trouble getting it the right way up again.

And here were the calves. At the foot of the haystack, bales had been shifted to form an enclosed, warm place. Angus was behind them, a dark figure in a dark coat, out of the pool of light from a lantern he'd set up. He was holding Bonnie as if holding a shield.

'How did you find them?' Maggie asked, and he appeared to shrink even more.

'Bonnie,' he said at last, and it was as if the words were dragged out of him. 'Brought 'em along the beach. Came up to find me. Knew something was wrong when you come home in that car. Bonnie made me go down the beach.'

'Oh, Bonnie,' Maggie said, and she sounded close to tears.

He wanted to hold her. He couldn't. He was holding Betty, and Betty was awake and looking across at the calves.

Maggie was looking at Betty and in the lamplight he could see the shimmering of her tears.

'What…what do you think of them?' Gran whispered. Gently he set her down on a couple of hay bales, still wrapped in the blanket he'd carried her in. The calves shifted nervously as he stepped back, but they were still close enough for Betty to reach out and touch them.

There was a long silence. Max thought maybe he should say something but Maggie's hand came out to catch his. She leaned on him, heavily, and instinctively his arm wrapped around her waist to support her.

She leaned on him some more, and the pressure of her hand told him to stay silent.

He stayed silent. He held onto Maggie.

Family, he thought suddenly, and the same feeling he'd had when he'd seen the farmhouse came over him. It was a longing, deep in his gut, for something other than the solitary path he'd elected to travel.

Family? This? There were commitments all over this place. For Maggie to accept such responsibility… Her strength left him awed and his hold on her tightened instinctively.

Betty had asked Angus if he liked the calves. She was waiting for him to answer, and Max could see Angus knew he had to say something. And he knew by the tension in Maggie's body that she was desperate for Angus to respond.

'Yeah,' he said at last, and it was a beginning.

'They'll be milkers,' Gran whispered. 'It's just the start. Now Maggie's here you can have your herd again.'

'We could use the milk from these for cheese,' Angus said, in a voice that sounded rusty from disuse. 'Until we build the herd up enough to sell milk to the co-op again.'

'Yes!' It was still a whisper but Gran's tone was almost triumphant. She turned to Maggie. 'Four calves are a start. If you buy Angus another every time you can afford it… Promise me you will. Promise.' The last word was such a fierce demand that he felt Maggie flinch against him.

'I'll do my best,' she said.

'And you'll help her.' The old lady was suddenly staring at *him*. 'You'll help her. Yeah, you will, I know it.' She closed her eyes, as if exhausted and Max was spared having to answer. 'It'll be okay. Farm's safe. Will's son'll be here. It's okay.'

'Gran,' Maggie said roughly, sounding desperately anxious.

'Yeah, it's time to go to sleep,' Gran said, without opening her eyes. 'And if your fella'll give me another shot of that morphine stuff, I'll take it with pleasure. You'll do that?'

'I will,' Max said, because there was nothing else to say, and the pressure of Maggie's hand in his increased.

Thank you, the pressure said. Thank you.

More and more he had no idea what he'd been propelled into. This was a weird setting, so strange he felt as if he'd been transported to another world.

But there was peace here, of a sort. Angus was waiting with ill-concealed impatience for the people in the tableau to disappear so he could be alone with his animals. Maggie was leaning against him, taking strength from him and giving him warmth in return. An old lady was saying goodbye.

Maggie was weeping openly now, tears slipping down her cheeks unchecked. He held her tighter, and he felt her shudder against him.

'Can you carry Gran back to bed?' she whispered.

'I'll do that, and then I'll come back for you.'

'I'll make my own way,' she whispered. 'I always have and I always will.'

He looked down at her in the moonlight, a woman who needed to be cared for, yet who was worrying about everyone around her. She worried about more than just these two people, he knew. She worried about the whole community.

Maggie. The word alone was making him feel strange, like he'd never known what a woman could be until now.

He was involved until the morning, he told himself. No more.

Did he believe it?

First things first.

Leaving Maggie—as ordered—he carried Gran back to the house. She roused enough to direct him to her bedroom, a room of grand proportions overlooking the front garden. He tucked her into a huge bed heaped with faded eiderdowns, he injected more morphine and he thought she was asleep. But as he made to leave, her hand came out and grasped his.

'Thank you,' she whispered. 'You've made it perfect. I can go now. Look after them for me.'

Her eyes closed again and he stood looking down at her, trying to take in what she'd just said.

It was a farewell, and by the look of her...

She desperately needed fluids, he thought, touching the back of her hand, pressing the dry skin back a little and watching it stay where he'd pressed it. She was so dehydrated.

She was emaciated. Weary. Done.

If this woman presented at Emergency right now, the wheels of medical technology would move into overdrive.

He should at least set up a drip to get fluids in.

But he knew instinctively that this woman wouldn't thank him for extending her life. He didn't need to talk to Maggie to know it. The decision had already been made.

She was dying and she knew it. So how did he react to the old lady's request. *Take care of them?*

What sort of request was that?'

Should he rouse her and say 'Hey, I'm a passing stranger, stuck for the night but out of here first thing in the morning.'

As if he could rouse a dying woman and tell her that. But not to tell her…

He could tell her nothing. She was already asleep.

He flicked off her bedside lamp and left, feeling that a promise had been made regardless. By failing to deny her…

Nonsense. She had no right to ask anything of him, and he had no need to answer.

Move on, he told himself harshly. Move on to Maggie?

He came out into the living room, expecting her to be there, but there was no sign of her. He'd come ahead with Betty, and he thought she'd have struggled back on her crutches. Apparently not.

He swore and went out again, to find her sitting on a low stone wall by the garden gate. Just sitting, staring into the night.

She should be in bed, too, and those wounds still needed dressing. He came up behind her and saw her shudder. Involuntarily his hands rested on her shoulders. She flinched, and then, unexpectedly, she leaned back into him.

'She'll go now,' she whispered. 'Thank you for caring for her.'

The night was growing more and more surreal. He'd turned into Gran's treating doctor?

There was nothing for it but to agree. 'I expect she will,' he agreed. 'Unless we get proactive.'

'There's no point. But today… It would have been a disaster without you.'

'I suspect it was a disaster because of me,' he said ruefully. 'If I hadn't driven around that bend…'

'You had every right to drive around that bend.'

'Come inside, Maggie,' he said gently. 'Can I carry you?'

'No point,' she said, and sighed. 'Sorry. That sounded ungracious, but there's not a lot of use in getting accustomed to leaning on anyone.'

Yet still she leaned on him.

'You're cold.'

'I do need to go inside,' she agreed with reluctance.

'You don't want to?'

'I want to run,' she whispered. 'I'm so tired.'

He hesitated. There were things he should be doing. Carrying her inside, cleaning her face, strapping her knee, putting her to bed as he'd just put Gran.

But out here the stars were hanging low in the sky. From over at the haystack came a soft lowing as the calves settled down for the night. Angus would be with them. As Max had left, carrying Gran, he'd turned back and seen the elderly man settling onto the straw with an expression on his face that was almost joy. Angus and Bonnie wouldn't be leaving their charges.

They wouldn't be coming to the house to help Maggie, either.

How alone was this woman?

What was he doing? There was still something inside him yelling go no further, ask no questions, back off. He couldn't. The old lady's words were like a spell cast across the night. *Take care of them.*

It wouldn't hurt, he conceded. For one night he could help, and maybe he could help by staying outside with her for a little. Instinctively he knew she didn't want to go into the beautiful old house. No matter how Maggie had filled it with flowers, no matter how she'd fought to keep it lovely, for now age and infirmity had taken over, leaving an intangible air of impending sorrow.

His hands rested on her shoulders, gently, yet with a

message he didn't need to say. I'm with you, was his unspoken message. You're not alone.

But he had to leave her for a moment. She was growing colder.

'Wait,' he said, and strode swiftly into the house, searching for what he needed. When he returned she hadn't moved.

He set an eiderdown around her shoulders. He put another across her knees, tucking it under her, and then, because he had no taste for martyrdom, he wrapped a third around himself. Then he sat down beside her. Close.

'That's piles taken care of.'

'Piles,' she said, cautiously.

'Never let your backside get cold,' he said seriously. 'First thing they should teach any medical student. Nasty things, piles.'

He felt rather than saw her smile, and felt also a tiny lifting of tension. Great. Those smile lines round her eyes had come from somewhere. He didn't like it that they seemed to be getting rusty from disuse.

His arm wrapped around her waist and held. He could feel the warmth of her body through the eiderdown. That meant she could get warmth from him. That felt okay, too.

More than okay.

'You want to explain the calves?' he said, for want of a point to start. For a little while he didn't think she'd answer, but then she started, staring out at the stars like her story was written there.

'It's Gran's dream. The great plan. To get me back here, to have William's son inherit the farm, to give Angus back his milking herd.'

'William's son,' he said cautiously. 'As in the little girl you're incubating right now?'

'Yeah, and Archibald turning into Annie's the least of our

problems. It's all a bit of a dream,' she said dryly. 'Gran's dream and my dream, all mixed up.'

'Do you want to share?'

'Do you want to listen?' But then she seemed to catch herself. 'Look, this is nothing to do with you. There are probably places you should be. To ask you to stay the night is big—to make you share any more is crazy.'

'I'm not volunteering to fix anything,' he said. 'Just listen if you want to talk.'

And it seemed she did. She sighed and unconsciously leaned closer. 'Okay, potted history. I'm English and so was William's mother. William's father—Betty's son—is a hot-shot businessman who left the farm when he was eighteen, moved to England and has never been back. William was therefore brought up in London. We met as interns, we fell in love, we married, and we were typical Londoners. Only William used to talk about the Australian farm his parents had sent him to when they'd wanted to get rid of him over the school holidays. He spoke of an awesome gran, a fabulous farm and a wonderful community at Yandilagong. He kept saying we'd move here one day, set up practice, have bush kids.'

'Dreaming?'

'It was more than that,' she said softly. 'Neither of us had happy childhoods. The thought of a farm and country medicine and family sounded so magical we thought we'd get the training we needed and go. Only then Will died. I was miserable and alone, working in a dreary little haze, until I got a letter from Betty.'

'Reigniting the dream?'

'That's a good way of putting it,' she said, still staring out at the stars. Still letting her body share warmth with him. 'I have no idea why Will told his father he'd stored sperm, or why his dad told Betty, but she knew. She wrote and said if I wanted to have Will's baby then why not come here and live. She told me there's a self-contained apartment at the back of the house so I could be as independent as I wanted. She could help with the baby. I could get a part-time job helping the doctor in town. She even enclosed a lovely letter from the Yandilagong doctor saying there was a vacancy here for as much work as I wanted.'

She gave a wry chuckle then, which made him think she should laugh more. Her laugh was rusty, with traces of bitterness, but still he liked it.

'And so?' he asked, and she sighed and the chuckle faded.

'So then I got dreamy and impractical. I'd been in a fog of grief and apathy since Will died, and suddenly I thought why not? I don't intend to marry again—not after the sort of heartache Will and I went through—but to have Will's baby seemed like a giant leap into the future. I thought if it didn't work out at the farm I could always leave. There'd be lots of jobs for part-time doctors in Australia. So I went through IVF in London and when I was four months pregnant I came.'

'To find…'

'What you see,' she said, and he could tell she was trying hard now to keep bitterness at bay. 'Betty's here, and Angus. Angus is Betty's son, Will's uncle. Will had met his shy Uncle Angus who lived in a separate house on the farm, but he knew little about him. Now I realise how disabled he is. He has high-level Asperger's, which means he's intelligent enough to care for himself, but he's pathologically afraid of the outside world. Betty's been in and out of hospital for the last couple of years, and by himself Angus has let the farm fall apart. Betty's had to sell the milking herd and half the land to recoup, and she's now terrified that when she dies he won't be able to stay here.

So her plan was to induce me to come, help her care for Angus, and work as a doctor while she minded the farm and the baby.'

'But she must have been ill when she wrote to you.'

'Yes, but she didn't intend the chemotherapy not to work. Hope has to feed on something. So I walked straight into a mess, but by the time I'd been here for twenty-four hours I knew I couldn't walk away. I am…I *was* William's wife. William loved Betty. He loved this farm. To turn my back on them…I can't.'

'I see,' he said slowly, and he did, and he was seeing chasms everywhere. He'd also seen the way she'd looked at Betty. Maggie's husband had loved his grandmother. Like it or not, deception or not, Maggie's allegiance was inviolate.

She was some woman. A feisty, loyal, doctor.

A woman to make his heart twist…

'It's not a great story,' she said across his thoughts. 'I…. Thank you for listening.'

'I wish there was more I could do.'

'There isn't.' She hesitated. 'So why gynaecology?'

'Sorry?' he said, startled.

'I've told you mine. You tell me yours.'

'We need to get those wounds dressed.'

'You've been saying that for hours. Another ten minutes won't hurt.'

'There's nothing to tell.'

'I watched your face as you watched my baby. There's shadows.'

'My shadows are none of your business.'

'They're not,' she agreed obligingly, and tugged her eider-down closer and pushed herself to her feet. 'Sorry. Of course I don't want to know if you don't want to tell me.' She looked thoughtfully out to where he'd parked his car beside the last tractor in the row. 'There's probably a really logical reason, like gynaecology makes more money than obstetrics.'

'So it does.'

'And you can sleep uninterrupted at night.'

'So I can.'

'But that's not the reason.'

How did she know? He couldn't figure it out, but there was something about this night, something about this woman, that said only the truth would do. It was none of her business, but suddenly it was.

'I lost my wife when she was six months pregnant,' he said, and she plumped straight back down beside him. Close. Her hand took his and held it.

'Oh, Max…'

'Past history,' he said. 'Six years ago. A case of the doctor's wife getting the worst care. I was an obstetrician. She died of pre-eclampsia.'

'You're saying it was your fault?'

'I should have monitored her more closely.'

She frowned. 'You wouldn't have been the treating doctor. She'd have had her own obstetrician?'

'Yes, but—'

'So how often would you have checked her blood pressure if you'd been in charge?' To his astonishment she was sounding indignant.

'That's not the point.'

'It is. Unless you ignored swollen ankles and puffy hands and breathlessness and any of the other signs.'

'She didn't—'

'She didn't have obvious signs until too late,' she finished for him, as if she knew. As indeed she might. 'You know as well as I do that pre-eclampsia can move really fast. Terrifyingly fast. You'll be pleased to know I take my own blood pressure twice a day, but I'm paranoid and if I was your wife and you tried to take mine twice a day I'd be telling you where you could put your cuff. Tell me about your wife. What was she called?'

'Alice.'

'That's a lovely name,' she said warmly. 'Was she lovely?'

'I… Yes.' But he said it hesitantly. Sadly even. Aware that the memory of the lovely, laughing girl he'd met and married so long ago was fading. Aware that photographs of her were starting to superimpose themselves over real memory.

'It's awful, isn't it?' she said confidingly, breaking a silence that was starting to be too long. 'You think you'll remember for ever. You think how can you ever move on? It's impossible. And all of a sudden…' She paused, then gave herself a shake, tossing away thoughts she obviously didn't want. 'And your baby?'

'A little boy. He lived for twenty-three hours.'

'And you called him…'

'Daniel,' he said, and he was suddenly aware that it was the first time he'd said it since the funeral. Daniel. A tiny being, robbed of his mother; robbed of his life.

Odd that his memories of Alice were fading, yet the memory of that tiny part of him, Daniel cradled in his hands, his son, was still so strong. Still so gut-wrenchingly real.

'I'm so sorry,' she said, and the pressure of her hand was warm and strong. Maggie would certainly be a great doctor, he thought. Empathic and caring and…lovely?

Lovely. There it was again. It wasn't a professional word, he thought, but it was in his head and it wouldn't go away.

'So?' she said.

'So I abandoned obstetrics, left England and came to Sydney to be a gynaecologist,' he said, too briskly, and rose to his feet. 'End of story. You need to go to bed.' He sounded rougher than he'd intended.

'I do,' she admitted.

'Let me carry you. That leg must be giving you hell.'

'It's not tickling,' she admitted, and somewhat to his surprise she didn't object as he gathered her up in her pile of eiderdowns.

'Maybe it's time we both moved on,' she said as he carried her through the roses, and he didn't disagree at all.

The fire was dying in the grate. He settled her on the settee again, loaded the fireplace with logs, found a can of soup, made them both soup and toast—he was hungry even if she wasn't—and bullied her into eating.

Then, finally, he tended her face and her knee. And all the time…

Lovely.

The word kept echoing over and over.

Which was crazy. And impossible. She was seven months pregnant. He was mixing her up with his memories of Alice, he thought as he worked. He had Alice in his mind—that it was Alice he was helping, It was Alice he could save.

No!

But there were memories coming at him from every-where and the only word that kept superimposing itself on all of them was…

Lovely.

He had the gentlest hands.

She was drifting. He was cleaning her face, carefully ridding it of every trace of dirt, then making it secure with wound-closure strips and dressings. Occasionally what he was doing hurt, but she hardly noticed.

His face was so close to hers. Intent on what he was doing. Careful.

Caring.

How long had it been since someone had cared for her? How long since someone had even opened a can of soup and made her toast?

It was an illusion, she told herself. This man was trapped by circumstances, in the same way she was trapped. The only difference was that tomorrow morning he'd leave and she'd stay.

But somehow the bleakness had lifted. For tonight she could let herself drift in this illusion of tenderness. She could look into his face as he worked, watch his eyes, abandon herself in their depths. Feel the strength and skill of his fingers. Watch his concern.

He was worried about her. She should reassure him, she thought. She should say she had things under control, everything was fine, that she'd bounce up in the morning like Tigger. As she'd bounced before.

Only right now she didn't feel like Tigger. Surprisingly, though, neither did she feel like Eeyore, for who could feel sorry for herself when a doctor like Max Ashton was right in front of her? He was so close she could take his face between her hands and…

And nothing. Get a grip, she told herself, and something in her face must have changed because Max's hands lifted away and his brows snapped downward.

'Did I hurt you?'

'I… No. I believe I'm nearly asleep.'

'I need to wash your knee.'

'Go right ahead.'

'You want to wriggle out of what's left of those jeans?'

'I can do that,' she said with an attempt at dignity, and then tried and it didn't work, and when Max gave up watching and helped she was pleased. Only then his hands were on her thighs and she thought that was pretty good, too.

Whoa. Keep it in focus, Maggie. He was a doctor and she was a patient.

She felt like she was drifting on painkillers, yet she'd had nothing. She felt drifty and lovely, and like it was entirely right that she was lying half-naked on a settee in front of a roaring fire with the man of her dreams taking her leg in his hands.

The man of her dreams?

'Ouch!'

Yikes, that brought her down to earth. Earth to Maggie? It was about time contact was made.

'Sorry,' he said ruefully. 'But it's not looking as bad as I thought.'

'Good,' she said sleepily. 'Excellent.'

'Have you been worrying?' he asked, sounding bemused.

'I guess I'll worry if it's about to drop off,' she said. 'Speaking of dropping off…'

'You want me to carry you to bed?'

'I'm fine here.' The thought of going out to her apartment at the back of the house seemed suddenly unbearable.

'You are fine,' he told her. 'Some of that initial swelling's already subsiding. I think you've simply given this one heck of a bang. I suspect the X-ray tomorrow will show a nice big haematoma at the back of the knee and nothing else.'

'Excellent. Then life can get back to normal.' She hesitated. 'You know, I don't really need you to stay.'

'I need to stay,' he said. 'You banged your head, you shook

your daughter about and you need to be in hospital under observation. If that's not possible, you're stuck with me.'

'Or you're stuck with us. I'm sorry.'

'Forget it,' he said roughly, and then looked contrite. 'Sorry. 'It's okay, though. Just forget the sorry and think of it as one colleague helping another. You look like you need far more help than I can possibly give, but one night out of my life isn't much.'

Put like that, it even sounded reasonable that he stayed, she thought. And there was no way she was arguing any more. Not when she wanted him to stay so much.

For all the right reasons, she told herself hastily. For very sensible reasons, which had nothing to do with the way her insides did this queer little lurch when he looked at her.

'"You want to use Gran's settee?' she managed.

'You want me to stay here with you?'

She did. It sounded wimpy and she had no right to ask him. There were plenty of spare bedrooms. But…

'This room's warm.'

'So it is,' he said, and suddenly he was smiling.

'I—it seems a waste to heat another.'

'It does,' he agreed. 'And it'll mean I can check your vital signs during the night without getting up. Also it'll mean I don't need to get my sleeping bag from the car.'

'You don't need to check my vital signs.' But the night was getting fuzzier and she was getting past arguing. 'You have a sleeping bag?'

'For camping. At the music festival. Not that I needed to. My friends organised us a camp that'd make a Bedouin sheikh jealous.'

'Your friends?'

'Fiona did most of the organising. She's a radiologist and she's a very organising person.'

Fiona. He had a girlfriend, then. Of course he did. Anyone with a smile like that would have a partner. There was no reason then why her somersaulting insides would suddenly somersault in a different direction.

It was too much. She was too tired. She needed to sleep and not think of problems and how she was going to manage with an injured knee and how she could check Gran through the night when she was so tired and what she was going to do tomorrow.

Without Max. Who had a girlfriend.

'Do you need help with the bathroom?' he asked, and she had to think about it before answering.

'I can manage,' she said with another of her dumb attempts at dignity.

'Really?'

'Really.'

'Very well,' he said, and smiled and lifted her eiderdown and tucked it up under her chin. And then, before she knew what he intended—before she could even guess he'd thought of such a gesture—he bent and kissed her.

It was a feather kiss, maybe a kiss of reassurance, of warmth and of comfort. But surely such a kiss should be on the forehead. Not on the lips.

But on her lips it was.

His mouth brushed hers, and it was as if the heat of the room was suddenly centred right there, and it was a surge of warmth so great it was all she could do not to reach out and hold him and lock the kiss to her.

Only her hands were under the eiderdown. Thankfully. Because to hold this man…

To hold him would be a shout that she needed him, that she was alone, she was bereft and he was everything she most wanted but could never have.

William…

She made herself say her husband's name in her head but it didn't work. There was nothing there.

William. Gone.

Max. Here. All male.

'Goodnight, Maggie,' he whispered, and she could have wept as he drew away.

'Goodnight,' she made herself whisper back.

She closed her eyes. She didn't want to, but she did.

William, William, William.

As a mantra it had no strength at all.

Max. She wanted him to stay. Right here. Right now.

For ever.

CHAPTER FIVE

SHE woke and sun was streaming in the windows. Max was kneeling in front of the fire and it was morning.

It was well into morning. Her eyes flew open, she stared at the sunlight flooding the room and thought this was no dawn light.

Her eyes flew to the grandfather clock in the corner and as if on cue it started to boom.

Nine booms. Nine o'clock!

'And how any of you ever sleep with that thing is a mystery,' Max murmured, kneeling to blow on the embers as she stared at the clock as if it had betrayed her. The embers leapt to life—of course. Would they dare not if this man ordered?

He looked… He looked…

Much cleaner than last night, for a start. He looked like he'd showered. He was wearing clean jeans and a clean shirt, though he had the sleeves rolled up as if he meant business.

He looked like he should always be here. Making her fire in the mornings. Living in her house. Just being here.

But then he turned to her and she saw the strain on his face and inappropriate thoughts went right out the window.

'Betty died at six o'clock this morning,' he told her, and her world stilled.

'Died…'

'You were sleeping so soundly that short of a bucket of cold water I couldn't rouse you. I couldn't bring myself to do it. I'm sorry.'

'Betty,' she whispered, and she felt a wave of grief for the old lady, a grief so strong it threatened to overwhelm her.

Though she'd known Betty by her correspondence and via William for longer, she'd only known Betty personally for a few months. For most of those months she'd been angry. Betty had conned her into coming, had trapped her. But despite her anger she'd never doubted Betty's motives. She'd manoeuvred Maggie into coming for love of a son, for love of her son she had no other way to protect.

Maggie's hands went instinctively to her own belly as her baby gave a fluttery kick inside her. Who knew what she'd do to protect this little one?

When did a mother's love die?

'Angus…' she whispered.

'Angus was with his mother when she died.'

'Angus was!' She stared at him, incredulous. In the whole time she'd been here Angus had never been in the house. It was almost as if he was afraid of it.

'I thought they'd both want it,' he told her, squatting back on his heels and meeting her gaze with steadiness and truth. 'I thought if Angus has been farming for years he'll understand what death is.'

'But how did you make him come?'

'I told him what was happening. I told him what I thought he should do and he agreed.'

'But to make him listen…'

'I know. I went over to the haystack, he backed away so I simply said his mother was dying and needed him to sit with her. Then I came back and sat on one of his tractors until he came. It took him half an hour to work up the courage, but he came. I stayed on the tractor and told him what Betty's condition was, and finally he decided he could come into the house. Betty woke, just for a moment, as he arrived. He held her hand until she died.'

'Oh, Max,' she said, awed. And then, 'Oh, I should have done that.'

'I think your body was simply demanding you stopped,' he said gently. 'And to be honest, Maggie, it wasn't you Betty wanted. She had a tiny sliver of awareness left, and it was all for Angus.'

'Oh, Max,' she said again, and burst into tears.

He moved then, like a big cat, covering the distance between them as if it was nothing. She'd half risen but he gathered her into his arms, as if that was where she'd been heading all along, and he held her close.

And maybe his arms were where she had been heading. She didn't know—all she knew was that right now she needed him. She clung to him, he held her close and in those first few moments of grief she let out the emotions that had welled within her for years.

How long since she'd wept? Even the night William had died... His parents had been there and they'd been angry with her because she and William hadn't consented to some new and amazing treatment they'd heard of in the States. It didn't matter that William was far too ill to travel by the time they came on board with their offer to send him. Their anger had surrounded her, deflected her grief, making it seem like she had no right to a grief that was all theirs.

So now here she was, three years later, sobbing out grief for William's grandmother instead, being held in the arms of a complete stranger, letting it out, letting it out.

She didn't care. She simply sobbed until she was done, and when he laid her back on the cushions and she finally managed a watery smile, she knew the time for crying was over.

'Thank you,' she said simply. 'If Betty had Angus with her then, yes, she had everything she wanted. And she saw him with the calves last night.'

'And he saw *her* with the calves,' Max agreed. 'He knows they were a gift from his mother. He's back with them now. He even talked about burials.' He smiled. 'He seemed to think the back paddock'd be a good place but I managed to talk him out of it. We discussed where his father was buried and thought that'd be okay. I believe you'll be able to talk it through with him when you're ready.'

'But—'

'I've organised the undertaker to come in a couple of hours,' he said. 'And I've rung the coroner. He agrees that since the old doctor left detailed notes before you arrived, outlining Betty's condition as terminal, I can certify her death, even though I didn't see her until last night.'

'How did you know all this?' she asked, dazed.

'You have her medical file on the dresser,' he said. 'I read it during the night.'

She took a deep breath. This was huge. She couldn't sign Betty's death certificate herself—not when she'd been sharing a house with her—but without a certificate from a treating doctor, the police would have had to be called; a coroner's inquest required.

Max had circumvented it all.

'You've been awake all night?'

'Most of it,' he admitted, and motioned to the grandfather clock and grinned. 'Ben here kept me company.'

'You could have moved,' she said, but then she thought back to vague memories of the night. Once or twice, early in the night, she'd stirred. She knew she had. Both times Max had been right by her, asking about her pain, just there until she'd drifted off again.

She'd slept because he'd been right beside her.

Clearly not all the time.

'I checked on Betty just after midnight,' he continued. 'I thought she was slipping then, but it was faster than I thought.'

'Oh, Max.' She gulped and swallowed, not knowing what to say. There was nothing to say.

'There's more,' he said. 'If you're up to listening.'

'More…'

'I've had the night to think,' he told her. 'In between Ben's timely announcements to the world. Maybe I should warn you that my theatre staff consider me a little bit…well, maybe their term might be domineering. And organised. Maybe to the point of obsession. I do like a good plan.' He shot her another of his disarming grins. 'So I've done some preliminary planning.'

'I don't understand.'

'I know you won't be able to take it all in right now,' he said sympathetically. 'So just listen and take in what you can. Ideally you need time to say goodbye to Betty, to plan her funeral, to let your leg heal and to get over the shock of the last twenty-four hours. I think you need to lie on this settee for the next week—possibly even until your baby's born. Only there's no one to take over your work. I took four days off for the music festival, which gives me today clear but that's it. I have a huge surgical waiting list—I do all the major public gynaecological surgery for South Sydney—so, like it or not, after today I'm no help at all. So I need to act fast. First we get you showered.'

'*We?*'

'Objection at step one?' he demanded quizzically. 'You're hardly steady enough to shower alone.'

'If you've already showered,' she said with another of her futile attempts at dignity, 'you'll see there's rails and a seat set up for Betty.'

Betty. So much emotion.

'Okay, you have rails,' Max conceded, watching her face. Obviously seeing her need to get independent fast. 'Next item on list is letting people know about Betty. William's parents? Will they come? Your own parents?'

'Not happening.' She shook her head, trying to rid herself of a wave of self-pity. Of want. Of need.

Because her need wasn't for her parents, who'd been a tiny part of her life before they'd sent her to boarding school at six, or William's, who simply wouldn't care enough to come, but for this man who she'd known only since last night and she had no right to need at all.

'Friends?'

'Betty has a town full of friends, but if you've let the undertakers know, the word will be around town already.'

'Okay,' he said. 'That's easy. So now we move to stage three of my plan.'

'Your plan. For world domination?' she asked, cautiously, trying to smile.

'Better. I've found you a locum.'

'Max!'

'Yeah, I know this is way too much organisation,' he said,

and raked his fingers through his dark hair with the air of a man who wasn't sure where to start. 'But, hell, Maggie, you're a basket case.'

What? Imperceptibly her spine stiffened and her eyes flashed. 'What did you call me?'

'A basket case.'

'I am not!' *A basket case.*

'Okay, only a tiny bit of a basket case,' he said hurriedly. 'The rest of you is pure, brilliant competence. But for the little piece of you that might need to put her leg up for a time… Maggie, do you need the income from your medicine?'

For a moment she thought about not answering. This was so not his business. But he was looking at with such concern, how could she not?

'I have William's insurance,' she conceded.

'Excellent. So if you aren't emotionally committed to practising medicine for the next few months, then you don't need to. You know you've had two calls this morning already?'

'Two calls?'

'Neither of them serious, both of them I've referred to the medical tent at the festival,' he said. 'But I can hardly leave you to run yourself into high blood pressure.'

'I'm not like Alice.'

'No,' he said, and caught himself. 'No.'

'So?'

'So nothing,' he said, suddenly cool and professional. 'Blood pressure or not, you've been overworking and undereating and it has to stop. So here's my plan.'

Grief and shock had taken a back seat for the moment— fascination had taken its place. This was a man in move-a-mountain mode. Bemused, Maggie decided it might just behoove a girl to lie back and let him move it.

I have an internist friend who's looking for work,' Max said. 'John's a forty-year-old doctor from Zimbabwe. His wife, Margaret, is a dentist. John's a highly trained doctor and he's just finished his supervised assessment for accreditation in Australia. He had a job lined up in northern Victoria but it fell through last week. I rang him this morning and sounded him out about taking on the position of locum here for a while.'

'You rang him?'

'Just to check he's still available,' he said, still sounding clinically detached. As if he was handing out a prescription. 'But to say he's eager is an understatement. He has two young daughters who think the beach sounds great, and he's free right now. If they can stay here while they size the place up, they can be here tomorrow. John can act as locum and if you're interested in a long-term arrangement—even a partnership—that might work, too.'

'Tomorrow,' she said, and flabbergasted wasn't too strong a word for it.

'I have a surgical list first thing tomorrow morning so I need to leave tonight,' he said apologetically. 'But I rang the first-aid people at the festival. Until John arrives they're happy for you to divert your phone through to them. They'll cope with minor stuff and call for help on the big stuff. So today and tonight are covered. And then… John's great. I'm sure he and his family will be sensitive to Angus and to your independence. Maggie, it'd mean someone would be here when you went into labour.'

And the professional detachment was gone. He was suddenly sounding hesitant—coaxing—as if he was trying to persuade her to do something against her will.

Against her will? Was he out of his mind?

She'd advertised for a locum but there'd been no applicants, yet here was Max, pulling doctors out of hats. To have another doctor here…

'You're kidding me, right?'

'I'm not kidding,' he said, seriously. 'And I've done nothing you can't undo.'

'Why would I want to undo it?' she demanded, feeling breathless. 'I mean, I haven't met John but if you say he's good…'

'He's good.'

'They *could* stay here,' she said, trying to take it in. 'I mean…for the short term. But there's lots of places in town for long-term rent. They might prefer it.'

'You need someone to be here when you go into labour.'

'Whoa. You sound like my mother.' Then she heard what she'd said and corrected herself in her head. *You sound like my mother ought to sound like.*

Or not. There was nothing maternal about Max Ashton.

There was nothing maternal about the way she was feeling about Max Ashton. Or the way the concern in his eyes made her feel.

'I'm very maternal,' he said, and grinned, and, wham, there it was again, that smile.

She couldn't afford to get sucked into that smile.

What was she thinking? Betty was dead, she reminded herself frantically. That ought to be enough to deflect her. She should be grief stricken. But after last night…

No. Grief had very little place here. She and Betty had grieved together during the final stages of the illness. Now there was an aching sense of loss, but with it a huge relief that Betty had gone as she'd wanted, in her own bed, with her son by her side, knowing all was safe with her world.

And that was because of this one overbearing, domineering doctor with a heart-stopping smile. Whose plans she had to focus on because she was feeling as if she was about to be swept up in a tidal wave. Any minute now he'd offer to paint her baby-crib pink.

Or not. She looked again at his face and saw strain behind his smile, and thought this was hard for him—planning for her when he wanted nothing to do with pregnancy.

'You don't need to worry about me in labour,' she said, fighting to get her face in order. 'I'm having my baby in Sydney.'

'You are?'

'That was about my only sensible stipulation before I came here,' she said. 'I've organised an apartment in Sydney before and after the birth. I told Betty I was doing that before I even came to the farm.' She gave him a shame-faced smile, thinking she sounded a wimp. 'I thought there'd be a family doctor here, but I wanted back-up. And, yes, I realised going to Sydney will leave Yandilagong without a doctor, but there's nothing I can do about that. I can't be on call when I'm in labour.'

'You don't think?' he demanded, and suddenly the tension was easing. 'What's wrong with you? What a wuss.'

'I am,' she said, and discovered she was smiling back at him. And more—the lump of grief around her heart since she'd learned that Betty was dead was lifting away.

Was she fickle as well as cowardly?

'Hey,' he said softly, and he cupped her chin with his middle and index fingers, lifting her face so her eyes met his. 'It's not wrong to smile now,' he said softly. 'Betty knew it was her time. She planned everything and it happened exactly as she wanted.' He smiled gently into her eyes, forcing her to smile in return. 'Yes, she might be somewhere now where she has inside knowledge that her carefully orchestrated grandson is, in fact, a girl, but she can hardly come back and demand a rerun. So let's send her up a little message that girls can run farms, too, accept that she died happy and move on.'

'I will,' she said, and suddenly, inexplicably, she sniffed. It was the way he was looking at her. Like he cared…

What was it about this man? He was turning her into a sodden heap.

'Good girl,' he said softly. 'Will you accept John and his family to help you?'

'I… Yes.' What else was a girl to say?

'Great. Are you sure you don't want help with that shower?'

'No, thank you,' she told him, but it was a lie. She'd have loved help with her shower. Only she was a big girl and big girls didn't lean on big boys. Doctors didn't lean on their colleagues.

Maggie didn't lean on Max?

Without Max it would have been a ghastly morning. As it was…showered and fresh, she said her goodbyes to Betty while Max hovered in the background, filling in technicalities, smoothing the way for Betty's departure.

It was he who contacted the priest from Betty's church, and who let him in as Maggie finished a needfully long shower. It was Max who hiked his brows as Maggie produced a list of instructions as long as her arm to give to the priest. It seemed Betty had planned her funeral right down to the Wellingtons and moleskins she wanted to be buried in, but it was Max who went through the list with the priest, ensuring Betty could have exactly what she wanted.

It was Max who stood beside her as she rang William's parents—as she heard their irritation that Betty's death had come at such an inconvenient time and really they couldn't come right now.

'Told you so,' she mouthed at Max as they talked, and he smiled and gave her a thumps-up, you-were-right sign, and what would have been an appalling call was made lighter.

Then he made calls to more distant relatives for her—yes, sadly Betty was dead, no, sorry, Maggie couldn't come to the phone right now, she was understandably upset, the funeral arrangements would be in the local paper tomorrow if they wanted to come. While Maggie nursed her third mug of tea for the morning and watched and thought this was hero material and all Max needed was a Superman outfit and he'd be right up there, leaping tall buildings, with her tucked neatly under his arm.

No one could deny Superman.

So calls made, he accepted no more arguments, but put her in the car and headed for Yandilagong. It took half an hour to navigate the main street as the festival was still going full swing but finally they reached the clinic. This had been set up by the old doctor, and Maggie now used it as her surgery. She went to clamber out of the car with her crutches but there were crowds of people on the pavement and someone jostled her, and Max swore and was at her side in an instant, picking her up yet again and carrying her through, regardless of her protests. Superman still.

But then he paused.

'Max!' It was a shout from across the street. Max turned with his burden still in his arms.

A woman was running lightly across the road. Beautiful. Sleek, cream jacket, casual jeans, lovely silver ballet flats. Gorgeous blonde hair, straight and glossy as a shampoo advertisement, the fringe pushed back with designer sunglasses. A wide, white smile.

'Fiona.'

Fiona. The girlfriend.

Lois to Superman's Clark Kent, while the wimp in his arms was simply some woman he'd rescued before he moved onto the next task.

'I thought you had a call back to Sydney,' Fiona said, clearly astounded.

'I did,' he said. 'But I had an accident on the road and was forced to stay. Fiona, meet my accident. Dr Maggie Croft, meet Dr Fiona Hamilton. I told you about Fi last night. She's a radiologist.'

'Hi,' Maggie said, feeling really, really at a disadvantage. Lying back in Superman's arms was scarcely a way to endear yourself to Lois. Or to Fiona.

This woman was also a doctor. That made three of them, but there wasn't a lot of professional recognition in the way Fiona was looking at her. Well, what do you expect if you go around carried in Superman's arms, she demanded of herself. She was the victim here. The rescuee. Superman's armful.

'You didn't go back,' Fiona said blankly, looking from Maggie back to Max.

'No. As I said, I was stuck.'

'You really did have an accident?' Fiona's gaze shifted to the Aston Martin. As if to verify the claim, there it was, a smashed headlight, a crumpled left panel and a crack running the width of the windscreen.

'Oh, your car,' she said in horror, and put her hand to her eyes as if she couldn't bear such hurt. 'Oh, your gorgeous car.'

'Maggie was hurt, too,' he said brusquely. 'I'm taking her in for an X-ray.'

'You're X-raying her here?'

'Apparently it's not as much a backwater as you might think,' Max said. 'I gather there's basic X-ray equipment.'

'I don't understand,' Fiona said. 'Why are you carrying her?'

'Because he's bossy,' Maggie said, finally deciding she needed to be helpful if she was ever going to get this over with. 'Max won't let me use crutches. The fact that I was fine on them last night…'

'Max stayed with you last night?' Fiona asked, incredulous.

'Yeah, and with Grandma and Angus and our cows and our dog,' she said, deciding to pre-empt trouble before it got a hold. 'He was really useful. But I don't want him to drop me, so…'

'I'll come in with you,' Fiona said, sounding bemused, and stood aside and let them both pass. 'You stayed with her last night, Max? You stayed in the same house as real people?'

'Don't be impertinent,' Max retorted, and Fiona grinned as if it was a shared joke.

Great. She so didn't want to be here, Maggie decided. If they were in Superman territory she wouldn't mind a telephone box to disappear into.

Or was she thinking Doctor Who? A bit of time travel to a different place.

But there was no avoiding practicalities. Max had to let her down to unlock the building. She opened it, entered her security code, then sat down speedily in the chair next to the door, because to tell the truth both knees were wobbly now. She could cope with Max here, but Fiona's presence completely unnerved her. She made her feel about ten.

'The X-ray machine's in there,' she told Max, pointing to the next room. 'If you set it up, I'll come in when you're ready.'

'How out of the ark are we talking?' Max said cautiously, while Fiona looked on in obvious bewilderment.

'State of the art,' Maggie retorted. 'Or,' she added honestly, 'it was state of the art ten years ago. The old doctor got it second hand from Gosland hospital when they extended. For nice plain skull and knee pictures it's fine.'

'You've used it recently?'

'It really is fine,' she said, growing incensed. 'What, you think we should have brought a small animal to test it on first? How about if Fiona volunteers a toe?'

Maybe that was uncalled for. Dumb, really. She didn't know this woman, and to include her in a stupid joke...

But Fiona looked as if she hadn't even heard. She tugged open the door and stared through at the X-ray equipment, becoming efficient. 'I'll check it for you, Max,' she said briskly.

'Wow,' she muttered. 'I have my own gynaecologist *and* radiologist.'

She was ignored. They were both in clinical mode. She had a sudden vision of them both back in Sydney, two hugely qualified specialists, totally focussed on their work.

Beside them she felt like a country hick. A patient to be cared for with clinical efficiency and kindness.

That's what Max had been doing all night, she thought dully. Caring for her with kindness.

'There's nothing complicated here,' Fiona called. 'So what were you intending to do today? Make sure she's okay and then come back to end the festival with us?'

She? *She's the cat's mother.* A saying used to teach children it was impolite to refer to people impersonally.

She, the patient. She, the inanimate object, causing trouble.

'I'm still heading back to Sydney,' Max told her, equally brisk, 'just as soon as I know Maggie's not going to do anything dramatic.' Without waiting for a response—or an okay—he lifted Maggie again and carried her through. Still talking to Fiona. 'We were always going back separately anyway. You know I have a list in the morning, and Clarissa and Doug are staying until it ends. I can't wait until then.'

'It's pretty dreary,' Fiona said. Max laid Maggie down on

the prepared trolley, and Fiona manoeuvred the overhead X-ray machine over her knee. She slid a pillow underneath with the ease of a professional, as if she'd done it a million times before. As she must have. This was a simple technical procedure. She wasn't X-raying a patient. She was X-raying a knee.

'Clarissa and Doug are bickering,' she said. 'Brenda's boyfriend turned up and I've had enough music. I'll come home with you, as soon as you're ready.'

'Fine,' Max said. 'Are you okay there, Maggie?'

'Fine,' she repeated. Feeling like a sack of potatoes. Wanting, pathetically, to say, 'Hey, this is about me.'

'Do you have leather shields?' Fiona demanded, still not looking at her. 'We need to protect the pregnancy.'

The pregnancy. Not the baby. Not *her* baby.

'In the side cupboard,' she said through gritted teeth, and Max fetched them and set them up so they formed a barrier between the X-ray machine and her belly. Her daughter.

Annie? Not Archibald. She had a bit of thinking to do on that one.

Chloe didn't seem right any more.

'Right. Keep still,' Fiona said. 'Hold the position. Max, get out of range.'

So Max moved back behind the door and Fiona clicked and then clicked again.

'And her head,' Max said,

'Her head. Why?'

'She gave it a bang when we hit last night.'

'So why didn't you X-ray it last night.'

'Maggie's grandmother died last night. We couldn't leave her.'

'She died…'

'Of old age,' Maggie said wearily, not wanting any more questions, wanting this conversation to be over. 'That's why Max stayed. He was wonderful. But I don't need him any more and you both need to be in Sydney. Can we get on with this, please, because, like you, I need to go home.'

Her X-rays were fine, beautifully read by Fiona. Torn ligaments in her knee that would heal in time. Nothing wrong with her head. Fiona wished her all the best for her recovery—and for her pregnancy—and left to go back to their 'camp' to pack. Max drove Maggie back to the farm and the closer to home they got the drearier she felt.

Why had meeting Fiona made everything seem worse? Heavier?

They pulled into the driveway and she recognised the vehicle at the front gate. Who wouldn't? A silver hearse is unmistakable in anyone's language.

Max cut the motor and went to get out, but she put her hand out and stopped him.

'You don't have anything inside?'

'No, but—'

'But then it's time for you to go,' she told him, trying to make her tone firm and sure. A man and a woman were waiting for her on the veranda, dressed in sombre grey. That was her future, she thought. Grey.

Grey with a baby daughter? She gave herself a mental slap to the side of the head and made herself smile. Maybe grey until she'd buried Betty and her knee stopped hurting, but in the long term she'd be fine. More than fine. Max had conjured up a locum. Even the sight of the staff from the Yandilagong Funeral Parlour didn't have the capacity to dim that.

'You've been wonderful,' she said. 'But Fiona's waiting.'

'She's not—'

'You know she is. And I don't need you any more. Last night I did need you, and I'll always be profoundly grateful that you were here for me. And you've found me a locum. You have no idea how grateful I am for that.'

'You know that John might stay long term if you want to share.'

'I might just want to,' she said. 'But that's for the future. So thank you again.' She tugged her crutches over from the back seat and opened the car door.

'Maggie?'

She turned back to him.

'I could stay another night and leave at dawn. I don't want you on your own.'

'I have a sore knee,' she said, pushing herself out of his gorgeous car. 'That's all. I can manage by myself. And, besides, I have Angus and cows and dog and tractors. What's alone about that? Meanwhile, you have your own life you need to get back to. Thank you.'

He looked across at her—and then before she knew what he intended he was out of the car, coming around to her side, taking her crutches and placing them against his precious but increasingly battered car.

'Maggie, thank *you*,' he said heavily. 'You've reminded me…'

He paused. Reminded him of what? she thought, but she looked at his face and knew he wouldn't answer. Knew he didn't know how to answer.

'John's good,' he said inconsequentially, and she nodded.

'If he's worked with you I imagine he must be.'

'He can work with everyone. Kids. Babies. He's okay.'

'Are you saying you're not okay?' she asked gently. 'Because you no longer work with babies?'

'I'm fine.'

'I hope you are.' And then, because he looked…lost? No, surely that was too strong a word for it, just a little bewildered, as if Superman's world was a bit out of kilter and he didn't know how to put it right. And she thought, Why not?

Why not? She really wanted to do this. She wouldn't see this guy after today. What was the harm?

When she really, really wanted to do it. Fiona or not. What difference would a kiss make?

And before she could examine the thought any further, her hands came up to take his face and draw his mouth down to hers.

Only his mouth was already moving. To hers.

And for one long, sweet moment sanity flew out the window.

There was nothing sensible about kissing Maggie. There was nothing planned. He only knew that her lips were on his, that his hands were on her waist, drawing her into him, feeling a blast of want and need so great it threatened…

Well, it didn't threaten. It simply did. Did remove sanity. Did remove acknowledgement of how crazy this was, how inappropriate, how stupid.

Nothing mattered but the surety that he was kissing her.

She tasted of honey. Honey, he thought, and had a flash of recall, hours ago, sharing toast and honey. It must have stayed. Or maybe honey always clung to this woman.

As did sweetness.

As did heat.

For heat was what he was feeling—heat surging through the linking of their mouths, through the fire he felt in his hands at her waist, through the way her body curved and clung as her lips parted to welcome him into her. She was aching for him to deepen the kiss, showing a need that was at least as great as his own.

Did he need her?

That was a crazy thought, too, for of course he didn't need her. He never could need. To expose himself to that sort of pain… No!

So he'd leave this afternoon and never come back. She'd get on with her own life and he'd get on with his. But strangely, unaccountably it made his immediate need even greater. Knowing that this might be the only time—this *would* be the only time—that he could hold her in his arms and let desire hold sway.

She was so lovely—achingly lovely. She was simply dressed in pregnancy jeans and windcheater, she was battered and tired and very pregnant—yet lovely had been one of the first things he'd thought when he'd seen her, and he thought it again now.

Her body was all soft curves. Her pregnant belly moulded against him and he found himself curving to accommodate it. A man taking his woman unto him.

He was deepening the kiss—deepening, deepening, deepening, until all he felt was her and all he knew was her, and the rest of the world could float away for all he cared.

Only, of course, it didn't. It couldn't. The woman on the veranda was clearly not amused at being kept waiting. She'd walked down to meet them. She'd stopped four feet away from them and coughed, a cough that said this wasn't appropriate, she could understand sympathy this morning but she couldn't understand passion.

Dammit. He felt Maggie shift in his arms, withdraw, become conscious again of her surroundings, and he wanted to shout 'No' and tug her closer, but the woman coughed again and he wanted to strangle her.

Reluctantly, achingly, he let Maggie pull away, then stood, holding her at arm's length, gazing down at her bewildered eyes. Her mouth was lush and full, her lips just kissed…

But behind them the woman was looking confused.

'Dr Croft?' she said.

'That's me,' Maggie said, and there was a definite shake to her voice. 'I'm sorry I've kept you waiting. 'Dr Ashton was just kissing me goodbye.'

Goodbye.

The word stung—but that's what this was. For one long moment he teetered, a part of him wanting to say, no, it's not goodbye, this is just the beginning. But then Archibald—or was it Ernestine?—kicked, and Maggie glanced ruefully at her abdomen and so did Max. And there was her baby between them.

Reality slammed back, and remembered pain. No. He wasn't ready for this. He'd never be ready. Exposing himself to the pain he'd felt six years ago… No and no and no.

Where to go from here?

Nowhere.

To leave seemed impossible. To leave seemed like leaving part of himself behind.

'Fiona's waiting,' Maggie said. 'I'm sorry about the kiss. You don't have to tell her.'

'Fiona's not—'

'Max, just go,' she said, and her voice was really trembling. 'Please. I can cope myself. I will be fine. I'll be better if you go.'

'I don't want to leave you.'

'You must,' she said gently. 'You have your world and I have mine.' Her chin jutted a little and she forced herself to smile. 'You go and get back to your life. But thank you for being wonderful. My hero.'

She hesitated for a moment, then lightly stood on tiptoe and kissed him again. Only this time it was different. It was a fleeting, final kiss of farewell.

And then, very deliberately, she turned her back on him. She nodded decisively to the woman waiting. 'Let's go inside. I've kept you waiting long enough.'

She made her way slowly on her crutches up to the veranda and he watched her go and she didn't turn back once.

Max was free to go.

She didn't look back. If she had she would have wept. As it was, the woman from the undertaker kept giving her odd glances.

This was a small community. It'd be all over town by night-fall that she'd kissed a stranger—that Dr Maggie had a love life.

She didn't have a love life. She'd kissed him and it was entirely inappropriate. He had a girlfriend. What was she thinking?

She was grief stricken, she decided as she let the two undertakers into the house. Of course she was. That was it. Anything could be excused on the basis of shock and loss.

She wasn't herself. Tomorrow she'd wake up and be back to nice sensible Maggie, who knew her place and was properly horrified by today's behaviour.

Was he gone?

It was so hard not to look back.

He drove back to town to collect Fiona and the further he drove the worse he felt. He'd left Maggie alone with the undertakers. How would she cope?

She'd cope magnificently. She was one magnificent woman.

She was bereft, alone and hurt.

She'd kissed him.

There were so many conflicting emotions he didn't know where to start sorting them into any sensible order. For, of course, there was no sensible order, and when he collected Fiona and she started talking serious clinical medicine, serious hospital politics and the difficulties of progressing up the hospital's hierarchy, he was grateful.

Medicine blocked out the white noise. He'd learned that when Alice died and he retreated back to it now.

Only…when he arrived back to the hospital the white noise followed him, ready to descend at any sliver of opportunity. He worked until midnight, he did a session in the gym and confusion followed him to bed.

Maggie, Maggie, Maggie.

He'd organised her a locum. John seemed delighted at the chance to help, and he was having a tough time not shoving him aside to take the job himself. He was jealous?

How stupid was that? Really stupid.

But still he lay and stared at the ceiling until dawn.

Maggie. Babies. Family.

The whole heart thing.

He could still feel Daniel in his arms. He could remember every wrinkle, every precious feature of his tiny son. He could remember the joy of being married to a woman he loved, but superimposed on that joy was aching, tearing loss.

To open himself again to that sort of pain…

No.

So stay away.

But the funeral…

He could bear everything else, but the thought of Maggie at Betty's funeral was too much. The thought of her standing at a graveside as once she'd stood at William's grave, as he'd stood at Alice's and Daniel's…

No.

So… This last thing he'd do for her. He'd arrange work so he could go to the funeral. He'd stay well back—if possible she wouldn't even see him. If she was surrounded by family and friends then he didn't have to go near. If she saw him he was simply paying his respects, visiting John to see if things were working out, taking his car for a run.

No harm there.

The decision released a twist of pain in his gut and he closed his eyes in relief.

But still he didn't sleep.

Maggie.

CHAPTER SIX

As FUNERALS went it was a biggie. Betty had lived and worked in Yandilagong all her life, so even though it rained—sleet, in fact—half the population of the district turned out for the service.

But as Betty's only close family member, Maggie was left alone, regarded with deference and respect. When William had died, her friends and colleagues had surrounded her. No one in this community knew her well enough yet to think they had that right. So the undertaker's assistant held an umbrella over her while she tossed roses down onto the coffin in the little graveyard overlooking the sea, and she felt more alone than she'd ever felt in her life.

Angus hadn't come. Of course not. He'd said his goodbyes the night his mother had died and that was that.

He was okay, though, Maggie thought, for now he had two little girls intruding on his solitude. John, the locum Max had miraculously found, had been at the farm for three days now. It had taken John's children—Sophie, six, and Paula five—about three minutes to find the calves and Bonnie. Angus was attached to them, so they attached themselves to Angus. Angus watched them with the same kind of wariness he used for anything he didn't understand, but after only a day he decided they were just like the calves, not posing any threat to his personal space.

Neither did their parents. John and Margaret seemed wary about sharing a house with Maggie, cautious of her privacy and carefully respectful. They were lovely people but they let her alone.

But right now she didn't want respectful isolation. She wanted to be hugged.

It wasn't going to happen.

The ceremony was over. She turned away from the grave and the undertaker's assistant left to bring the car close. People moved respectfully back from her. She looked bleakly out toward the road—and Max was coming towards her.

He was dressed for a funeral, in a dark suit and tie, a magnificent, deep grey overcoat—cashmere?—and a vast, black umbrella. He looked absurdly handsome. He was moving toward her as others moved back.

She was still on crutches. He waited until she reached him and then he smiled, that crinkly, tender smile that made her heart do back flips.

'Why are you here?' she asked, suddenly breathless.

'I thought you might like me to be.' He glanced around at the crowd, backed to a respectful distance. 'I'm so sorry I'm late. I had an emergency at dawn that took a lot longer to sort than I expected, and I couldn't leave halfway through. But now I'm here, can I help? Do you want a ride to the wake, or do you need to ride in the hearse?'

'I don't…I don't…'

'I've put my hood up,' he said enticingly, and he sounded so eager she almost smiled.

She did smile. *It was so good to see him.*

And then he had his arm around her waist, tugging her

against him so she was under the shelter of his umbrella with him. She was wearing a raincoat with a hood. It hadn't been working. Now she was held hard against him, protected from every quarter.

It was so good to feel him.

'I came via the farm,' he told her as he ushered her into his lovely car. 'John and Margaret told me where to find you.'

He'd had the paintwork fixed, she noticed. She was glad. She really liked this car. Or maybe it was the way she felt about its owner.

Maybe…maybe she should listen to what he was saying.

'John thinks this place is great,' he said, sliding in behind the wheel. Taking charge with smooth authority. 'He can't believe the medical set-up. I gather Margaret's already talking about setting up a dental practice. You guys have done a lot of organising in three days.'

He was deliberately making his voice practical. He must know instinctively that emotion was the last thing she needed now.

Of course he knew. He'd been to funerals himself.

'There's work for half a dozen doctors in this district if I could ever get them to come,' she said, struggling to come to terms with too many emotions and match his composure. That was what she needed—composure. No matter that the man beside her made her feel so breathless she was practically gasping.

'No one wants to be the only doctor in a small town, because there's no back-up,' she managed. 'To find John was a miracle. You want to wave your magic wand and produce more?'

'I'm no magician.'

'No.' She paused. Maybe no was the wrong word. He felt like a magician. Her personal genie, appearing when she most needed him.

'No family at all?' he asked gently, looking back at the clusters of people dispersing into their cars, and his look acknowledged that she wasn't a part of any cluster.

'No.'

'Surely there's someone…even back in England… Someone who cares.'

Hey, this was getting personal. What about composure?

'I have lots of friends,' she said, drumming up indignation, and he smiled.

'I'm sure you do. But do you have any friends who might drop everything and race to the aid of a Maggie who needs them?'

'I don't need them,' she said with dignity. 'I… Thank you for coming, though.'

'My pleasure.' He hesitated. 'If I'm welcome I thought I'd stay for the wake—or whatever you call it here. We've both done this,' he added strongly, as she made to shake her head. 'I've buried Alice and Daniel. You've buried William. This can't be nearly as bad, but from what I remember it's an endless process of standing, tepid tea in hand, thanking, thanking, thanking.'

She couldn't think what to say. She glanced across and saw in his eyes the recognition of shared pain.

A funeral of an old lady should be a celebration of a life well lived—and this was—but it inevitably brought back memories of funerals that hadn't been timely. Funerals where pain had been raw and deep.

'You've got the whole day off?' she asked.

'I've rearranged things. I need to be back in Sydney tonight but I thought I could give you this day.'

'Gee, thanks,' she retorted before she could help herself, and his smile returned, deepening, making his grey eyes dance.

'Noble's my middle name and I'm addicted to tepid tea. You want to make use of me or you want me to go away?'

What was he asking? Was he mad?

Did she want to stand in the funeral parlour's reception rooms, as he'd said, alone, drinking endless tea, receiving words of consolation from hundreds of people she didn't know? Or did she want Max's solid presence beside her? Just there if she needed him. There if she just wanted him.

This was an extraordinary gesture. If he'd phoned last night and said 'Should I come?' she'd have said no, but he was here now. He was here and it'd take a stronger woman than she'd ever be to knock back his offer.

'Yes, please,' she said, in a rush before either of them could change their minds.

He was offering his strength for a day and she'd take it.

Secretly, she knew she'd take anything this man was prepared to give.

It seemed, as he'd predicted, an endless day, and at the end of it, when everyone had gone, when the last neighbour had wrung the last bit of nostalgia from the occasion, Max drove her back to the farm.

It was still raining. They drove along the long line of tractors and Maggie felt herself trying to work out a way she could make him stay longer.

That wasn't fair. She knew it. But...

'Would you like to come in and have dinner?' she asked as they pulled to a halt. 'Margaret's cooking for me as well tonight. I...I'm sure there'll be enough to share.'

'She already asked me,' he said gently. 'I refused.'

'Oh.'

His face grew suddenly grim. 'Maggie, I don't think I can

ever go down the road I went with Alice. I can't get involved again.'

Well, that was blunt to say the least. 'Involved?' she said cautiously.

'I think we both know what I mean.'

Whoa. Suddenly things were going where they had no right to be going. At least he was being direct, but…

'You're thinking I'm on the catch for another husband,' she whispered, and suddenly anger was there, surging whether she willed it or not. She did will it.

He thought she was a victim, she thought suddenly, incensed by the knowledge. A passive, needy woman who might cling. A woman who'd kissed him the last time they'd met, whether he'd willed it or not, and he probably hadn't willed it; he was probably just being kind. To a sex-starved widow, seven months pregnant with another man's child.

'I don't think that,' he started.

'Just as well,' she retorted. 'So what about Fiona?'

'Fiona?'

'Your girlfriend.'

'Fiona is my colleague. I don't have a girlfriend. There's been no one since Alice.'

'How very noble,' she snapped. 'I hope Alice is up there polishing your halo, ready for you to join her.'

'Look, it's just that I can't do relationships any more,' he said, forcing out the words. Trying to explain something he didn't fully understand himself. The impotence and the grief of not being able to help his lovely Alice, and the knowledge that such pain again would kill him. 'It's not fair to mess you around.'

But Maggie wasn't looking at him with sympathy, or with understanding.

Whew. Anger was good here. Anger was great. It pushed

away any embarrassment, gave her the words that needed to be said and the dignity to say them.

'How can you be messing me around?' she said, stiffly and coldly. 'I kissed you—yes, I did kiss you, and very nice it was, too. Given half a chance I'd do it again. Only that's all it was—a kiss—nothing to do with my life. And if you think I'm about to turn into some helpless, clinging female…'

'I didn't say that.'

'You didn't need to.' She gritted her teeth. 'Thank you very much for today. It was very kind. You've been very kind to me all round, and if there's any way I can repay you, please let me know. But I don't need anything else. I'm sorry you can't stay for dinner, because you know what? John and Margaret are fun and the kids are gorgeous and it would have made a grey day better. You might even have enjoyed it. But for anything else, forget it. Okay, enough. Thank you again.' And she grabbed her crutches from the back and climbed out of the car.

The rain was pelting down. He grabbed the umbrella and headed for her side of the car but she turned away from him.

'No,' she threw over her shoulder. 'Go away. You don't want to get involved and neither do I. And you never know when a desperate widow might change her mind, grab you by the hair and drag you into her lair before you can fight back. Get out of here, Max Ashton, and keep safe.'

'I didn't mean—'

'Yes, you did,' she retorted, and limped away fast through the tangle of garden. 'Yes, you did,' she yelled again. 'Go find some other maiden to rescue. This one's been rescued enough, so you need to move right on.'

CHAPTER SEVEN

SHE was right. He needed to move on.

He didn't hear from her for six weeks. He put her right from his mind. Or he tried to.

Work was his salvation but he extended his operating schedule to the point where Anton, his anaesthetist, finally said cull it or find a second anaesthetist to share the load.

'That break was supposed to do you good,' he said morosely. 'Instead you've come back ready to work the rest of us into the ground. You know what? We were hoping you and Fiona might have worked something out. You could both do with a love life.'

'I don't want a love life,' he growled.

'But you need one,' Anton said bluntly. Anton had a wife, a three-year-old and one-year-old twins, he was permanently sleep deprived and he thought the rest of the world should join him in his glorious domestic muddle. 'A good woman and half a dozen kids would take the edge off your energy and protect us all.'

'You do the procreating for both of us,' Max growled. 'You're good at it. I'm not.'

'Practice, man. Just find the right lady. I'll admit Fiona's not perfect—I can't see the chief radiologist of Sydney South having much time for diapers—but there must be someone to suit you somewhere.'

There was, Max thought grimly. He'd found her. He just didn't have the courage to take it further—to step into the abyss of commitment.

So he'd stay clear of entanglement and he'd work.

But like it or not, as he worked he realised he was feeling the same roller-coaster of emotions he had felt in the months after he'd lost Alice. There was an abyss in front of him, only he didn't know where. If he put his foot down he wasn't sure the ground would still be solid. The feeling left him even more sure that the only way forward was to keep right away from Maggie.

But his thoughts weren't staying away from Maggie. A dozen times a day he wanted to get in his car and go to her. Only the fact that his workload was horrendous saved him. He was always needed in Theatre, in the wards, in his consulting rooms.

The situation wasn't sustainable. He'd thought the inexplicable magnetic attraction he'd felt for her would fade but if anything it strengthened. And then, at the end of the sixth week, he had a phone call from John at the farm.

'How's Maggie?' he demanded before he could help himself.

'We're all fine,' John said jovially. 'It's working out brilliantly. There's so much work here, and it's a great little community. But, hell, Max, the place is the epicentre of a medical desert. I'm run off my legs already, and the moment Margaret put up her plate she had so many teeth coming through her door she was tempted to take it down again.'

'Yeah, but Maggie…'

'She's fine, too. Except… That's why I'm ringing.'

'Except what?' He was right back there again, feeling the

terror he'd felt when Alice had shown the first signs of pre-eclampsia. Leaning against the wall for support. Knowing this was illogical and emotional, but there was nothing he could do about it.

'Margaret's worrying.'

'Why?'

'Because she's alone,' he said, and Max's world righted itself again. Alone. That wasn't terrifying.

It wasn't great, though. Alone? Why the hell was she alone?

'She can't have the baby here,' John said. 'The only doctor's me, and I'm not prepared to give obstetric support without back-up. All the women from around here need to go to the city to have their babies. Mind, if we had a really good obstetrician…'

'Get on with it,' Max growled. Damn, he'd sussed John was good, but he didn't appreciate him being this good—not only helping Maggie but starting to put pressure on others to help. Namely him.

'Okay,' John said, chuckling, and Max thought briefly through jumbled emotion that Zimbabwe's loss was Maggie's gain. 'It's just Maggie's organised herself an apartment at Coogee for the next couple of weeks until she has the baby. She chose Coogee because it's a beach location where she can walk and swim, and it's close to the hospital she's booked into. Which also happens to be our hospital. I mean, your hospital.'

Coogee. A suburb of Sydney not ten minutes' drive from where he was taking this call. Max drew in his breath, suddenly feeling trapped—pulled towards the abyss. 'She's coming here?'

'She's already there. She left on Sunday. So I thought I'd give you a heads up so you could look out for her.'

The implied responsibility rattled him further. 'She's not a friend, John,' he said, before he could think about it, and there was a moment's stunned silence from the end of the phone. He could almost see John's brows snap down in surprise—and disapproval.

Fair enough. Maybe he even disapproved of himself.

Maybe what he'd said had been stupid. And cruel?

But would Maggie think of him as *her* friend? Maybe not, he conceded. She'd been so angry the last time he'd seen her...

'She's *my* friend,' John said at last, gently chiding, and Max caught himself.

'Sorry. I mean...I was just thinking... Why did she book herself in here for the birth? There are many hospitals in Sydney.'

'I believe she booked herself into Sydney South before she even came to Australia,' John said, growing more disapproving by the moment. 'I don't believe she did it to annoy you. But if you don't think of yourself as her friend...'

'I do.' He raked his fingers through his hair. 'Sorry, of course, I mean I guess I do. It's just that I hardly know her.'

'You came to her grandmother's funeral. The locals said you held her up all afternoon. Physically.'

'She needed holding up.'

'Well, maybe she needs holding up again now,' John said brusquely. 'She's left here and gone to stay in a hotel apartment until the baby's born. She doesn't know anyone in Sydney and we're worried. So worried, in fact, that Margaret says if you won't promise to keep an eye on her then she'll leave me here with the kids and go and keep her company herself. So I'm asking you to check on her.'

'She'll want solitude,' he said, clutching at straws.

'You're kidding me, right?' John demanded. 'She's not like Angus. She's a sociable, chirpy, intelligent colleague. The girls and I are already half in love with her. We can't bear to think of her being alone. But if, as you say, you don't see yourself as her friend…'

'All right,' he said, goaded, and then heard himself, heard his anger, and felt small. 'Sorry,' he said. 'I've had one hell of a morning. I'm run off my feet.'

'Yeah, I'm hearing that, too,' John said. 'So why are you running yourself into the ground?'

'There's work…'

'And there's delegation,' John said. 'You ever heard of it? Yeah, I know, it's none of my business, only Margaret and I worked in that place ourselves and gossip travels fast. We still hear things. So you met Maggie, you hugged her all through the funeral but you haven't phoned her since, you're working yourself into the ground and now you react like a scared wimp when I suggest you keep tabs on her.'

'Why would I be scared?'

'You tell us and we'll both know,' John said cheerfully. 'Okay. Margaret wouldn't let her go without giving us her address. You want it, or do we have to figure some other way of taking care of her?'

Max raked his hair again. Did he want her address?

Short answer, no.

Long answer? Long and very complicated answer?

Of course he did. Yes.

The beach was glorious and she had it almost to herself.

It was early September. There were lifesavers watching her with lazy care, and she liked that. She also liked it that she was almost the only one in the water apart from a couple of German tourists whooping it up in the shallows.

It was Wednesday. A working day. Even those not at work

thought it was too cool to swim. Too bad for them, she thought, backstroking lazily along the backs of the waves. She'd swum this morning and now, in the late afternoon, she was swimming again. After the rush of the past few months this was bliss. She had nothing to do but swim and float and watch the expanding bump that was her daughter.

She was so-o-o pregnant. Her belly button had turned inside out. She felt the size of a small whale. A whale's natural environment was water, she thought, rolling happily over and over in the surf. This was where she was meant to be. Wallowing.

Ooh, it was lovely to be off her feet. Ooh, it was lovely to be here, even if she was alone.

She wouldn't be alone for long, she told herself. She had a week to go, give or take a few days. Very soon now she'd have her daughter.

It wouldn't stop her being lonely.

Now, *that* was crazy talk. She gave herself a mental scolding, as she'd been doing a lot since she'd left the farm. She wasn't alone in the least.

John and his family had moved into the farmhouse. They were lovely and they were giving her all the support she needed. Angus was happy, with his tractors and his calves and his dog. So she had John, Margaret, Sophie, Paula and Angus, plus the community of Yandilagong. After Betty's funeral she'd learned just what belonging to a small community really meant. She had enough tuna casseroles and jelly cakes and cream sponges in her freezer to last her a lifetime.

Her future looked far less isolated and a lot more calorie laden than she'd ever dreamed possible.

So why was she lonely?

It's because I'm alone right now, she told herself, in the

manner of one talking to someone being deliberately dull-witted. Lonely means alone.

You've been alone since William died.

I haven't felt alone. Not for a while now. Or not achingly alone.

Not until I met Max.

And there it was, the crux of the matter. One drop-dead gorgeous doctor and her whole world had been thrown out of kilter.

So put him out of your head, she told herself for about the thousandth time since Max had left. Just swim and don't think of him.

She did a couple more laps of the patrolled part of the beach, then watched the German couple decide it was time to call it quits. Maybe it was time for her to do the same. Reluctantly she turned toward the shore—and saw a man striding down the sand toward her. A man who looked vaguely familiar.

Really familiar.

She stared in disbelief, thinking she was dreaming.

She wasn't dreaming.

Max.

For a moment she thought wildly about swimming out to sea. The last time she'd seen him she'd been so angry. So humiliated. She tried to dredge up that anger now—and failed.

She floated and watched him greet the lifeguards, haul his shoes and socks off, roll up his chinos and stroll down to the shallows. He was shading his eyes with his hand so he could see better.

She was doing the same. Treading water, shading her eyes, trying to watch him.

Max.

A wave, bigger than usual, rose behind her. Acting on impulse, she caught it and let it carry her all the way to the beach. Or almost all the way. Her bump grounded her about twenty feet before the rest of her would have.

She surfaced, wiped the water from her eyes, pushed her curls back and he was about six feet away.

'What are you doing here?' she managed, and he looked down at her for a long moment without replying. As well he might, she thought.

She'd decided buying a pregnancy swimsuit was a waste of time—who was there to appreciate it except her? Her modus operandi was to wear a sarong to the beach, tug it off at the last minute and get into the water fast. She was wearing a faded pink bikini. The top was respectable—well, almost, though her bust had grown considerably bustier in her pregnancy. She couldn't see her bikini bottom. It was somewhere under her bump.

Max, on the other hand, looked cool, collected and casually fabulous. Business shirt without a tie and the top buttons unfastened. Rolled-up sleeves. He was carrying shiny black shoes, socks tucked inside.

Very neat, she conceded. Whereas she…

She didn't want to think about what she was.

'John said I should check on you,' he told her, and she winced. Of course. It wasn't like he was here because he wanted to be.

'I'm good,' she said. 'John should have called. I would have told him I was okay and spared you the trouble of making the trip.'

'I wanted to see you.'

She stood up, awkwardly because of her bulk. He made an instinctive movement to help—and then stopped.

She saw it. He didn't want to help. He didn't want to touch her.

Okay, then. She stood knee deep in the shallows and shook herself like a dog, her curls flying every which way. She'd braided her hair but it refused to stay braided in the surf. She looked whale-like and wild, she thought.

Not Max Ashton's sort of woman at all.

'So there you go,' she said tightly. 'You've seen me. Okay?'

'Maggie, can we talk?'

'If you get any closer you might mess with me.'

'That was a dumb thing to say,' he said. 'I'm sorry I said it.'

She glowered, but then she thought, no, this was childish. She could be the grown-up here. Maybe it'd even make her feel better to act magnanimously. 'It's okay,' she conceded graciously. 'I was acting a bit needy. I needed to be pulled up.'

'You didn't. I was out of line. I'm sorry.'

Was this what happened when you were magnanimous? You got someone feeling nicely off balance and guilty in return. Excellent. 'Thank you,' she said, still attempting grace. 'Apology accepted.' She didn't move, though. Walking forward, out of the water, seemed a bad idea, and walking closer to him seemed worse.

Not to mention the fact that her walk was now more like a waddle. Not a lot of grace there.

'You swim amazingly,' he said, still sounding stilted.

'For an Englishwoman,' she finished for him, eyeing him with caution. Trying to figure where to go from here. 'William spent most of his summers at Yandilagong. Betty taught him to surf and he taught me. Just after we finished medical school we did a rotation at Durness in Scotland. Do you have any idea how cold the sea water is around Scotland? This place is a sauna in comparison.'

Was she gabbling? Maybe she was.

'This still looks winter-cold to me,' Max said, and, yes, he was looking at her as if she was gabbling. He still seemed wary.

Did he still think he had the capacity to get to her?

However true that might be, she refused to be got to.

'You're dreaming.' She eyed him challenging. He looked so collected. So not part of this beach scene. She desperately wanted to get things on an equal footing. 'It's not cold,' she lied. 'Come in and try it.' She raised her brows in mock challenge.

'I don't have swim gear.'

'Are you wearing boxers or jocks?'

'I...' He seemed thoroughly disconcerted, as well he might be, she thought. Even more excellent. She wanted him disconcerted and she wasn't backing off.

'Well?'

'Boxers,' he conceded reluctantly.

'Then where's the problem?' she demanded, amazing herself at her effrontery. What was she doing? She didn't care, though. What was there to lose? 'Your audience would be two male lifesavers and me. You'd hardly be playing to a packed gallery, Dr Ashton.'

He'd never do it. Or would he? She stayed right where she was and watched the cool, collected, man of the world, his expensive jacket flung over his shoulder, his Italian brogues in his hand, think about his dignity.

Saw the exact moment when he decided to lose it.

He gave her a long, considering look—then walked twenty yards up the beach, dropped his jacket and shoes on the dry sand and then dropped everything else except his boxers. Taking her breath away.

The first time she'd seen him she'd thought he did serious gym work. Stripped to his boxers she was sure of it.

This man was a doctor. He spent his days in hospitals with sick people. What was he doing having a body like this? It was all she could do not to gape.

Maybe she did gape, but luckily he was already hitting the water, running into the waves as if he was a man decided on a mission and determined not to let a little thing like icy water stand in his way. She saw the first shock as he hit the water, and she saw his determination deepen. She watched as he launched himself into the surf by diving head first into the first wave, swimming out past the breakers and then body-surf back in again. She watched, and she thought there were serious things going on here, serious things in her head that she didn't know what to do with.

He was worried he'd mess with her head?

He already had.

She had to get herself together. He surfed back to her, right to her feet, then stood up. Water was streaming down his face. His hair was flopping wetly onto his forehead. He looked ten years younger, ten years more…more…

Whoa. This seriously pregnant woman does not need complications, she told herself, and knew she already had complications in droves.

'You lied. This is c-cold,' he muttered, abandoning bravado, and she grinned and sank back down into the water and rolled herself over and over in the shallows.

'Wuss. I've been in for half an hour.' Then she relented. 'Okay, at first it's cold. You need to swim to warm up.'

'You've been swimming that long?'

'And loving it. I'm getting wrinkly now—it's time I got out—but if you want to keep swimming I'll join the lifesavers on guard duty.'

'Maggie…'

'Just swim,' she advised him kindly. 'You look like you're a man who needs to get something out of his system. I don't know what it is but, whatever the problem, I've always found exercise helps. Off you go and enjoy yourself.'

'You're not going to swim with me?'

'Closeness isn't a good idea,' she said, and she knew that she was suddenly sounding stiff and formal but she couldn't help it. 'You said it yourself. You get the gremlins out of your system, Dr Ashton, but you need to do it alone.'

It was a weird, almost out-of-body experience. He swam the length of Coogee Bay and back again, twice, then a third time for good measure. Up on the beach Maggie was wrapped in what looked like an enormous beach towel—bright blue with yellow splodges. She was sitting on the sand, chatting to the lifesavers, watching him.

He was too far away to see their faces, to have any idea what they were saying, but they looked cheerful. Maggie was waving an expansive arm in his direction. Was she talking about him?

Did it matter?

Maybe it did—but that thought wasn't going anywhere. He put his head down and swam some more.

He'd checked on her. She was obviously coping splendidly by herself. There was no need for him to have come.

There was no need for him to stay.

So finally he surfed to shore and strolled up the beach. Maggie was laughing at something the lifesavers were saying and they were laughing back. They seemed at ease together, like old friends, but then he got close enough to watch the guys' faces and he knew that, pregnancy or not, they were totally aware that this was one attractive woman.

Was he jealous?

Yes, he conceded. Yes, he was, which just went to show how dumb this whole set up was.

Get out of here, he told himself. Get out of here fast. But then Maggie rose to greet him and he stopped thinking about anything but Maggie.

Her towel was amazing. It was vast, sky blue and dotted with brilliant yellow sunflowers. Draped around her very pregnant body she looked…she looked…

'Like an elephant,' she said before he said a word, and he blinked.

'Pardon?'

'That's what these guys here say I resemble. An elephant with sunflowers. Elegance-R-Us.'

'You look cute,' he said lamely, and the lifesavers looked at him like he was a sandwich short of a picnic. Which maybe he was. Cute didn't cut it.

Sexy did, though.

'I don't think anything this big can be classified as cute,' Maggie retorted. 'But I'm going for whale rather than the elephant. A cute little sexy mama whale. You say I'm cute? The guys here say I'm sexy. I say I'm just enormous.' She twirled around, full circle, grinned and unwrapped herself, then proffered her towel. 'Meanwhile, would you like to borrow this? You need to dry yourself or you'll get cold.' And before he could stop her she'd handed her over her sunflowers.

He was dripping. He had no other towel, so it'd be churlish to refuse.

But her towel smelled of her. There it was again, that faint citrusy thing, mixed now with the salt from the sea. She must use it in her washing powder, he thought. Or maybe it was just Maggie. Maggie exuding lemons and limes, tangy, clean and beautiful.

She was smiling happily at him as if she was really pleased he'd dropped by, and she was really pleased that he'd seemed to enjoy the swim she'd persuaded him to take.

Yep, beautiful. And sexy. And cute. The whole lot wrapped together.

But she was reaching into her bag, fetching out a sarong and wrapping it round herself. Sliding her toes into sandals. Preparing to leave.

'That was wonderful,' she said. 'It was great to see you again, Max, but it is getting cold. Thank you for coming. Goodbye.'

So there it was. He'd been dismissed. His duty was done; he could leave.

'You're not going to ask me back to your place for a drink?' he said before he could stop himself, and she looked him up and down, appraisingly.

'Risky,' she said.

'Risky why?'

'You know why.'

'That's ridiculous,' he said. 'And I'd rather not drive back to my place covered in sand. Your apartment's just over the road. It was your concierge who told me where to find you.'

That was what his mouth was saying. Was he out of his mind? He needed to leave, yet here he was, arguing.

Something was driving his tongue that wasn't his head.

'You'd be second in line to the shower,' she said cautiously. 'It's my shower. I get to go first.'

'Deal,' he said, and that was that. The lifesavers looked almost disappointed as Maggie turned to them and waved.

'See you tomorrow, Craig, Simon,' she said happily.

'Unless you're in hospital tomorrow,' one of the men said, and for a moment a shadow flitted across Maggie's face.

Was she worried about it, then? The birth?

Of course she would be. How many pregnant women had Max cared for? Every single one of them worried.

But Maggie was putting on a cheerful front and he watched her deliberately put the shadows aside. 'I'm not due for a week,' she told them. 'And first babies are always late. I'm guessing there's two more swimming weeks to go.'

'Well, good luck if there's not,' the same guy said. 'And let us know what happens. We're starting to feel like we know your daughter already.'

They walked up the beach together, slowly. Max had tugged on his clothes but he still felt…different.

Maggie had introduced the lifesavers to her daughter. She'd made them her friends. This woman could make friends with anyone.

She was beautiful. The word was echoing over and over in his mind. She had the sunflowers draped over her shoulders. She was a huge blue and yellow whale.

Gorgeous!

'I wouldn't mind an ice cream,' she ventured as they neared the street, so Max bought two ice creams and in silent consent they sat on a park bench and ate them.

She was a very neat ice-cream eater, Max noted. Methodical. Cute.

'And you're a biter,' Maggie told him, and he stared.

'Pardon?'

'You bite your ice cream. I've never been able to figure why people do that. You risk freezing your insides. Licking's much more sensible.'

'How did you know what I was thinking?'

'I just know,' she said smugly and then relented as she saw his look of bewilderment. 'You have a very readable face.'

'Gee, thanks.'

'My pleasure. I practise reading people's faces,' she explained. 'So much more dependable than palm-reading—and I like doing it.'

'I don't like you doing it.'

'Whatever,' she said happily. 'But biting ice-cream cones is nuts. You've finished already, and mine's only quarter way down. So…do you always take your pleasures this fast?'

She eyed him sideways, her eyes twinkling, deliberately appraising, deliberately teasing, and he felt himself respond— maybe exactly how she hoped he'd respond. Trying not to blush like a schoolboy!

First the boxers, now this. She was enjoying herself at his expense.

He'd found her expecting her to be lonely, maybe anxious, maybe depressed. Maybe she was all those things, but she was making a good job of hiding it.

'When did you last have an antenatal check?' he demanded, trying to get back to sounding businesslike, but instead sounding like he was feeling, out of his depth and flailing.

'Yesterday—*Doctor*,' she said, raising her brows, still laughing. Still teasing. 'I'm being *very* good.'

She had him off balance and she knew it. All he could do was flounder on. 'So what did he say?'

'*She*. A lovely obstetrician called Helen.' She says my baby's head's not engaged yet so I could be at least a week.'

'So what are you doing with yourself?'

'Reading,' she said, and looked virtuous. 'Reading, reading, reading. And no—*Doctor*—not a romance or a thriller or even a trashy magazine. Medical journals. If I'm going to be a family doctor I'm going to be a good one. Did you know bed bugs are on the rise?'

'Bed bugs,' he said faintly.

'World travel's getting so common that the little pests are spreading,' she said. 'Apparently, if a patient comes in covered in red welts I should check if they've been in a hotel recently. And if a local hotel gets infected then there's a whole list of things that need to be done. I've been reading Health Department Guidelines. As district medical officer—that's me now—I need to know what to look for. Did you know they hide in the seams of mattresses during the day? And you can't just spray the place with an insecticide bomb and move on either. There's serious health implications. I need to know what to do—and I get to close the place down if they won't comply.'

'Really,' he said faintly.

'Really,' she said, sounding reproving. 'And don't sound dismissive. You get bitten by bed bugs and you'll be the first to complain to the local health officer. There's so much to learn.'

'I see there is.'

'Don't belittle it,' she said, even more reproving, and stood up. He looked up at her—wrapped in her sarong and towel, balancing her ice-cream cone—and thought there was no way he could belittle this woman.

And suddenly the focus was no longer on bed bugs. Or ice creams. Or even mischief and teasing. Suddenly he didn't know where to go from here.

'Look, I'd better go,' she said, as he rose to stand beside her. 'That shower... Maybe it's not a good idea.'

'Maybe it's not.' What was going on here?

But he knew. What he was feeling was an irresistible attraction to a woman who represented everything he didn't want. Commitment. Giving himself. Emotional entanglement.

Everything he didn't want?

How many doctors did he know that'd take bed bugs on as a commitment? But he knew that Maggie would take on everything she cared about as a commitment.

The farm. Angus. The community of Yandilagong.

Him?

See, there it was. He looked down into her eyes and thought he could read her. If he wanted her...

He did want her.

No. To leap into that abyss...

'Maggie...'

'No,' she said softly. 'You don't really want...what's between us. Not now, maybe not ever. It's better you go.'

'John wants me to keep checking.'

'You can ring me at the hotel. John can ring himself if he wants. Come to think of it, he does already, so you needn't bother.'

'Is there anything at all that you need?'

'No.'

'So that's it, then.'

'Yes,' she said, and turned away.

And then...

They were standing near where pedestrians were streaming over the road from the beach-side park to the shops beyond.

The traffic lights across to the shops didn't appear to be working. At some subconscious level while they'd been eating their ice creams Max had been conscious of confusion, cars slowing, honking at each other, pedestrians scurrying between cars.

The car came from nowhere, overtaking others that had slowed to a crawl. Its tyres were screeching into acceleration where others were braking. It was bearing straight down on the intersection like there was no question it had right of way. It was travelling way beyond the speed limit, a crazy speed, even if people weren't there.

Only, of course, people were there. Families were leaving the park. Tourists were holding ice creams and cameras, chatting to each other as they headed to the shops. A couple of office workers, their suits at odds with the casual crowd, looked like they were heading home. A young mother was pushing a stroller.

All were frozen by the noise of a car out of control.

There was no time for screaming. Just the roar of the car's engine.

It didn't even slow. It came straight through.

There was a flash of yellow, a sickening thump, a crash of breaking glass. A body flew high, above the car's bonnet. All the way over.

It crumpled to nothing on the road behind.

The car didn't pause; indeed, the scream of its engine increased. The bright yellow motor with huge wheels and about a dozen exhaust pipes behind simply kept right on accelerating, screaming along the esplanade, through the next set of lights—also not lit—around the corner, up the hill and out of sight.

Leaving behind mayhem.

CHAPTER EIGHT

FOR a moment nobody moved. It was like some sort of Greek tragedy—players turned to statues where they stood.

Then someone screamed, and Max was gone from Maggie's side in an instant.

She hardly saw him go. He was simply no longer with her, and by the time she could take in the enormity of what had happened—what was still happening—he was crouching by a body crumpled on the roadway.

Dear God, it was a child.

She dropped her ice cream and her bag and ran.

Triage. Max was with the child. What else?

No one else seemed to have been hit. Or maybe there had.

Yes, there was another. A woman was standing in the middle of the road, behind a stroller, staring numbly at the child who was now more than ten yards away from her.

Maggie's eyes dropped from her face and saw her arm, which was streaming with blood. Far, far too much blood.

Maggie was with her in a heartbeat, seizing her hand and raising it above her head.

'Sit,' she said, and the woman looked wildly toward the child Max was tending.

'No. I…'

'Help me,' Maggie said harshly to a kid standing by—a teenager with green-spiked hair and a T-shirt with a message that was shocking. If she was in the mood to be shocked. She wasn't.

'Give me your shirt,' she said, and to the kid's enormous credit he peeled it off almost before she'd finished saying the words.

'Help me sit her down,' she said, and the kid took the woman's good hand and Maggie gently pressured the woman to sit. And then, as she sagged, to lie down.

Her arm was gushing, blood pumping out at a rate that was terrifying. Maggie had it still in the air. She grasped one of the kid's hands and placed it on the woman's wrist so he was holding her arm up. 'Hold it high,' she snapped, 'Keep it there.' She was twisting his T-shirt into a tie, twisting, twisting.

'Grace…' the woman managed.

'I'm a doctor,' Maggie said as she wound the T-shirt round her upper arm. 'There's two of us here. Dr Ashton's looking after Grace while I look after you. I need to stop your arm bleeding before you can go to her.'

It sounded simple. Stop the bleeding. Stopping a gushing artery was an almost impossible ask.

She'd do it. She had the twirled T-shirt right round the woman's arm now and was twisting it cruelly. The woman cried out in pain.

'Ambulance!'

To Maggie's astonishment—and relief—the kid—Spike?—was holding his cellphone with his spare hand, barking orders. The kid looked all of about fifteen, yet he was acting with the responsibility of a trained paramedic.

'Esplanade, Coogee. Traffic accident. Two hurt, bad. Bleeding all over the place. Get here fast!'

'I'm going to be sick,' someone moaned faintly behind them. The kid turned and snapped, 'Get away from us before you do, then. And give us your cardigan. We need a pillow.'

'Great,' she said, as someone else handed over a jacket—not the woman who was threatening to vomit but it didn't matter who gave it, as long as they had it. 'Keep that hand raised.'

'Got it,' the kid said—and not for the first time Maggie thought how impossible it was to predict from any group of people who could be called on to help.

Who was helping Max?

Did he need her?

She couldn't look. Not yet.

The bleeding was slowing. Thank God. Heaven only knew how much blood the woman had lost in those first seconds—her arm had been ripped almost from elbow to wrist and spilled blood was impossible to quantify—but the bleeding was easing now to almost nothing.

'I need another shirt,' she yelled back into the crowd, and someone handed one over. 'And a towel.' She'd dropped hers and there was no time to return to the side of the road to fetch it. But someone handed one over.

In seconds she'd fashioned a pad to fit over the whole wound. She placed it on, then wrapped it tightly with the shirt, using the sleeves to tie and tie again.

She now had a tourniquet and pressure on the wound itself, and Spike was still holding the arm high.

'Grace,' the woman moaned again, and finally Maggie let herself glance across to Max.

He was working furiously. Alone. No one had moved to

help him. There was a gathering crowd of onlookers but that was all they were. Onlookers.

She had Spike to help her, and the woman's bleeding was controlled. Triage said she had to move on.

'Can you tell me your name?' she asked, and the woman's pain-filled eyes stared up at her like she didn't hear.

'Your name,' she said again, softly but urgently, and put her hand fleetingly on her cheek. 'It's okay. Spike and I have stopped your arm bleeding. You're going to be okay. But I need your name.'

'J-Judith.'

'The little girl—she's yours?'

'I… Yes. Thomas is in the stroller. Grace is…Grace is…'

'Dr Ashton's looking after Grace,' Maggie told her. 'He's good. He'll take good care of her. I'll go now and see how she is.'

'Thomas…'

'Thomas is fine.' She looked around her at the onlookers. Met the eye of an elderly woman who was looking shocked, but was already turning away as if she was about to leave. That was what sensible people did at the scene of an accident. If they couldn't help, they left.

She wanted sensible.

'Can you help with the baby in the stroller?' she called and the woman paused and pointed to herself.

'Me?'

'Please. What's your name?'

'Mary. I know these people,' she ventured. 'They live near me.'

'Great.' She motioned her to come close, so Judith could see how comfortingly grandmotherly she looked. 'Judith, Mary's one of your neighbours and she'll be looking after

Thomas. Spike here is holding your arm up until the ambulance arrives, so it doesn't start bleeding again. You're going to be fine. I need to help Dr Ashton with Grace. If you promise to stay still then there'll be two doctors looking after Grace.'

'Go,' the woman whispered without hesitation. 'Go.'

He heard her in the background and he blessed her for it. He'd never questioned her competence, but now... She was skilled and she was fast and she was sure. People jumped when she said jump, recognising her natural authority even if she was nine months pregnant, covered with sand and dressed in a bright yellow sarong.

There was so much blood... The woman Maggie was working on must have torn an artery but he couldn't help her. He had urgent work to do himself.

Vaguely he heard the voices in the background, the woman's voice naming her children. The blonde-ringletted child under his hands was dressed endearingly in a pink tutu over a bathing costume stained with rainbow ice cream. She was called Grace?

She was conscious. Just. Considering the force with which she'd hit the road, consciousness was a miracle. But like her mother, there was far too much blood. From her leg. Torn femoral artery? It must be.

He'd ripped his shirt—he was getting good at this! —and was twisting a tourniquet. Slowing the bleeding. Her leg was twisted at an appalling angle. There was a gash across her abdomen, bleeding sluggishly, and the bitumen had ripped her skin like sandpaper. Her tutu was bright with blood.

'It's okay, sweetheart,' he murmured as he worked, and she gazed up at him in pain and confusion and shock. 'It's okay. The car hurt your leg. I'm a doctor and I need to fix it.'

'M-Mummy…'

And then her eyes rolled back in her head. Her tiny body was suddenly limp.

No!

Blood loss. Haemorrhagic shock.

He dropped the shirt-cum-tourniquet he was working on and moved to cup her face in his hands. Breathed. Hit her chest.

Her leg started spurting blood again.

But suddenly Maggie was beside him, kneeling on the bitumen, taking in the situation in one sweeping glance.

'I'll stop the bleeding, you get her breathing,' she muttered. 'Go.'

He had help!

It was blood loss—lack of blood pressure—that'd caused her heart to stop. He knew that. He had to get her breathing. But it was no use getting her heart to work again if the blood loss didn't stop. The task was impossible.

But with Maggie beside him he no longer had to think about the bleeding. He could move to CPR as he'd practised it so many times, at medical school and afterwards.

Breathe, one, two, three…

Breathe, one, two, three…

'The ambulance is on its way,' Maggie snapped as she worked, and he glanced across to where a kid with spiked hair was supporting the mother. So did Maggie.

The kid gave Maggie a thumbs-up sign, and she turned back and kept on working.

Breathe, one, two, three…

'I'm shifting this leg,' she said. 'The compound fracture means we'll never stop the bleeding while the artery's this exposed.' But she hadn't stopped to speak. She was simply doing. She was twisting the shirt-tourniquet one last time, holding it in her teeth—in her teeth!—taking the leg in both hands…

One fast movement and the leg was suddenly in alignment.

Not that Max had time to care.

Breathe, one, two, three…

Please.

Breathe, one, two, three…

And the little girl's chest heaved. Heaved again, all by itself.

'Dear God,' Maggie whispered, and Max was saying it too, over and over in his head.

Please, please, please…

The child was breathing.

The bleeding was slowing again now, but not because of death. Not!

'The ambulance,' Maggie whispered, and he heard it then, the scream of the siren above the traffic. Help was on its way. Plasma. IV fluids for both mother and daughter. If they could get them on board before the little girl's heart shut down again, she stood a chance.

And then the professionals were there. There were suddenly four skilled paramedics, assessing in an instant what Max and Maggie were doing, skilled hands taking over, smoothly, efficiently.

IV lines were going in. Oxygen masks. Pain relief.

Stabilisation, stretcher boards, transfer.

Curt questions, to the point, to each of them. Who was involved? The blood…was any of it Maggie's? Max's? Spike's?

The baby in the stroller… Identification?

'I know who they are,' Mary said. The elderly lady had lifted the toddler from the pram and was cuddling him. 'If you want, I'll come to the hospital and hold the baby until someone can come for him. I can give you details.'

'And you?' The ambulance officer turned to Maggie. 'Do you need help?'

'I'm f-fine,' she managed, knowing she didn't look fine. Nine months pregnant, soaked in blood, shocked.

'I'll look after her,' Max said, and his arm came round her waist and she let herself lean into him.

'I feel funny,' Spike said suddenly, and there was another moment of drama where the paramedic moved fast before the kid's knees buckled under him.

'He's a hero,' Maggie said shakily as they loaded Spike, too, into the ambulance and the paramedic looked at her and then at Max.

'It seems we have a surfeit,' he said dryly. 'We were lucky to get here as fast as we did—the power's off all over the city and the traffic's crazy. But in the meantime you guys seem to have saved a couple of lives.'

And then they were gone.

The police were taking statements and were collecting fragments of broken glass for forensics. Someone had started cleaning blood from the road.

In a few minutes all evidence of the accident would have disappeared. The stone had been tossed into the lake, it had splashed, the ripples were moving outward and in minutes life would be smooth again. Only Maggie didn't look the least bit smooth.

'Maggie, you know we agreed that shower wasn't a good idea?' Max murmured, and she looked up him and he saw her react to what he must look like. Which was a reflection of what she looked like.

Texas Chainsaw Massacre, version two.

'I'm not sure they'll even let us into the apartment block now,' she muttered, and her voice was shaky.

'You should have gone with the ambulance.'

'Why? My voice always shakes after drama. I'm fine.' She shook her head. 'Of all the criminal…'

'Don't think about it. Come and get clean.'

'You'll talk your way past my concierge?'

'I'll do whatever I must to get this off us,' he muttered grimly. 'But we did good, Maggie.'

'We did, didn't we?' she said—and burst into tears.

She sobbed. She sobbed all the way back to the apartment, while Max told a stunned concierge what had happened. The power was out and the reception area was dim. 'There's been power outages a couple of times already this week,' a shocked concierge told them as he ushered them toward the stairs. 'That'll be what happened with the traffic lights.'

Maggie was no longer listening. She was simply limp.

What was wrong with her? She'd done her share of stints in emergency rooms. She was a doctor, for heaven's sake. What was she doing, collapsing like a sodden rag?

But collapse she had. She couldn't stop shaking. If Max hadn't been holding her up she'd simply have sat where she was and not moved until morning.

Her tears had stopped—finally—but the numbness was ongoing. She made no protest as Max propelled her into her apartment, into the bathroom and straight into the shower. Then, as she stood limply under the warm water, sagging against the far wall, he swore, pulled his shoes off and came into the shower with her. He tugged her close and held her while the water ran and ran, and the red slowly turned to pink and then slowly turned clear.

Max had ripped off the remains of his ruined shirt along with his shoes. He was wearing chinos and nothing else. She was wearing her sarong. It might be clean but it still felt bloody. Ugh. She didn't want it on. She hauled it free and the water turned red again with the movement.

There was a crimson smear on her bikini top. She tugged at the strap and Max hesitated, then helped her unfasten it.

Then, as the shaking continued, as her bikini top fell to the floor, he swore and tugged her in hard against him.

What was she doing? She didn't care. She didn't have the energy to care. She let herself be pressed to Max's bare chest, skin against skin.

She needed the contact so much. She needed him.

And something else.

She wanted to be beautiful for him, she thought through a haze of shock and tears. It was a silly, dumb thing to think but think it she did.

She wanted *him*.

'Maggie…'

His voice was unsteady.

'S-sorry,' she whispered, trying to get her voice under control. Trying to figure out what on earth she was thinking. 'I'm sorry. I… It's just… It must be being nine months pregnant. Hormones or something. I'm not… It's not exactly medical treatment you're giving me here.'

'I'm trying hard to feel like your treating doctor,' he said, and she felt a fierce stab of denial. No.

'You don't feel like my treating doctor,' she whispered.

The warm water was running over them. There was no light apart from the filtered daylight from the window in the bedroom beyond. She felt like she was in a warm, sheltering cave, held by her man.

She was so close…

Closer than she'd felt to William?

That was an impossible question, and the truth was she didn't know. But it didn't seem to matter.

Up until now, grief had been with her every time she thought of him. Now, shocked out of any trace of a comfort zone, thrown into such intimacy with this new man in her life, it seemed that William had become a memory that couldn't be betrayed, a gentle ghost taking his rightful place in her life, watching her move on.

And with the thought—move on—came knowledge of where her heart was taking her, and the surge of self-knowledge made her gasp.

She made to pull away but Max was holding her against his chest. Against his heart.

Her bump was in the way. Apart from her tiny bikini bottom she was totally naked, but she was still huge. But Max was holding her as if he loved her; as if this child she was carrying was his.

No. He didn't want this. How could he?

'You don't want this,' she whispered.

'Want what, Maggie?'

What did she want?

She knew exactly what she wanted. The unsayable. But she had to figure another answer.

'You don't want a pregnant woman stark naked against you.'

'I don't believe you're quite stark naked.'

'I might as well be. And I'm so…so…'

'Beautiful,' he said softly. And then as she looked up at him in confusion, he added, almost ruefully, 'Pregnancy's beautiful. I've seen this before, Maggie. I'm a doctor, remember.'

That got to her. No way was she going down that route. She pulled back from him, swiped water out of her eyes, tried to look up at him with determination. 'You're not *my* doctor.'

'You needed someone. You sobbed.'

'I didn't need a doctor,' she managed. 'I needed someone who knew what I was feeling. Didn't you feel like sobbing, too?'

He wasn't answering. He was fighting to act as if this was professional care.

She didn't want to be treated with professional care.

Why had she let herself sob on him? What sort of a baby was she?

Enough. She hauled open the shower and grabbed a towel. It was big but not big enough. Beautiful? Ha! Winding the towel round her as best she could, she backed into the bedroom, leaving Max looking after her.

Still not answering.

She'd fallen in love, she admitted as she towelled herself dry with grim intensity. With someone who saw her as a patient.

So get dressed. Get this finished with. Fast.

How had that happened?

Maggie had been covered with blood and she'd been distressed. She'd needed to get her clothes off. It was natural that he'd help her.

So? He was a doctor helping a heavily pregnant woman in distress. He should feel professionally detached.

He felt no such thing.

She'd asked him if he felt like sobbing. The answer to that was easy. The way he'd felt…sobbing didn't come close.

But what he was feeling was nuts. To look at a nine-months-pregnant woman and ache to take her to him…

It was inappropriate. It was mixed up with his memories of Alice.

If she wasn't pregnant, would he still feel this desire?

He needed to get away, he thought, until after Maggie's baby was born. Until he could see how much he wanted Maggie for herself.

He suspected it was a lot.

So don't rush it, he told himself harshly. Leave her until you can see the whole picture. Get the emotion of pregnancy out of it.

Meanwhile, she didn't need him.

But, damn it, he wanted her to need him.

There wasn't even a light in this apartment. There'd been a couple of weeks of rolling power cuts—apparently there was a major problem with the city grid. If he wasn't here she'd be by herself in the dark.

Maybe she had enough resourcefulness to buy herself a candle?

Of course she did, he thought, hauling off his soaking chinos and wrapping himself in a towel. It might be seductive to think of himself as a white knight on a charger, but she didn't want that.

And maybe playing the protector now might mess with things later.

How much later?

Later she'd have a baby and a farm and friends. She still wouldn't need him.

He came out of the bathroom and she was at the apartment door. Thanking the concierge. Not being needy at all.

'They'll get him home. Great.'

She turned and he copped another blast of how gorgeous she was. Her hair was still wet, her flaming curls clinging to her lovely face. She was standing in bare feet, wearing maternity smock and jeans, lit by the afternoon sun from the outside window. And as he watched her, the tangle of emotions surrounding him fell away. Hunger hit him with such force that he almost took her in his arms right then.

But she was holding out gym pants, measuring them for length. The gym pants acted like a shield, giving him pause.

Somehow sense prevailed. Just.

'I've found you some clothes,' she said, cutting across his thoughts with such brisk efficiency that he blinked.

'Pardon?'

'Don—the concierge—has loaned you his gym gear. You need to bring it back tomorrow. Clean.'

'Um…thanks,' he said. Resourceful? Yes, she was. Clinging? No.

'You can hardly drive home in your towel,' she explained, quite kindly. 'We both need to get a bit of dignity back here.'

'We do.'

'Right, then,' she said, and waited—politely—for him to disappear back into the bathroom. To get into another man's gym gear and leave.

What else was a man to do?

Take her in his arms and kiss her senseless?

Let himself fall into that abyss?

He was so close—but not close enough. For as she turned away, he saw her put a hand to her back and wince. Backache in advanced pregnancy was common, but with that tiny gesture the pain he'd felt on losing Alice came flooding back. Maggie was beautiful, brave, intelligent—and vulnerable and pregnant and alive. How would he feel if he took her to him, if he loved her with all his heart and then…and then…?

No.

And she'd turned away. She was being sensible for them both.

* * *

By the time he was dressed in Don's classy gym gear he was almost thinking clearly, but still he didn't want to leave her. What had happened seemed too big. Outside, the sun had gone behind clouds and the apartment was gloomy.

'Do you have candles?' he asked, and she looked at him like he wasn't very bright.

'Of course I have candles. I have enough to light the whole apartment. We had power cuts for a while last night, too, if you remember, and the night before that. Did the lights go off where you were?'

'No.' But maybe they had. The hospital had its own generator and by the time he'd left work—at midnight—the power had been on again.

Work. That was the way to go, he thought. Get back to work and get a grip on your emotions. But to leave her here alone seemed wrong.

But maybe there was an alternative.

'I do need to go back to work,' he told her. 'But I also want to check on Judith and Grace. The ambulance was taking them to Sydney South. Would you like to come with me? I can put you in a cab to come home afterwards.'

'Thank you,' she said, picking up her purse.

Just like that. 'Yes?'

'I'd decided I'd go before you offered,' she admitted. 'I know I should be professionally detached, but you're looking at a woman who's so undetached she just sobbed her naked heart out on your manly chest. And you know something? I might have sobbed even if it wasn't manly so let's not get too personal here. So, yes, please, Dr Ashton, I need to find out how they are.'

'You should rest,' he said, belatedly.

'So I should,' she agreed. 'But I'm never going to rest until I know.'

'Maggie…'

'No more sobbing,' she promised. 'No more chests. Just two doctors checking on two patients. Let's go.'

CHAPTER NINE

SO ONCE again Maggie got to ride in his seriously sexy little car, but despite her bravado she wasn't feeling sexy, or brave, or anything other than totally disoriented. She was feeling disconcerted by the way she'd reacted over the last couple of hours. She was feeling...bereft.

Because she wanted this to be different?

For her mind had moved on from drama and was now playing tricks. Max was driving her to the hospital to see how two people they'd helped were faring. That was all that was happening but she was feeling sensation of warm wind in her hair, she was watching Max's strongly boned hands—surgeon's hands, she thought—on the steering-wheel, and she was feeling like she was part of a couple again. She felt cared for. She felt like she was a woman beside the man she loved.

The sensation was insidious in its sweetness—and it was a lie.

For Max was being efficient and kind. Nothing else.

But it didn't stop her soaking it up. True or not, she was holding to the moment, thinking if this was all she had then she'd enjoy every minute of it.

But sadly it was only a short drive. At the hospital Max pulled into his personal parking place—impressive!—and her illusion of togetherness dispersed. It was back to being Maggie on her own.

But still she hesitated before getting out of his car, holding back for just a moment but long enough for him to come round to her side. He was holding the door wide for her, looking at her in concern. Proffering his hands to help tug her unwieldy body upward.

'Are you okay?' he asked uneasily. 'Maggie, this is too much. Shall I take you home again?'

'I'm fine. It's just this car's too low. I need a crane.' She looked at his hands—thought about how she should refuse his aid. Contact with this man was doing dumb things to her head—and then she thought, no, dumb or not she'd take any contact she could get. She took his hands, he tugged her to her feet and she came too fast.

She was hard against him. Only she wasn't. Her bump was in the way.

She had to get herself under control. Max was on the other side of her bump, holding on, waiting for her to steady herself. Looking at her in concern.

She steadied. Took a deep breath. Tugged her hands away.

Then… 'Spike,' she said.

This was exactly what she needed. Not to look at Max. Not to let him see her need. Spike was on the far side of the car park, accompanied by a couple—a man in paint-spattered overalls and a woman in the uniform of one of the local supermarket chains. They looked about to climb into a battered family sedan.

'Spike,' Maggie yelled, and then, as he didn't respond, she put two fingers in her mouth and whistled.

Max hadn't seen Spike, and he hadn't expected it. He was a whole eighteen inches away from Maggie, and the whistle came close to bursting his eardrums. It was a whistle a farmer might use to call a dog in the next county.

'It's Spike,' Maggie said happily, and headed across the car park.

He followed. Bemused.

'Where did you learn to whistle like that?'

'Betty,' she said over her shoulder. 'Great legacy, huh?'

Maggie had Spike's attention now. Of course she did. He— and his parents?—stood by their car, immobilised by Maggie's whistle.

The whole car-park looked immobilised by Maggie's whistle, but Maggie's sole attention was on Spike.

The kid still looked pale and subdued, dressed in the non-descript clothes that emergency departments give out after accidents. His spiked hair was sagging at the tips and he looked…smaller? But Max watched his face as he recognised Maggie, and thought this was a kid who'd had a life-or-death situation thrust at him and who'd reacted with courage and honour. It had left its mark.

Like Maggie, sobbing her heart out on his chest. Life's tragedies were something that affected both them deeply.

'Spike,' Maggie said joyfully as she reached him, and she hugged him before he knew what had hit him.

'I'm C-Colin,' the kid managed, trying to sound defiant. 'Not Spike.'

Maggie grinned and turned to Max. 'He's Colin,' she said happily. 'Our hero's Colin.'

'Hero?' the woman beside Spike said faintly.

'Hero,' Maggie said definitely. 'Is Colin your son?'

'I… Yes,' the woman said. 'And this is his father.'

'I'm really pleased to meet you,' Maggie said warmly. 'We helped at the accident, with your wonderful son.'

'The hospital called us,' the man told them, glancing at Spike as if the thought of Colin as wonderful was clearly ludicrous. 'They said Colin had been in an accident.'

'We were so scared,' the woman added. 'Only then we found out he wasn't actually in the accident. He'd just seen it and fainted.'

Someone needed to explain, but even as Max thought it, Maggie was on the case. She was like a lioness with a cub, he thought, bemused. Maggie, fierce and loyal and true. He watched the indignation on her face and he thought this was a woman who, once she gave her heart, would give it for ever. Spike had earned her loyalty and she'd repay it a thousand times over.

And he wondered suddenly—out of left field—whether he could find the courage to ask for that commitment to himself.

'Is that what Colin told you?' she was demanding, indignation personified. 'That he'd seen an accident and fainted?'

'What else is there?' his father asked.

'Did he tell you he saved a lady's life?'

The couple stared. 'He just said he saw an accident,' Spike's mother said. 'He said he had to give his T-shirt to the doctor and the ambulance guy said he fainted.'

'Not until he wasn't needed any more,' Maggie retorted. 'Tell them, Max. This is Dr Ashton, by the way. Dr Ashton, tell them about how Colin was just plain wonderful.'

So Max told them, while Spike's parents looked bemused, and then disbelieving, and finally awed. Spike flushed and looked like he didn't know where to put himself, but he didn't have a choice. Like it or not, Maggie hugged him again, and then his mother was lining up for her share.

And suddenly, fiercely, Max was wishing he was somewhere in the middle of that hugging. It was dumb but there it was. Things were shifting inside. A huge hunger he'd ignored for years was suddenly refusing to be ignored.

The abyss of emotional connection seemed suddenly no abyss but something wonderful. Something that if he dared move forward could be his again.

If he dared.

Maybe…maybe that abyss was simply a blockade that had to be battered down. It was a blockade built from fear and loneliness but on the other side…

'You must be so proud,' Maggie declared, as Max's world shifted, while Spike's mum took over hugging duty.

'An' the doctor said they'll live,' Colin said, muffled by the closeness of his mother. 'I asked. But I can't believe I fainted. Bloody souk.'

'You didn't faint until the drama was over,' Max said firmly, putting his arm round Maggie and holding her against him. Finally taking a hug for himself. The hug felt good. No, it felt excellent. It felt right.

But somehow he had to keep talking to Spike and his parents. Maggie expected it of him, he knew. This was a lady who'd expect a lot of her man.

'Colin, I fainted for the first time when I was a medical student,' he told him. 'It was during the first Caesarean birth I ever attended. The mother was conscious—*she* told the nurse she thought I was going to faint. She even told her to help me. Colin, you did better than the average medical student. You did what had to be done, and you kept your personal, emotional reaction until afterwards. That took guts.'

And beside him Maggie nestled closer and beamed up at him. He had her approval, he thought, and maybe what he was feeling was corny and clichéd and soppy, but corny or not it felt right.

'Did he really do that?' Spike's father demanded, staring at his son like he'd never seen him before.

'He was the only one in the crowd with the courage to help,' Maggie declared, and Max could feel her wanting to hug Spike again. He was doing Spike a favour by holding onto her, but that certainly wasn't the reason he was holding on. He was holding on for himself alone. 'Maggie and I are trained medical professionals,' he said, hugging her tighter to solidify the 'Maggie and I' connection. 'Colin came in cold and did brilliantly.'

'Hey,' Spike's dad said, and his eyes were filling. 'Hey.'

'Weren't nuthin',' Spike said.

'It was everything,' Max said.

And then, as Spike's parents showed every sign of bursting into tears, he said farewells for both of them and dragged a reluctant Maggie away. He held onto her all the way to the other side of the car park. He'd drag her further if he could, he thought. There were far too many people around for what he wanted to do; for what he wanted to say.

But it'd have to wait. Maggie wanted to see how Grace and Judith were faring and something told him nothing would ever get in the way of Maggie's intentions.

But then he paused as he heard her sniff. 'Maggie?' He took her shoulders and looked down into her eyes. She sniffed again and glared.

'I don't cry,' she managed. 'I never cry.'

'I know that,' he said, managing to keep a straight face. 'So why are you not crying now?'

'I just thought…' She swiped her eyes angrily with the back of her hand and sniffed again. 'I watched their faces. His mum and dad's.'

'They were very proud.'

'It's what I want,' she said, and she put her hands under the bump that was her baby and tried to smile. 'You know, I was at the pictures last year. Life was grey. I was just working, just living, for me, for me, for me. William had said if ever I wanted his baby I should go ahead but there was no way I could. How could I ever have a child on my own? Only then I went to the pictures and this mum came out, arguing with her son. It was a silly, soppy picture—a romance—and she'd obviously dragged her kid there against his will. He was giving her such a hard time and she was saying leave it alone, you loved it as much as I did, and he was rolling his eyes at her, and she was saying if he didn't say something nice about it she'd make him broccoli sandwiches for a week. And he rolled his eyes again—and then he grinned. Then he looked around to make sure no one was noticing that he'd grinned, and I thought, That's what I want.'

'You want a teenager?' he said faintly.

'Like Spike,' she said. 'All contradictions and prickles and lovely underneath.' She patted her bump with pride. 'I'm going to refuse to let her get her ears pierced. That'll be such a fight. My best friend Rachel and I pierced our ears with ice and needles when we were thirteen.'

'You didn't!'

'My mum didn't even notice,' she said, with a touch of sadness. 'She wouldn't. I didn't have that kind of a family. But Rachel's did and she swabbed us with so much disinfectant the sides of our faces were yellow for a week. Then she marched us both off to her family doctor. She and Rachel yelled at each other all the time and I loved it. I so wanted someone to yell at me.'

'You're looking forward to yelling?'

'I am,' she said, sniffing again but finally managing a watery smile. 'I'm going to be the yellingest mother.'

'Maggie…' Someone pushed past them on the path. If he didn't get her to himself right now he'd go nuts.

But she wasn't thinking about him. 'Let's go,' she said, and suddenly, unaccountably, she seemed happy. She tucked her arm into his and tugged him forward. 'Let's go find Judith and Grace and make sure what Spike said is true. I'm so in the mood for a happy ending.'

So was he. He had some figuring out to do, but suddenly so was he.

Instead of going into the emergency waiting room and asking through normal channels, because Max worked at the hospital he took her straight into the emergency room itself. He introduced Maggie to Sue-Ellen, the director of the emergency department. Sue-Ellen greeted Maggie with pleasure, eyeing her bump with friendly interest.

What Spike had told them was the truth. Judith was in Theatre, having her arm stitched. She'd been given blood and would be fine. Grace was still being stabilised. 'That compound fracture of her leg needs work. She'll need grafts for the skin on her tummy, but every indicator is that we'll have a good result,' Sue-Ellen told them. And then, as if unable to contain her curiosity, she said, 'So you're the lady Max collided with the weekend of the music festival. We've been hearing rumours.' She grinned at the bump. 'I'll assume this isn't fast work, then, Dr Ashton.'

'Sue…'

'Just kidding,' she said, and gripped Maggie's hand. 'Good to meet you, Maggie. But you don't look like you should be here as a doctor. Midwifery's that-a-way.'

'There's a while to go yet,' Maggie said, and Sue-Ellen looked at her bump more closely and raised her eyebrows in polite disagreement.

'Really? I've had ladies come in looking smaller than you and leaving with a carry cot not all that many hours later.'

'Not me,' Maggie said firmly. 'Not yet. I'm not sticking round here now. I only wanted to know how Judith and Grace are.'

'You know, they're probably better than Judith's husband,' Sue-Ellen told her, and motioned through the glass doors to where a young man sat in the waiting room. He was holding a baby—Thomas? Thomas was asleep in his arms. The young father was staring straight ahead, holding the baby like his life depended on it. He looked grey.

'He came in looking worse than he looks now,' Sue-Ellen said sympathetically. 'I think he'll have lost ten years of his life on the way here.'

'That's the downside of loving,' Max said, flinching as he watched him, and Maggie cast him a look of reproach.

'Don't,' she said softly. 'You can't keep thinking like that.'

'How can you stop?'

'You're not cut out to be an emergency physician, then,' Sue-Ellen said bluntly. 'Sometimes I wonder how on earth can I go home at night expecting Bill and the kids to still be there. But amazingly they are. You just have to keep faith.' She smiled and motioned to Maggie's bump. 'Like you. There's a mound of hope if ever I saw it. Good luck with it. Oh, and, Max, Anton's been looking for you. Have you had your phone turned off? There's a crisis upstairs.' She disappeared, leaving them standing by the admissions desk, expecting them to leave.

He'd have to leave. A crisis. Max swore under his breath.

Of course. He'd slipped out to see Maggie during a quiet time. He'd called Anton after the accident saying he'd be longer than expected and it had still been quiet, but peace in his department never lasted long.

Anton needed him? He'd have to go. But what should he do with Maggie?

Maggie was looking through the glass doors that led into a waiting room. She'd be wanting to go and hug the young father, he thought. But then the door to the waiting room swung wide and Mary—the neighbour who'd helped at the scene—and a couple of other people arrived. Grandparents?

In moments the young father was surrounded. Others were doing the hugging, and Maggie was looking almost wistful.

'I need to go home,' she said, and suddenly he knew she was fighting not to sound forlorn.

He badly didn't want her to go back to the hotel by herself. Why had he set up his department so he was indispensable? Of all the stupid…

'If you wait until I've checked with my department I might be able to take you,' he told her, knowing already how doubtful it was that he could. And maybe she heard it in his voice.

'A cab's fine.' She was still looking through the glass. 'Oh, I wish there was something I could do.'

'You've done enough,' Max said. In truth he was having trouble pulling his attention away from the little group as well. They'd come so close to the edge…

He'd been over that edge. So had Maggie. Surely as a professional she knew she needed to protect herself.

But was it possible to protect yourself? He thought he'd built armour that was invincible. Only now… Suddenly he didn't know where that armour was.

'I'll just go talk to them before I go,' Maggie said, and her eyes were glistening again. 'But thank you, Max. I mean… just intending to visit was great. Even before the accident. It was very nice of you.'

'I'll come back to the hotel after work to make sure you're okay,' he growled.

'I'll be asleep,' she said, 'two minutes after I get home. Of course I'm okay. There's no need to worry.'

'There is a need.' The thought of her going back to her hotel alone seemed unbearable. 'Maggie, have you arranged for anyone to be with when you go into labour?'

'I don't need anyone.'

'You do need—'

'No. I've learned not to.'

'I could—'

'No, because you don't want to,' she said bluntly. 'We both know there's stuff between us that's messing with your head.'

'Maybe my mess is getting clearer. Maybe my head is saying loud and clear that I want to help. Maggie, I want to be involved.'

That gave her pause. She gazed up at him for a long moment and then she shook her head.

'No,' she said, and he thought she was trying to sound firm for both of them. 'Not after today. I just sobbed on you, naked in the shower, and if that didn't confuse the issue then I don't know what would.' She hesitated but then her voice became more certain. 'Okay, Max, I'll be honest here and confess that right now I look at you and my knees turn to water. Now, if that's not a confession to make you run a mile I don't know what is. But I'm also thinking that maybe it's my hormones playing tricks. Would any nine-month pregnant woman be hard-wired to latch onto the first available male and cling? I've never been pregnant before. I have no idea what's hormones and what's not. I only know that this isn't the time to find out. And I also suspect you don't ever want to find out. You see that pain?'

She motioned out to the waiting room where the young father sat in a surge of hugs and tears. 'That's what I want to be part of,' she confessed. 'That's why I made the decision to have William's baby. I want to open myself up for all that again. Hurt, grief, but the joy that goes with it. That's what I want but I don't think you do.' She tried to smile, tried to make him smile with her, but he wasn't smiling. He glanced out at the little family and saw again the grief that he'd sworn never again to endure.

He turned again to Maggie and he knew he was exposed again, like it or not. But they were standing in the middle of the emergency room. The woman behind the admissions desk could probably hear them—he could practically see her ears flapping. In another part of the hospital patients were waiting for him, and he knew they'd be urgent. How could he talk to her now?

He needed time to sort his head out. He needed time to get the words right.

All he could do now was to address immediate need. Which was to keep her safe.

'Maggie, I will not let you go back to the hotel,' he said. 'Let's find you a bed here until I can take you home.'

'Are you kidding?' she demanded, astounded. 'I'm not staying in hospital.'

'If you go into labour…'

'Then I'll come back. I'm not stupid.'

'Look,' he said, and suddenly he was in no man's land—

no longer sure of anything. Reason had gone out the window. He only knew that this woman had changed his world, and to leave her now seemed physically impossible. 'Maggie, I don't know what the hell I'm feeling but I can't let you go home by yourself.'

'The reluctant martyr,' she groaned.

'What?'

And suddenly she was angry. 'How do you think this makes me feel—that you're being dragged into my life by your toenails, kicking and screaming. Butt out.'

'Maggie, I—'

'I've already confessed how I feel,' she snapped. 'How much pride have I lost? There's only one thing you can say after a confession like that and it's goodbye.'

'I don't want to say…'

'No, and neither do I,' she confessed, still furious. 'But we don't have a choice. Maybe we can think about things after the birth, after I get some normality back into my life. But not now.'

'You need help.'

'Stop it,' she said. 'Just cut it out or you'll have me agreeing with you, and how scary's that?'

'It's not in the least scary.'

'What, to have me clinging to you?'

'Maggie…'

'Stop it,' she ordered. 'Max, just cut it out and go back to your life. Please.'

'Do you really want me to?'

'Of course I don't, but it's the only sensible thing to do.'

'Do you want to be sensible?'

'No!' She was practically yelling at him. Patients were looking at them. Staff were looking at them. Maggie glanced around and suddenly she shrugged and a spark of mischief replaced the anger. Mischief and something more. 'Of course I don't want to be sensible, but I do need to go home. But if you're really intent on following… Maybe I'd better warn you what you'd be in for if you really let me need you. Let's see me not be sensible.'

And before he knew what she intended—before he could begin to guess—she seized his shoulders, she stood on tiptoe and kissed him.

And this was a *Kiss*. It was a seize the day, claim the man, take what you want for there might be no tomorrow kind of kiss, and it possessed him utterly, from the time her hands grasped his shoulders, from the time her lips met his, from the time she melted into him.

For that was what she did. She melted. Her lips were like fire, and the heat she gave him, the strength, the passion, the surety… It took his breath away.

It took him away. His sensible self. The Max who thought things out logically. The Max who thought he was in control.

This was a man and a woman, and between them was a need as primitive as time itself.

He was holding her close and he was falling…falling… For it was no longer Maggie who was doing the kissing. He was kissing her, holding her, taking her to him. Claiming her as his own.

And they were being cheered.

At a subconscious level he heard the cheers and knew he should pull away, only that would mean letting her go, and to let her go was impossible.

He'd never felt such heat. Never felt such fire.

Her mouth was open under his and he felt her tongue start

its own sweet exploration. His hands tugged her closer and he kissed her back, demanding as well as giving, taking passion, taking sweetness and heat, taking joy…

The clapping and laughter around them was growing louder. More raucous.

And then there was an apologetic murmur. A hand on his shoulder was tugging him back. There was laughter right beside him, and the hand on his shoulder was insistent. Someone—not Maggie—was determined that he move.

Reluctantly he propelled Maggie away from him, holding her by her shoulders until she was steady. She stood back, looking astonished at her own temerity, while around them patients and staff erupted into applause. The guy at his shoulder was an orderly at the head of a trolley, wanting to get past. The patient on the trolley was laughing, too, but the orderly was inexorably pushing them both aside.

'Bedrooms are upstairs, mate,' he said, smiling.

'It's young love,' an old lady on a nearby examination table said.

'At it like rabbits,' a kid on a trolley called out, and Max found himself blushing from the toes up.

'I just rang Anton and told him you were here,' Sue-Ellen called from behind them, apologetically. 'He needs you right away.'

And to Max's astonishment, Maggie grinned at their audience and gave Sue-Ellen a cheery wave.

'Take him,' she called. 'He's all yours now.'

'I don't think I want him,' Sue-Ellen said, grinning back. 'He's looking used.'

'If he's second hand I'll take him,' the old lady called. 'He looks like there's still a bit of life in him yet.'

'All the same—out of here,' Sue-Ellen said, laughing. 'If

we can't deliver your baby, Maggie, you'll have to leave. We've got an influx expected.'

'Trouble?' Max asked, fighting hard for composure, and Sue-Ellen's smile faded.

'Probably. This power grid problem's not going away and half the city seems to be affected. The power cuts over the last few days seem to be minor in comparison. You'd think drivers would think no traffic lights means slow down. Try telling that to the moronic driver who caused your accident. We're hearing there's accidents all over the place. The only reason we're not rushed off our feet already is that the traffic's so gridlocked it's taking ages getting ambulances to us.'

And it seemed as if the outside world was breaking in from all directions. 'Max!' Through the swinging doors burst Anton. 'Where the hell have you been? I've been trying to contact you. We've got a bleeder. Theatre three.'

'Maggie, if the traffic's a problem…' Max started, but Maggie was already backing away.

'It wasn't a problem on the way in,' Maggie said. 'Even if it is, I'll just find a café and sit it out until the power comes back on.'

'I don't want you—'

'No,' she said, giving a firm nod. 'You don't. You have work to do and I'm in the way.'

'Max,' Anton said, warningly. 'This can't wait.'

'Goodbye Max,' Maggie said, and tried to smile. She walked away, leaving him staring through the glass doors after her.

'Max,' Anton said again, sounding more urgent.

'I'm coming.'

'Should I find someone else?' Anton demanded, watching his face.

'No. No,' he repeated, more firmly. 'She'll be okay. She has time.'

'Time until the baby's due, or time until you go after her?' Anton said.

He didn't answer but he didn't have to. He knew what Maggie wanted. Her body had just told him, and he knew he wanted the same.

How soon could he go to her?

There didn't seem to be any cabs, so Maggie took a bus, and, as Sue-Ellen had warned, the traffic was a nightmare. Every set of traffic lights was out.

The city was descending into darkness but, weirdly, people were being friendlier than she'd ever known. The lack of traffic lights, the series of mostly minor accidents at uncontrolled intersections meant that traffic was going nowhere. People sat patiently on Maggie's bus, discussing whether the supermarkets would be open for candles, where they could get long-life milk, ice, something for dinner that didn't need cooking.

Someone had a tiny keyring pig from a Christmas cracker that oinked every time he shone its nose light. 'I'm going to do my supermarket shopping by pig,' he told his fellow passengers as after two hours on the bus everyone gave up waiting and decided the only way anyone was getting anywhere was on foot.

Maggie tried to smile. Normally she'd think this was fun, but too much had happened today and her back was starting to ache. She was still half a mile from her apartment when the bus stopped. Weariness and the shock of the day was taking its toll. She really didn't want to walk.

There were no cabs. She had no choice.

It was hard to keep herself steady on the pavement. Without streetlights, people were jostling, good-humoured and laughing, but with each step Maggie felt less like laughing. Her back hurt!

This was tiredness, she told herself. Shock. She'd been bending over the two accident victims, not being careful. She'd been swimming before that. She'd done too much.

And… She wanted Max.

Maybe she'd never see Max again.

She deserved not to see Max again, she told herself dismally. She'd kissed him like a…like a hussy.

Ooh. She gave herself a mock hoot of horror. A hussy?

She didn't feel like a hussy. She felt alone and clumsy and huge, and as she walked steadily onward she was also starting to feel more than a little scared.

A stab of hot pain jabbed at her back and she thought, no, it couldn't be. Please.

She had to be sensible. If there was a chance she was in labour… No, she was imagining things. She was over three miles from the hospital now—it was impossible to walk back. She'd be okay.

But her back hurt. A lot.

Her feet slowed. What to do?

What would she tell a patient to do?

Call an ambulance.

That was good advice. She was nine months pregnant with bad backache. Calling an ambulance was only sensible.

The decision made, she felt better. She stopped walking and searched in her purse for her phone.

It wasn't there.

Damn, she could see it, her phone, sitting on the charger on the bedside table in her apartment. She'd left it there when she'd gone swimming and she'd been in too much of a rush when she'd left with Max to think about taking it.

Don't panic. Don't panic!

She had no phone here, but she could get to her apartment and phone from there.

She could phone Max?

Or not. What could Max do that an ambulance couldn't?

She kept walking. She could see the glimmer of the moon over the sea. The sea was where her apartment was. Great. Two minutes' walk and she'd be there. She'd let herself in, make herself a cup of tea, ring the ambulance and then watch the moonlit sea while she waited.

No power. She wouldn't be able to make tea.

Oh, for heaven's sake, she was crying again! She wasn't a hussy—she was a total wuss.

CHAPTER TEN

MAX spent the night with his thoughts returning again and again to Maggie. Uneasy, and getting worse.

As the city's traffic became more and more gridlocked, the hospital became quieter. Apparently people were abandoning their cars and walking, or finding accommodation where they could. Once the traffic was truly gridlocked, accidents lessened, and even when they happened ambulances couldn't get through the blocked roads.

'Contact your local medical centres if you need to,' radio announcers were telling those with battery-operated radios. Suburban doctors were operating emergency clinics. The population was coping as best it could.

Tomorrow there'd be questions asked in parliament, Max thought. Heads would roll over this unprecedented mess. Only…

Only Maggie.

Dammit, Maggie.

He needed to know that she'd got home safely, but he rang her apartment block between patients, at ten and again at midnight, and got no answer. He fretted about it to Anton as they worked together on what they hoped would be their last surgical case for the night, and Anton provided an answer.

'Most small apartment blocks don't man their front desks at night,' he explained patiently, as he monitored their patient's air supply. 'Phone in the morning when the concierge comes back on duty.'

'There should be an after-hours emergency number.'

'Every apartment will have its own number,' Anton said, staying patient. 'Maggie will be able to ring out if she needs to.'

'I need to ring Maggie.'

'You don't have her cellphone number?'

'No!' he snapped, so harshly the nurses looked at each other and thought whoa, tread lightly here, surgeon annoyed.

He just needed to know she'd got home. The radio was reporting total gridlock. Even when he finished here he wouldn't be able to drive and find out.

In desperation, when he finally finished in Theatre—after two in the morning—he rang John and Margaret at the farm. Woke them. Frightened them.

For nothing.

No, Maggie's apartment number didn't work at night but if he rang in the morning the concierge would put him through. Her cellphone number? Actually, she'd given her usual phone to John because the locals used it at need. She'd said she'd buy another for private use but, no, she hadn't given them that number either.

Why hadn't they asked her for it?

Why hadn't he asked her for it?

'So what's the problem?' Margaret asked sharply.

Max caught himself and said, no, it's only that the city's in the grip of a blackout, and he was probably worrying unnecessarily.

He left the ward and walked slowly across the quadrangle

to his apartment. Thanks to the hospital generators everything seemed normal. He felt stupid.

But he also felt increasingly apprehensive, and the feeling wouldn't go away.

Maggie.

This was not how it was supposed to be.

And as he stood there he thought… They were supposed to be together. One man and one woman and one baby.

The knowledge was suddenly so strong it was almost primeval, kicking in where any pretence at intelligence left off. Maggie and her baby weren't here, so why was he here?

He stopped and stared southward, toward Coogee. Three miles or so as the crow flew. How long would that take him to walk?

How long would it take him to run?

The pain wasn't too bad if she lay still.

She lay still.

The backache grew. It seemed to be coming in waves.

The apartment was dark.

She was *not* afraid of the dark.

She was afraid.

Okay, get sensible. Yes, the contractions were indeed contractions. Yes, they seemed to be getting stronger and closer together.

She rang the ambulance yet again.

'There's a massive traffic jam,' a sympathetic operator told her. 'I'm trying as hard as I can to get a car to you. Can someone take you to your local medical centre? Can you call a neighbour?'

'I'll call a neighbour,' she agreed, sweating.

She staggered up from the settee. Went to the door,

unlocked it—just in case the ambulance could get here. Looked out into the pitch-black hallway.

Tried to remember seeing any of her neighbours. Tried to figure which door she could knock on.

Thought again she was being stupid.

This was her first baby. She was hours away from delivery. Maybe a day.

No, she decided as the next contraction hit. Not a day. But hopefully hours. It was stupid to stumble about in the dark waking neighbours she didn't know.

She groped her way back into her darkened living room and collapsed back onto the settee.

Dammit, she wasn't going to lie here in the dark and be terrified. She wasn't!

Max…

'Don't think of Max,' she told herself between gasps. Between contractions. 'Max has less chance of getting here than an ambulance does, so there's no use even thinking of him. Think of your daughter instead. Do you want her to meet you sweating with fear in the dark?'

'No!'

'So do something about it.

She took a deep breath, which was supposed to be steadying but wasn't. 'This isn't a scary time,' she told herself, trying hard to believe it. 'It's looking more and more like it's your daughter's birthday, so put your party hat on. When the ambulance arrives I want to look brave.'

As if…

At least light some candles.

'Okay. I think I can do that,' she gasped, clutching at her back and trying not to cry out. 'Maybe. If I don't have something else happen first.'

* * *

Three miles wasn't very long as far as marathons went, but this wasn't a marathon, this was a sprint. Max was fit but he kept fit by working out between cases in the hospital gym. He had strength training. He didn't run. He especially didn't run in the dark without benefit of streetlights.

It'd be a sight easier if his heart hadn't been hammering in his chest before he'd started. The more he ran the more it kept right on hammering.

He was being dumb, he told himself, over and over again. He was imagining problems when there weren't any. There was no reason at all for a sane doctor to run across a darkened city, growing more fearful by the minute. But the mantra had started in his head and once started it wouldn't go away.

Maggie, Maggie, Maggie.

He'd let her go home. Of all the stupid, criminal, irresponsible...

It wasn't stupid, the sane part of him said. He'd assumed the electricity would come back on as it had come back on last night and the night before.

He'd never imagined this totally irrational certainty that he'd lose her.

She wasn't his to lose, the sane portion of his brain reminded him, but the sane portion of his brain was getting smaller by the minute, replaced by raw emotion. Maggie was *his* woman. His heart was telling him that, with every sound of his feet hitting the pavement. And his woman was having his baby.

His? Irrational? Maybe but it didn't matter. He knew truth when he heard it and he was running.

* * *

And in an apartment in Coogee… 'I will not have my baby in the dark. I will not have my baby in fear. I will not have my baby lying on a rented hotel apartment settee with no beauty. Not!'

Her apartment block loomed solid and black in the night. There was a faint light coming from one of the terraces above his head, but none of the windows were lit.

Maggie hadn't lit her candles, then?

Of course not. Maggie would be asleep. She wouldn't thank him for barging in and waking her. Terrifying her for nothing.

He made himself slow. Made himself catch his breath. Went into the foyer. Wondered why the door into the foyer was unlocked. Then thought maybe it was attached to some electrical security system that wasn't working. If the concierge had faced the choice of locking tenants out or letting the foyer stay unguarded overnight, that's what he would have done.

So he could climb up the stairs to Maggie's apartment.

Just walk up and knock?

That's what he was intending to do. Walk up and knock. It's three in the morning. Wake up, Maggie, I'm here.

Breathe.
  Breathe.
  Breathe.
  Surely the books hadn't said it hurt this much.
  Breathe…
  You can do this.
  '*I can't…*'

* * *

He knocked on the door and the impact of the knock had the door swinging inward. What the…? She hadn't locked it? She hadn't even closed it properly?

The corridor he felt his way down was in complete darkness. So was the apartment through the door. Maybe stopping to fetch a torch would have been sensible.

He wasn't feeling sensible.

He swung the door wide and called. 'Maggie?'

Nothing.

Did he stumble round in the dark and see if he could find her? Hell, he'd scare the living daylights out of her.

He raised his voice. 'Maggie?'

Still nothing.

It wasn't completely dark. There was a faint glimmer from the hall mirror, reflecting light from outside. His eyes were finally adjusting to a darkness that was more intense here than in the moonlight outside, but it was still a less intense dark than the corridor. He could see shapes. A bench in the kitchenette. A hall lamp. The living-room settee.

'Maggie?'

He was feeling his way in, wondering if he had the right apartment. There were four doors in this corridor and he'd got here by feel.

It'd be just his luck to have the wrong apartment.

'I'm a doctor,' he called, just in case some stranger was sitting bolt upright in bed, preparing to have a heart attack because of a prowler in their apartment. 'I'm looking for Maggie. I'm looking for a pregnant woman in trouble.'

He sounded stupid, he thought, edging into the sitting room as he called.

The drapes were wide open and he could see the moonlit sea beyond. Then, as he drew further into the room, he saw there was another light source outside. Low light, hidden until now by the bulk of the settee.

He moved cautiously forward, hit his knee on a coffee table and swore.

'Maggie?' He tugged open the big glass door to see where the light from outside was coming from. 'Maggie?'

'Did you bring gas?' a voice demanded from floor level, and the words were a series of breathless, pain-filled, gasps. 'If you didn't, kill me now. Oh, Max…'

She'd set up a birth centre. She was on the tiled balcony floor but on bed of sorts, a mound of soft bedding right at the edge of the terrace, where the open protective rails gave her a sweeping vista of the sea beyond.

There were candles everywhere. She was surrounded by a sea of light, a complete circle apart from the line of sight between her and the sea. The moon was hanging low, casting a silvery trail of moonbeams over the ocean. They looked almost a ribbon, reaching out to touch the woman on the cushions at his feet.

Apart from the hush-hush of the waves on the sand below there was complete silence. All this Max absorbed in a fraction of a second. And then…

'Mmmmmmmmmpf…'

It was a long, low moan, so low that unless he was right next to her he'd never have heard it. For Max, who'd delivered a thousand babies or so, it was the quietest birthing moan he'd ever heard.

Forget the moonbeams. He was frantically shifting candles so he could get to her. He wanted so much to take her in his arms, but there was still a part of him that was sensible. 'Obstetrician Goes Up In Flames' wasn't a headline he wanted to hit the newsstands any time soon.

Obstetrician? Maybe he was.

Indeed he was. For even as he took in what was happening, even as emotion hit him like a kick in the guts, his professional side was kicking in as well. Making him sensible; making him take the time to make the scene safe before he could kneel beside her and tug her into his arms and hold her close.

It took seconds and then he had her.

'Mmmmmmmmmmmpf....'

Another contraction already...

He held her tight until it passed, and then he kept on holding her. Yes, he needed to be her doctor, but first there was an urgent need to be...Maggie's man.

'Max,' she whispered, and he simply held her until the next contraction hit and beyond. Maggie's man? Some truths were beyond question. Then...

'No gas?' she demanded.

'I didn't bring my bag,' he said ruefully. 'I ran.'

'You ran.'

'Dumb,' he said. 'Like you having your baby in the middle of a power strike. You didn't think to call for help?'

'I've called for help.'

'To me?'

'I called the ambulance. You're not an obstetrician,' she said, with a breathless attempt at dignity.

'I'm an obstetrician. Can you bear me to examine you?'

'Mmmmmmmmmmpf...'

'That was a yes?'

He didn't want to be Maggie's doctor, he thought. He wanted to keep right on holding her. He also wanted a full birthing suite. A full obstetric team.

'I did call...the ambulance...' she repeated. 'Hours ago. I

hoped the ambulance could get through. I didn't think you could.'

'I'd have been here earlier if you'd phoned me.'

'You want me to apologise for not phoning?' she gasped. 'You didn't bring gas. I'm holding it against you for ever. Mmmmmmmmmpf…'

'I'm holding you against me for ever,' he said shakily, but he couldn't. He had to set her down again on the cushions and be her doctor.

'I'm…I think I'm going to push,' she managed.

'Try not to till I've seen.'

'Then hurry up and see,' she said, and moaned again.

'You want to yell?' he asked.

'I'll wake the neighbours.'

'Someone might have gas,' he said. 'Did you think of that? If you yelled someone might have come and helped you.'

'I only want you. Mmmmmmmmpf….'

The head…

'Maggie, she's crowning.'

'Don't care. Mmmmmmpf…'

'You do care,' he said, hauling the candles closer to where he needed to see. Then as another contraction rippled through and he realised how close she was to delivering, he suddenly changed direction, shifting candles, cushions, shoving Maggie's whole makeshift bed and Maggie with it along the balcony so she was hard against the wall. So he could haul her into sitting position and leave her propped up, gasping, fighting, bearing down, so she could see….

So she could see her daughter enter the world.

And then… There was moment's stillness. A moment's peace where the world held its breath. Where even the moonlit sea seemed to hush. Until…

She screamed, a scream to wake every neighbour from Coogee to Bondi, a truly excellent birthing scream that came with that last triumphant push.

'Slow… Slow…' he said urgently, and she did, backed off, stopped pushing, while his fingers found…cord.

Not a problem—he had it free in seconds.

Oh, thank God he was here.

'Go,' he said, and she sighed and groaned and held her knees and pushed with one mighty heave—and managed to see…

As her baby daughter slipped into Max's hands and into the world.

No one came. The scream that could have woken the dead evoked no response at all.

There was no sound at all as Max cleared the baby's airway, checked her breathing, felt this tiny, perfect being come to life in his hands. Maggie's daughter didn't cry. She simply stared upward, dazed, incredulous, vernix-coated, slippery as hell.

And inside him, something that had been missing for a long, long time settled back into his heart and stayed.

What could ever be more perfect than this? This moment of birth.

And *this* birth was the best. Delivering Maggie's baby… Quite simply he felt like the luckiest man alive, and as he slipped the tiny girl onto Maggie's breast, watched the baby slide against her mother's skin, saw Maggie's hands cradle her daughter, watched her eyes fill with tears, saw the two of them mould into one moment of absolute perfection, he knew his world could never be the same again.

He knew he could never want it to be the same.

He didn't speak. Instead he simply watched, and smiled and smiled and smiled.

Finally Maggie looked up at him, her eyes shimmering with tears, and whispered simply, 'Thank you, Max.'

'It was my privilege,' he said softly. 'I believe that I love you.'

The world held its breath once more.

She stared at him for a long moment. Awed. Then slowly the corners of her mouth curved into a smile

'It took only that,' she whispered, and the world started again. Back on the beach the waves began again, life began again. 'Oh, Max, my love. My heart.' She was smiling and smiling, her eyes misty with love and with happiness. 'For you to love me… How can you mean it?'

'I never say things I don't mean. Maggie, how can I not love you?'

She hesitated, and he saw her smile falter. 'But…'

But? He didn't want to hear a but—and he wouldn't do anything to mess with that smile.

'Maggie, I won't rush you into anything,' he said quickly, touching her face lightly with his fingers. Wondering how this wonderful woman could possibly call him her love. Her heart. But with that one word—'*But*'—reality had broken in a little. Sense was starting to prevail.

The professional side of him was still playing a part. Right now, Maggie was at the most vulnerable moment of a woman's life. The emotion she was feeling must be overwhelming. To take her to him—to claim her as his own—was what he wanted to do more than anything in the world, but not now.

'I'll not push you further,' he whispered. 'Not this night. I swear I'll feel the same, now, tomorrow and for ever, but if it takes months for you to believe me, then so be it. I'll wait for however long it takes.'

He was watching Maggie's daughter find her breast, take her first taste of Maggie's milk. Wondering how she could doubt his love. But if Maggie needed time, he had to give it to her.

'Oh, Max, I do love you,' she whispered, and he felt the last trace of the heavy load of armour he'd placed around his heart disappear to nothing. 'My Max.'

But her instinctive *'But'* still had him shaken. It had reminded him that this was no time to demand commitment. It wasn't fair.

There was a reason laws were in place to protect the doctor-patient relationship, he thought, forcing himself to be sensible. He wasn't about to play on her gratitude and her emotions. He must hold back!

'What…what will you call her?' He was struggling hard to return to being professional—he needed to, because the birthing process wasn't quite over. But as far as Maggie was concerned it was done. Life was here now, complete. For all of them.

'Rose,' she said.

'Is that a name you and Will picked out?'

'We didn't choose,' she whispered. 'We didn't dare to think there'd ever be a baby. I did wonder about Chloe, only now I see her…she's just Rose. And I'll add an Elizabeth for Betty.' She smiled shyly up at him, looking almost anxious. 'What do you think?'

'Pretty much perfect.'

'I think so,' she said. 'Stitches?'

'Nothing to stitch.'

'Too perfect,' she said, shy giving way to smug. She was relaxing again now, and she was looking just about as happy as it was possible for a woman to be. 'I'm so good at this.'

Right. He didn't mention the cord around Rose's neck. There were some things Maggie didn't need to know. How close she might have come...

It didn't bear thinking about.

'I'd like you up this end of the bed,' Maggie said, sounding suddenly like the old Maggie, like the strong and imperious woman he loved.

'I believe I need to clean up.'

'It can wait,' she said. 'I need to be kissed.'

So much for the doctor-patient relationship. He touched her face again, loving her with every part of his being.

He still needed to be sensible. He still needed to remember that instinctive *'But'*.

Okay, Maggie needed to see that what he was feeling wasn't the result of need and loss and all the things that had been messing with his head for so long. But right now...

'Max, right now I'm holding my daughter and I believe my world is wonderfully, amazingly fabulous,' she whispered, loving him with her smile. 'The only thing that could make it more perfect is if you kissed me. So...'

So he'd never know how she was going to finish that sentence, for he had her in his arms, her daughter gently cradled between them, and he was kissing her as she wanted to be kissed.

As he wanted to kiss her.

Which was pretty much as perfect as a kiss could be.

They slept—or Maggie and Rose slept, and Max lay with Maggie in his arms, with tiny Rose wrapped and snuggled between them.

If he slept he might move too close, put in peril this tiny, precious creature who already felt a part of him. He had her nestled between them so Maggie could feel her daughter's closeness, but Max could feel the baby's warmth as well, her tiny snuggling movements, her flawlessness.

With the roads still blocked from the night, the usual sounds from the street below were silent. There was only the ocean, the moonlight over the water, this woman, this baby.

Life was perfect.

There were complications. He knew it. He was a surgeon in a major teaching hospital and Maggie had committed herself to be a country doctor and farmer. Were the two compatible?

Could Maggie leave Yandilagong to be with him?

The decision was too hard for now. They needed time to think.

Only there wasn't much space in his head to think. All he could think was how right Maggie felt in his arms, and how wonderful life felt right now.

Maggie stirred some time toward dawn. It was still dark. She could close her eyes and sleep again, only right now she was too happy to sleep. She felt her daughter nestled beside her. Max's arm was under her shoulders, his chest was her pillow, she was cradled against him and she felt so happy she was almost floating.

Yet she'd said, *'But.'*

Why? It had been an instinctive reaction, a stab of acknowledgement of every barrier that lay between them. *'But it's impossible that you love me.'* Only right now she couldn't even think what those barriers were.

So why had she said it?

It had changed things, she thought, no matter how he'd reassured her. She'd told him she'd loved him, but he'd moved onto practical things again. She had allowed the real world a glimpse in.

But she wanted to love him in the real world as well. She wanted to be with him. In Max's arms, with her daughter by her side, she felt like the luckiest woman in the world.

There were problems. Even within her haze of relief and love and happiness she could dimly acknowledge that. Maybe that's what her *'But'* had been about. She'd promised Betty that she'd care for Angus, she'd care for the farm, she'd even told her the medical needs of Yandilagong were settled. How could she simply abandon that promise and walk into Max's life?

She would if he asked her. She must. She'd find a way.

Max loved her. How wonderful was that? How wonderful was life?

It was too wonderful to let herself think about problems right now, she thought dreamily. Problems were for tomorrow. Right now she was in the arms of the man she loved with all her heart, and her daughter—*their daughter?*—was between them.

She smiled a cat-got-the-cream smile and she nestled closer into Max. His arm tightened instinctively around her.

She was loved.

She slept.

CHAPTER ELEVEN

SOON after the sun rose, when the power finally came on, when the city slowly came back to life, an ambulance arrived. Maggie was bundled up to be taken to hospital, so Rose could have all the checks she needed, and Maggie could be cared for.

If Maggie had her way she'd stay right where she was, but it wasn't possible. Max couldn't stay with her—or wouldn't. The impulsive declarations of the night were over.

'For we do need to take this slowly,' he told her as he helped lift them both into the back of the ambulance. 'I need to go back to work. You need to go back to the farm.'

'I don't want to go back.' Impulsive, stupid or not, that was an absolute.

But Max was made of sterner stuff than she. Some time during the night a decision had been made.

'Maggie, I said I won't rush you and I won't,' he said. 'Last night you had a baby. You're an emotional—'

'Mess? I am not,' she said, ready to be indignant, but he smiled and placed a finger on her lips.

'Of course you're not. But there's all sorts of things to be thought out before we decide where to take…what we're feeling for each other. You promised Betty you'd stay on the farm. Yes?'

'I…' Her face clouded. 'Yes.'

'Today's not the day to make a decision to break that promise,' he said gently. 'I love you and I want you but I will not pressure you. You go to hospital, then you go back to the farm and we'll take things from there. Maybe in three months…'

'Three months!' She was on a stretcher, settled into the ambulance and she said the 'three months' as a wail. If she hadn't been cradling her daughter she might have got up and told him where he could put his three months.

But Max's expression was firm. A decision had been made. 'Maggie, it's life-changing decisions we're talking here,' he told her, and he kissed her lightly on the lips—and then, as if he couldn't help himself, he kissed her more deeply. 'I want no regrets when we move forward together,' he added.

'Will you still want me in three months?'

'I'll always want you,' he said simply, and he kissed her again, so deeply this time that the paramedics sighed and looked at their watches. He pulled away at last, smiled ruefully and climbed out of the van. 'Off you go, then, you and Rose. I'll clean up here and bring a suitcase to you later. And then…I'm working in the same hospital, my love. I won't be far away. Three months, my Maggie. We'll live that long.'

'Only if I have you waiting for me at the end,' she muttered, but she knew in her heart that what he was saying was sensible. She even managed to smile back. 'Oh, Max, I love you so much.'

Three months… Why had he said it? But even as he questioned himself he knew he was right. Maybe the time frame could be shorter but he doubted it. There were so many things that needed thinking through.

At least he hadn't been stupid enough to say he'd stay away from her. Yes, she needed space to think. Yes, her need of him might be hormonal. Yes, it was fair to give her time to recover from the emotions of the birth and, yes, he needed time to work out an idea that was still only a vague possibility—but staying away from her was impossible.

So Maggie was admitted to South Sydney, and if he happened to pass her ward a dozen times a day it wouldn't be proper not to check on her. Rose decided to be jaundiced, and there was another reason for him to be there. Yes, Maggie was a doctor, but she couldn't be dispassionate about her own daughter. It was hard enough for Max to be dispassionate, watching this tiny creature wearing her sunglasses under the lights. This tiny girl who held his heart in her hands almost as tightly as her mother did.

Their hospital stay was thus extended, but finally the jaundice resolved, and when Rose's colour faded from golden back to pink it was Max who drove them both back to the farm.

And if he hugged Maggie as he helped her into the car, if he kissed her as he closed the car door, and if he drove down the coast road feeling all the smugness of a man with a new family, who could blame him?

Beside him Maggie smiled and smiled. She was happy to be going home, he thought, and there was another stab of disquiet. Home to the farm. How to make this work?

Angus was watching for their arrival from the back of an ancient Lanz Bulldog. Angus was a part of Maggie's family. There were complications everywhere. How could he ask her to abandon Angus?

He couldn't. He wouldn't.

Maggie had attempted to raise the issue with him but he'd shushed her. 'It's not time,' he'd said, and he wouldn't be budged.

His wonderful idea was growing. There were still so many factors, though. Somehow Max had to figure a way around them.

Was three months long enough? It had to be. He had to figure out a way.

Focus on now, he told himself harshly. One step at a time. Angus was watching them and Maggie was smiling at him. Angus wasn't smiling back. He was holding onto his tractor as if it was his refuge.

'She needs headlights,' Max called as they pulled up beside Angus's tractor. 'I might know a source where I can find some.'

'Yeah?' Angus said.

'Leave it to me,' Max said, and then, offhand, 'You want to meet your niece?'

The elderly farmer stared at both of them in apprehension but Maggie didn't move, didn't speak, and Max didn't either.

Slowly Angus ventured down from the tractor. Max flicked the switch of the sunroof so it slid back, exposing Rose in her cocoon in the back seat, swathed in pink, gazing in astonishment up at the sky.

Angus edged nearer. Neither Maggie or Max said a word. Nearer.

He put a hand on the car—and then cautiously, cautiously put a finger out to touch.

Rose's little hand was just there. He touched her fingers and they curved and held, and Angus stared down at her in incredulity.

No one spoke but Max felt a knot of emotion in his chest that had lots to do with the expression on Maggie's face— but also something to do with Angus himself. With this farm. With the night of Betty and the calves in the haystack.

Family.

And the ideas that had been drifting since Rose's birth became more than ideas. An ambition?

No, a certainty. If he could pull it off.

He must.

And then there was a whoop from the house and Sophie and Paula were tearing along the driveway to meet them. Angus backed away, but only as far as his tractor.

'You've met her first, Angus, not fair,' Sophie yelled, and then Margaret and John were outside, too, and Maggie and Rose were enveloped.

Max could go now.

Only Maggie clung to him, and he had no intention of leaving until he must. In truth, all he wanted was to bundle Maggie and Rose back into his car and take them back to Sydney. To leave them here seemed wrong—but there were plans to make. If he could do it in three months… He must. He needed to get back to Sydney and get things moving right now.

But still he stayed and had dinner with them, knowing he'd been a fool for not accepting dinner the night of the funeral. One dinner missed was one too many. Then Maggie walked him out to the car and it was entirely logical that he take her into his arms and kiss her and kiss her and kiss her.

'I love you,' he whispered into her hair, for it seemed impossible not to say it.

'I love you right back,' she whispered. 'Max, three months is crazy.'

'It is,' he said ruefully. 'But I need to sort stuff out. Can you bear to be patient?'

'What do you need to sort out?'

'A happy ever after,' he said. 'If that's what you want.'

'How can you doubt it?'

'Then be patient,' he said, and kissed her again—but then

as Rose's indignant wail sounded from inside the house he put her away from him.

'I need to go and so do you. Go feed your daughter.'

'You'll come back?'

'Soon.'

'That's not soon enough,' she said, distressed. 'Max…'

'Hush,' he told her. 'Hush, my love. Let's take this one day at a time. Let's figure out where we go from here.'

She went back into the house to feed her baby, feeling bleak. Empty. Lost. That he was returning to Sydney without her…

He was giving her room to make her decisions. He was being honourable.

She didn't want honourable. She wanted Max.

And why had she made those promises to Betty?

The promises were closing in on her now. Back in Sydney she'd thought she could break them. It had seemed possible. But here, with echoes of Betty all around her, it seemed less so. For her to walk away from Angus, and the farm, and the community…

Oh, but to walk away from Max…

Inside the house Margaret met her, holding Rose out for her to take. When she saw Maggie's face she hugged her.

'Oh, my dear, he'll be back.'

'Will he?'

'Of course he will,' Margaret said stoutly.

But for how long? Maggie thought, but she didn't say it.

Max seemed to have faith in their future. Maybe she should, too.

He stayed away for almost a week and that was long enough. Then he made a mercy dash back, to give Angus his headlights, and bonnet badges he'd found for his 1949 Newman WD2. That was a good moment. Angus almost smiled. Maggie did.

Then he found someone to take over part of his role in Sydney so he could work reasonable hours. His car soon seemed to know the route back to the farm all by itself, and the more he visited, the more sure he was of what he felt. His thoughts were finding a centre, a purpose, but three months might not be long enough to finalise his plan.

Would she agree? Once the emotion of the birth had faded would she still feel the same? He daren't ask, not yet, but he rang, twice a day, sometimes more, and the pleasure in her voice said she might, she must.

'Your grin's getting fixed,' Anton told him. 'It's stretching your face.'

'Yeah,' he said.

'Don't do it,' Anton said morosely. 'Three kids and it's the end of life as you know it.'

'Would you want your old life?'

'Hell, I can't remember my old life,' Anton said. 'It's in the bottom of my wardrobe with my blue suede shoes. Figuratively speaking, that is. I'm not quite that old. I just feel it.'

'But for all the whinging…'

'Yeah, I wouldn't give it back.' Anton said, smiling at his friend. 'And if you take that final step, neither will you.'

She loved him, she loved him, she loved him. She wanted him here. That he wasn't next to her, seeing Rose's first smile, waking in the night next to her, loving her, felt wrong.

The promise she'd made to Betty seemed more and more impossible. To stay here for ever when the man she loved was in Sydney… How could she?

But Max wasn't asking her to go to Sydney. His phone calls and visits were all about now, all about what Rose was doing, how the farm was going, what was happening with the ancient Sift TD4 diesel Max had found and had shipped to the farm.

'So who's the tractor fanatic?' Maggie teased.

'Just taking a polite interest,' he said innocently. And she laughed to think of him, her swish Sydney surgeon, now with a secret passion for tractors… Max. Her man.

He wouldn't keep coming unless he wanted her. And she knew that she'd go with him. Despite her promise.

But the promise still lay heavy on her heart. The problem was that she'd become part of this community. Betty was gone but her ghost lingered through the house, a gentle, approving presence Maggie felt as a blessing all around her.

Betty had manoeuvred this into a happy ending, for the farm, for the community and for Angus, and in a sense Maggie had her happy ending as well. She had her precious daughter who was already gurgling her delight at her world. She was surrounded by people who loved her.

She and Rose had their own part of the house. The apartment Betty had built was large, sun-filled and lovely, but Sophie and Paula were constantly in and out, fascinated by Rose, bringing the house to life with their chatter and laughter. And John and Margaret were wonderful. They were looking to buy their own home but there was no rush. No rush at all.

This situation could extend indefinitely, Maggie thought. If not for Max.

Three months. He was gently patient, but she knew now that patience disguised steady purpose. He loved her, he wanted her and he was making her fall more and more deeply in love with him at every visit.

A couple of months after Rose's birth Maggie started doing two clinics a week—morning sessions, with no house calls. It took some of the load from John, and it felt good. She was back to serving the little community of Yandilagong that had been such an important part of William's past. The reason she was here.

The farm—the second reason she was here—was great as well. The tractors were like benign spirits, with Angus as their leader. His calves were half-grown now, and friendly. Maggie watched Angus and the calves, and Sophie and Paula with Bonnie, and she started to think maybe a pup of her own would be fun.

But if she was to move to Sydney…Max had a hospital apartment. A pup? No.

How could it matter? How could she put a pup above Max?

He loved her. There was no doubt about that, and every time she saw him she knew deeper in her heart that this was the man she wanted to share her life with.

So what was the problem?

She could sell the farm to John and Margaret. She knew that. They'd take care of Angus and she could visit constantly.

She'd done the best she could for Betty, for Angus, for the farm, for William's beloved community. It was only…only…

No. She loved Max and every time he phoned, every time he visited, she knew that her love was returned and more.

She was his woman. His gaze lingered on her, his kisses told her he wanted her, that he was waiting only from some misguided sense of chivalry. The wait didn't mean he didn't want her—the warmth of his voice on the end of the phone confirmed it. He'd said three months and he was sticking to it, but after that… She belonged to him as he belonged to her.

So she knew how this must end. At the end of three months she knew he'd come to claim his own.

And she knew what her answer must be.

And three months to the day he came. He'd rung the night before. 'Tomorrow,' he'd said, in a tone she couldn't mistake. He'd hardly said anything about three months for…well, for three months, but here it was and of course he'd remembered.

'I'll be there at lunchtime,' he said. 'Wear something pretty.'

So here she was, at lunchtime, wandering the house feeling like…

Like she'd made her decision and it was the right one, even if it did involve a sense of loss.

Rose was asleep in her little pink crib in her bedroom overlooking paddocks that swept down to the sea. Maybe they could find a house by the sea in Sydney. Maybe her longing to be a country girl had been irrational.

She'd be with Max.

If he still wanted her.

He wanted her. For months the sizzle had been building. It was in his voice, in his laughter, even in his silence. She couldn't mistake his desire, for she felt exactly the same about him. He made her toes curl.

Speaking of toes…she looked down at her feet. She was wearing sky-blue, open-toed sandals and she'd painted her toenails crimson. She was wearing a blue and white gingham dress with a bow at the back and Sophie had tied her hair up in a blue ribbon.

He'd ordered pretty. She felt a bit like Sandy from *Grease*, before the leather.

* * *

He was late.

'What time are we expecting him?' Margaret called from the kitchen. 'My roast'll spoil.' She wandered out to join Maggie on the veranda and then turned toward the road. 'Is this him now?'

Maggie gazed out, sizzle building like petrol on wildfire— and then her sizzle faded. This wasn't Max. It was an SUV, bright crimson, with two surfboards on the roof rack.

'Wrong place?' Margaret said.

'So what's behind it?' John asked, joining them. The SUV was slowing and turning into the driveway, and a truck was following. A huge truck, big enough to hold the contents of a small house.

'Maybe Angus has ordered another tractor,' John said, looking out to where Angus and Bonnie were sitting on the Sift TD4 diesel that Max had found. The Sift had been built in 1950 in France. Maggie knew that now. She was starting to feel almost as affectionate toward the tractors as Angus.

She'd be able to come home to visit.

Back, she reminded herself sharply. Not home. Home would be in Sydney with Max.

Max or not, the truck and the SUV were certainly coming in. The SUV drove slowly along between the tractors, followed by the truck. Who was in them?

The sun was in her eyes, but as the SUV passed Angus, the window slid downward. 'Hey, Angus. Hey, Bonnie.'

It was definitely Max. But what was with the truck? Had Max brought Angus another tractor? A going-away present?

She hadn't told Angus she was going away. She hadn't told John or Margaret, but maybe they'd guessed.

She didn't know herself yet, she reminded herself sharply, but that was stupid.

There was no choice.

Max.

But why was he driving an SUV? With surfboards?

Both truck and SUV were pulling up now, under the gums by the house. A couple of burly guys climbed out of the truck and stood, waiting. Max climbed out of the SUV. He was wearing jeans and boots and an open-necked checked shirt with his sleeves rolled up. His hair looked sort of unruly.

He looked great, she thought. He looked…free.

He reached back into the SUV and lifted out a black and white ball of fluff. Set it gently on its feet.

A puppy. A Border collie, like Bonnie. Ten or twelve weeks old? Cute as a button.

The puppy looked around in astonishment, and Bonnie was off Angus's tractor in a flash, bounding down to check out the new arrival.

The puppy rolled onto its back while Bonnie sniffed from all angles, paying special attention to the rear.

No one moved. It was like a very special test was being conducted. But then Bonnie's tail wagged, the puppy righted itself, put a paw up and gently swiped at Bonnie's nose.

Bonnie bumped him gently with her nose in return, wagged her tail, then turned and bounded back toward Angus. Puppy in tow.

'Hey, he's for Maggie,' Max called, and Angus even grinned.

'Share,' he said.

Not if I'm going to Sydney, Maggie thought wildly, but still she couldn't say anything.

But he wasn't walking toward her. Max was unroping the surfboards from the roof of his car. He lifted them down with loving care, and laid them on the ground.

Behind him the men had tugged open the van doors. They were carrying out…a sea kayak?

Aren't you going to help?' Max demanded of the group on the veranda. 'I'm paying these guys by the hour.' And John gave Maggie a push that nearly sent her off the veranda without benefit of steps.

'Go help your man,' he said.

'He's not—'

'Maggie,' Max called, sounding exasperated. 'I've brought you a surf board all the way from Sydney, and you don't even want to come see it? Oh, and the front berth in this kayak is for you.'

'But—'

'And there's more stuff,' he called. 'It might be a bit of a squash but it seemed too much bother to rent storage in Sydney. We can sort out what we don't want later.'

'But…' said Maggie.

'I think you'd better go see, dear,' Margaret said, smiling and smiling. 'I might go in and turn the roast down. John, girls, inside, all of you.'

Don't leave me. She didn't say it. She thought it. She was feeling like the veranda was swaying under her.

'Come and look,' Max called, peremptorily this time, and finally she did, walking cautiously down from the veranda and out through the garden. The puppy came bounding to greet her, and that gave her a moment to get her thoughts together. Or as much as she could, kneeling to hug a squirming mass of black and white pup.

How had he known she wanted a puppy?

'We'll never keep him happy in Sydney,' she said, and then heard what she'd said and blushed from the toes up. She was making all sorts of assumptions—or she'd made assumptions and now they were being stood on their heads.

In a good way?

'I always wanted a dog,' Max said, and she rose and watched while the pup wheeled back to Bonnie. 'Her name's Bounce.'

'So he's not a gift,' she said cautiously.

'He's a gift.'

'But you said *you* want a dog.'

'He's a gift to all of us.'

'I don't understand.'

'Maggie, this is a moving van,' he said, motioning behind him as if she might not have noticed the van, the two burly removalists, the sea kayak, the vast, leather-topped desk they were now carting out. 'It's full of my stuff. Last time I was here I checked out a couple of empty sheds out the back. I was hoping I might be able to unload it here.'

'Why…why would you want to do that?'

'Ah.' He crossed the distance between them in a heartbeat, but stopped six feet away, as if reminding himself not to rush. 'I was hoping you'd guess,' he said. He motioned back to the surfboards. 'I'm also hoping you might teach me to surf.'

'You know how to surf,' she said, struggling to breathe.

'I can body-surf. I can't stand up. I didn't have William to teach me.'

'So you brought all your furniture—so I could teach you to surf?'

'Not all of it, but I did bring my grandfather's desk. Isn't it great? It's big enough for both of us. We can teach Rose to read at this desk. Then there's my great-grandmother's piano. I have this really strong feeling that Rose will be a piano player. It can't go in the shed, by the way. It'll need to have a bit of the sitting room. Do you think it can have a bit of your sitting room?'

'I'm living in a one-bedroom apartment at the back of the house,' she said, with an attempt to get things clear.

'Yes, well, there's moves afoot to change that,' he said, smiling so much her heart felt like it was turning somersaults. 'I hope I haven't pre-empted things.'

'Pre-empted…'

'You see, John thinks this place could be a really wonderful medical centre.'

'*Here?*'

'Yandilagong,' he said patiently. 'The town itself is small, but the surrounding farming population is enormous. The farmers all end up going to the city for their major medical needs, but if there was a really good medical centre they wouldn't need to. John and I have been talking to the politicians and there's nothing but enthusiasm.'

'John and you?'

'John and I.'

Her head was spinning. 'So what's this got to do with pianos?'

'You're not giving me time,' he complained, but still he smiled, his lovely, slow, lazy smile, and her heart was giving up somersaulting and going into freefall. 'Do you know how beautiful you are?'

'No, I…'

'Someone ought to tell you,' he said. 'Only that someone needs time. Like a lifetime.'

'Max…'

'You're right, I'm getting ahead of myself,' he said. They were still standing about six feet apart. Stupidly formal. His eyes weren't leaving her face.

'John thinks a big medical centre would work here,' he said. 'He's a family doctor. So are you. Margaret's a dentist. That's two and a half medicos already, if we count you not going back to work full time.'

'I need to go back to work full time.'

'But do you want to, with Rose so young? If there were supports in place so you didn't need to?'

'Max…'

'Maggie, don't distract me,' he said. 'Or don't distract me more than you're already doing. Blue hair ribbons, hey?'

'You said you wanted pretty. I let Sophie and Paula choose.'

'Sophie and Paula have fine taste,' he said, and grinned and then schooled his features into mock gravity. 'Enough. Let me get it all out in one hit so I can figure whether I should unload this van or just hightail it out of here.'

She was trying to figure out whether he was laughing or he was serious. She wanted to be closer to him, but still he stood back, watching her, as if he had to lay it all on the line before any movement was possible.

'We need more doctors,' he said.

'More doctors.'

'For our hospital,' he explained, as if she was a little bit thick. 'You know the old hospital out on the headland? It's used now as a holiday camp, but apparently it's still government owned. There's such medical need in this area it's becoming a political hot potato, and I have assurances that if we can guarantee staffing, they'll reopen it. So John's written to a friend of his who's also emigrating from Zimbabwe. She's a surgeon, her husband's a farmer and her sons dream of surfing. They think this place sounds great. And then there's Anton, my anaesthetist. His wife's going nuts, him leaving home at six in the morning and not getting home until well after the babies are in bed. This place is just what he needs as well.'

'You've done… John's done…'

'Nothing you can't undo,' he said, smiling, and smiling was all he had to do to have her so deeply in love she could never climb out. 'All you need to do is say the word,' he said. 'John and I didn't want to say anything to you until we knew it was possible, but we're almost sure now. So sure I've quit.'

'You've quit.'

'You sound like a parrot,' he said, and his smile widened. 'My beautiful parrot. Yes, I've quit.'

'Wh-why?'

'Because I want to be a baby doctor again,' he said, simply and surely. 'Maggie, I want to deliver babies. There's a huge population of young families locally, and if Anton and I are here then the mothers won't need to go to Sydney for their confinements. So that's what I want. It's what I want almost as much as the thing I want most in the world. The really big thing. The thing on which everything else depends.'

'I don't…I don't…'

'You don't know what that is?' He paused, a long drawn-out silence where the world stretched out before them, infinite in its possibilities.

'I told you the night Rose was born,' he said softly. 'I'm saying it again now. Maggie, we've both been battered,' he said softly. 'But we both know what love is and how wonderful it is that we've found it again. It's time now we acknowledged it, took it in both hands and never let it go. The night Rose was born I knew that you had my whole life in your hands. I love you, Maggie, with all my heart. For now. For ever.'

His words took her breath away. It was like there were

suddenly a thousand gifts, showering down like the Christmas morning of a child's dreams, only better and better and better.

'I also want to live here,' he said, and it was like a tiny prosaic jolt that had her thinking, no, this wasn't dreaming. This might even be true.

Why didn't he move? Why didn't he take her in his arms? Was this a dream? She couldn't quite believe it could be real.

'John's found another farm,' Max said, and there was that in his eyes that said he understood exactly what she was feeling. Maybe he was feeling like that, too. 'He's put in a provisional offer.'

'Provisional…'

'Provisional on you marrying me.'

She loved this man.

Marriage.

'So…so let me get this right,' she stammered. 'You want to leave Sydney and come here. For…always?'

'I never wanted to live in Sydney anyway,' he said, and his smile was a caress all by itself. 'When Alice died I walked away from my career and I didn't much care what direction I was heading. There's a few of us like that at Sydney South. John, escaping from the troubles in Zimbabwe. Anton, who came from France after a broken love affair and never left. And then there's John's friend, the surgeon. There's a whole queue, waiting for you to say the word.'

'The word?'

'Yes,' he said softly. 'Just say yes.'

There was too much to take in.

She'd spent three months trying to work out how to break a promise, yet here was the man she loved with all her heart telling her she needn't break it. That the dream that had started with William was still precious, but he was willing—no, he was demanding—that she share it.

It was too big. It was making her head explode.

'You'd seriously come here to live?' she whispered, awed.

'And work. It's what I should be doing, Maggie,' he said, his smile fading. 'I should be taking care of mothers having babies. That's what I'm trained for. And I should be taking care of you.'

'I don't need—'

'To be taken care of? I think you do. But, Maggie, if I can take care of you I promise to let you take care of me right back.' He said it quickly, as if he seriously thought she was going to argue. 'I want you to yell at me if you think I'm spending too much time working and not enough time with you. I'd even like you to yell at me if I squeeze the toothpaste the wrong way. I might yell back but if that's what you want...a spot of yelling...I don't see me objecting. I want you to teach me to surf, and I want us both to teach Rose. I want to help Angus with his tractors. I want to help train Bounce. I want us to have more babies.'

'You want...'

'Most of all I want what you want, Maggie,' he told her. 'I want a happy beginning. A family. Love and laughter from this day forth. So what do you say, Maggie? Will you marry me?'

'You're too far away,' she whispered, and he was with her before she finished saying it. Taking her in his arms. He smiled down at her, loving her with his smile, and then suddenly he was kneeling before her.

And suddenly Margaret, with Rose in her arms, and John and Sophie and Paula were out on the veranda again. Not making a sound. Bearing witness.

Suddenly the removalists had put the desk down to watch.

And suddenly Angus was standing up on the tractor, holding a dog firmly under each arm, as if he was afraid they might interrupt.

Nothing interrupted.

'Marry me,' Max said again, and he took her hand in his and held it to his lips.

This was crazy. Mad.

It was muddy. He was kneeling in the mud, asking her if she'd marry him.

She had an audience hanging on her response.

Joy began to well up inside her—clearly, this could be no dream.

She knelt down, too.

'Your dress,' he said, in mock horror.

'Blue and brown's great,' she said, and her eyes were inches from his. She had both his hands in hers. She had him right where she wanted him.

'Ask me again,' she said.

'I think I've forgotten. What was the question?'

'Something about marriage.'

'Right, that,' he said, sounding dazed. And then he swore. 'I knew I forgot something. Hang on a minute.' And he reached round to his back pocket and found a box. A tiny crimson box.

He flicked it open.

It wasn't a ring. It was a single diamond, perfect, sparkling in the sunlight. Making her catch her breath with wonder.

'I didn't know how you'd like it set,' he said. 'So I thought… There's so much you've done because you had no choice. I thought if you said yes…'

'If I said yes…

'If you said yes,' he went on resolutely, 'we can get it set any way you want. We can surround it with rubies. We can embed it in gold or mount it on platinum. You can have a woven plait band or a smooth one. Anything you like, my love. As long as you take me.'

'A package deal, huh?'

'A package indeed,' he said, and cast an amused look around at their audience. 'A family. A medical centre. A medical partnership. Love. All or nothing, my beautiful Maggie. So I'm asking you again, and I'm thinking surely this time you need to answer. Maggie Croft, love of my heart, please will you marry me?'

And what was a girl to say to that?

She put her hands on his face. She drew a deep breath and she smiled into his loving eyes.

And she cast her future to the wind, to blow where it willed, with this man beside her.

'Yes,' she whispered. 'Yes, I will. My love. My heart. My life.'

BACHELOR DAD, GIRL NEXT DOOR

BY
SHARON ARCHER

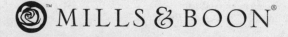 MILLS & BOON®

First published in Great Britain 2010
Harlequin Mills & Boon Limited,
Eton House, 18-24 Paradise Road, Richmond, Surrey TW9 1SR

© Sharon Archer 2010

ISBN: 978 0 263 87878 3

Harlequin Mills & Boon policy is to use papers that are natural, renewable and recyclable products and made from wood grown in sustainable forests. The logging and manufacturing process conform to the legal environmental regulations of the country of origin.

Printed and bound in Spain
by Litografia Rosés, S.A., Barcelona

Born in New Zealand, **Sharon Archer** now lives in county Victoria, Australia, with her husband Glenn, one lame horse and five pensionable hens. Always an avid reader, she discovered Mills & Boon as a teenager through Lucy Walker's fabulous Outback Australia stories. Now she lives in a gorgeous bush setting, and loves the native fauna that visits regularly… Well, maybe not the possum which coughs outside the bedroom window in the middle of the night.

The move to acreage brought a keen interest in bushfire management (she runs the fireguard group in her area), as well as free time to dabble in woodwork, genealogy (her advice is…don't get her started!), horse-riding and motorcycling—as a pillion or in charge of the handlebars.

Free time turned into words on paper! And the dream to be a writer gathered momentum. With her background in a medical laboratory, what better line to write for than Mills & Boon® Medical™ Romance?

Recent titles by the same author:

MARRIAGE REUNITED: BABY ON THE WAY
SINGLE FATHER: WIFE AND MOTHER WANTED

CHAPTER ONE

LUKE DANIELS ran an idle glance over the sleek silver motor-cycle stopped in the lane beside him at the traffic light. Through his closed windows he could hear the throb of the powerful engine. An unexpected spark of interest fought with deep unease.

It'd been years since seeing a bike had had any sort of effect on him. How odd that it should be now, when he was back in Port Cavill to stay—at least for the year-long term of his contract.

But perhaps that was why.

Port Cavill. The scene of his first medical failure.

'Are we nearly there?' His daughter's sulky voice inter-rupted his dark thoughts.

'Not far, Allie.' He rolled his neck, feeling the tiredness and tension in his muscles.

'Alexis,' she corrected with all the disdain a ten-year-old could muster.

Luke stifled a sigh. He wasn't popular and there wasn't anything he could do about it.

Except get on a plane back to England.

Even the weather conspired to make things unpleasant.

The earlier sunny heat had given way to oppressive humidity, which the car's air-conditioning was struggling to cope with. Glowering banks of cloud still pressed down with the threat of more rain to come.

He studied Allie's sullen profile and debated whether to point out again that they'd only be here for a year. Long enough for him to help his father get back on his feet. Long enough to seem like a lifetime in a child's eyes. Times like this he longed for Sue-Ellen's wise counsel. But his wife, Allie's mother, had been buried two years ago. So loving, so giving. And too damned young to die.

'That person on the bike's waving at you, Dad. Who is it?'

He looked in the direction of Allie's pointing finger.

'I don't know.'

The pillion passenger began pulling at the rider's shoulder until the person must have retaliated with an admonition to keep still. Catching Allie's eye, Luke smiled. 'Kind of hard to tell with that helmet on, isn't it?'

His daughter shrugged, letting him know a moment of shared humour couldn't woo her.

The lights changed and the bike pulled away sedately enough to merge into his lane ahead. Following slowly, he allowed the distance to stretch because of the wet road. The pillion passenger turned to check behind. Luke shook his head in irritation. The action would shift the weight, unbalance the bike. He felt a twinge of sympathy for the poor rider.

Movement from a side road caught his peripheral vision. A car fishtailed into the intersection.

Had the motorcyclist seen it?

Heart pounding, hands clenched on the steering-wheel, he waited for the inevitable disaster. Suddenly the rider reacted, the brake light flicked on.

'Too late,' Luke muttered. 'Counter-steer.'

A split second later, the rider obeyed his command. Relief quickly swooped into despair as the wheels skidded precariously on the slick surface.

In the time it took for rider to control the bike, graphic memories of another, less fortunate motorcycle leapt out of the past to assault him. A battered racer, twisted metal. The smell of hot tar and spilled petrol.

The smell of blood.

His cousin's moans of pain.

A line of sweat chilled Luke's upper lip as he remembered the helplessness. The hopelessness when he'd realised the extent of Kevin's injuries. Nausea rolled through his stomach.

Super-sensitised now to the progress of the bike and the actions of the cars around it, Luke could feel irrational, burning anger growing. He'd successfully suppressed the anguish for the thirteen years since the accident. Now in the blink of an instant it was all there, raw and powerful.

He wished the rider would turn off so he could stop worrying about them but they were travelling inexorably in the same direction. Slowing more, he let the distance widen, until several other cars filled the gap.

By the time he got to his turn-off, they'd disappeared.

Relief was short-lived. He turned into his parents' driveway to see the bike parked on the gravel.

Still helmeted and astride the machine, the rider seemed to be delivering a well-deserved lecture to the dismounted pillion passenger.

'That's Aunty Megan,' said Allie.

Hell! Luke clenched his jaw as a cold chill swept his body. What was his baby sister doing hooning around Port Cavill on the back of a bloody motorcycle?

'Stay here,' he ordered his daughter as he flicked his seat-belt catch off.

He stalked towards the pair at the bike, relishing the thought of tearing strips off them after the fright they'd given him.

'Luke!' Megan launched herself at him, enveloping him in an enthusiastic hug. He clamped her close, intensely thankful for her vitality and safety. Determined to make sure she stayed that way. 'We weren't expecting you until tomorrow.'

'We came straight through from the airport,' he said after a moment. Holding her away from him, he frowned. 'Your bad luck I was here to see that stunt you and your friend here pulled back in town. You think I want to spend my first day home scraping you two off the road?'

'Oh, don't you start, too.' Megan threw her hands up. 'Terri was just going off at me about it.'

'Yeah?' Luke aimed a black look at the rider. 'Maybe he'll think twice before he takes you on the bike again.'

'But Terri's—'

'In fact, let's make that official.' God, he'd been back in town for less than half an hour and he was already standing toe to toe with his sister. Part of his anger was tiredness. But most of it was fear. If he had the power to prevent it, he wasn't going to lose another member of his family.

And this was definitely within his power. 'You're grounded.'

'Honestly, Luke!' Megan planted her hands on her hips.

'Does Mum know what you're up to?'

'I'm nearly eighteen.' Her chin jutted defiance as she glared at him.

'Is that a no?'

'No, it's not a *no*. She doesn't mind if I'm with Terri.'

'She will after I've spoken to her,' he said grimly.

'But Terri's a really careful rider.'

'Too bad. I don't want to see you on the back of this bike, any bike, again.' He directed a narrow-eyed look at the rider.

Brown eyes, so dark they were nearly black, watched him. The hint of wry amusement in them had him clenching his jaw against a scathing comment.

The motorcyclist took off the padded gloves and began fiddling with the helmet strap.

Luke was reluctantly impressed that the boy was prepared to stay in the face of the conflict. 'Look, Terry, this is a family argument. You don't want to get involved, mate. All you need to know is Megan's off the social circuit until further notice. There's no point hanging around.'

'Gee. That's going to be kind of tough, Luke,' said Megan smugly. 'Since you guys are going to be working together.'

'What?' He turned on his sister. 'You mean Mum's letting you go out with one of the hospital staff?'

'One of the doctors.' The sly look she slanted him should have been a warning. 'Terri's taught me heaps.'

Luke felt his anger crank up several notches.

'That's a recommendation I can do without,' said a husky feminine voice beside him.

The tirade he'd been about to unleash faltered on his tongue.

The rider slipped off the helmet and balanced it on the handlebars. Long black hair slithered over the protective leather jacket as the woman dismounted and turned to face him.

'Hello, Luke. Long time, no see.'

'Terri?' He gaped, his stunned brain struggling to put the name together with the evidence before his eyes. 'Theresa O'Connor.'

'Close enough. How are you?' She held out a hand and he stared at it stupidly for a long moment.

'Bloody hell. Theresa O'Connor.' He used her hand to tug her into a hug. It was quick, lasting only a second. Meant to be social, asexual. Nothing to precipitate the volcanic heat that swept through him.

He swallowed and set her away at arm's length.

Her continued stillness, her composure, unsettled him out of all proportion. Especially the small smile curving her lips.

Suddenly, Luke remembered the last time he'd seen her. On the moonlit beach at the bottom of the hospital grounds. Could it really have been twelve years ago? The memory felt too intense. She hadn't been so calm then. Though neither had he. He'd just kissed her.

He focussed on her mouth. Those lovely full lips had been soft and hesitant then eager, even demanding, beneath his.

Until he'd pushed her away.

He blinked and dragged his gaze back to hers. She stepped away, unruffled by their contact except for a tell-tale wariness in her eyes. 'It's Terri Mitchell these days.'

'Yes, of course.' He had so many questions but he felt oddly tongue-tied. His body's unexpected response to her, that hot fizz of recognition, left him unbalanced.

His memory tripped in with details supplied over the years by his mother and Theresa's brother, Ryan. Theresa was widowed, her husband killed when they'd been working with an aid organisation in Africa. An explosion. She'd been injured, too.

He cleared his throat before speaking into the lengthening silence. 'Theresa, I was sorry to—'

'No harm done.' She cut him off quickly, a tiny flare of dismay in her dark chocolate eyes. The smile on her lips looked stiff, unnatural and he realised her misunderstanding had been deliberate. Theresa didn't want to hear his words of condolence.

She glanced behind him, her smile warming. 'You must be Alexis. Your grandmother's told me all about you.'

'Alexis, this is an old friend of the family.' Luke drew his daughter forward, leaving his arm across her shoulders as he made the introductions. He was pleasantly surprised when she leaned into his side instead of shrugging him off.

She glowed under Theresa's attention. Gone was the surly, uncooperative child of mere minutes ago.

Theresa's serene surface was so firmly in place, the moment of panic seemed as though it was a figment of his imagination. Still, there was something…a hint of sadness shadowing her eyes and smile. With her attention on Allie, he could see it much more clearly.

After a few minutes, Theresa said, 'I'll leave you all to catch up properly.'

'Mum said for you to come to tea tonight, Terri,' Megan said.

'Oh. Thank your mum for me, Megan, but I have some paperwork to do before tomorrow. See you later, Alexis.' Her friendly smile faded as she raised her eyes to his. 'Luke.'

He wondered if her refusal of the dinner invitation was because of his arrival or if the paperwork excuse was genuine.

She mounted the bike, slid the helmet over her luxurious hair. Her long slender fingers worked quickly to buckle the strap beneath her chin before she reached out to turn the key in the ignition. The machine throbbed to life.

Much to Luke's surprise, she rode down the extended driveway beside his parents' house.

'So, I guess that means I can keep riding with Terri,' Megan said.

He sent her a noncommittal look. 'We'll see.'

'Luke!'

He grinned at her wailed protest and slid his question in casually. 'Is Theresa staying in the beach cottage?'

'Terri. She prefers Terri.'

'Terri, then.' He raised an eyebrow.

'Uh-huh. She's been renting it since she came back.'

He wondered why his mother hadn't told him when she'd been giving him updates on the latest Port Cavill gossip.

'And that was, what, six months ago?'

'About.' Megan shrugged.

'It's a hovel.'

'That's when *you* used to live there, Luke. Terri's done it up.'

'Really.' Perhaps he might find an opportunity to wander down for a visit, see how his old bachelor pad had scrubbed up. Learn more about the intriguing tenant…

Or perhaps not.

He was here for a year and would have his hands full with the hospital, his father and Allie. Meeting Terri again like this had tipped him out of kilter, that was all. He was tired, maybe even a little jet-lagged. Not thinking straight.

The last thing he needed was to complicate his life. Especially with someone who must thrive on excitement if the bike and her previous job were anything to judge by.

Seeing her had plunged him into an odd time warp where he relived their kiss on the beach. Could it really have been twelve years ago? He hadn't treated her particularly well that night, rejecting her soft sympathy, allowing his bitterness and guilt over his cousin's death to colour the things he'd said.

Still, she was obviously made of stern stuff. She'd gone on to do her medical training.

He'd had no interest in women during the two and a half

years since Sue-Ellen's death. How damned inconvenient that
the sexual spark missing in his life since then should choose
to wake up now.

In Port Cavill. Of all places.

With a colleague. Someone he needed to work with for the
next year. The time and place and person couldn't be worse.

Terri parked the bike beside the cottage, thankful to have
made the short journey without disgracing herself by stalling
or missing a gear. Or dropping the bike. She huffed out a long
breath before putting down the stand and dismounting on
shaky legs.

Luke was back.

Helmet tucked under one arm, she collected her handbag
from the top box. She'd known he was coming home, of
course. Most of the Daniels family had been in a happy buzz
of anticipation for the last couple of weeks.

Except for Will Daniels. He'd been upset that, despite his
recommendation, the board had appointed Luke to the
position of hospital director. A position she'd been acting in
since Will's myocardial infarct. Worse was that the notifica-
tion had only come yesterday.

Terri had stifled her disappointment so she could reassure
her convalescing boss that it didn't matter.

But it *did* matter. She'd been relishing the responsibility.
It was good for her, challenging, restoring her sense of self.
Giving her a much-needed focus for her shattered life.

She sighed. Perhaps even more distressing was her ridiculous fluttery reaction to Luke. How long had it been since
she'd felt that disturbing feminine awareness of a man? Such
lightness had had no place in her life for so many years. To
have it now felt wrong, frivolous.

She crossed to the door and let herself into the cottage. Her hand lingered on her helmet for a moment after she'd placed it on the hall-stand. When Luke had confronted her and Megan, the temptation to stay inside the fibreglass dome and hide behind the smoky Perspex visor had been overwhelming. Behaviour much more in keeping with the starry-eyed teenager she'd been last time they'd met.

Why couldn't she have been caught on the ward, performing some marvellously complex medical procedure? Saving lives, saving the world, she mocked herself silently. That would have been too perfect.

She slipped off her jacket and hung it on the peg by the door. Naturally, Luke *had* to arrive a day early, catch her kitted out in motorcycle leathers and then mistake her for Megan's boyfriend.

Still, she thought she'd handled the meeting with reasonable aplomb. Thanks to the helmet, she'd had a chance to gather her wits a little before revealing herself. If anything, it had been Luke who'd been nonplussed. Embarrassed by his mistake probably.

He'd hugged her. Spontaneously. She wrapped her arms around her body, remembering the feel of his firm hold, his torso pressed to hers for those long seconds. Not that it meant anything. The Daniels family was naturally, delightfully, demonstrative.

Unlike the O'Connors.

Unlike the Mitchells. Her husband's family had saved their affections for their causes. And those they'd pursued with dedication and passion. No sacrifice too great. She grimaced, chiding herself for her disloyalty. Hating the bitterness of her thoughts.

In the kitchen, she filled the kettle. While she waited for the water to boil, she scanned the scrubby trees that bordered the back yard. The sandy path to the beach was well hidden. Astounding that she'd had the temerity to follow Luke down the track all those years ago. What a crush she'd had on him, poor sad child that she'd been.

She shook her head then spooned a scant teaspoon of coffee into a mug.

That was the past. This was now and she wasn't an angst-ridden teenager any more.

She'd been married…and widowed. The explosion that killed her husband had ripped her life apart. She'd come to Port Cavill to give herself a chance to recover, to regroup. She'd come here for peace. Nothing more.

As she contemplated the future, she pursed her lips.

Stepping into the role of director had given her a new sense of purpose. She'd been doing a damned good job even if the paperwork part of the job wasn't her forte.

Now she had to step aside.

Gracefully.

Luke's return was difficult on so many levels. Peace would be in short supply while he was around.

She sighed. At least, their first meeting was over now. Next time she encountered him, she'd be working for him.

CHAPTER TWO

DRESSED only in jeans, Luke stood in the darkened room at the back of the house and stared moodily across the moonlit lawn. He could make out the hump of the small cottage sheltered by trees at the edge of the lawn.

Theresa's place. No, not Theresa—Terri.

Was she tucked up, asleep? He glanced at his watch. Half past one in the morning. He'd be willing to bet she wasn't lying awake thinking about him, the way he was about her.

He leaned his forearm on the wooden window-frame and contemplated his reaction to her that afternoon. Surely, it had to be a product of his recent upheavals—the move, travelling, worry over his father and Alexis.

He'd had eight happy years of marriage to Sue-Ellen. He'd loved his wife, damn it. During all the time they'd been together and since she'd died, he hadn't looked at another woman.

Yet one tiny and very public hug with Terri had evoked such a powerful memory that he'd been swept back twelve years to the last time he'd held her in his arms. To a five-minute interlude on the beach.

Ridiculous. Potentially disastrous.

Luke rubbed his jaw, feeling the rasp of stubble. Perhaps

he was over-thinking this. Perhaps it merely demonstrated that it was time he did start thinking about a relationship. Or at least start preparing Allie for the possibility that he might one day date. Bring someone, a woman, into the family. He tried to picture that day but long dark silky hair and hot chocolate eyes stayed stubbornly in his mind.

He gave up, let his thoughts dwell on the brief meeting that afternoon. The way Terri had deflected his condolences made him wonder about her. Was her grief still raw? Did she suffer any long-term post-traumatic stress symptoms? A gnawing ache settled in his chest for the pain she'd been through. He could only begin to imagine the difficulty of losing someone the way she had. So brutal and sudden.

He and Allie had had time with Sue-Ellen. Poignant time for words of love, reassurances, promises. Heartbreaking but enriching moments to cling to in the days, weeks, years that followed her death.

Terri hadn't had that. She'd had no chance to say goodbye before her husband had been snatched away.

He needed to be mindful of that, sensitive to her needs, and be ready to offer counselling, in a professional capacity, if she needed it. As hospital director, the welfare of his staff was paramount. He was feeling the natural concern of a doctor for a colleague. Plus Terri wasn't just a colleague, but the sister of a friend. The least he could do was offer support to Ryan O'Connor's sister. Yes, that was more like it. He just needed to apply a bit of sound reasoning.

Through the loosely screening shrubbery, he saw the lights of the cottage come on. Almost as though the intensity of his musings had woken Terri.

He snorted out a small breath. How hopelessly fanciful. So much for the power of common sense.

A few minutes later, she walked across to the hospital in the moonlight. The ends of a stethoscope looped around her neck dangled darkly on her pale T-shirt. She seemed to look up at his window. A queer shaft of excitement made him draw a quick breath before he could block it.

One tiny glance from her and his heart was flopping around in his chest like a freshly caught flounder. He shook his head in disgust.

Terri was obviously the doctor on call tonight.

As his system settled, he watched her disappear through the back door of the hospital and then reappear in the glass-walled corridor. By angling his head, he could follow her progress until she turned the corner leading to Accident and Emergency.

He should go back to bed and yet something held him at the window. A moment later, slow revolutions of light—blue, red, blue, red—began flickering off walls and gutters, signalling the arrival of an emergency vehicle on the other side of the building.

He straightened and, moving quietly, walked back through to the main house to find a T-shirt.

Since sleep was so elusive tonight, he might as well spend the time working with his new colleague. Pro-pinquity in a hospital setting would be the best cure for this inconvenient fascination. Baggy, unflattering clothing, surgical caps, masks, booties. That should take the edge off her appeal quick smart. For his sanity, he needed to start the therapy now. Familiarity bred contempt—he had to believe it.

Anticipation quickened his pace as he retraced her footsteps along the silent hospital corridor.

No sign of any staff in the casualty waiting room. The ambulance was gone. He skirted the main desk and entered the treatment area.

A pale-faced woman sat in an open cubicle clutching a bowl, her eyes closed and head tilted back to rest against the wall.

The nurse attending the woman turned and frowned.

'I'm sorry, sir, you must stay in the waiting room and ring the bell if you need to see the doctor.' She yanked the curtain of the cubicle closed as she came towards him.

'Is Dr Mitchell around?'

'Yes, but you must—'

'I'm Luke Daniels. The new director. And you are?'

'Oh, Dr Daniels.' The line of her mouth thinned even further. 'I'm Dianne Mills, one of the nurses. Terri's busy with an urgent case at the moment.'

'I'm here to help. Where is she?'

'I'll take you through to her.' The woman's subtle unfriendliness seemed to say that his assistance wasn't required or particularly welcome.

Luke smiled grimly as he grabbed a gown from the shelf and followed her. Maybe she was right. Judging by the praise heaped on her by his parents, Terri was a very competent doctor. She'd recognised the signs of his father's myocardial infarct even though Will Daniels had insisted it was just indigestion. What had the stubborn old cuss been thinking? A call to the cardiologist had confirmed that Terri's prompt actions had minimised damage to the cardiac muscle. Tests had shown life-threatening partial occlusions in several other vessels and his father had been whisked in for triple bypass surgery.

'What's the urgent case?' he asked as he tugged the gown over his clothes.

'An unconscious teen brought in by two friends. The girls couldn't wake her when they got her home. We've got food poisoning cases coming in as well. I was just about to call for back-up.' She sent him a speculative look.

'I'll cover.' He smiled. 'We can reassess later with Dr Mitchell if necessary.'

Dianne nodded. Her brief response wasn't encouraging. Perhaps he needed to work on his people skills.

They were still a distance from a closed curtain when Luke heard a young woman's clipped voice say, 'I thought she should sleep it off.'

'But I s-said we should b-bring her here,' added a second, shakier female voice. 'Even th-though it's, like, two o'clock in the morning.'

'You've made the right decision for your cousin.' Terri's even husky tones sent a light shiver over his skin. Sudden doubt needled at the belief that familiarity with her would help him. He swallowed.

'Are you sure she hasn't take anything? Drugs?' Terri asked.

'Um, sh-she—'

'No, of course not,' said the aggressive voice of the first girl. 'Never.'

Luke stepped through the gap in the curtain and took in the situation with a sweeping glance.

Two young women in their late teens stood to one side of a gurney. Dressed to the nines in their party clothes, heavy make-up smudged beneath their eyes and an array of coloured streaks adorned their heads. He caught the tail end of the ferocious glare the taller of the two girls used to browbeat her friend.

Terri's eyes lifted to his briefly in a moment of intense silent communication. It was obvious she didn't believe the girls' denial. Her eyes slid away and she moved to the head of the gurney where she bent over the patient, laryngoscope in hand.

'Temperature up another half-degree to forty-one point five, Terri,' said a nurse as she pulled up the patient's skimpy knitted top and placed the diaphragm of her stethoscope on the pale skin.

'Thanks, Nina.' Terri glanced up. 'Dianne, could you get us some ice packs, stat.'

'On my way.' Dianne slipped out of the curtained cubicle.

Keeping an eye on the activity at the gurney, Luke crossed to the teens. 'I'm Dr Luke Daniels,' he said calmly. 'You're on your way home from a party?'

'A rave.' The taller girl gave him a superior look. She was busily chewing gum and her eyes had the dilated pupils of someone who'd taken some sort of substance. 'Over at Portland.'

'Apical pulse one forty. BP seventy over forty. Sats seventy per cent.' Folding her stethoscope, the nurse turned away to collect a monitor from the side of the room.

Luke turned his attention to the other teen. 'Was your friend able to walk out of the rave on her own?'

'We—we kind of, um, had to h-help her.'

'Was she talking to you then?'

'N-no.'

Out of the corner of his eye, he saw Terri slide in the endotracheal tube.

'Airway in. Ready for the ventilator, Nina.' She straightened, moving aside so the nurse could attach the unit

Stepping back around the gurney, Terri unwound her stethoscope and listened to both sides of the patient's chest and her abdomen.

Luke looked back at the shorter girl shivering beside him. Deliberately holding her eyes, he said gently, 'We need you to be honest and tell us how long ago she took something. Was it a tablet?'

'Th-three hours.'

'Shona!'

'Well, sh-she did. We all did. They were only l-little pills, j-just to give us a b-boost.'

'Thank you for your honesty,' said Luke, touching her arm to reassure her.

'They were only Es,' said the taller girl, tossing her head. 'There's nothing wrong with me and Shona so it can't be the that.'

'Those so-called party drugs affect everyone differently.' Luke clenched his teeth against the urge to shake some sense into the girl. 'You two have been lucky. You're friend hasn't.'

'J-Jessie had leukaemia. When she was a kid. Is that why she's so sick now?'

A wave of despair at their folly cramped his chest and stomach. He was aware of Terri's eyes on him, but he refused to meet her gaze. He didn't need to see the pity that she undoubtedly felt for him.

'She's g-going to be okay, isn't she?'

'We're doing everything we can for her.' He ushered them towards the curtain. 'We'll get you to wait outside.'

Dianne came back in with cloths and the cold packs.

'I'll organise those, Dianne, thanks,' said Luke, taking them from her. 'Can you show the girls to a room where they can wait, and get next-of-kin information from them, please?'

'C-could we have something to drink?'

Luke met the nurse's concerned eyes. 'A glass of fruit juice for them, please, Dianne, and perhaps see if there's an apple or two in the staffroom.'

As Dianne showed the girls out, Terri said, 'I'm going to have to set up a central line for fluids.'

'Right. You scrub, we'll monitor Jessie and get your equipment set up,' he said, wrapping the cold packs and placing them in Jessie's groin and armpits.

He'd organised a trolley with the required sterile packs by the time Terri had finished at the sink.

'Gown, gloves.' He nodded to the second trolley.

The soft rustling noises as she gowned up tormented him while he concentrated on opening the catheterisation kit and dropping drapes onto the sterile work surface.

'Do me up, please?'

He turned to see her encased head to toe in surgical green, her elbows bent and gloved hands held relaxed in front of her, maintaining her sterile working space.

He knotted the straps at the nape of her neck, then reached down to do the same at her waist. The warmth he could feel on the tops of his fingers made them clumsy. Try as he may, he couldn't close his mind to the enticing curve of the small of her back.

She turned to face him.

Brown eyes, huge and dark, stared at him from above her mask. His breathing hitched. He was a fool to think hospital clothing would instantly dissolve Terri's appeal. He'd never seen anyone look quite as...*sexy* while preparing for an aseptic procedure.

'Luke?'

He blinked, looked down to see she was handing him the tab for the outside string. She turned in front of him and took back the string. 'Thanks.'

He swallowed. Perhaps he *should* have gone back to bed after all. Let Dianne call in the emergency back-up. Turning away, he snipped across the shoulder of Jessie's top, exposing her clavicle and neck.

Nina came back with a bag of saline and began to set up the drip monitor.

A moment later, Dianne stuck her head around the curtain.

'I've got contact details for Jessie's mother. They're down from Melbourne, staying with relatives for the weekend.'

'Thanks, Dianne. I'll make the call now.' He took the paper from her and went to the phone. With the line ringing at the other end, Luke tucked the receiver under his ear.

'Terri, the ambos are at your uncle's place,' Dianne said. 'He's aggressive and hypotensive. They're concerned about trying to establish an IV so I suggested they scoop and run.'

'Good idea,' Terri said. 'How's Mary going with the rest of the race-picnic follow-ups?'

'All done now,' Dianne said. 'She's just managed to get through to Matt in Garrangay about the Macintoshes. I'll go and set up a cubicle for your uncle.'

'Thanks, Dianne,' Terri said. 'Nina, can you see if there's any word from the lab tech on call? We'll really need to be able to run some bloods through tonight.'

'Will do.'

Luke pressed redial when the ring tone timed out. With the receiver held to his ear he turned to look in Terri's direction. Her work was quick, neat, methodical. He congratulated himself on being able to view her nimble fingers with detachment. Sure, she was a pleasure to watch but, then, he always enjoyed seeing someone perform a task well. The peculiar feelings that keep threatening to muddle his mind when he was close to her, had to be a product of his stressful few weeks organising his trip back here.

'Hello?' The sleepy voice pulled his attention back to the phone. A short time later, he hung the receiver back on the wall cradle and allowed himself a brief moment to close his eyes. Weariness washed through him as his sympathy went out to Jessie's mother. What a nightmare for a parent.

He straightened and turned around to find Terri's eyes on him as she stripped off her gloves and mask. The beauty she brought to the everyday movements stopped the words in his mouth.

'She's on her way in?'

'Yes.' He cleared his throat, relieved when muscles moved back to normal function. Stepping back to the side of the gurney, he said, 'Her brother's bringing her in.'

Terri moved to stand beside him. Even with the pervasive smells of the hospital, he was piercingly aware of the subtle scent of soap she brought with her. Of her vitality, her fine-boned femininity, the warmth in her dark eyes.

'This must have been a hard case for you on your first night here.'

His mind abruptly went back to the night of the kiss, the parallels with the sympathy she'd shown him then. He wanted it just as little now. He wasn't sure what it was that he did want from her—but he knew it wasn't that.

He rolled his shoulders. 'It's always hard seeing someone as young as Jessie taking risks like this with the rest of her life.'

'Yes.' Her lashes lowered, but not before he'd seen a quick flash of hurt at his brush-off.

An apology hovered on his tongue. Instead, he picked up Jessie's chart and began detailing her treatment. 'We're looking at an ICU transfer for her?'

'I haven't made the call yet. The first priority was getting her stabilised.' Her voice was all cool business. He must have imagined the moment of vulnerability.

He nodded and recorded another complete set of observations. The girl seemed to be holding her own, with her oxygen saturation and blood pressure markedly improved. Her temperature was steady. 'You've done a good job, Terri.'

The curtain rattled beside them. 'Terri, your uncle's two minutes away.'

'Thanks, Dianne. Be right there.'

'You happy to take Mick's case?' Luke asked, glancing at her as he slotted his pen into the shirt pocket under his gown.

'Yes, of course.'

He nodded. 'I'll call the air ambulance, organise Jessie's transfer.'

'The number's on the wall by the phone.' Terri turned to leave. He couldn't stop his gaze from following her for the few paces it took her to clear the cubicle.

He breathed out a sigh, aware of the odd tension ebbing from his body with her disturbing presence gone. His physiology was more like that of a teenager.

He was a grown man.

A widower, with a daughter.

He dragged a hand down his face. The effect she had on him had to wear off.

Soon. For his sanity, it had to be soon.

Terri hurried through the department, confusion churning through her stomach. Luke had shut her out. Just as he had all those years ago on the beach. Well, what had she expected? They weren't friends. Ryan had been his friend. She was just Ryan's bratty little sister. It was probably all the years of hero worship and then that kiss on the beach that made her feel as though she knew Luke better than she did.

She sighed. Still, he'd be good to work for—which was a relief. She could see that much from this short stint. It had been a pleasure the way he'd fitted in so well, picking up the reins, knowing what she needed and facilitating treatment. He'd deferred to her position as the doctor on call while still commanding respect from everyone in the cubicle. The nurses, the teens, herself.

The teens' rebellion had melted away in the face of his charm, information just flowing out of them under his non-judgemental questioning. The way he'd spoken with Jessie's mother had been wonderful, his velvety voice so full of compassion and caring.

And he'd complimented her handling of the case. In all the years of working with Peter, her husband had never done that.

Luke's praise meant a lot.

More than it should.

Not good! Scratch the surface and there was still a really bad case of hero worship going on underneath.

She was going to have to keep clear of him as much as possible—at work and away from it. Which might be difficult as she lived at the bottom of his parents' garden.

Still, she had no reason to think that he would seek her out. She'd been the one doing the chasing all those years ago—even if she hadn't realised it at the time. Things were different now. She wasn't chasing anyone. She had enough on her plate.

To try to find her courage.

To learn to like the woman she was.

CHAPTER THREE

TERRI met the ambulance at the door, desperately trying to look as professional as possible. Her uncle lay still and pale, his beloved face slightly distorted beneath the oxygen mask. A large white dressing was taped to his forehead. Seeing him like this made her heart twist but she pushed the feeling away. He needed her competence now, not her love.

Frank began his handover as they wheeled the trolley through to the treatment room. She was aware of Dianne and the police sergeant following them.

Between them, they transferred him to the hospital gurney.

Frank stepped back and continued his report. 'There was a smashed bottle of beer on the floor. Looks like he'd slipped in it and hit his head on the corner of the sink. I've dressed the laceration on his forehead. It hadn't bled much,' he said. 'We found him sitting against the kitchen cupboard. After we got the go-ahead to scoop and run, all the fight went out of him. He's been as quiet as a lamb.'

'Okay, thanks, Frank.' Terri leaned over her patient, her hand on his shoulder as she tried to rouse him. 'Uncle Mick? Open your eyes if you can hear me.'

The lashes flicked up and his dry lips stretched into a smile that was more of a grimace. He fumbled with the mask and Terri helped him pull it away, noting the sweetish, ketotic odour of his breath.

'Tee.' He used his nickname for her and for some reason that gave her an instant of misgiving. Should she have stayed with Jessie, handed this case over to Luke as he'd offered? 'What're you doing here, love?'

She shook off the doubt. Responsibility for the emergency department was hers tonight. Luke being here was a bonus, not an opportunity to get him to deal with her family. 'Do you remember what happened, Uncle Mick?'

But his eyes closed again and he mumbled an indistinct response.

'BP is ninety over sixty,' said Dianne.

'Right.' Terri slipped her stethoscope on and listened to the irregular rhythm of his heartbeat. 'Let's get an ECG going, please, Dianne.'

As the nurse snipped off his T-shirt and began attaching the leads, Terri slipped a tourniquet on Mick's arm and bent over his hand. After a moment, she moved on to his wrist and then quickly to his elbow. Beneath her fingertips she could feel the tell-tale springiness of a small vein. Good enough to establish an intravenous line? She hoped so. It would be so much quicker and less complicated than putting in a central line. The sooner Mick started rehydrating, the sooner they could get him stabilised. 'I'm going to put a needle in your arm, Uncle Mick.'

She slipped the cannula into place and released the tourniquet, permitting herself a moment of relief as she taped it securely. She carefully drew off a syringe of blood. 'How's that ECG looking?'

'Typical hypokalaemic changes,' replied a deep voice. Luke.

Terri took a breath, willing her heart to settle. Surely Jessie hadn't been picked up already.

'Nina's specialling Jessie,' he said as though he'd read her mind. 'She'll call me if she needs me. The transfer chopper is still half an hour away.'

She glanced over to where he examined the ECG strip. He tilted the readout so she could see the flattened T peaks. 'Thanks. It's what I expected. Let's get him started on normal saline IV with thirty millimoles of potassium.'

'I'm on it.' Dianne pivoted away to the bench.

Luke held out his hand for the syringe. 'The lab tech's in. You'll want a priority on the electrolytes and glucose. When they can for the CBC, urea and creatinine?'

'Yes, please. Thanks.'

She'd just opened her mouth to add a request when he said, 'I'll organise a strip reading for the blood glucose so you can set the insulin infusion.'

'Right.' There it was again—that intuitive understanding of her work rhythm. It was fantastic and a little unnerving. With anyone else, she was sure she'd have revelled in the experience. But because it was Luke, there seemed to be a level of intimacy associated with it that she badly needed to deny. But what could she say? *Stop reading my mind—stop doing such a great job?* Terri shrugged mentally and settled for 'Thanks.'

She turned back to her patient and flicked on her pen torch. 'I'm going to shine a light in your eyes, Uncle Mick.'

She lifted each eyelid and watched as the pupils in the deep brown irises expanded and contracted readily. Equal and reactive. At least it looked like he didn't have a head injury to complicate things further.

'Blood sugar, twenty-three,' said Luke.

'Okay.'

Dianne appeared beside her. The nurse reeled off the potassium level in the saline bag then held it so Terri could check the label.

'Correct,' Terri said.

She walked around to the other side of the gurney so she could more easily examine the wound on his forehead. 'I want to have a look at your cut, Uncle Mick.'

'Fluids set, Terri,' said Dianne.

'Thanks.'

A jagged flap of skin had curled back from the triangular laceration but the area looked quite clean. A simple irrigation and suturing job.

'No! No!' Her quiescent patient erupted into unexpected action. So quick. One moment she was lifting the dressing and the next she was flying across the room. In slow motion she watched the horror on Frank and Dianne's faces from the other side of the gurney, their hands uselessly reaching towards her. She saw the sergeant step forward, his mouth tight as he restrained her flailing patient.

Any moment now she was going to hit the floor. Paradoxical that she had so much time to notice everyone's expressions but none to organise her limbs to save herself from the inevitable painful sprawl.

But it didn't happen.

Hands reached her, catching her from behind, cradling her against a hard, warm body. Her uncle lay back down in the milliseconds in which she struggled to understand what had happened. She turned her head and looked up into Luke's grim face. How had he managed to get across the room to save her?

'Are you all right?'

Pain bloomed in her cheekbone, replacing the numbness of a second ago. His face dissolved and she realised her eyes were tearing up. 'Yes. Thanks.'

She tried to move away but his hands held her firmly, preventing her escape. Short of an undignified struggle, she was helpless to free herself. Luke was so large and hot and solid. She felt fragile. Insubstantial. Utterly feminine.

Though it must have only been seconds, time seemed elastic, stretching to allow her to feel every square inch of contact. He turned her slightly. She could feel his bracing arm behind her back, the fingers that curved around the top of her arm.

'Go and get some ice on that.' He sounded gruff. His eyes, still fixed on her face, were dark.

She blinked the tears into submission, embarrassed at this sign of weakness. 'I have a patient to attend to.'

'I'm taking over.'

'I need to—'

'You need to stand down and let someone else handle this, Dr Mitchell.' His voice lowered, losing its sternness. 'I can feel you trembling, Terri. You need to go and sit down.'

Her defiance ebbed away, making her realise how shaken she felt. 'Yes. Okay.'

He frowned suddenly and tilted his head to look at her more closely. His fingers tightened on her flesh. 'You have a slight nosebleed.'

'Do I?' As soon as she spoke, she could feel the trickle just below her nostril. Knowing there was physical evidence of her injury made her feel even more vulnerable. An uncomfortable sensation.

She pulled out of his grip and this time he released her.

'Go and clean up. I'll finish here then come and have a look at you.' He turned back to her uncle on the gurney.

She hesitated briefly, then realised that the others had meshed into a team around Luke to treat her uncle. She spun on her heel and left the room.

'I found you at last.'

At the sound of Luke's voice from behind her, Terri jumped. The boxes of twelve-gauge needles she'd been handling scattered across the shelf.

'I wasn't hiding,' she said, not entirely truthfully. How long had he been standing there, watching her?

'Hmm. How are you feeling?'

'I'm fine.' When she'd re-stacked the boxes and regained some of her composure, she turned. He was leaning against the doorjamb, his arms folded, one foot crossed over the other. A plain black T-shirt stretched over the chest she'd so recently been clamped against.

'Good. Let's have a look at you, then, shall we?' A slow smile curved his mouth as though he read her reluctance and thought it amusing.

'I don't think *we* need to. But thank you anyway,' she said, shooting him a discouraging stare.

She'd never appreciated how absurdly claustrophobic the long narrow room was with the well-stocked shelves towering along the walls. It was all his fault, of course, the way he was blocking the only exit.

'I think *we* might let *me* be the judge of that.' His smile took on a distinctly determined edge. 'Just think of it as my self interest.'

Terri picked up her clipboard and hugged it tightly in front of her torso. 'Self interest? In what way?'

'If I don't think you're up to it, I'll take over the rest of your shift.'

He waited with an expression of polite interest as she thought of and discarded several weak excuses.

'Oh, all right. Let's get it over with, then,' she muttered. The thought of his hands on her, even in a professional capacity, was nerve-racking. The imprint of their earlier contact still plagued her. Her back to his chest, his fingers on her arms as he turned her...

She forced down a swallow and pushed away the distracting memory. 'Where do you want to do it?'

He raised a brow and his lips tilted.

She felt heat leap through her system. *Oh, God, had she really said that? Please, let the floor open up and swallow her now.* 'The exam.'

'Cubicle three is empty.' Still grinning, he moved to one side and stood with his back pressed against the shelf. Did he think she was going to squeeze past him? No way.

'After you.'

He shrugged. 'Sure.'

She breathed a sigh when he moved but it was short-lived relief. With his back to her, she could appreciate the broadness of his shoulders, the way his torso tapered to his waist and hips, the long, long legs, the easy way he moved. Her mouth felt suddenly dry.

Just outside the door, he turned, looking back at her, one brow raised quizzically. She realised her feet were still planted in the middle of the supply-room floor. Silently cursing her distraction, she tightened her fingers on the clipboard and hurried to catch up.

She walked stiffly to the curtained area, aware of him striding beside her. His lithe, trim body moving smoothly. Unlike her limbs, which felt all angles and awkward gracelessness.

Perched on the edge of the bed, she watched him bend to

wash his hands. Her eyes were irresistibly drawn to the denim pulling over the line of his buttocks. When he straightened to rip a piece of paper towel from the dispenser, she looked away quickly.

As he stepped in front of her, she let the deep breath she'd taken trickle out. This was a professional examination, one colleague of another.

Hospital director of staff doctor.

It would only take a few minutes.

'Look past me. You know the drill, hmm? Focus on a point on the wall.' He raised his hand and shone a thin beam of light into her eyes.

'Have you had bleeding from the nose before?'

'Um, a couple of times.' She was acutely aware of his face near hers as he assessed her pupil.

'Recently?'

'No.'

'How long ago?' He moved to her other eye and again bent towards her to do the examination.

'Oh, um. Years.' Then she remembered the exact occasion.

The landmine blast which had killed Peter.

And killed her future. Nausea rushed down on her, sweat popped out of her pores leaving her clammy and chilled. 'It…was…um, a—a couple of years.'

There was a small silence.

'Are you all right, Terri? You've gone very pale.'

The blood abruptly rushed back to her head, filling her face with heat, sweeping away the faintness.

'Yes. Yes. Really, I'm fine.' At least he hadn't commented on her stumbling hesitation. 'You—you asked about nose-bleeds. It's been a couple of years.'

'Nothing since?' He frowned as he straightened up, seeming to weigh her response for dissimulation.

She looked away from the measuring blue eyes. The last of the nausea receded. 'No.'

'How heavy were your previous bleeds?'

She frowned and pulled back, pulling herself together at the same time. 'I've had a tiny nosebleed here, not an arterial haemorrhage.'

'Yes, of course.' He appeared to shake himself mentally as he slipped the penlight back into his top pocket. 'I'm going to examine your cheek.'

'Fine,' she said through tight lips, closing her eyes, hoping to shut him out, so close, so threatening to her peace of mind. A rustle of fabric, the tiniest feather of air across her skin. Had he moved closer? Just the thought made her heart kick into a frantic, irregular rhythm. She was too scared to open her eyes to check.

A few tense seconds passed. Why didn't he just get on with it?

Then the subtle torture began. Gentle probing fingers travelled down her nose, across her cheekbone, around her eye socket.

Nasal bone, glabella, maxilla, zygomatic.

Breathe in and out. In and out. Perhaps if she recited the muscles. There were so many of them…

She couldn't think of a single name.

Closing her eyes had been a bad idea. Sure, it meant she couldn't see him but the other sensory information was overwhelming. The heat of his body reached out to her. His smell—part soap, part tantalising masculine musk—surrounded her. Small whispery sounds of each inhalation, exhalation. How much more measured and normal his breathing was than hers.

His touch was warm and deft. The skin beneath his finger-tips was alive with nerve endings. Nearby cells seemed to quiver in anticipation of their turn.

She swallowed, feeling so thoroughly shaken now that she didn't dare open her eyes lest he read her ragged state.

Think of something else. Now!

Work. The emergency department.

'How's Uncle Mick?' she said, dismayed to hear her breathlessness.

'Uncle Mick?' He sounded preoccupied. 'Oh, yes. Mick.'

After a moment, he cleared his throat. 'I'm just waiting for the blood results to come back. Particularly the sodium level. I noticed you had a half-strength saline bag standing by.'

'Yes.' She pushed the answer out, working hard to keep her tone even. Concentrate on work, on the technicalities. That would surely bring her back to an even keel. 'I was worried about hyperosmolar hyperglycaemia.'

His fingers stopped moving, the tips resting softly on her skin. The moment hung, oddly alive with possibilities. Had he finished?

Finally, she opened her eyes and looked straight into his, so close. He looked almost puzzled. His pupils were huge, making his eyes dark and intense. For a second, she thought she read a match to her own helpless awareness in the inky depths. Was it real? Or was she desperately trying to see something so she'd feel better? Something to tell her that she wasn't the only one caught by this sensual spell?

Hard on the heels of that thought, she realised it would be better if the weakness was hers alone. How much more difficult might it be to resist the temptation to explore this if she knew he felt the same way.

'Dr Daniels?' Dianne's voice broke the spell.

Shock shuddered all the way to Terri's toes.

Luke snatched his hands away from her face as though she were contaminated. He blinked and the earlier, intense look was gone. Now his expression was easy to read. Shock, plain and simple.

'The lab's just rung through the results for the sodium and blood sugar on Mick Butler,' said Dianne, seeming not to notice anything amiss.

Terri felt heat rushing to her face. She wanted nothing more than to cover her cheeks with her hands. Bowing her head, she brushed a crease on her scrubs.

'Results. Yes. Good.' Luke cleared his throat. His apparent discomfort was a small balm to Terri's frazzled system. 'Er, what are they?'

'Sodium, one hundred and forty. Glucose, twenty-four.'

'Right. Thanks, Dianne.' The rasp had gone from his voice. 'We won't need to change to the half-strength normal saline.'

Out of the corner of her eye, Terri saw him dig his hands into his jeans pockets.

'How's your nose, Terri?' asked Dianne. 'That was a real thump Mick gave you.'

'I'm fine.' Terri looked up, making her lips stretch into what she hoped was a reassuring smile. 'No lasting damage. Just a bit tender.'

'Are you sure?' Dianne's hazel eyes searched her face.

'Yes.' Oh, God, think of something to say, before Dianne says anything else. The woman was a fantastic emergency department nurse but no diplomat. But Terri's rattled brain didn't produce anything in time.

'You're looking very flushed. Almost feverish. Do you think you've got a temperature? Will you be all right to stay on duty?'

Terri scowled as she slipped off the bed. 'Yes, of course I'll be right to work the rest of the shift. If I look flushed it's because the two of you are looking at me as though I'm something squashed on a microscope slide. Perhaps you could both take yourselves off and find some other poor specimen to peer at.'

Unconcerned by the tart response, Dianne grinned then delivered her parting comment. 'You're going to have a shiner.'

'Such a good look for an accident and emergency doctor,' Terri muttered. She glanced at Luke. 'Are you going home now?'

'Will you be okay for the rest of the night?' His voice was low and warm.

'Yes, of course,' she said briskly. She needed to take herself in hand. His concern was *professional*. She couldn't let that lovely, rich voice fill her with this inappropriate neediness. 'Thanks for your help and, um, for catching me.'

'No problems.' He smiled briefly. 'I'll leave you to it, then.'

She watched him go. If her roiling confusion was anything to judge by, it was going to be a physically and mentally draining twelve months.

Perhaps it was time to consider moving on. Her contract only had six months left. But she didn't *want* to move. She'd been thinking about extending her contract. It felt wonderful to be home. Comfortable, safe, reassuring after the trauma she'd been through. It felt like the best place for her while she got back on her feet.

Port Cavill had everything. Wonderful people, gorgeous setting, a great hospital, a world-class motorcycle track.

Unfortunately, it also had Luke.

But it only had Luke for a year. Could she survive that long?

CHAPTER FOUR

TERRI'S cottage door was open but there was no answer to his knock. Through the window, Luke could see the small sitting room. A subdued golden glow from the lamp made it cosy and welcoming in the dusk. A far cry from the cramped and messy look he'd cultivated while using the cottage as his bachelor pad in his late teens.

He hesitated. She couldn't be far away, perhaps down on the beach. Should he follow her down there? Perhaps he should take her absence as an opportunity to slide away unnoticed. He'd been calling himself all the fools under the sun for coming down here anyway...

But when his feet moved it was to follow the path around the cottage, past her bike tucked in the rickety garage.

The shushing of waves grew steadily louder as he approached the line of trees edging the grounds. He picked his way through the grove and paused on the open sand, breathing in the salty tang of the ocean. Moonlight washed the scene with a ghostly aura.

A short distance away, Terri stood at the edge of the water, her hands tucked into the back pockets of her jeans. A floppy knitted top clung to her slender curves. Her head tilted slightly as she stared out to sea. She paid no heed to the wave ripple creeping towards her naked toes. At the last moment it paused and slid away again without daring to touch.

She seemed lonely, sad. He had a powerful urge to reach out to her, to offer comfort. Or was it something else?

He'd kissed her on this very spot. Hard to believe it was a dozen years in the past. He could remember how she tasted. Sweet with a promise of spice.

'Remember the night of the schoolies' party?' The question was out before he could think better of it. She had a powerful effect on him—a walk down memory lane with her was a torment he could do without. Besides, that night didn't reflect well on him.

'Of course.' Slowly, she turned her head to look at him. Dark shadows from the bruising beneath her eyes made her look mysterious, almost exotic, reminding him how little he knew about her.

'I wasn't kind to you that night.' He'd wanted to take what she'd offered...and more. Much more. He'd wanted to grab, to hold on, to lose himself in her sweetness, her gentle sympathy. Somehow, he'd found the sanity and strength to pull back, to send her away.

But he hadn't done it graciously.

She shrugged and looked away. 'I wasn't asking for your kindness. I only wanted to talk to you about getting a medical degree.'

'I know.' He frowned. Had the kiss that came back to haunt him after all these years meant nothing to her? She sounded so indifferent that he felt an inexplicable urge to push, to get a reaction from her. 'I'm surprised I didn't put you off.'

'You weren't that bad.' She took her hands out of her pockets and bent to pick something up.

He swallowed, unable to look away from the unconscious provocation of jeans pulled tight against her curved buttocks. The knitted top rode up, exposing a small wedge of pale skin, gone in a flash as she straightened. She bent to examine a curved shell in her long fingers, her face hidden by a curtain of wavy dark hair. It was a little shorter now than it had been when he'd buried his fingers in it twelve years ago.

He pulled his mind back to the conversation.

'Wasn't I?' Perhaps the incident loomed much larger in his mind because sobriety the following day had brought sneaking shame at his behaviour. 'That isn't how I remember it.'

'You were grieving for your cousin.' She slanted him a look as she pushed the thick curls back over her shoulder.

'This must be a first for gender interaction.' He huffed out a small laugh, feeling irrationally frustrated with her. 'I'm trying in a roundabout way to apologise for the things I said and you're busy making excuses for me. I took my anger out on you.'

She grinned at him, her teeth gleaming in the subdued light. 'Would you feel better if I said you'd been callous and cruel and I've never recovered? That I'm bitter and twisted with an abiding fear of beaches?'

He felt suddenly foolish. 'Maybe not.' But he realised that some tiny part of him wanted a sign that their exchange on that long-ago evening had meant something to her…even as he recognised his folly.

Her hands tipped the shell from palm to palm as she contemplated him for a moment. 'Want to walk?' she said, waving a hand vaguely along the beach. 'Just along to the rocks and back.'

'Sure.' He levered off his runners and hooked his fingers

into the heels. Sand sifted between his toes in a soft caress. When Terri moved away, he fell into step with her.

The gentle sibilance of the waves filled a small silence. He felt an odd mixture of relaxation and intense awareness of every move that she made.

'You said something important to me that night.' Her voice was deliciously husky, easy to listen to.

'Now I *am* worried. Wisdom brewed in a beer bottle.' He grimaced. Should he be embarrassed or pleased that she apparently remembered something after all? 'What pearl did I drop?'

'That one of the hardest lessons is not being able to save everyone.'

'Ah. Yes.' An echo of his harsh feelings trickled through his memory. Such bitterness and anger at the senselessness of his cousin's death. What chance had Terri had to soothe his pain? Yet she'd tried after he'd pushed everyone else away. And she'd succeeded to a degree. Their kiss had distracted him. It was that he remembered most clearly about that night, not his grief.

'You were right. Failure can be hard to live with.' She sounded sombre. Was she thinking about her husband? Had she tried to save him after the explosion? He was trying to frame a diplomatic question when she said, 'You were talking about Kevin, weren't you?'

A shadow darkened his mood for a moment. His cousin had been young, full of promise, full of male bravado—a reflection of himself. 'Mmm. I was still pretty raw.'

She tilted her head to look at him. 'You were very close?'

'We grew up together.' The simple sentence couldn't begin to describe their relationship. His throat grew thick. 'Mum used to say that we were more like twins than cousins.'

They reached the rocks and silently turned to retrace their steps.

She stopped to throw the shell into the water then scrubbed her hands together. When she turned her gaze met his. 'Dad said you were working on Kevin when he arrived at the scene.'

He'd forgotten that her father had been the local police sergeant at the time. It'd been her father who had pulled him away from Kevin's body when the paramedics had arrived. A band of stiffness tightened around his larynx. He cleared his throat. 'It wasn't enough.'

In the small pause that followed, he watched a wave ebb, its highest point marked by a thin line of froth. 'I felt responsible for the accident.'

'Why?' Her voice held only curiosity. Nothing more. Would she judge him when she knew the whole story? Every now and then he still wondered if he'd done things differently, if he'd picked his words more carefully…but thinking that way was pointless.

He flexed his shoulders, feeling the old weight of his dereliction. 'We'd argued about his recklessness. Kevin rode as though he was immortal.' He lifted his eyes back to hers. 'Hell, I suppose we both did. He didn't even make it through the first bend. I saw him hit the car head on.'

'Oh, Luke.' He could hear her distress, felt unexpectedly soothed by the knowledge it was for him.

'I grew up after that.'

'It wasn't your fault.' She put her hand on his arm.

He stared down into her eyes for a long second, feeling his heart twist. 'Still got that soft heart, haven't you, Terri? I know it wasn't my fault…now. At the time…' He shrugged.

After a moment, he reached out to stroke her cheek, her

skin soft and cool beneath his fingertips. She shivered and desire punched into him, shortening his breath, tightening his gut.

Would she resist if he pulled her close? Folded her into his body? Covered her lips with his?

Finished what they'd started all those years ago. Right here. Right now.

The connection stretched. Then she snatched her hand back, removing it from his elbow, and folded her arms.

He dragged in a huge breath and took a mental step back. 'You're cold. We should go in.'

'Yes.' Head down, she made a beeline for the trees at the top of the beach. Almost as though she was trying to escape. Had she sensed the desperation with which he'd held himself in check?

He smiled grimly. Surely if she had, she'd be running.

The silence between them wasn't comfortable. Touching her had created a tension that hadn't dissipated even though the physical link had broken.

'So how are you settling in? And Alexis?' Terri sounded slightly out of breath. Still because of him? Or was it the cracking pace she'd set?

He grasped at her change of subject, relieved one of them was functioning above waist level.

'Okay.' He thought of yesterday's asthma attack and the dramatics which had preceded it. 'Allie says I've blighted her young life by dragging her halfway around the world to the back of beyond. She wanted me to leave her behind with one of her friends.'

'She must miss them,' Terri said softly.

'We're only here for a year. She'll make new friends if she gives herself the chance.' He was dismayed by the defensiveness he could hear in his voice in reaction to Terri's gentle compassion for his daughter. Frustration mixed with self-disgust. At least talking about this took his mind off the other source of frustration walking up the sandy path ahead of him. *Though not entirely.* Even in the dim light, he could see Terri's slender hips swaying in her pale jeans.

'What are her hobbies?'

'Hobbies? Oh, hobbies. Yes.' *God, get a grip, man.* What were his daughter's hobbies? 'Soccer. She plays soccer.'

'There's a junior soccer league she can join.'

He reached up to push a low branch out of the way. 'Actually, that's a damned good idea. Thanks.'

'A year's a long time when you're her age,' she said a few steps later.

'It'll be a bloody long time when you're *my* age if she's going to sulk for the whole time.'

Terri chuckled.

'Thanks for the sympathy,' he muttered, holding back a self-deprecating smile.

'Sorry. I'm not really laughing at you.' Kind humour mixed with the understanding in her soft words. 'It must be difficult for both of you.'

'Mmm. I'm only being spoken to when she can't avoid it. The way she's behaving I'll need to get her intensive counselling to recover. Maybe I should book some for myself while I'm at it.' He was making light of the situation but his heart was weighed down by the knowledge of his daughter's unhappiness. There was no way around it. He was committed to helping his father for this year.

'I'm sure you'll work it out.' Terri stepped onto the veranda of the cottage. 'Well, this is my stop.'

He should go but her obvious relief made him push his

welcome. Just for a few minutes more. A chance to work on his familiarity plan, give it another opportunity to kick in. Besides, he needed the small respite before facing the tension back at the house. 'I wouldn't say no to a cup of coffee.'

Her pleased look faded. He suppressed a smile and waited.

'Wouldn't you?' She turned her head slightly as though she made a quick inventory of the rooms. It made him wonder what she didn't want him to see, but all she said was, 'You'd better come in, then.'

'Thanks.'

They wiped the sand off their feet at the door.

'It'll just be instant,' she said, glancing at him as he followed her into the compact kitchen.

In the artificial light, he clearly saw the purple-blue smudges forming under both her eyes and a faint bruise on the bridge of her nose.

'Coffee.' She froze with the jar clutched to her chest as he stepped closer. 'What are you doing?'

'How's your nose?' Cupping her face, he tilted it to the light. Her carotid pulse jumped against the edge of his hands. Masculine satisfaction surged through him.

'Fine.'

'No sign of any problems after last night?' Her skin felt soft and smooth beneath his finger tips.

'No. None.' She scowled. 'Have you finished?'

Was he? His gaze dropped to her mouth. If he leaned forward, just a little, he would discover if reality was as delicious as his memories of their kiss. Temptation wrestled with good sense.

Then the opportunity was gone as Terri pulled back out of his light hold.

'You won't get your coffee unless you get out of my kitchen,' she said tartly. 'Why don't you sit at the table?'

He stifled a sigh and retreated, slipping onto one of the chairs and allowing himself to follow her with his eyes. Watching her was like indulging in a visual feast. Filling the jug, getting out the mugs, spooning in the coffee. Commonplace, everyday things.

But there was nothing commonplace about his reaction. He shifted on the chair, easing the snugness of his jeans. To take his mind off her, he looked around the room. Ochre walls made the little room cheerful. At the end of the bench a distressed dresser displayed an eclectic collection of china. The cupboards had been stripped back and varnished to show off the warm grain of Baltic pine.

'You've made the place nice. A vast improvement on when I lived here.'

'Thanks.' She smiled slightly and switched off the jug. 'I must admit I prefer butterscotch paint to wall-to-wall centre-folds.'

'God, were they still up?' An unexpected wave of self-consciousness threatened to heat his face as though he was an awkward adolescent.

'Every single anatomically enhanced one of them.' She slid him a cheeky look. 'If I'd known you were coming back I could have saved them for you.'

He snorted, his momentary embarrassment evaporating. 'I like my women more natural these days.' *Like you.* The unspoken words reverberated in his head.

She smirked at him, obviously comfortable again now that he was at a distance. The devil in him wanted to see that composure shaken again, to know that he wasn't the only one affected by this inconvenient attraction. 'There's another reason why I was so hard on you that night on the beach.'

She eyed him warily. 'There was?'

'Oh, yeah,' he drawled. 'I fancied the pants off you.'

'No!' Her mouth opened in a perfect circle of shock. She blinked at him then burst out laughing. Nervous laughter that only lasted for a moment before she stopped and stared at him again.

'Yes.' He grinned, enjoying her reaction.

'Oh, come on.' Her movements were jerky as she turned back to the bench to pick up a spoon. The staccato clatter of metal on china filled the room. He could imagine her marshalling her defences. After a moment, she said, 'You barely knew who I was.'

'Oh, I knew all right,' he murmured as she turned with the hot drinks in her hand. The only sign remaining of her agitation was the heightened colour in her cheeks. 'You used to haunt your uncle's racetrack.'

She handed him a steaming mug.

'Thanks.' He considered her over the rim as he took a small sip. 'Your brother warned me off.'

'Ryan? Did he?' She wrinkled her nose in disbelief.

'Sure. He warned off a few of us. He'd have dismembered me if he'd known some of the things I'd thought about you.' Things he'd have liked to share with her...would still like to share with her.

'I never realised. I must make sure I thank him for his interference.' She shook her head, her lips curved with amusement. 'And here I thought I was the most unpopular girl in school. All the boys wanted to be my friend but never my *boy*friend.'

'It was self-preservation.' He grinned, raising the mug to take another mouthful. Flirting with her was fun—regardless of whether it was a good idea. It had been a long time since he'd done something just for the fun of it. 'I half expected a visit from your brother after I kissed you that night.'

'You thought I'd run home and tell?' She gave him an old-fashioned look and signalled for him to follow her along the hall. Over her shoulder, she said, 'Why would I advertise the fact that you'd rejected me?'

'I wasn't rejecting you,' he said as she led the way into the lounge.

'Oh, yes? I was kissed by the local heart-throb and then told he didn't want to babysit. That was a rejection in my book.' She curled into one of the overstuffed chairs and looked at him with a small enigmatic smile on her lips.

'Local heart-throb?' His cheeks warmed. This woman could really throw his system for a loop. 'Give me a break.'

'Tsk. *I'm* telling this story, not you.' She waved an airy hand, dismissing his protest. 'My poor seventeen-year-old ego was thoroughly battered.'

Luke grinned at her. 'You seem to have recovered just fine.'

'Some scars don't show.' She arched an expressive brow at him.

He felt his smile slip. God, she was so tempting. The offer to make amends was ready to leap off his tongue. With an effort he stifled the unruly impulse. That was *not* the sort of familiarity he needed to cultivate with Terri.

Shaking himself mentally, he looked around the room, his eyes settling on a collection of photographs on the mantelpiece. He stood and crossed the room to pick up one of the pictures. An unsmiling man stared out of the frame. Tanned, good-looking. Intense. He glanced at Terri. 'Is this your husband?'

'Yes.' Her fingers curled around her mug and she blew on the liquid as though cooling it was the most important thing in the world.

The easy relaxed atmosphere was gone in an instant and he

was sorry to have been the one to destroy it. He hesitated then said, 'Mum told me he was killed in a landmine explosion.'

'Yes.' Her monosyllabic answers discouraged further questions. She was obviously troubled and he wanted to get past the barrier she was putting up.

'Yesterday…' He put the picture back and moved to the sofa. 'You cut me off when I was going to offer my condolences.'

She shrugged. 'Nothing will undo what's happened.'

'You were with him when it happened,' he said gently as he sat down.

'Yes.' Her expression was shuttered.

'Were you injured?'

'I walked away.' She hadn't really answered the question and he sensed there was much more to the story.

'It must have been traumatic.'

'You could say that.' She hunched over her mug, resolutely keeping her gaze averted.

The healer in him wanted to help, find the key so she would let him in. Anguish radiated from her and he couldn't let it rest. 'Any ongoing problems?'

Her head snapped up and she glared at him. 'Why? Are you worried about working with me?'

Remembering his own grief after Kevin's death and then with Sue-Ellen, his heart ached for her. 'Maybe I'm worried *about* you, Terri.'

'It's not necessary and it's not your place.' Her lips barely moved as she grated the words out. 'I've done the counselling. Learned to live with it. I don't like giving people, *acquaintances*, chapter and verse on my life's tragedies.'

He ignored the sarcasm, hearing the residue of pain behind it. He knew well the twin burden of grief and guilt. Regrets over Sue-Ellen's death still tugged on his conscience.

'What about friends?' he asked softly. 'We're friends, at least, aren't we?'

She stared at him coolly. A tiny tremble of her chin betrayed her before she set her jaw.

'Well, if you need to talk…' He opened his hands, making a small conciliatory gesture.

'You'll be the first to know,' she said flippantly with a toss of her head.

'I'm sure I won't, but the offer stands. Any time.' He smiled gently. He'd failed to reach her. Worse than that, he suspected he'd caused her more suffering with his well-meant probing.

There was a small silence and then she said, 'Was there a particular reason for your visit tonight, Luke?'

He stifled a sigh. His communication skills with the opposite sex were not good at the moment. He'd alienated Allie and now he was doing the same with a colleague and friend. 'I wanted to see how you were after last night. Plus, we're going to be working together and—'

'So you'll be making these cosy calls on the other staff members as well, will you?' She looked at him then, one eyebrow raised, challenging.

'And I wanted to thank you for taking such good care of Dad with his MI,' he continued smoothly, ignoring her interruption. 'You saved his life.'

Her shoulders moved in a tiny shrug. 'I was just doing my job.'

'I know, but in this case the job was my father so thank you. He was lucky you were at the barbecue when it happened. Mum told me how stubborn he was about his *indigestion*.'

'It's hard for some people to face physical vulnerability. Especially someone as vital as your dad.' She studied the liquid in her mug.

Was she speaking from experience? He couldn't ask, not tonight. He'd already asked too much, definitely worn out his welcome. His heart squeezed and he felt the same frustrating helplessness as when Allie shut him out. The same...but different. This feeling was mixed with a potent attraction. More than anything, he wanted to scoop her into his arms, to comfort and reassure.

Bad idea. They had to work together. For a year. The sexual chemistry between them made it impossible for him to judge where altruism ended and lust began.

He had to keep reminding himself she was a colleague. Keep striving for that day when he'd know her so well this fizz of awareness would be a thing of the past.

The silence was broken by the catarrhal cough of a possum outside.

'I'd better go. Thanks for the coffee.' He placed his mug on the low table and waited a beat. 'I'll let myself out, shall I?'

At the door, he looked back at her. She hadn't moved.

'Goodnight, Terri.' That air of fragility about her tonight was probably entirely in his over-protective imagination.

''Night.'

Terri sat for a long time after Luke left, waiting for her equilibrium to return. Inviting him into this room had been a disaster. Why hadn't she thought of the photographs, realised he might be curious? But at the time she'd only thought of sitting somewhere other than the tiny kitchen table, where their knees would have touched every time they moved. Her eyes touched on the picture of Peter, her hand automatically sliding to her belly.

Protecting where there was nothing left to protect. Tears

stung her eyes, pushing to escape. She thought she'd finished with crying...

She'd been wrong.

CHAPTER FIVE

TERRI stared at the now-silent CB receiver in her hand, noting the tremor in her fingers with an odd detachment. The radio unit clattered slightly as she returned it to the base cradle.

A baby. Eight months. Fever of one hundred and two degrees for several hours. Part of her knew she should have suggested continuing with fluids and waiting another couple of hours before coming in. But the rest of her couldn't bear to take the risk.

Not today.

Babies were special, the small lives so precious.

Of their own volition, the fingers of one hand splayed across her abdomen. Her own baby would have been eighteen months old if she hadn't miscarried.

Eyes closed, she bowed her head. Abruptly, her sensory memory delivered a staggering tableau. The pungent stench of cordite clogging her nostrils, Peter's cries ringing in her ears. The cramping pain in her stomach as she'd crawled to try to help him. So much damage, so much blood. The very air had coated the back of her tongue thickly with the metallic taste.

She could still feel the puff of Peter's breath on her ear as he struggled to talk, to apologise, to ask her to look after their child. In his final moments, a connection between them, one that had all but vanished after they'd married.

A spasm low in her abdomen reminded her how she'd failed them all: Peter, her baby, *herself*.

In the aftermath of the trauma, her body had rejected its precious cargo.

Today was the second anniversary.

'Terri?'

'Luke!' Her eyes flew open and she spun round to face him. 'Luke.'

The room seemed to rock for a second and she put a hand on the bench to steady herself.

He stepped forward, his hand wrapping around her arm above the elbow. The warmth of his fingers a tiny comfort against the chill she felt. Concern filled the blue eyes drilling into hers. 'Are you all right?'

'Oh, yes,' she managed, faintly. Even to her own ears she sounded less than convincing. But she *was* all right…or she would be. He'd just caught her at a vulnerable moment.

'Come and sit down before… Sit down and tell me what the problem is.' His compassionate bedside manner flowed over her, making her want to believe he cared.

She swallowed and stood firm. 'Really, I'm fine.'

In a way, her turmoil was his fault. Talking to him the other night had left her more vulnerable than usual, that was all. His kindness, his offer to help had left her raw. She'd coped so well with the first anniversary. This second one was ambushing her, ruthlessly exposing the cracks in her defences. The skills she had used to keep herself functioning for the past two years felt fragile and unreliable. Twenty-four months. Would any amount of time be long enough to blunt the pain?

Perhaps she'd have taken today in her stride if Luke's visit hadn't unlocked her vault of painful memories, pitching her back into the emotional maelstrom of the tragedy.

But she would get past it, she had to.

'Terri?'

Luke's voice snapped her back to the present and she barely suppressed a start. If she didn't pull herself together, he'd be afraid to have her working in the department tonight. And she needed to work—she couldn't go home and sit alone with her thoughts. She had one constant, her ability to focus on her work. She was good at her job and that wasn't going to stop now. She couldn't let it—work was all she had left.

She took a deep steadying breath. With her eyes on the notes she'd made, she concentrated on the details.

'We've got two patients on the way in. A thirty-year-old male involved in a quad bike accident. Required resuscitation at the scene. He has head, chest and leg injuries.' Her voice was level and calm. No sign of the turmoil so close to the surface.

'Right. And the other patient?'

Her fingers tightened and the paper she held crackled a protest. She swallowed.

'The other patient is a febrile eight-month-old. Some vomiting and diarrhoea with a temperature of a hundred and two for several hours. There's no indication that his case is anything more serious than a childhood fever but I've suggested bringing him in for examination. Mum's extra-anxious because her niece had meningicoccal disease last year. The family live out of town and Dad's away on business so…' She clamped her lips to stop the flow of words. Her reasoning was feeble, the product of personal anxiety rather than professional concern. She needed to marshal a better argument.

'So you didn't want to leave Mum isolated in case things deteriorate during the night?' Luke shrugged. 'That's part of the reason we're here, isn't it? Better to have a patient come in and prove to be a minor case than to have us miss something major.'

Terri opened her mouth to defend her case for having the child brought in and then his words sank in. He wasn't questioning her decision, as she'd expected…as she deserved.

'Um, yes.' Grateful as she was for his attitude, the quick acceptance of her position made her feel like an inexperienced rookie. She suppressed a sigh and acknowledged the truth— the mood she was in tonight meant that whatever response Luke made, she would be hard to please.

She set the paper aside and glanced at her watch. 'The ETA on the quad bike victim is any minute now. The febrile infant will be at least twenty minutes.'

As soon as she'd finished speaking an ambulance glided up to the entrance, red and blue lights revolving.

'Let's get to work,' he said grimly, heading for the door.

With Luke's attention directed towards the unconscious patient being unloaded by the paramedics, Terri felt a subtle release of tension in her muscles. The quiet air of strength and competence that he radiated should have made him a pleasure to work with…it *did* make him a pleasure to work with, but it was also subtly threatening.

He saw too much and she had secret agonies she couldn't bear to have exposed. He'd already encroached where no one else had by asking her about the explosion that had killed Peter. Other people tiptoed around the issue, relieved when she moved the conversation away to safer topics. But not Luke. Had he sensed there was a problem?

She had to find the resolve to keep him out, not let his compassion weaken her. The guilt and responsibility, the burden for the terrible loss was hers and hers alone.

* * *

Luke watched the diminishing lights of the helicopter ambulance for a moment longer before turning wearily to walk back into the hospital. The future of the quad-bike victim was in the neurosurgeon's hands now.

The man's wife had wanted absolute reassurances that he'd recover but Luke couldn't give them to her. Even if her husband survived, he'd probably have months of rehabilitation ahead of him.

He and Terri had done everything they could. The skull X-ray had shown an intracranial haematoma, as he'd suspected from the blown right pupil. With the help of a telephone consult to a Melbourne neurosurgeon, they'd evacuated an epidural clot through a burr-hole. They weren't ideally set up for the procedure but they'd had to do it as soon as possible for the man to have any chance of a full recovery. Now stabilised, with the pressure on his brain released, the accident victim was on his way to facilities where he could be monitored by regular CT scans.

The only good thing about the situation was that the couple's five-year-old daughter had hopped off the bike moments before the performance of the tragic stunt.

Luke stripped off his blood-stained gown, lobbing it into the laundry bin beside the sink before scrubbing his hands.

He wondered how Terri was getting on with the dehydrated infant.

Odd how she'd behaved earlier when he'd first come on shift. She'd been so obviously upset that all his protective instincts had gone on high alert, demanding that he do something, anything, to help. After avoiding him for the best part of a week, she'd seemed positively delighted to see him. A disproportionate leap of pleasure had rushed through him in that split second when she'd turned to look at him, her eyes shining. Until she'd put her hand out on the bench to steady herself and he'd seen the desperation underlying her veneer of composure. For a moment, he'd been afraid she was going to collapse at his feet.

But there'd been no sign of hesitation or diffidence when she'd helped him with the quad-bike trauma case. He'd watched for it, been ready to take over if she'd faltered. But she'd been great. Better than great.

She'd been fantastic since day one, taking direction from him with no hostility at all. After his father had explained to him the hospital board's poor handling of the filling of the position he'd wondered how their working relationship would function. But it was a pleasure…in every way. And if there were any undertones of resentment, he couldn't detect them. If anything, he was the one giving out the mixed signals.

He enjoyed working with her. And on a personal level, he enjoyed being close to her. Perhaps just a little too much. Since that first night when he'd had his hands on her, he'd wanted nothing more than to touch her again.

Professionally, it was a potential time bomb.

She impressed the hell out of him.

As a doctor, she was strong and competent.

As a woman, she was an enigma. One he wanted to solve. The more he *knew* about her the less he understood her.

Those occasional flashes of uncertainty and fragility he saw in her cut straight to his heart. They were so out of keeping with the rest of her.

What had upset her tonight? Obviously not the trauma patient. Could it have been the infant?

It didn't make sense. That case appeared to be so straight-forward. Perhaps Terri had been a little on the cautious side but he preferred that in the staff he worked with than someone who was negligent about cases.

He knew Terri had taken the infant and her mother through to one of the double rooms. The woman had a toddler to look after as well and Terri's suggestion of a family room for them had made sense. His runners made no noise as he padded through to the quiet corridor

At the door of the room, he stopped dead.

Terri held the happy chortling baby on her knee. He could see her profile, see the loving smile on her lips. The boy's trusting eyes looked up into Terri's face as a stream of unintelligible words tumbled out of the rosebud mouth. The fingers of one chubby hand wrapped around Terri's thumb and he tried to stuff it between his lips.

'Aren't you a gorgeous wee man?' cooed Terri, her voice a warm, maternal caress. Luke's breath choked up in his throat.

'Ga!' said the child, responding enthusiastically to her tone.

'Yes, you are.'

The sight rocked Luke to the core, raising age-old masculine instincts to protect, to possess. He swallowed hard, waiting for the world to settle.

He adored being a father. From the moment he'd laid eyes on his daughter, his soul had been filled by her sweet invasion of his life.

A sharp, uncomfortable hunger stirred in his heart as he watched Terri with the child.

He must have made a small noise because Terri looked up suddenly. Her smile was filled with a warm uncomplicated love that slammed into him. The charged moment was packed with intimacy. His heart made a slow painful revolution in his chest and a shudder of recognition fizzed through his brain.

He wanted…He refused to let his mind finish the thought.

Terri's smile faltered and he wondered what she read on his face. Then she blinked, and a quick puzzled look filled her lovely dark eyes before she looked away. She was still seated in front of him but he had the oddest feeling she'd withdrawn from him, mentally fled.

He moved closer, compelled by a wholly male desire to pursue.

'Someone's looking a lot happier.' He sat beside her, putting one hand on the back of her chair as he leaned towards the child. He suppressed a grin when Terri flicked him a wary look. Her senses were spot on. Though he tried to present an unthreatening appearance, she had stirred a primitive corner within him.

He smiled as he stroked the baby's soft cheek with the back of one finger. The small mouth drooled saliva as it made chewing motions on Terri's knuckle. 'Teething as well, is he?'

'Yes. Which is possibly why he wasn't settling for his mum.' Her voice was soft and tender. 'Poor little fellow.'

Luke's eyes were drawn to Terri's profile. She wore her hair up twisted in a loose bun on the crown of her head, making it easy for him to study her profile, the curve of her cheek, the neat straight nose, stubborn chin.

Another wave of need spiralled through his gut. He hadn't felt such compelling sexual awareness for a long time. Experiencing it now so powerfully was exciting and unnerving.

He had some thinking to do. His situation with Terri was a sensitive one. He was her boss, they worked in a small hospital. They were both here for a limited time.

But there was something between them. Would Terri allow him to pursue it?

Or perhaps the more important question was, was pursuing it wise?

* * *

'Come on, kiddo. You can't sit there all day.'

Luke's head lifted at the sound of his sister's voice coming from just outside his line of sight. He knew Allie was reading a book on the patio. His fingers paused on the pawn he'd been about to move as he strained to hear his daughter's mumbled response. He picked up his father's black knight and left his piece on the square.

Not deterred, Megan chirped, 'It's time for some girl stuff. Let's go and see if Terri's home.'

Terri. A hot thrill streaked through him before he could suppress it. Sharp angles on the chess-piece dug into his palm as his fingers clenched around it. God, he had it bad if just her name being spoken unexpectedly could affect him like this.

'I don't know if Dad will let me.' Allie sounded bored and sulky.

'You won't know unless you ask him, will you, bunny? Come on. He's just inside playing chess with Dad.' Megan stuck her head around the corner of the French door. 'Hey, Luke, I'm going down to see Terri. Okay if Allie comes with me?'

His daughter's head appeared beside Megan's, her face anxious. Was she worried about going? Or worried he wouldn't let her? Everyday life required the skills of a wiser man than he.

'Do you want to, Allie?' he asked, keeping his tone neutral.

'I guess, sure. It's not like there's anything else to do.' She shrugged, trying to look nonchalant, but he'd seen the gleam of interest in her eyes. More than he'd seen in a long while.

'Okay, then,' he said, letting her comment slide. 'Don't stay too long.'

'Thanks, Luke.' Megan grinned as she turned to Allie. 'See. What did I tell you?'

Luke watched them go, his silent daughter walking beside

his ebullient sister. It should have been the other way around—the teen with the world-weary attitude and the ten-year-old with the naïve enthusiasm.

He was failing her in some way that he couldn't understand. The things he'd tried to reach her fell dismally short of success. He was beginning to wonder if they needed a counsellor to help them through this patch. But if Allie steadfastly continued to refuse to talk, then the sessions might just cause more of a problem than they solved.

What would Terri make of his unhappy child? This week, he'd found out that she was great with children of all ages. Maybe she could see what was troubling his daughter's spirit. He would ask.

Perhaps when the girls came back he could wander down to the beach cottage.

Yeah, right. And perhaps Terri would see through him.

'She's not settling, is she?' said his father.

Allie?' Luke said, earning himself a quizzical look. 'No, she's not.'

'Maybe you should have planned a day out with her today.'

He met his parent's faintly critical gaze. 'I did. She didn't want to go.'

'Ah.' His father nodded sagely and turned his attention back to the board.

Luke contemplated the elegantly carved black and white chess pieces. White was in a hopeless position. The defence was shot and he had no offensive pieces in good positions. In short, no matter what he tried now, he was going down.

His thoughts drifted back to Allie. Every approach he'd tried had been grimly rebuffed. He'd hoped the move to Australia might have ultimately sparked some interest in her. He'd know it wouldn't be easy but he hadn't expected it to get so much worse. He had to do something soon. He couldn't stand by while his daughter sank into depression.

His father made a move, taking the white queen with his remaining knight. 'Well, maybe she needs some female company. Meggie and Terri might sort her out.'

'Maybe.' He hoped so. 'Megan's been great since we've been here.'

His father grunted. 'Wants to be a nanny. Did she tell you?'

'No, but she'd be good at it.' He castled, without much hope of salvaging his position. 'She got Allie moving, which is more than I can do these days.'

'Your mother and I have christened her the relentless angel.' There was a small pause.

Luke looked up to catch the thoughtful narrow-eyed look his father gave him over the top of his glasses.

'So, how are you finding Terri to work with? I hope you're cutting her some slack after the way the board treated her.'

'Terri doesn't need any slack to be cut from anyone, least of all me. As you well know.'

'Well, just so long as you're doing the right thing by her,' his father said gruffly. 'I don't want the hospital to lose her.'

'Neither do I.' And his concern wasn't just for the hospital.

'She's been through a lot, that girl.'

'Yes.' Luke looked back at the table. 'Has she told you what happened to her husband?'

'Just the basics. She's not much of a talker.'

'No.' So it wasn't just him that she was shutting out, thought Luke grimly.

'Hell of a tragedy, losing someone that way.'

'Yes.'

His father grunted then leaned forward to move his queen. 'Checkmate.'

* * *

'Hey. Got time for a couple of pests?'

'Always.' Terri looked up to see Megan walking around the side of the cottage. A moment later, to her surprise, Allie followed. 'Out for a walk?'

'As far as your place,' Megan said with a cheeky smile.

'I see.' Terri grinned back. 'In that case, let me finish planting the last of this punnet then I'll get us something to drink.'

'Cool,' Megan said.

Terri was aware of Allie's solemn eyes following her every move as she and Luke's sister chatted. The child was much too quiet, even allowing for natural shyness. Megan's irrepressible bubbliness wasn't succeeding in drawing her into the conversation.

'Do you like gardening, Allie?' Terri asked when there was a small silence.

Allie shrugged.

'These are herbs. When they grow bigger, I'll be able to use them for cooking.'

'Mummy has some.' Allie's toe dug into the dirt as she muttered, 'Had some.'

'Did she?' Terri patted the earth into place around the last seedling as she thought about Allie's slip and then correction. 'What did she have?'

Another shrug.

'You don't remember?'

Allie shook her head.

'When these little guys grow up, they might look more familiar.'

'I won't be here then.'

'Well, if you are. They don't take long to grow. Now, about that drink I promised.'

Terri led the way into the kitchen and went to the sink to wash her hands. When she turned, Allie was standing by the hutch. One tentative finger was stroking her old china soup tureen.

'Do you like that, Allie?'

The girl snatched her hand back, her cheeks tinting. 'Mummy's have the same pattern. I can't remember what it's called.' Her expression was infinitely sad and Terri's heart ached for her.

'It's the willow pattern. My great-great-grandmother brought a whole dinner set over to Australia with her on the ship when she came from England.'

'Same with Mummy. Not the ship. But it was from her great-, um, grandmother,' Allie said. 'I think they're pretty.'

'I think you're right.' Terri smiled and was rewarded with a tentative smile in return. She was about to ask if Allie's mother had the full set when an urgent beeping broke the moment.

Megan dug in her pocket for her phone. 'Uh-oh, it's my study partner. She wants to go over our English Lit. assignment—we're presenting it next week.'

The teen's vivid blue eyes pinned Terri with a speaking look. 'Is it okay if I leave Allie here with you?'

'Sure.'

'Thanks.' Obviously feeling that she'd delivered whatever message she'd been silently sending, Megan bounced to her feet. 'See you later, Allie cat.'

In the silence that Megan left behind, Terri and Allie eyed each other.

'I suppose you want me to go,' Allie said colourlessly.

'Stay for a bit longer if you want to.'

'Can…can I?'

'Sure. You can help me in the garden for a while. I hate seeing a willing pair of hands go unused…even an unwilling pair,' Terri teased gently.

She kept up a steady patter of information about different plants and answered Allie's occasional question. As Terri had hoped, working in the garden helped the girl to relax a little.

'There.' She sat back on her heels and looked at the garden bed they'd finished preparing. 'Haven't we done a great job?'

Allie looked at it doubtfully. 'It's just dirt.'

'Ah, yes, but it's happy dirt that's going to nourish and pamper my next crop of tomatoes which will taste extra-good. Better than anything you'll buy in a supermarket.' She smiled then glanced at her watch. 'Let me clean up and then I'll walk you home.'

'I can go by myself.' Allie sounded belligerent, ready to defend her position.

'I'm sure you can,' said Terri mildly. 'But today's special because it's your first visit and I'd like to take you home.'

'O-okay.'

As they walked across the yard together, Terri had the impression that Allie wanted to say something. After another handful of paces, the girl finally blurted out, 'So, if this was my first visit…'

'Yes?'

'Does that mean it would be okay if I visited again? Please?'

'I don't see why not as long as it's okay with your dad.'

'It won't bother him,' she said flatly. The corners of her mouth pulled down.

'Why do you say that?'

The slender shoulders twisted into a shrug. 'Because it wouldn't.'

'I'm sure that's not true, Allie.'

Another shrug. The girl had turned the gesture into a whole new language of subtle nuances. No wonder her father was concerned. Terri felt for both of them. Allie seemed to be stuck in denial about her mother's death. Which left Luke with the sad task of helping her face the sorrow.

'Anyway, maybe I can help with your garden some more.'

'If you'd like to.' Terri smiled.

'I—I used to help Mummy sometimes.'

'Did you? Well, I'd be delighted to have you come and help me sometimes, too.'

Luke was sitting on the patio when he saw Allie and Terri come through the line of bushes. Allie was talking animatedly to Terri, much more like her old self.

And Terri was…well…Terri. Looking gorgeous in shorts cut just above the knee and battered tennis shoes. The thin knit material of her old T-shirt clung in all the right places. Her hair draped in a ponytail across one shoulder, the ends curving around her breast.

He stood, shoving his hands into his pockets, and walked across the lawn to meet them. Terri lifted her head and gave him a small smile. A moment later, Allie saw him, her face falling. He suppressed a sigh.

'Had a good time?' he said to his daughter, ignoring her sudden mood change.

'Yes. Terri said I could visit again as long as it's okay with you.' Her tone was terse. 'So may I?'

He raised one brow and his daughter's eyes slid towards Terri in a shamefaced look.

'Please?'

Luke glanced at Terri, who gave him a small nod. 'All right,' he said slowly. 'As long as you understand that Terri might have to say no sometimes.'

'Yes.'

'Okay, then.'

Her quick thanks were perfunctory but the grin she gave Terri was more open. 'Thank you, Terri.'

'Thank you for your help in the garden.' Terri smiled.

Luke cleared his throat. 'Nana's nearly ready for dinner, Allie, so how about going in to wash up?'

He watched his daughter disappear then turned to find Terri watching him, her dark eyes filled with soft sympathy. He realised abruptly that it was not the look he wanted to see when she focussed on him.

'Allie's struggling with her mother's death, isn't she?'

Shock and hope jolted through him. Had Terri managed the impossible? 'Did she talk to you?'

'Not really. I just got the impression that she hasn't accepted what's happened.'

'You're right. She hasn't. I can't seem to reach her or get her to open up at all.'

Terri looked towards the house, her face pensive. She opened her mouth as though to say something, then must have thought better of it.

'Whatever you were thinking just then…tell me,' he demanded. She gave him a startled look. 'Please,' he said, moderating his tone, 'Don't worry about offending me, just say it.'

He could see her hesitate but after a small silence, she said, 'Your daughter seems almost…angry with you.'

Conscious of a sense of disappointment, Luke slowly released the breath he'd been holding. Unreasonable though it was, he'd expected Terri's answer would provide a breakthrough for him with his daughter.

'Too true.' He gave her a wry grin.

'But it's more than that, Luke. Watching her with you just now, it's like she's made up her mind not to let you get close.'

She gazed off into the distance again. 'Maybe she's punishing you for something.' Her words came haltingly, as though she was choosing each one with great care. 'Or…'

'Or?'

Her deep chocolate-brown eyes came back to his, the expression in them puzzled. 'Or maybe it's herself she's punishing.' She shook her head. 'But for what, I can't imagine.'

'Neither can I.' He silently turned over what she'd said. Perhaps there *was* an answer in her impression. He just had to find it, use it to untangle whatever was going on in Allie's mind. After a moment, he said, 'I don't know what the answer is but you've obviously worked some magic with her today.'

'Me? I haven't done anything.'

'I think you'd be surprised. It's the most enthusiasm I've seen in her for a long time so thank you.'

'Poor little girl,' she said softly as she stared in the direction that Allie had disappeared.

Luke ran his eyes over Terri's profile, taking in the thick spiky black lashes that fringed her eyes, the lovely apricot tint of her cheeks. Her lack of awareness of a tiny smudge of dirt high on her cheekbone was endearing.

Without thinking, he reached up to brush it away for her.

She jerked back, her eyes wide and alarmed. 'What are you doing?'

'You have a bit of dirt just…' He indicated on his own face as she so obviously didn't want his touch.

'Oh. Well. Thanks.' She scrubbed it as she eyed him warily. 'I, um, I'd better go, then. Bye.'

'See you tomorrow, Terri.'

'Yes, tomorrow.' She swung away. Her long easy stride carried her quickly out of his view. With a small sigh, he turned towards the house. Terri making sure Allie got home safely was laudable but now his excuse for dropping in at the cottage was gone. He smiled wryly at his disappointment.

Probably just as well.

'How are you going, Joe?' asked Terri a few days later as the patient on the bed wriggled slightly.

'Okay. Got an itch.'

'Hold still just a little longer. I'm nearly finished.' Using the dissecting forceps, she pulled back the last section of the skin flap and pushed the curved needle through the subcutaneous tissue. The needle holder made soft ratcheting clicks when she grasped the sharp tip to pull the thread through. With the final neat stitch secured, she snipped the ends and disposed of the needle in the sharps bin.

Luke wasn't on the same roster as she was today. She should have felt relief but when she tried to define her feelings, they weren't at all clear cut. If anything, she felt…flat. As though some indefinable ingredient for sparkle in the day was missing. She frowned. That nonsense needed to be stamped on quick smart.

'All done, Joe. We just need to dress that before you move.'

Joe arched his neck to look at her handiwork. 'Woah. Cool.'

'A thank you would be good, Joey,' said his mother.

'Thanks, Dr Mitchell.' The freckled face flashed a puckish grin.

'You're very welcome.'

'Terri?' Susan poked her head around the curtain. 'We've got a ten-year-old with ARD on the way in.'

'Okay. Thanks, Susan. I'm just finishing up here.'

An odd look crossed Susan's face as she hesitated a second. 'Shall I send someone in to dress that for you?'

'Okay. And a tetanus booster, too, thanks.' Something was definitely worrying the nurse. She stripped off the gloves and said to her delighted patient, 'You'll need to keep the dressing on and dry for twenty-four hours and we'll see you back here in a week to have the stitches removed.'

'Okay.'

'The wound was very clean,' she said to Joe's mother. 'But if you have any concerns, don't hesitate to come back and see us.'

'Thanks, Terri.'

'Someone will be here in a minute to put a dressing on that and give you a sheet of instructions.' Terri smiled and excused herself.

She found Susan in the office, making a note on the patient tracking board.

'Problem?' Terri said.

'Maybe.' Susan looked up, frowning. 'The message was a bit confused but I think the ARD patient is Luke's daughter.'

Terri's hands stilled. 'What makes you think that?'

'The teacher who called it in was very shaken but she kept saying it was Alexis and asking for Dr Daniels.'

'Ambulance dispatched?' Terri swallowed a stab of foreboding. Luke had mentioned Allie's worsening asthma attacks.

'No. The child was already in transit with one of the other teachers when the call was made.'

'Right, what's their ETA?'

'Now. The class was on a field trip to the museum. They decided to make the dash straight here rather than wait for an ambulance as they're only a couple of blocks away.'

Terri suppressed a sigh. She could understand the temptation to make the dash, but it was precious minutes that the child should have been having treatment.

'Okay. I agree, let's assume that it is Alexis. Have we got medical records for her?'

'I've rung Admin,' said Susan. 'They're on the way.'

'Great. Thanks.' Terri glanced at the clock. Ten o'clock. She wondered what Luke had planned. He wouldn't be too far away because he was on duty this evening. She didn't want to page him unnecessarily but she knew he'd want to be there if it was Allie having the attack.

'Let's confirm the identity of our patient…' She trailed off as a car drove into the emergency drop-off point and the sliding doors swished open. The child in the passenger's seat was hunched forward so that she couldn't see a face. But the bob of straight dark hair looked all too familiar.

Her stomach swooped.

'Call Luke, stat, please, Susan,' she called, picking up an oxygen cylinder and mask as she raced for the door.

CHAPTER SIX

'OH, DOCTOR, thank goodness,' gasped the young pale woman rushing around the car to intersect with Terri at the passenger door. 'The attack's so bad. I didn't think we were going to make it.'

Terri leaned into the car, conscious of the teacher hovering behind her as she ran a critical eye over Allie. Hunched shoulders, hands pressed to her sides as she laboured for breath, audibly wheezing with each hard-won lungful.

'Hi, Allie. Can you understand me?'

The glossy head gave a tiny nod.

'I'm going to put an oxygen mask on you.' She fitted the soft plastic mask over the blue-tinged lips and flaring nostrils. Frightened blue eyes clung to hers briefly before closing.

'I've got a gurney here, Terri,' said Susan.

'Okay, let's get her inside.'

Terri was shocked by how frail the child felt in her arms. She settled her on the gurney, seating her as upright as possible.

Susan wheeled the gurney through to a cubicle as Terri took a set of obs. Allie's slender shoulders rose and fell at a rate of about forty respirations per minute. Beneath her fingertips, Terri could feel the child's radial pulse rocketing at one hundred and sixty beats per minute.

'I know it's hard, sweetheart, but I want you to try to relax as much as you can, slow down your breathing.' Terri clipped a pulse oximeter onto one dainty finger.

Another slow nod.

'We're looking after you now and we'll have you comfortable in no time,' she said soothingly.

'Where's Daddy?'

'He's on his way, sweetheart. Susan's taking your shirt off now so she can attach some dots to your skin.'

With the clothing stripped away, Terri could see the way each desperate breath hollowed out the soft tissues around Allie's clavicle, leaving skin gleaming white over angular bone.

Terri placed the stethoscope diaphragm on Allie's chest and listened to pounding heartbeats accompanying the harsh wheeze in the girl's lungs. No sound at all would have been a very bad sign.

'Do you think you could do a peak flow for me?'

The dark head bobbed and Allie reached for the tube.

'Good girl.' Terri glanced at the scale on the side of the tube. The baseline reading was forty percent of what she'd expect for a child of Allie's age and size. 'Allie, have you been taking preventative medication?'

'Didn't. Take.'

'What about your puffer, sweetheart? Did you have it with you at the museum today?'

The cubicle curtain clattered and suddenly Luke was beside the gurney.

Allie raised shadowed eyes to her father then looked at Terri and shook her head tiredly.

'Okay, sweetie,' Terri said. 'Susan, a gown, large, and a pair of gloves, please.'

'Allie, honey, what happened?' Luke stroked the hair off

her forehead with hands that shook visibly. 'Try to relax, sweetheart.' He looked up at the oximeter and then pinned Terri with a fierce look. 'What's going on? Her oxygen sat is only eighty-nine per cent. Why isn't she on a nebuliser?'

'We're just about to start one,' Terri said gently. 'Luke, you have to let us do our job. Your job is to be calm for Allie.'

His face worked as he pulled himself back under control. When he spoke, his voice was rough but more measured. 'I'm staying.'

'I know. Susan's beside you with a gown and gloves for you. So, let's get this nebuliser started.' She was aware of him moving, pulling on the gown, as she broke an ampule of bronchodilator into the nebuliser cup. Oxygen gurgled noisily through the liquid, delivering a fine mist of life-saving bronchodilator. The clear plastic frosted with Allie's urgent rasping breaths.

Terri glanced at Luke. How hard it must be for him to see Allie's battle. His strong features reflected the suffering his daughter was going through. The naked emotion brought a hot lump to her throat.

She turned away to check Allie's readings.

Little response. She prepared a second inhalation and bent to swap the nebuliser cup. 'Do you think you could swallow something for me, Allie?'

The girl nodded.

'Have you got a favourite jam?'

Another nod.

'Apricot?' The dark head shook.

'Strawberry,' Luke said, his voice hoarse. A nod from Allie.

'Susan, could you mash prednisolone in jam, please? We're going with the strawberry.'

Luke watched Terri smile at his daughter. He could see the situation was desperate. As a father he wanted to yell and rage and demand she do something to help Allie, to relieve his daughter's suffering, to make it better.

Stat!

As a doctor, he knew everything that could be done was being done.

Thank God for Terri. Calm, competent, caring. Confidence-inspiring. He was grateful for the small tasks she assigned him. He was there to be with his daughter, that's what mattered. It helped him that he was doing something, no matter how small.

Three hours later, Terri opened the door to Allie's room and tiptoed across to the bed where Luke sat keeping watch. They'd worked for two hours to stabilise Allie. He'd been ready to slay monsters to save her if necessary. His protective concern appealed deeply and Terri realised she felt acutely vulnerable having seen him this way.

Only now that the frightening attack was over could she admit how serious the situation had been. The thought that she might have failed Luke, failed Allie, sent a shaft of nausea into her stomach.

She touched Luke's shoulder. He stirred, turning to look up at her. His expression was dazed.

'She's going to be okay now.'

'Yes, thanks to you.'

'Thanks to the team.' She looked at his drawn face, lines of exhaustion etched around his mouth, and her heart squeezed. 'Take a break, get something to eat and drink, Luke.'

He opened his mouth, refusal in his eyes.

'Just for a few minutes. I'll stay here with Allie.'

She could see he still wanted to refuse.

'I promise I'll be right here when you get back.'

'Okay.' He stood slowly and arched his back. 'Thank you. I won't be long.'

'I know.' She smiled.

Alone with Allie, Terri smoothed the sheet at the edge of the bed and allowed herself a moment longer to watch the sleeping child. It was a pleasure and a relief to see the steady respirations and better skin colour. To check the monitor and see pulse, oxygen saturation and respiratory rate all nearly within the normal range. A stark contrast to the girl who had presented in the emergency department.

For the initial one hundred minutes of her admission, it had been all too possible that her condition could have deteriorated disastrously. She'd been so tired, using accessory muscles as she'd fought for breath.

Terri stroked Allie's forehead, watching the fragile eyelids flutter open above the oxygen mask. Blue eyes, startlingly like her father's, flickered and focussed slowly.

'Hey, sweetheart,' Terri said softly. 'How are you feeling?'

'Okay.' Allie smiled weakly. Her pale skin contrasted with the purple-grey crescents that shadowed her eyes.

As her eyes cleared, she looked around.

'Your dad will be back in a minute,' said Terri. 'He's been sitting with you since you came in.'

'I know. I don't know why,' she said, her voice filled with pain as she closed her eyes and turned her head away.

Terri blinked and stood lost for words for a long moment. 'What do you mean, Allie?'

The girl's mouth trembled. 'H-he hates me.'

'Oh, honey—' Denial sprang to Terri's lips, her tongue started to form the words. She stopped, stifling the automatic response. Allie believed what she was saying.

'Can you tell me why you think that?'

Allie flicked her silent sideways glance, her eyes tortured beneath the lake of brimming tears.

'Your dad's very worried about you,' Terri said softly. 'He loves you very much and he wants to help you. I think he's sad because he doesn't know how. Maybe if you talked to him—'

'You don't understand.' The soft tortured words were ripped from a deep anguished place and tears spilled over to stream down Allie's cheeks. 'I don't deserve to be happy.'

'Oh, Allie.' Terri reached for the slender shoulders, drawing the crying girl into an embrace. 'Tell me what you mean, sweetheart.'

Terri rocked her gently and waited.

'D-Dad was w-with me when Mummy died. It's m-my fault.'

'Oh, sweetheart,' Terri murmured as she rubbed the girl's back and listened to the story of guilt and anger and unresolved grief that tumbled out. Interspersed with sobs and hiccups, it wasn't easy to understand, but she didn't interrupt the flow. Finally, Allie wound down.

'It's not your fault that your mum died.' Terri squeezed her gently, her heart swelling when Allie's arms crept around her waist and clung. 'You're grieving and your thoughts are all jumbled up, aren't they?'

'It f-feels bad.'

'I know, sweetheart. I know.' She stroked the girl's hair and pressed her lips to the top of her head. 'Have you tried to talk to your dad about this at all?'

'No,' came the whispered response. 'I can't tell him.'

'He'll understand, Allie.'

'He'll be angry.'

'Never. He might be sad for not seeing why you've been

so unhappy. But he'd never be angry with you for the way you're feeling now.'

Eyes framed by spiky drenched lashes lifted to cling to hers. Panic and a tiny growing spark of hope swam in the blue depths. 'Your dad will be back in a few minutes. What say we tell him together then?''

'Y-you'll help?'

'Of course. In the meantime, how about I check you over? Sit forward for me so I can listen to your chest.' Terri recorded Allie's obs while she kept up a steady stream of chatter and questions to keep the girl's mind occupied.

Terri knew the moment Luke slipped quietly into the room. All her senses quivered with awareness. 'Here's your dad now.'

Allie's smile dimmed and Terri suppressed a sigh. She waited until Luke was standing on the other side of the bed. 'Allie told me some things she's been worrying about, Luke. She's going to be very brave and tell you about them.'

'Allie, that's great, sweetheart,' he said softly.

'Allie?' Terri prompted after a pause.

The girl plucked at the sheet, her eyes averted. Luke's eyes filled with baffled hunger as they settled on his daughter.

The silence felt thick with accusation. Terri's stomach clenched painfully. In her eagerness to help, had she made a monumental error? Would professional counselling have been the wiser course?

But she was so sure they didn't need an intermediary; they just needed to start. Terri bit her lip as she debated what to do next. Her instincts told her it would be better if Allie could tell her father herself. Much more therapeutic. But perhaps the stress was too much for the child.

'Allie, darling... I know you're unhappy.' Luke's voice was gentle and coaxing. 'I know it's not easy but I want you to know that you can tell me anything, anything at all. I won't be cross with you.'

Terri's throat blocked with tears and pride for the man as he tried to connect with his daughter. His words were just right. So honest and brave and perceptive. No defences. No armour. He'd lost people close to him and yet he was still prepared to put his feelings on the line for those he loved.

Perhaps this was a lesson she needed to learn. She'd thought she'd lost her physical courage in the landmine explosion. But maybe she'd never had what really counted—the raw emotional courage she was witnessing now between father and daughter.

Allie's head stayed bowed, her shoulders rounded.

Luke's eyes were soft with hope and love. 'I promise I'll listen and between us we'll try to find a compromise.'

There was a long tense silence. Terri held her breath and willed Allie to answer.

Luke glanced up and she gave him a tiny nod of encouragement. His throat moved as he swallowed, then he looked back at the top of his daughter's head.

'And even if I can't make it better,' he said, 'I will always love you, Allie.'

'How can you?' The girl sucked in a slightly wheezy breath, her arms wrapping tightly around her thin body. Terri's heart ached at the sight of the defensive movement. Then, in a tiny, unsteady voice, the girl said, 'Mummy died because of me.'

'No!' The last vestige of colour drained from Luke's face. He laid his arm on Allie's shoulder. 'No, baby.'

'Yes!' she whispered.

'Oh, Allie.' His face twisted. 'Why, sweetheart? Why do you think that?'

'You could have fixed her b-but you were looking after me so she d-died.' Tears streamed down Allie's flushed cheeks and her words came out haltingly between spasmodic sobs. 'She'd still be alive if it w-wasn't for me.'

'No, Allie. I'm sorry.' Luke could hardly get the words out through the constriction in his throat. Why hadn't he intuitively understood the cause of his daughter's anguish? He was her father, for God's sake. 'I wouldn't have been able to fix your mum.'

'B-but I get sick,' she said. 'You always f-fix me.'

'Sweetheart, your mum's sickness was different. The cells in her blood multiplied and multiplied and we couldn't find a way to stop them.' He sat on the edge of her bed, wanting to gather her into his arms but not wanting to push while she was so defensive. 'I'm sorry, Allie. I didn't realise you were feeling this way. I let you down.'

'No.' With a choked cry, Allie suddenly launched herself at him. He hugged her close, her thin arms wrapped around his neck tightly. The frail body against his shook with great sobbing shudders.

He breathed deep. His child, his baby, had thrown herself into his arms. The stamp of this small person's scent affixed itself on his soul all over again.

It had all been made possible by one extraordinary woman.

He lifted his head in time to see Terri swiping her hands across her cheeks as she turned to leave.

'Terri?'

She hesitated a moment then lifted brimming eyes to meet his. His chest swelled at the unsteady smile she gave him. He owed this woman more than he could ever repay. He wished he could reach out and draw her into the circle of his embrace with Allie.

'Thank you,' he murmured.

She nodded, nudging a box of tissues along the bedside dresser until it was within easy reach for him. 'I'll let the switchboard know that I'm taking your calls until further notice.'

His heart was full as he watched her slip out of the room, shutting the door behind her.

He held Allie until her sobs subsided. In a small silence he grabbed a couple of tissues and proffered them.

'Thanks.' She blew her nose with unselfconscious vigour, then sighed. After a moment, she said, 'I miss Mummy.'

The wobble in her voice tore at his heart.

'I do, too, Allie.'

'We left her.'

He frowned. 'When we came here?'

'Yes. W-we left her behind.' She tilted her head to look at him. 'We left all the places she loved.'

'She loved it here, too,' he said. With his thumb, he wiped the moisture from her cheeks. 'Remember last time we were here together? She taught you how to snorkel.'

'Yes. But it's not the same.' Her voice was thick with unshed tears. 'We left her garden.'

'I know, baby, I know.' Luke understood immediately. The garden had been Sue-Ellen's pride and joy. She'd lavished love on her plants with the same generosity she'd lavished it on her family. He swallowed as a quick stab of grief pierced his heart. 'You know Mr Owens is looking after it for us.' He laid his cheek on the top of her head. 'But it's not the same as us being there, is it?'

Allie's hair rubbed his skin as she nodded. 'He won't love it as much as w-we would.' Her voice shook anew.

'I know.' He gave her a quick tight squeeze. The silence was comfortable, soothing. He rubbed her back in slow circles, enjoying the closeness after so many months of friction.

'T-Terri said maybe we could get a plant.'

'To remember your mum by? Would you like that?' How brilliant. How elegantly simple. Bless Terri and her insight.

Allie's head, cuddled against his chest, nodded.

'I think that's a great idea. We can go to the nursery and you can pick something out.'

'I already know what I want to get. A pink rose like the one we had by the front door.' She lifted her eyes to his, the lashes spiky with tears. 'The climbing one.'

'Okay. We'll get the very best pink climbing rose in the nursery.'

Allie rewarded him with a radiant smile, a glimpse of the healing process that had begun. The moment was precious. 'Can Terri come, too? When we get it?'

Luke quelled a pinprick of apprehension. *Terri.* Both he and Allie wanted more of her in their lives. It seemed like a potential disaster. He didn't want Allie to get hurt.

For him the want, the *need*, was on a very different level. In an instant of uncomfortable clarity he realised he was projecting his fears for himself onto his daughter.

He didn't want to get hurt. Didn't want to risk losing someone else that he cared about. Didn't want to put his heart on the line.

He stifled a sigh. He was afraid that his options for choice in the matter were well gone.

'Can she, Dad?'

'Of course. If she wants to.' He shook off the shiver of disturbing self-awareness. A family outing with Terri might help to take the magic out of her presence, give him a bit of perspective where she was concerned. 'We'll talk to your granddad, too, and see where we can put the rose.'

'Somewhere special.'

'Somewhere extra-special.'

'Thanks, Dad.' She reached up and hugged him spontaneously again. The lump in his throat got bigger. 'I feel better.'

'So do I, Allie. So do I.'

He had his daughter back. Right now, this was what counted. Allie relied on him to make sensible choices.

For her and for him.

A short time later, Terri filled out a biochemistry form requesting urea and electrolytes and slipped it into a laboratory collection bag with a tube of blood.

As soon as she'd finished, her mind strayed towards the room at the end of the emergency department where Allie had been moved once she'd been stabilised. How were Luke and his daughter? When Terri had left them half an hour ago, Luke had had his hip perched on the edge of the bed and Allie wrapped in his arms.

A cocoon of paternal protection.

A beautiful snapshot of love between parent and child.

Terri swallowed. What sort of parents would she and Peter have been? Her hand ran down the flatness of her abdomen. She already knew he'd had no time for her pregnancy. The changes in her body, which had so delighted her, had left her late husband cold. She tried to imagine him enfolding a child, their child, in his arms.

That picture wouldn't come.

Suddenly she needed to see Luke with Allie, to see that affirmation of pure, unconditional love. Her feet carried her past the curtained cubicles to the door of Allie's room.

There they were. She rested her fingertips lightly on the glass of the window and felt the tension in her chest ease.

They were going to be okay, this father and daughter who had each carved a niche in her heart.

As she watched, Allie's arms came up to wrap around Luke's neck. The scene in the room blurred. Terri lifted her hands, pressed her fingers to her eyelids as she willed away the unexpected rush of moisture.

The moment between parent and child was infinitely precious. They'd been through some very tough times, but they would get through it together and be even closer on the other side.

As though he'd felt her presence, Luke's head lifted and looked straight at her. Her pulse gave a treacherous leap.

He smiled crookedly, tilted his head in an invitation to join them.

Terri swallowed then opened the door.

'Hi,' she said softly. Her smile felt wobbly.

'We've got something to ask you, haven't we, Allie?' Luke's voice was husky.

'Yes.' Allie grinned. Her cheeks were tinged with pink and the strain had faded from her eyes. She looked like a normal happy ten-year-old. 'Please, will you come to the nursery with us when we chose the plant for Mummy? Please say you will. Please.'

'Of course. I'd be honoured. When's the big day or haven't you got that far in the planning yet?'

'There's no school tomorrow.'

'I think Sunday week perhaps.' Luke touched his daughter on the nose. 'Terri and I are rostered off then and it'll give your granddad a chance to decide where he wants the garden.'

Terri blinked in surprise. He knew her roster that far ahead? She stifled a foolish glow of warmth. He probably knew everyone's shifts—it wasn't as if they had a huge medical staff.

'Sunday week, then,' she said.

Luke smiled. 'We'll let you know what time.'

'Okay.' She slid her hands into the pockets of her coat. 'I'd better get back to work. I just wanted to look in and see how you were.'

'We're good. Aren't we, Dad?'

'We are indeed.' His eyes were filled with light and warmth and something more. Something that made Terri's heart lurch. 'I'll catch up with you before you go off duty, Terri.'

'Sure,' she managed. 'I'm off at five, all being well.'

'I know.' His slow smile sent a hot shaft of excitement sizzling along her diaphragm.

'It's a pleasure, Edith,' Terri said as she opened the door to let her last patient out. 'Keep off that foot as much as possible and we'll see you again next week.'

'Next Friday. Thanks again, dear.' Leaning heavily on her walking frame, the woman hobbled a couple of steps then stopped in the doorway. 'Oh, Luke. How are you?'

'Good, thanks, Edith.' His smile seemed tense to Terri's eye but he stopped to exchanged pleasantries with the elderly woman. 'If you'll excuse me, I need an urgent word with Terri, with Dr Mitchell.'

'Of course, dear. We'll chat another time.'

'Absolutely.' He nodded. A muscle rippled in his jaw as though he was keeping his emotions on a tight leash while he chatted with Edith. He stood aside so she could move through the door. 'You can count on it.'

As soon as the patient had gone, he shut the door. The latch snicked loudly in the silence and he stood for a moment with his hand on the doorknob.

Terri's mouth went dry. 'Luke. Is there a problem with Allie?'

'No. No. Just the opposite.' His voice was gruff as he turned.

Terri found herself scooped into a tight hug. For a split second she froze as sensations tumbled into her brain. The feeling of his solid body aligned with hers, the heat and strength of his arms wrapped around her. The fresh essence of him, faintly tangy, masculine and clean. She flattened her hands on his back, feeling the hard ridge of muscle on either side of his spine.

She shut her eyes, savouring the contact as her knees turned rubbery. The embrace felt wonderful and for a magical instant his touch erased her sorrow and filled empty places in her spirit. In his arms, she felt more whole than she had for a long, long time.

After a moment, he held her at arm's length, his eyes burning down into hers.

'Thank you.' His throat worked as he struggled to speak. 'I owe you more than I can ever repay.'

'Oh, Luke.' This glimpse into his vulnerability was wrenching. Terri ached for him. She reached up to cup his cheek.

He brought his hand up, held her fingers more firmly to his face. The very faint roughness of his clean-shaven jaw tingled on her skin. Her heart squeezed.

'You saved my daughter's life and you've performed a miracle by getting her talking to me.' His head dipped and his lips touched her palm for a tiny thrilling moment.

She sucked in a quick breath at the caress, reminding herself that it meant nothing. Luke was naturally demonstrative and this moment was an emotional one for him. His love for his daughter and his relief at their reunion was spilling over into his actions. But her stubborn heart somersaulted wildly, refusing to listen to common sense.

'You've given her back to me, Terri.'

With her senses so overloaded with physical awareness, she struggled to bring her mind back to their discussion. *Allie*. 'You never lost her, Luke. She loves you very much. You know she does. She's just confused right now. You were the person she asked for when she was brought in today.'

'Was I? Thank you.' His grip tightened on her hand briefly when she tried to withdraw her fingers. After a moment he released her and a grin lit up his face. 'She hugged me.'

'Yeah, she did.' Terri's smile felt quivery. 'I saw.'

He sobered. 'My poor baby. Thinking her mother's death was her fault. I didn't see it. I still don't know how she could have believed it.'

'Children have their own view of the way the world works.' She curled her fingers into her palm, as though by holding tight she could lock the sensory memory of his skin on hers. Maybe part of the reason she had been able to tap into Allie's feelings was because of her hyper-sensitivity to the girl's father. 'They sometimes feel responsible for things in a way that an adult wouldn't consider.'

'Yes.' He paced away from her, lifting one hand to his forehead. His fingers furrowed through his hair, leaving endearing tufts standing in their wake.

Terri allowed her gaze to stray over his broad shoulders. The soft woven fabric of his white shirt showed off his powerful torso to perfection. With the sleeves rolled up to elbow level, she could appreciate his muscular forearms. She smiled wryly. She'd always had a weakness for nice arms and hands.

And firm thighs and posteriors. She sighed. The navy denim of Luke's jeans fitted him very well indeed.

He spun around and his eyes drilled into hers. Heat crawled

into her face as though she'd been caught doing something she shouldn't.

'No wonder I couldn't reach her. I should have listened to you the other day when you suggested she was punishing herself.' He moved restlessly to the side again and Terri released the breath caught in her lungs. 'She was so ill. I can't get the picture of her struggling for breath out of my mind.'

'Luke—'

He looked back at her fiercely. 'I nearly lost it in the emergency room.'

'But you didn't.'

'Only thanks to you treating me like a raw intern.'

'Allie is your daughter. Of course it was difficult for you.'

'I don't know what I'd have done if—'

'Stop this. Right now.' She knew too well how he'd have felt. She might not be a parent in the full sense of the word but she knew what it was like to lose a child. The guilt could be paralysing. 'Stop torturing yourself. Allie has recovered and she needs her father. All of him. Not someone fractured by guilt. It's a pointless emotion when you should be concentrating on each other.'

'Yes. You're right.' He dragged a hand down his face then gave her a gorgeous, lopsided smile. 'Thank you. For everything. Including the pep talk. You see things beyond the physical. It makes you an extraordinary doctor, Terri.'

Terri swallowed and looked away. She shoved her hands into her coat pockets. His praise was almost more than she could bear because she knew exactly how limited her abilities were.

He trusted her.

It was priceless.

It was an almost intolerable burden.

She wanted to warn him not to think too highly of her. Warn him how very flawed her judgement could be.

'Luke, please…' Her voice was croaky. She cleared her throat before continuing. 'I was just doing—'

'Don't say you were just doing your job. It was much more than that. We're lucky to have you here at Port Cavill.' He looked deeply into her eyes and there was no doubting his sincerity. '*I'm* lucky to have you here.'

The warm approval was too much. She needed to shrug it off, find a way to keep him at a distance, to quash this intimacy that seemed to have sprung up between them.

'Well,' she said, struggling for a light note, 'I'm glad you think so. Please remember this when I do something to blot my copy book.'

Her smile felt ghastly as she blinked back the urge to cry. She needed to go, find somewhere private to pull herself back together. She cast unseeing eyes in the direction of her watch and said, 'I must catch the lab tech before she goes for the day.'

She all but fled, not caring what he thought. As the barrier of the door clicked shut behind her, she sagged with relief.

Too much, too soon. Being close to him showed her how very flimsy the shell of her carefully mended persona was. She wasn't ready for the powerful, conflicting emotions that Luke awakened. She wondered if she ever would be. She shivered. How long would she be able to hold the façade together under the pressure?

Luke stared at the door after Terri had gone.

He frowned. She'd seemed embarrassed by his thanks. More than that, she'd seemed ashamed, as though she was somehow undeserving of them. But that was ridiculous— she'd saved his daughter's life today.

He'd been there, he'd seen how hard she'd worked, seen her skill and determination. He couldn't praise her highly enough for what she'd done.

He owed her. He respected her.

And he wanted her.

Needy hunger that clawed at him. He'd held her in his arms twice now—embraces that had started out with the very best platonic intentions. But he'd felt the heat grow in his lower abdomen on both occasions, giving the contact with her a sizzling, inappropriate energy.

Familiarity wasn't kicking in as quickly as he'd hoped. He just had to keep holding himself in check until it did.

He huffed out a breath. An armful of Terri Mitchell would test the restraint of a saint. All he had was the very tenuous control of Luke Daniels and it was no match for the temptation of her.

CHAPTER SEVEN

LUKE pushed open his car door and stood listening to the high-pitched howl of hard-working motorcycle engines.

He was escaping. Just for the day.

At his mother's behest, he'd left Allie with her for a girls' day out. Shopping. His daughter was really excited about it. He smiled wryly, hard pressed to think of anything he'd like to do less.

He was also escaping from the lure of Terri. She had the day off but he had no good excuse to invade his colleague's off-duty hours. Other than the fact that he wanted to.

With Allie gone for the day, he couldn't casually suggest a walk on the beach…via Terri's cottage on the off chance that she was around. Having her so close, at the bottom of the garden, was a refined form of torture.

He sighed. Rather than hang around home testing his self-discipline, he was going to face a personal demon. He'd loved hanging out at the racetrack with his cousin Kevin, and Terri's brother Ryan. He hadn't been back since Kevin's accident.

Hadn't been on a bike either. But that was something to tackle another day…perhaps. For now, being here was an accomplishment.

He'd talk to Mick Butler while he was here, too. An informal follow-up after the diabetic episode. He smiled wryly. Maybe he would earn himself some Brownie points with Terri.

He walked through the tunnel under the track to the pit area and watched the speeding bikes for a few moments. Just an initial tightening in his chest, he noted dispassionately. Nothing unmanageable.

He took a deep breath and looked at the people standing trackside. His lips curved when he spotted a familiar profile. Terri's uncle.

'G'day, Mick!'

The man turned. 'Luke Daniels!'

Their palms smacked together as they used the handshake to draw into a quick, hard embrace of uncomplicated masculine friendship.

Mick stood back, his wide smile and dark eyes familiar and uncannily like Terri's. 'About time you showed your face around here!'

'Yeah, I know.' Luke shrugged. 'Time gets away. You know how it is.'

'I know.' Mick patted his arm, the gesture awkward but the emotion behind it genuine. 'I was sorry to hear about Sue-Ellen. She was a bonzer girl.'

Luke nodded. 'Yes, she was. Thanks. I got your card.'

'How's that gorgeous daughter of yours?'

'Giving me grey hairs.' Luke smiled.

'It gets worse.' Mick chuckled. 'I remember when my girls—'

He was interrupted by loud whoops and clapping from the men nearest them. Mick's head whipped back to the course.

'She's just taken Russ,' called one of the appreciative audience. 'Boy, he's going to be dirty about that.'

'She?' A corkscrew of unease twisted through Luke's gut. No, it couldn't be…could it?

'Terri.' Mick craned his neck, following the action. 'She's on the yellow Honda.'

Luke's heart leapt into his throat. His eyes followed the motorcycle as it tipped into another sweeping bend in a blur of red leather and yellow bike.

'That's Terri?'

Terri! Oh, God.

Desire and fear congealed into a solid lump of cold ice in his gut.

Leaning, leaning… Surely the bike must slide from under her. That long crouching form would be thrown, fragile bones crushed, gentle curves mutilated.

How dared she risk her precious life like this?

The woman. Was going. To drive him. Insane.

'Yeah, good, isn't she? Could've gone pro if she hadn't been so set on medicine.' Obviously unconcerned, Terri's uncle turned away as one of the other riders came in.

Good?

Good!

Luke wanted to demand that she be called off the track, stat. He folded his arms, feeling the tightness pinch around his eyes and mouth. Acid churned in his stomach. He'd been watching the speeding riders with reasonable detachment, congratulating himself for managing that degree of calm. The accident which had killed his cousin had been years ago. Past time for him to let go his visceral antipathy to motorcycles.

But now…

Now he knew it was Terri on the track, he felt sick.

And angry.

Angrier by the minute.

Two circuits later, she slowed and pulled into the pit area. Oblivious to his glowering presence, she stopped to chat briefly to a couple of the mechanics further along the lane. Her long legs braced on either side of the machine. With a quick nod, she rode forward slowly. The machine's throaty growl sounded a protest at the restrained speed as she turned into the empty garage.

Luke stalked across the tarmac, driven by the desire to give her a verbal blast. He turned into the wide door. Terri stood beside the bike, stripping off her gloves.

The skin-tight red leather suit moulded to her lithe body.

His gaze was drawn irresistibly down over each feminine curve.

Breast, waist, hip, thigh.

At the knee, the bright supple covering disappeared into long black boots.

Luke swallowed, his steps slowing as an unexpected shudder shook him.

His eyes made the return trip.

She was gorgeous, sensual.

Dangerous to his sanity.

As he watched, she unclipped her helmet and shook out waves of long dark hair.

Perfection.

And she would risk it all for a thrill, a momentary pleasure.

His daughter had made a confidante of this reckless creature. Allie wouldn't be able to cope with another flood of grief in her young life. Terri needed to consider that when she indulged her whim for danger.

Bubbling anger dimmed a tiny internal alarm that sounded in his brain. *Walk away. Don't do this, don't do this. Walk away, now.*

His entire system twitched with the need for an argument, even relished the prospect in a perverse way.

His feet moved purposefully until he was only a few feet from her. She turned. The radiant smile on her lips tilted higher. He could see the high of exhilaration was still pumping through her system.

'Hi, Luke.' Her buoyant greeting was the last straw.

'I suppose you're proud of that display out there,' he said softly.

She tipped her head slightly to one side. 'The riding?'

'Yes, the riding,' he grated.

'Oh, yes. I suppose I am a bit. Did you see?' She still hadn't realised his dangerous state of mind. Enthusiasm shone through her voice. She stuffed her gloves into the hollow of the helmet and then stood with it dangling from one hand.

'I saw,' he said grimly. 'What sort of example do you think you're setting?'

'Example? Well…a good one, I hope. I was in absolute control of the bike at all times,' she said, her voice confused.

'All it takes is a loss of concentration for a split second.' He ground his teeth together. The muscle tension in his jaw was painful. 'People rely on you. Patients up at the hospital. My family. My daughter.'

And me. What about me? How am I going to feel if your broken body ends up in Accident and Emergency? He managed to clamp his mouth shut before the telling words escaped.

'You have a responsibility to this community.' He sounded foolish but, even realising that, he was powerless to stop himself.

'Luke, I—'

'What if something happened to you?'

She gave him a long, searching look. Her expression melted into a look of profound compassion. 'Oh, I'm so sorry. This is about Kevin, isn't it? How insensitive of me. I know it was hard for you, the way he died, but you can't hold onto that grief, Luke. For your sake and for Allie's, it's time to let it go.'

He swore a brief, earthy oath. 'You think this is about Kevin?'

'Well, yes.' Her beautiful face was uncertain and he could see her trying to read his mood. 'Isn't it?'

'No. God damn it. This is about *you*, Terri.'

She took a step back, retreating from the fierceness he knew he was radiating.

'I—I think you need to calm down and then maybe we can talk about this. Perhaps later.' She pivoted and started to walk past him. 'For now, I—'

Without thinking, he reached out, snagging her elbow. The force of her momentum spun her around and landed her hard on his chest, one hand braced at his waist. His fingers flexed around her upper arms where he'd reached out to steady her. Her well-worn leathers felt warm and soft, oddly intimate against his palms.

He gulped in a lungful of air, starting the move to set her back on her feet.

Then she lifted her head. Her lips trembled only inches from his and all his good intentions evaporated.

'Terri.' His voice, so ragged, sounded shockingly needy, desperate.

'Luke.' His name was little more than a whisper.

Dark, nearly black eyes held his for a long moment before slipping, heavy-lidded, to his mouth. Instead of freeing her, he pulled her closer, tilted his head, slanted his lips over the fullness of hers.

No awkwardness, no hesitation. The delight of unexpected familiarity mingled with the wonder and excitement of discovery. She made a small humming sound, almost a moan.

The hand at his waist relaxed, then tightened again before creeping around his back as she pressed into him. The pressure of each fingertip burned through the thin fabric of his shirt. He revelled in the touch, wanted more, wanted it on his skin.

All his anger with her carelessness, his fear for her safety, everything, drained away. Her lips parted in a sweet moist caress, so soft and mobile. Delicious.

A thrill streaked through him, blotting out coherent thought, reducing his world to the sensation of her body pressed to his. She made him want to give more—take more—than was sensible.

A single resonating crunch ripped through the moment. Terri's head jerked back, her torso arching away from his. She stared up at him, eyes wide and stunned. As he watched, the dazed expression cleared from her eyes. Her hands, which had been clasped across his back, now flattened on his chest as she shoved herself away from him.

He swallowed. His system was revved, heart pumping, muscles ready to take on dragons.

The only thing he wasn't ready for was Terri. She looked utterly shattered. Her breasts rose and fell shakily with each shallow, rapid breath.

The helmet, the source of the noise, rocked back and forth on the floor beside them.

Terri started to raise her hand to her face and he saw the tremor in her fingers. As though she suddenly realised what she was doing, her fingers closed in a fist that was pulled sharply back to her side.

'What did you do that for?'

'I'm sorry.' His voice was hoarse, the words meaningless. He wasn't sorry. Not at all. Given the option this moment, he'd take up where they'd left off.

'You're s-sorry?' Her voice rose and she looked momentarily as shocked as he was by the note of hysteria. She glowered at him. Then her face slowly crumpled.

'Oh, God. What have you done? I was okay when I though it was just m…' she trailed off, her expression appalled.

'Just you?' His heart bumped. She felt the same way he did.

She stiffened, pulling herself together before his eyes. 'Just… This thing… Us… We can't…' She touched her forehead with her fingers, rubbing hard at the skin. 'Oh, what am I saying? There is no us. We're colleagues. Nothing more. Do you hear me?' She looked up at him then, the expression in her eyes desperate, daring him to disagree.

She was wrong. Though he couldn't point that out. Not right now.

Not when he could see how devastated she was.

Not when his own system was shaking and shuddering in the aftermath of the kiss.

He didn't understand what was behind her reaction but he needed to find a way to soothe her. He lifted a hand to reach out, make a tiny physical connection…

She nearly leapt away from him.

'Terri—'

'I have to go.'

He watched her long legs powering her away from him, agitation clear in every rapid step.

She didn't want anything more than a professional relationship, that much was clear. But it didn't alter the fact that she'd kissed him back.

Wildly.

Wantonly.

He felt like a teenager, giddy and stupid after the voluptuousness of his first kiss.

And it was a first…his first passionate kiss since his wife had died. He scrubbed his hands down his face. Why had he done it? He hadn't felt as though he had a choice—once she had been in his arms, blind instinct had taken over. For both of them.

He didn't want to think about replacing his wife. He wasn't ready.

Was he?

He could almost feel his reality shifting around him. He swallowed. Maybe he was ready.

Kissing Terri didn't feel like the betrayal he'd have predicted if there'd been time to consider before acting.

Quite simply, the kiss was the most important thing to have happened to him, as a man, for two and a half years.

It'd been electrifying. Physical, demanding, consuming.

Utterly sublime.

Twelve years ago her kiss had been sweetly innocent with a hint of the spice to come. Now her flavour was piquant, rich and complex.

Terri tasted *right*.

He wanted to kiss her again, explore the spark between them. To rejoice in being alive and savour the stirring of his masculinity.

But they had some issues to sort out first.

Luke huffed out the breath. He was sorry he'd upset her. The last thing he wanted was to hurt her. He needed to talk with her, find out what the problem was, help her deal with it.

He made up his mind. She had until tomorrow to calm

down. Then he was going to apologise for ambushing her and get to the bottom of her reaction.

He walked out slowly to find Mick.

The next day, Luke spotted Terri at the bench in the emergency department kitchenette. He ran his eyes hungrily down then back up the green scrubs that draped her slender body. He smiled wryly. She had no business looking so damned desirable in the baggy work gear. Her hair was caught in a loose bun at the nape of her neck and he itched to tug out the tortoiseshell comb holding it in place, sink his fingers through the long silky strands.

He took a deep breath and dredged up some self-control. He was here to apologise, smooth over any awkwardness. Not create new problems. He needed to talk to her, pave the way for them to discuss what had happened at the racetrack.

Arranging his face in what he hoped was an affable, non-threatening expression, he went into the room. Her head was bent, the nape of her neck looked so vulnerable he wanted to reach out, to comfort. She seemed to be staring into the drink she was preparing. She held an empty teaspoon over the rim of her mug as though she was trying to decide what to do with it.

'Terri?'

She started violently, jerking the handle of the mug in her hand. Dark liquid slopped over the bench. She muttered something under her breath, put the teaspoon down and reached for the dishcloth.

'Luke.' A quick flush of red ran under her pale skin.

He stopped beside her. 'I'm sorry,' he said gently. 'I didn't mean to startle you.'

'Did you want something?' Her voice was even as she mopped up the spill. The pattern on the bench would be scoured off if she was any more thorough.

He stifled a sigh. 'I wanted to see you—'

'Well, here I am.' She still hadn't looked at him.

'I wanted to see how you were.'

'I'm fine.'

'Terri…' Voices in the doorway made him glance round. At least one of the people obviously intended to come into the room and Luke didn't want to be interrupted or risk the discussion being overheard. 'We need to talk. Somewhere private.'

'Talk? As hospital director to doctor on duty or something else?' She rinsed the cloth under the tap and hung it over the tap.

Refusal was plain in her stiff spine and he was tempted to lie. 'Something else. Personal.'

'In that case no, I can't spare you any time just now.' She topped up her mug from the urn, then flicked him a brief glance. 'If you'll excuse me…'

He held his hand out in a motion of appeal and she froze. Then took a small step back and looked at him fully. Her eyes were puffy and tired and all the colour had drained out of her cheeks. She looked fragile, as though she hadn't slept well.

He nearly groaned with the need to put his arms around her. 'Terri—'

'I need to go. Please.' The words were calm. Yet he had the distinct impression she was holding herself together by willpower alone. Guilt stabbed at him.

'Of course.' He curled his fingers into his palm and dropped his hand. She waited until he stepped aside before she moved past him.

His gaze followed the graceful sway of her hips until she turned into one of the offices. She must intend to catch up with some paperwork.

He ran a hand through his hair and smiled philosophically.

Terri wasn't going to make it easy for him.

Sue-Ellen would have. His wife had smoothed his life for him wherever she could. He'd appreciated it. Their love had been a quiet, comfortable emotion. Not a grand passion.

Nothing like the volatile mixture of emotions he was starting to feel for Terri.

He sighed. She was complex. Combustion to Sue-Ellen's serenity.

Terri tested the limits of his self-control—which, to his chagrin, were diminishing with each passing day.

What the hell was he going to do about her?

He had to think of something or they were both going to be wrecks by the end of their time together. Though he realised he didn't like thinking of that in terms of a finite period.

CHAPTER EIGHT

TERRI sifted cool sand through her toes beneath a shallow wave. Her walk along the beach had restored a degree of calmness.

Seeing Luke today, being near him after the explosive embrace yesterday, had been impossible. She'd reacted like the gauchest schoolgirl. Embarrassing, but she'd been unable to help it. He'd seen, of course. The pity in his eyes had been hard to take. What did he think of her now? She'd wager that the glowing opinion he'd expressed the other day had been amended.

She turned and walked up to the path through the trees. A small part of her wanted to know what he'd been going to say in the kitchenette. Most of her was just plain afraid. She wasn't sure what scared her the most—that the kiss meant something to him or that it didn't. How contrary.

As she approached the cottage, a figure rose from one of her verandah chairs. She stopped.

Luke.

Her heart stuttered then raced into an erratic uncomfortable riff. Damn, damn, damn. She longed to turn and run, but that was ridiculous…especially as he'd seen her.

Forcing her feet to move, she squared her shoulders and climbed the steps.

'I guess you get to see me after all.' She was proud of the drawl she managed. Her internal tremble was scarcely noticeable. A miracle, considering the way her traitorous heart was still pounding at her larynx.

'I won't stay long,' he said softly, his expression sombre. 'I wanted to make sure you were okay. You were upset today.'

She shrugged, hoping for nonchalance. 'You caught me by surprise after…'

'After yesterday,' he finished for her. 'I owe you an apology for the way I treated you at the track.'

An unexpected dart of pain lanced through her chest. That was one question answered. Her first kiss since her husband's death and the man who'd given it to her was falling over himself to apologise. While he wished it hadn't happened, she'd been shattered by the terrifying beauty and power of it. She couldn't let him see how much.

'Oh, that,' she managed, praying she didn't sound as brittle as she felt. 'Let's consider it forgotten, shall we?'

'I'm not apologising for the kiss, Terri.'

She stared at him, trying to make sense of his words.

'You scared the daylights out of me with the way you were riding that motorbike.' He held up his hand when she would have spoken. 'I know. You're a good rider. Better than good— you're outstanding.'

'Thank you,' she said faintly. 'I guess.'

'Don't thank me. I wasn't watching you and admiring your technically brilliant performance.' He smiled thinly. 'The way you threw that bike into the corners made me angry.'

'Angry?'

'I don't want to lose you.'

She swallowed, looking away uncomfortably.

'*We* don't want to lose you. Allie and me. We've lost too

much already. You're her new best friend and confidante. She needs you, I need…I don't want to see her hurt.'

'Of course you don't.' Her heart melted. He was such a good father. 'Neither do I.'

'I know.' There was a small silence then he smiled at her. A slow delicious smile that curled her toes. Her heart skipped a beat and then tripped over itself trying to catch up. She should excuse herself, send him home now he'd said his piece.

'Do…do you want to come in for a drink?' She heard the words leaving her mouth with a sense of astonishment. 'Er, don't feel you have to…I just…I'll understand if you're busy.'

'Nothing pressing,' he said firmly. 'Thanks, I would like a drink.'

'Right.' She stood indecisively for a moment then turned away to open the door. 'Coffee? Or a cool drink? Maybe a beer.'

'A beer would be great.' He followed her inside. Even with her back to him, she felt as though she was aware of every sound and movement he made as he followed her through to the kitchen.

'I've only got light beer.' She opened the fridge. 'Stubbie? Or would you prefer it in a glass?'

'Stubbie will be fine. Thanks.'

She handed him the bottle. His fingers brushed hers and a ripple of sensation ran up her arm. 'It's, um, a nice evening, let's sit on the chairs out the back.'

'Sure.' He held the door open and ushered her out.

As she settled into the wicker chair, she suddenly realised how romantic the setting was with the rapidly dimming pink wash of sunset. The golden glow from the kitchen light behind them did nothing to dispel the illusion of cosy intimacy. The glare of a harsh fluorescent tube would have helped—but to get that, she'd have to get up and walk past the source of her angst to the switch.

Luke twisted the top off his bottle as he subsided into the chair beside her.

'Cheers.' He leaned forward. There was a small musical clink as he lightly tapped his bottle to hers.

'Yes, cheers.' She watched as he lifted the bottle to his mouth, his lips settling on the rim. Looking away hastily, she took a swig from her own bottle. The liquid fizzed in her throat as she searched for something to talk about.

Something other than the thing that suddenly filled her mind.

His mouth, his lips.

His kiss.

Seconds crawled by as she sat in tongue-tied discomfort, her mind utterly stuck on the interlude in the garage. She glanced sideways at him, only to find him watching her intently, his face thoughtful.

She could almost see him gathering words for a discussion she didn't want to have. Not the kiss. She really *didn't* want to discuss that.

'Terri—'

She had to forestall him. 'Do you think you'll ever get back on a motorbike?'

As soon as the words left her lips, she felt ill.

He grimaced. 'I'm not quite ready for that yet.'

'Oh, God. Luke.' Her voice shook with her distress. 'I'm so sorry. I don't know where that came from.'

'Don't worry.' He lifted one shoulder. 'The thought did cross my mind at the track. That was before I saw you, of course. Then all I could think of was talking some sense into you.' He gave her a lopsided smile. 'And look what a good job I did of that.'

She wet her lips. Oh, dear. He was back to the kiss, she knew it. Talking about it meant acknowledging it out loud, holding it up to the light for examination, making it even more compelling. She wanted it to fade away. As it would surely do given enough time and *no* discussion with the man who'd made her feel so raw and conflicted.

When she didn't say anything, he said, 'Refusing to discuss it isn't going to make it go away, Terri.'

She raised her eyebrow and sent him a sidelong look. 'How can you be sure?'

He laughed softly. 'I know some of how you're feeling. It's a shock, isn't it?'

'A shock. Yes, that's one way of putting it,' she said with a sigh of resignation.

'It's two and a half years since I lost Sue-Ellen. I loved my wife. You're the first woman I've kissed since my wife died, and you knocked me sideways. I never expected to feel this way again. Ever.'

Terri contemplated the bottle she held loosely in her hand. Luke and Sue-Ellen had obviously had a very happy, loving relationship. Terri was surprised by the shaft of grief she felt. By the time the landmine explosion had killed Peter, she and her husband had had no marriage left to betray. Her stomach cramped at the memory. She was a fraud, letting Luke assume she was in the same predicament as he was.

He was right about one thing, though. Her equilibrium hadn't been this upset by a kiss since she'd been…

Eighteen, and it had been his kiss then, too. Heat swept through her.

'What I really want to do is kiss you again,' he said. 'Soon. I would do it right now, in a heartbeat, if I thought you would let me. But I'm guessing that's not going to happen…is it?'

'No. Oh.' Her pulse bumped hard. *He wanted to kiss her again.* 'You shouldn't. We mustn't.'

But it was what she wanted too—regardless of all her good sense telling her otherwise.

'I figure I'll give you a bit of time to get used to the idea.'

Her breath caught. 'G-get used to the idea?' she managed.

'Before I do it again.' His eyes tracked down to her mouth and lingered there for a moment.

'I'm only human, Terri, and I'm attracted as hell to you. I've tried to ignore it but that isn't working for me.' He tilted his head, giving her a self-deprecating smile when she remained silent. 'Am I mistaken in thinking you feel the same way?'

'We can't do anything about it. We mustn't.'

'Why not?' He paused. 'Do you feel like you'd be betraying Peter?'

Coldness gripped her at the sound of Luke speaking her late husband's name.

'That's...' Her throat closed and she had to force the words out. 'It's...not the same.' She stood and held out her hand. 'It's getting late. Have you finished your drink?'

He frowned, staring up at her for a long moment before slowly handing over his empty bottle.

She knew she was handling it clumsily but for the life of her couldn't think of a smoother way to signal that the evening was over. She walked past him, into the house. Hopefully, he would go now.

Bottles in hand, she walked to the sink and stopped.

'Not the same...how?' Luke's voice was soft, persuasive.

She turned slowly to see him standing across the room, just inside the door. His expression was tender with sympathy she didn't deserve.

How? Such a simple little question. But the answer had the power to rip her apart. Could she bear to see disgust in his eyes once he knew?

She was a foolish woman who'd stayed too long in a danger zone.

A sad, tragic creature who'd been too slow to accept her husband didn't want her or the baby she carried.

Her folly had cost her everything. Her marriage, her husband.

And the biggest price of all, her baby.

Perhaps Luke had been right that evening in her lounge. Perhaps he did need to know the worst about her. As a colleague, as her boss, as a friend. Maybe most of all as the doctor to whom he'd entrusted his daughter's well-being.

'My marriage wasn't like yours, Luke. We had… problems.' How laughably feeble and mild that sounded.

Solemn blue eyes examined her face calmly. 'Tell me. Whatever it is. I won't think less of you.'

Her throat closed on the urge to be sick. She knew better. Her hands tightened on hard smoothness and she looked down, surprised to see she still held the bottles.

'Peter was taking me to the airport when the explosion happened.' Her larynx felt raw and tender. 'I wanted to come home. He d-died because I wanted to come home.'

'Oh, Terri.'

In two strides, he was there in front of her. She watched numbly as he removed the bottle from one hand then the other. With her hands empty, he gathered her into his arms. His body heat was startling.

'You can't think that way,' he said. 'You'll destroy yourself.'

She wound her hands around his waist. With her ear pressed to his chest, she could hear the steady beat of his heart. After a long silence, she said, 'We were arguing when the car hit a l-landmine.'

'Poor sweetheart,' he murmured. 'And you feel bad because of that.'

She didn't deserve his understanding. She had to make him see, push out the ugly facts until he turned from her as he should. 'If he'd been p-paying more attention, he might have seen something to warn him, a flaw in the road surface. Or something.'

'Hush.' Luke hugged her tighter. 'You know it's pointless to think like that. He probably wouldn't have seen anything. That's why mines are such bloody awful weapons. You know that.'

His body curved over hers, holding her as though she was precious, reminding her of the way he'd been so protective with Allie. With his strong nurturing instinct, he was so unlike Peter.

Peter had loved mankind. He hadn't had time to cater to the needs of a wife. His need to serve had been noble and laudable but so very hard to live with. She'd felt petty and selfish asking for more for herself. For needing more.

Being enveloped in Luke's caring was glorious.

And it was torture.

She wasn't entitled to his good opinion. He still didn't know everything.

She swallowed and gathered the courage to let go the next piece of poison. 'I was leaving him, Luke. My marriage was over. I c-couldn't be the person he needed me to be. I failed him. I f-failed…I failed.' The words to make him understand the rest choked in her throat.

'No, you didn't. Marriages don't always work, sweetheart. It's sad but it's life.'

He thought she'd finished but she hadn't. She couldn't

bring herself to tell him the worst. She'd failed again. She was a coward.

His warm hand cupped her neck, the fingers stroking her sensitive skin gently. She stood passively in his arms, her attention on each delicate movement, storing the sensory memories for the future.

'What's so bloody unfair for you is the way you lost Peter and the timing. But it's not your fault, Terri.'

'Don't.' She squeezed her eyes shut as a hot lump in her throat threatened.

'Don't what?'

'Just don't.' She turned her head, pressed her hot face into the cool skin of his neck, feeling the steady bump of his carotid pulse against her forehead.

He shifted and her awareness of the hard body clasping hers changed abruptly. Her pulse sped up.

She should pull back…started to move. His head bent slightly and his breath whispered across her cheek. If she tipped her head a little and reached up, she'd be able to press her mouth to his.

It wouldn't be right to take more than the comfort he'd given so generously, especially when she had so little to offer in return.

But suddenly she didn't care. She wanted something for herself. A kiss, his kiss. Whatever he was prepared to give her in this moment. She wanted to feel desirable again, to remind herself how that felt.

She tilted her chin, but still he didn't move. Another millimetre nearer and still he waited with infinite patience. Each beat of her pulse pushed her a little closer.

And then the perfect, heart-stopping moment when her lips touched his.

Just the gentlest caress, the barest pressure. Exquisite. His mouth moved on hers, rubbing, nibbling, until the nerve endings in the sensitive skin were alive.

A gift to herself. The beauty of it held her enthralled. She whimpered when he pulled back. Not enough. More. She wanted more.

His hand lifted to tidy a strand of her hair. She suppressed a gasp as he tucked it behind her ear. As his fingers touched the rim, she could feel the tremor in them. Her heart squeezed painfully.

His hand dropped back to her shoulder and after a moment he said, 'I should go.'

'Should you?'

'Oh, God. Terri.' With his forehead resting on hers, he rubbed his hands slowly up and down her arms. 'This is too important for us to rush. I don't want you to do anything that you'll regret.'

'I won't. I wouldn't be.'

He pulled back and looked down at her. His throat moved in audible swallow and then he smiled. 'Don't tempt me,' he said with mock severity. 'I'm trying to do the right thing here.'

'I know.' If she pushed him now, he would give her what she wanted—sweet relief from the thoughts in her head. He was as vulnerable to the chemistry between them as she was. But she couldn't do it, he deserved more.

'We need to talk some more before we go any further.'

'Luke…' She suppressed a sigh. 'You can't solve everything by talking about it.'

He cocked his head, his smile teasing. 'Is this the same woman who solved my problems with my daughter by getting us talking?'

'That was different.'

'In some ways. We do have to talk and we will, but not now.' He pressed a quick kiss to her forehead and stepped away from her. 'Sleep well, darling.'

'Yes,' she said, knowing she wouldn't. 'Thank you.'

'My pleasure.' He reached out again and stroked his fingers down her cheek as if he couldn't resist touching one more time. 'See you tomorrow.'

'Sure. Tomorrow.' Terri watched him go, knowing it was for the best. Much as she ached for his embrace, he was right. She should be grateful he'd decided to leave before she did something they'd both be sorry for.

She wondered what he'd have done if she'd begged him to take her to bed. If she'd begged him to help her forget for a whole night. Not just the precious minutes when his kindness, his touch, his kiss had given her respite from her pain.

She'd wanted to be selfish. To beg, cajole, humiliate herself, until he gave her more. Until he gave her everything.

Her marriage had been far from a meeting of soul-mates. Friendship with Luke was richer and more fulfilling than all the sacred vows she'd taken with Peter. Too valuable to risk on the fleeting satisfaction of something more physical.

Besides…Luke was her boss, her colleague. And most importantly, Luke was a father with a daughter who needed him very much right now.

Terri took a deep breath and faced the truth. The last thing Luke needed was someone as broken as she was, clinging and demanding his time and attention.

Luke jammed his hands into his jeans pockets and took a deep lungful of air. The sweet smell of freshly mown grass mingled with the damp of the evening, helping to soothe his frazzled nerves. Leaving Terri was torment. But if he was to have any integrity at all, he had to.

He blew out a long breath.

She'd opened up to him, told him things that made his gut ache with the agony of them. He'd held her slender frame, felt the silent bottled-up grief in her trembling body, and he'd wanted to weep for her. Regardless of the state of her marriage, having Peter ripped from her life like that was a tragedy almost beyond comprehension.

Any hopes, any dreams, any chance of reconciliation had been lost in an instant. Cruel, senseless, irrevocable.

He was almost sure there was more. But why hadn't she told him? She was a very private person. Perhaps telling him as much as she had was all she could handle to start with. He could respect that and when she was ready to tell him more, he'd be there for her.

They'd made a start and he'd been content with that…

Until she'd instigated the kiss.

Then his altruism had evaporated and he'd wanted everything a red-blooded man wanted from a beautiful woman.

He'd wanted to break all his self-imposed rules.

He wasn't proud of himself. Knowing that, given the tiniest bit more encouragement, he'd have taken shameful advantage of a grief-stricken widow.

He'd nearly been unmanned when she'd looked up at him with her big brown eyes. She'd seen worse things than he could imagine. He'd wanted to take away her pain and heartbreak. To hold her, kiss her, touch her.

But he knew it wasn't that simple and, rather than risk the small progress they'd made, he'd chosen caution. It had taken all his strength to let her go, do the honourable thing. He didn't want her to do anything she'd regret. Their relationship was new, complex and far too fragile for a quick tumble into bed.

Why, then, did he have the nagging feeling that he'd let her down tonight?

His restraint hadn't been what she'd wanted, but he knew it was what she needed. Could she have read his retreat as rejection?

His footsteps slowed. He could go back, explain he wanted her more than life itself. Explain he wanted them to get it right, that it was too important for a quick grab at gratification.

Undecided, he stood looking at the cottage then with a small sigh he reluctantly turned for home. Going back now wouldn't be a good idea.

He'd make sure they talk again soon.

He'd make sure she understood how much he wanted her.

CHAPTER NINE

THE next day, Terri hung her white coat on the hook on the clinic-room door and turned to look at her reflection in the mirror. She smoothed her hair, straightened her shirt and ran a quick eye over the profile of her lower half in the new black jeans.

Then she looked herself in the eye and wrinkled her nose. How much more comfortable it was to fuss with her appearance than to think about the thing that was really bothering her.

Luke.

She didn't want to run into him yet. Last night he'd seen her at her worst. She'd been so vulnerable, so needy.

She didn't want to remember that he had the strength to resist her advances. He did a charming line in rejection, very gentle but firm. She grimaced. Too much self-respect to allow himself to be used. She should appreciate that…she *did* appreciate that. But a tiny part of her couldn't help but think it would be nice to have someone lose their head over her…just a little.

At least she'd slept well last night and for that she was grateful to Luke, his insight, his pushing. It had helped rather than harmed to talk about Peter. She'd expected to relive the explosion in vivid, torturous nightmares after Luke had gone. But she hadn't. Her sleep had been dreamless and refreshing.

She moved across to the desk and stacked the patient

records she'd used that morning. Scooping them up into he
arms, she walked to the door.

With her hand on the knob, she paused and took a deep
breath. No point skulking in the office. Seeing Luke was un
avoidable as they were both on duty for the day. Her only hope
was that he'd been called out for an emergency case but tha
seemed unlikely as she hadn't been notified that she'd need
to take cases from the second list.

She marched out of the room and was nearly at the fron
desk when surprise had her halting in mid-stride.

'Uncle Mick.' Perhaps she wasn't finished after all. 'Wha
are you doing here?'

'Tee.' His smile was quick and nervous, almost guilty.

'Have you got an appointment now?' she asked. 'I didn'
see you on my list but I can see you now if you like.'

'Um, no. Didn't want to trouble you, love. So, I, um, well
you know…should be running along.' Colour ran into hi:
cheeks and he shuffled his feet.

'Are you sure? You seem upset.' Terri was perplexed.

'Fine, I'm fine, love. I just…' Her uncle cleared his throa
and then his gaze slid past her. His expression was a mixture
of relief and consternation. 'Um, thanks, Luke. I'll, er, catch
up with you about those results.' His face turned even redder.
'See you at the track, Tee.'

Frowning, she watched him hurry away. She turned to see
Luke slide his used files into the tray. He added a couple of
blood tubes to the laboratory test basket. She glanced at the
name on the top file.

'Uncle Mick's been to see you?'

'Yes.' Luke looked a little uncomfortable. 'Look, let's grab
a cuppa and have a chat.'

'Is there a problem?'

'No, of course not.'

Her spirits plummeted. 'There must be if he's asked to see you. It's just that I thought after I'd diagnosed his diabetes…he's been feeling so much better… Oh, dear, this is such a backward step—I thought he finally believed that I knew what I was doing after all.'

'He does. Your uncle has nothing but praise for you.' Luke leaned across and wrapped his hands around the records she held. She released them quickly as his fingers brushed the skin on her forearm. He placed the files into the tray and said, 'On second thoughts, let's have lunch. We've got some other things to discuss as well and—'

'But he can't be happy with me if he's come to see you.'

'Terri, there are some things that make a man draw a line.'

'Oh. Is he still embarrassed about the incident the other night?' She frowned. 'I thought we'd got past that. I told him it wasn't his fault. That he only behaved that way because he was so ill.'

'Yes, but that's not why he didn't want to come to see you.'

'Then there was another reason?' She suppressed a squeak of surprise when Luke took her by the elbow and ushered her towards the door.

'Nina, we're going for a bite of lunch at home. Page us if you need us.'

'Sure thing, boss.'

'I'm…I don't know if I want to eat lunch with you.' Feet still moving in the direction he was guiding her, Terri looked back over her shoulder at the grinning nurse.

'Sure you do. I make a mean cheese omelette and we've got the kitchen to ourselves today as Mum's taken Dad into Melbourne for a check-up. And besides, you want to know why Mick's been to see me.'

'Yes, I do, but will you please stop making a spectacle of us by dragging me around the hospital?'

He muttered something under his breath and released her. He stopped when she did, a muscle in his jaw rippled giving the impression of tightly leashed emotion. They stood alone on the pavement between the hospital and his parents' house.

'Terri, Mick is fifty five years old.'

'I know.'

'So don't you think that he might be a little uncomfortable getting his first routine prostate check from someone who used to run around in the backyard with his own children?'

'Oh.' She swallowed, feeling like an idiot. She was dimly aware of his hand in the small of her back ushering her down the path. 'Of course. How stupid of me.'

'It's thanks to you that Mick was in here getting the check up today,' Luke said evenly. 'He said, apart from the hiccup after the races the other night, he's never felt better. *There might be something in this prevention is better than cure rubbish.*' He opened the back door of the house and gently steered her into the kitchen. 'That's a direct quote.'

'Oh.'

'His coming to see me had nothing to do with lack of faith in your ability, Terri.'

A quick expression flitted across her face. If he'd had to define it he'd have said it was pain. Her vulnerability punched him again.

'Well, that's…good, then.'

He saw the faint frown on her face as she stood in the kitchen, looking around. She looked lost, almost as though she wasn't sure how she'd got there. God, he wanted to look after her, protect her, smooth out the bumps in her life for her

He'd set himself a hard task. Terri Mitchell was fiercely in-dependent.

At least, with the surprise of Mick's visit, there hadn't been a chance for her to feel any awkwardness after last night. He'd wondered how their first meeting would go this morning. One bump had been avoided but it had created another that he didn't understand.

'Now, cheese, onion, mushroom?' He turned to the fridge and put the items on the bench as the reeled them off.

'I'm sorry?'

'For the omelette I'm making you for lunch.'

'You don't have to make me lunch.'

'Here's the grater for the cheese. We don't need much,' he said, pleased when her hands automatically began the task he'd set for her. He started breaking eggs into a bowl. 'This is a good opportunity for us to talk.'

'Actually, you're right. We *do* need to talk.' She stopped grating. 'What on earth were you thinking when you told Nina you were taking me home for lunch? She was grinning like the Cheshire cat. Heaven only knows what rumours will have started circulating by the time we get back to work.'

'I don't care.' He wiped the mushroom caps then sliced them thinly with a sharp knife.

'What do you mean, *you don't care*. This isn't London,' she said tartly. 'We're doctors in a small community. You *have* to care.'

'Nope. Do you want to cut up the onion for me?' He looked at her hopefully.

'No, damn it, I don't want to cut up your blasted onion.'

'Pity. Okay, I'll do it.' Suppressing a smile at her palpable frustration, he began slicing the vegetable thinly.

'Luke. Are you listening to me?'

'Absolutely.' He leaned down and got a frying-pan out of the cupboard and put it on the stove over a low heat. 'You're worried that the hospital grapevine has got us over here indulging in a bout of hot sex.'

A quick glance showed him that she was standing with her mouth open. He would be willing to bet that it wasn't because she was speechless. Much more likely that she had too much to say and didn't know which scathing retort to fire at him first.

'Knives and forks in that drawer, salt and pepper on the worktop.' He whisked the eggs and tipped them into the warm pan. Using a spatula, he lifted the edge of the mix to stop it from sticking.

With the eggs cooking gently, he risked another look at Terri. 'Don't you think the people you've worked with for six months have a better opinion of you than that?'

'Maybe.' She sighed. 'Probably.'

He spread the chopped and grated filling over the top of the egg and reached up to grab a couple of plates out of the cupboard. With a deft flip, he folded the omelette then cut it.

'Let's eat,' he said, carrying the laden plates across to set them on the table.

Terri followed slowly and slipped into the chair opposite his. 'Thank you.'

'Bon appetit.' He reached for the pepper. Out of the corner of his eye, he could see her pick up her utensils.

They ate in silence for a few moments.

'You're right, you do cook a mean omelette,' she said. 'It's delicious. Thank you.'

'My pleasure.'

Feeding her filled him with a warm glow. Basic, instinctive. Primal. He was surprised how much he wanted to provide food and shelter for this woman. Get close to her, to pet her and love her. To have her return his feelings.

He waited until she took the last mouthful of omelette. There was no easy way to start this discussion so he may as well plunge right in. 'If we're going to have a relationship, we need to set some ground rules up front.'

She stared at him, her mouth stopping briefly in mid-chew, then he could see her trying to force the food down her throat.

He got up to fill a glass with water then took it back to the table and held it out to her. 'Here.'

She waved it away. 'A relationship? Are you crazy?'

'No, not at all.' He put the glass on the table. 'We agreed last night that we're attracted to each other. There's chemistry between us.'

She gave him a hunted look and pushed away her plate. 'Yes.'

'Good.' He let out his breath. For a moment he'd thought she was going to deny him, but she was no coward.

'Luke, this is a small country town. We work together. You're my boss. Any sort of entanglement outside work has disaster written all over it.'

'We'll go slowly, be sensible. Start off with normal social interaction. Everyday, routine stuff. See where it takes us.' He watched the expressions flit over her face. 'I'm not suggesting that we flaunt it with public displays of extravagant affection but neither do I want to hide it away as though it's a furtive hole-in-the-wall affair.'

'What if we get down the track and realise it isn't working?'

'We're adults, professionals. We deal with it.'

She looked at him sceptically. 'What about Allie?'

'She'd be delighted. My daughter thinks you're the best thing since sliced bread. I know you care about her and I know that wouldn't change.' He leaned his elbows on the table and looked into her eyes. 'Even if you thought her father was the biggest swine this side of the black stump.'

She gave a snort of surprised laughter. 'And is he?'

'He tries hard not to be.'

Terri was still looking at him doubtfully, but Luke sensed he'd crossed some invisible boundary with her.

He smiled. 'So how about it?'

'Slow and sensible?'

'As you want.' And may the powers give him the strength to keep his word without causing him physical injury.

A loud discordant beep made her start. She reached for the paging unit on her waistband and looked at it. Tucking it back into position, she got to her feet. 'I'd better go.'

Hell. Was she going to leave him in limbo? Luke swallowed and stood to pick up the plates. Surely she wouldn't be so cruel.

A second later she looked him squarely in the eye. 'All right, then. Yes. Slow and sensible.'

He stifled the yell that threatened to rip out from gut level and managed a moderate 'Great.'

She nodded. 'See you back at work.'

'Yes.'

As soon as the door closed behind her, he let his smile escape. *Yes!* Now all he had to do was get the balance right. He didn't want her to feel crowded or stampeded by him, but he did want them to spend as much time together as they could.

Terri's heart somersaulted wildly. She'd just agreed to have a relationship with Luke Daniels. Should she applaud herself for bravery for taking the step or chastise herself for being foolish? Apologise to Luke for leading him on? For not telling him all the reasons why he shouldn't get involved with her?

She was too weak. The love that shone between him and

Allie beckoned her closer. Made her want to catch some of the warmth for herself. Was it so wrong of her?

Somehow she would find the courage to tell him what he had a right to know. Soon. Before they got too deep. First she would store precious bright moments in her memory.

She shivered as she walked through the warm spring afternoon. Was she fooling herself?

Everyday routine stuff, he'd said.

She was very much afraid that the *normal, everyday* could be addictive with Luke.

CHAPTER TEN

FIVE days since Terri had agreed to a relationship with him.

Five days of caution and restraint.

Five *whole* days.

Not long in terms of world affairs. Not even a week.

In terms of self-control, it was an aeon.

Luke looked across to where Allie was showing Terri the information tag on another nursery plant. At his daughter' behest, Terri obediently bent to sniff a white bloom. Helples to resist, he watched the way her red shorts clung to the curv of her buttocks as she leaned forward. A familiar tug of desir caught him low in his gut and he suppressed a groan Frustration was his constant companion these days.

He'd played it cool all week, not making any overt moves not giving Terri any excuses to retreat, to change her mind The first few times he'd joined her for coffee in the staff te room, he'd felt her wariness. As though she expected him to say something, do something, in front of the other staff. A though she'd known how hard he'd had to tether his need to stake a public claim on her.

By the end of the week she'd almost relaxed and he con gratulated himself that his softly, softly approach was working

Allie flitted to another plant like an overly fussy worker bee. Her face radiated enthusiasm as she turned over the tag, read it, then moved on. He smiled. She'd inherited her mother's love of gardening.

His eyes slid back to the woman who followed a pace behind his daughter. Long dark hair formed a thick gleaming mantle across Terri's shoulders.

Five whole days since he'd kissed her. Since he'd held her in his arms…threaded his fingers deep in her hair.

The sable silk would look glorious spread over his pillow…as her lips moved in a mysterious, womanly smile, inviting his kiss, inviting his touch. Inviting—

'Dad-dy!'

The plaintive cry slapped him out of his fantasy. He focussed to find himself staring straight at Terri. Her soft brown eyes held a quizzical expression. His pulse stopped and then lurched into an erratic bounding rhythm.

Hell. What was she reading from his face?

He swallowed.

'Sorry, miles away.' He walked towards them, forcing his mouth into the best smile he could manage. It felt feeble. 'What did I miss?'

'I want this rose for Mummy's garden.' Allie looked at him anxiously. 'Do you think Mummy would like it, Dad? It's not exactly the same as the one at home but the colour is so pretty.'

He looked from his daughter's wistful face to the plant with its cluster of small coral-pink buds. 'I know your mum would love it because you chose it, sweetheart. It's perfect.'

Allie beamed. 'Cool. Can we get some small plants, too? I talked to Granddad and he said we should. He gave me a list to choose from.'

'Did he? Then if Granddad said so, we'd better get some.' He grinned.

'We need a trolley. They're over there.' Allie pointed then skipped away.

'It's lovely to see her so happy.' Terri's husky voice sent a quiver down his spine.

'Yes.' He watched as his daughter manoeuvred an awkward flat-bottomed trolley back towards them. He tilted his head towards Terri, his eyes following the line of her jaw to her stubborn little chin. 'Have I mentioned how much I appreciate you giving me my daughter back?'

'You might have a time or two.' Her grin was alive with mischief.

'Perhaps I should mention it again,' he murmured, reaching out to capture a ringlet of hair that had caught on the simple gold chain of her necklace. Masculine satisfaction surged at her quick shiver as he stroked the strand back over her shoulder.

'It's not necessary.' There was a slight catch in her voice and when her eyes darted up to his they held a dark flare of awareness.

His gaze moved down to her mouth, watched as she caught her bottom lip. Her teeth sank into the tender flesh until he wanted to protest, wanted it to be his teeth nipping at the plump cushion.

'Terri—'

She blinked and looked away, a strained smile curving her mouth. 'Well done, Allie. Let's grab your rose and see what else we can find.'

Rooted to the spot, Luke watched as one of the attendants lifted the pot of the chosen rose onto the trolley. His daughter chattered to Terri and pushed the trolley a little further along the aisle. When they stopped, a trick of the light bathed the two of them in a glowing, ethereal halo. Terri bent her head towards Allie, whose upturned face was filled with trust and hope.

And love.

He stared at their smiling profiles. The seconds moved with a syrupy slowness as his heart compressed painfully. A shudder ran through him as though a foundation had shifted deep in his psyche.

He blinked and looked away, waiting for normality.

He wanted Terri badly.

He ached for her, but this sensation was something more. Something powerful, elemental.

Frighteningly important.

He'd promised to take things slowly and sensibly but there was nothing temperate about the emotions storming through him.

He frowned, abruptly certain he didn't know enough about her. She'd opened up so much the other night. Wrenching details about her marriage and about her last moments with her husband. Was there more? If there was, she'd baulked at the idea of sharing it with him. Why? What could be worse than the things she had told him?

Perhaps his unease was because he sensed the trauma of the explosion and her husband's death had left Terri with even deeper emotional scars than those she'd revealed. How could it not? Did a soul ever truly heal from such cruel wounds?

Despite the heat of the sun on his back, a chill spread across his skin. As though an unseen threat lurked just beyond his comprehension.

He huffed out a long breath, shrugging away the shiver of unwelcome intuition. The only thing he could do was take it one step at a time, build trust, hope they'd create something worthwhile together.

'Okay, you two, let's get this show on the road.' He aimed a smile at them as he strode forward. 'Plants. We need plants. Allie, you've got the list so you're in charge of choosing. Terri, you're with me behind the trolley.'

Allie giggled and relinquished the handle to him.

Luke captured Terri's hand and tugged her to his side. 'Now I've got you right where I want you,' he said under his breath so only she could hear.

'Luke!' Her gaze flew to where Allie was comparing a tag to the list she held.

'What? I'm only holding your hand.' He gave her a wicked grin. He lowered his voice and said, 'Would you like me to show you what I really want to do?'

'No,' she all but yelped. 'No, absolutely not. Behave.'

'Then you'd better hold my hand tight, hadn't you, sweetheart?' he said, his gaze roving over her anxious face.

'What about Allie?' Terri's eyes were fixed on his daughter. She cared very much for Allie's well-being.

Suddenly his peculiar mood dissolved and he relented. 'Don't worry. I've had a talk to her about going out with you.'

'You have?' Terri's eyes came back to his, wide and uncertain.

'She thinks it's a good idea. In fact, I think I've gone up in her estimation. See what a good influence you're being on me.'

'Mmm.' Her lips pursed in a moue of doubt and his pulse spiked. *Conversation, concentrate on the conversation.*

'Yes, she even wanted to give me some dating advice.' He strolled down the aisle towards Allie, who had moved on further. 'I should take you to the movies and buy you ice cream apparently. It's what all the girls like.' He gave Terri a thoughtful glance. 'What do you think…will it get me to first base?'

'Not likely,' she muttered darkly. 'You promised we wouldn't flaunt it.'

'I also said we wouldn't hide it.'

'I think we need to have a discussion on definitions. Yours versus mine.' Her tone was astringent. 'I'm starting to sense a lack of compatibility.'

'I'm always ready to discuss our relationship with you.' He grinned at her. 'Just say the word.'

He laughed when his impertinence was rewarded by an old-fashioned look. This subtle dance of courtship between them was a pleasure. It had been a long time since he'd done something just for the fun of it.

At the checkout, he said casually, 'Mum's issued a not-to-be-refused invitation to you for dinner tonight. Hasn't she, Allie?'

'Oh, yes, please come. Ple-ease,' said Allie.

'Dad said you used to be a regular at *chez* Daniels before we arrived.' It was short notice and his pressure was less than subtle, but he didn't care. He didn't think Terri was the type to play games. If she was free, she would come. If she wasn't, he wouldn't like it but he'd have to be philosophical. He layered on some more pathos. 'We'd hate to think we'd scared you off. Wouldn't we, Allie?'

'Yes.' His daughter looked faintly confused but game to agree.

'Since you asked *so* nicely, I'd love to,' Terri said, her narrow-eyed stare letting him know exactly what she thought of his tactics.

He grinned, unrepentant, and tried hard not to look too smug. Judging from the look Terri gave him, he hadn't succeeded.

He was falling hard and quick. Too hard? Too quick?

His senses told him Terri Mitchell was solid gold. His

doubts weren't about her. They were about her past and the pain she was still carrying.

With care and patience, they could handle anything that was thrown at them. He was sure of it...

He pushed away a second shadowy whisper of prescience.

CHAPTER ELEVEN

'TERRI! You're here!' squealed Allie.

Luke's head snapped around as his daughter dropped the cutlery she'd been setting out on the table to race over and hug their guest. Hard to believe from Allie's behaviour that she'd seen Terri only a matter of hours ago. Though he certainly couldn't chip her on her over-enthusiasm, given the great line of somersaults his own gut was doing.

'Come and see where we've put the rose I picked for Mum,' said Allie. 'We planted it as soon as we got home. Granddad had the garden all ready.'

'Give Terri a chance to say hello to everyone else before you start dragging her off, Allie,' Luke said, placing the chairs he'd been carrying around the table. *Give her a chance to say hello to me.*

'Hi, Luke.' Terri's smile was wary as he drew near and put his hand on her shoulder. He leaned forward to give her a peck on the cheek. Low down, right beside her mouth. Her skin was soft beneath his lips. She smelled delicious, fresh soap, light fragrance. All woman. All Terri.

'I brought a bottle of wine.' She stepped back and thrust a bottle into his hands.

He looked at the label, giving himself a precious moment to regroup. A South Australian white wine. 'Thanks. You must be psychic. Mum's baking fish on the barbecue.'

'Not so psychic.' She grinned. 'I spoke to Vivienne when we got home from the nursery earlier.'

'Clever, then.'

The back door opened. 'About time you showed yourself around here, young lady,' said Will as he carried the large bowl of salad to the table and then crossed to hug Terri. 'I was starting to wonder what that new hospital director had done with you.'

Unexpected heat crept into Luke's face. He knew what the new director had been doing with her.

And what he planned to do, given half a chance.

'Oh, just the, um, usual. You know, work, work ,work,' Terri said with a weak laugh. Her cheekbones flushed becomingly as her eyes slid in Luke's direction and then quickly away.

Will frowned. 'Humph. I still say the board did the wrong thing by you.' Luke stifled a sigh when his father shot him an ambiguous look. 'I told Luke he was stepping on toes. You did an excellent job as acting director.'

'Thank you, Will, but it's working out well having Luke in charge.' This time, when she slanted a look at Luke, she met his eyes. He enjoyed the tiny conspiratorial moment. 'We've got the new boy licked into shape now and you know how much I detest paperwork. We don't let Luke go home until he's cleared his desk.'

'Like me with my homework,' said Allie with a big grin. The way his father and daughter responded to Terri was beautiful.

'Exactly like that.' Terri smiled as she ran a hand down Allie's stubby ponytail. 'Yes, I think your father's proving to be quite satisfactory, Allie.' She looked at him from under her lashes. 'All things considered.'

'Thank you for that faint praise,' Luke murmured, feeling close to tongue-tied. She was flirting with him. His heart wobbled and then melted.

'Oh, it's important to give encouragement…where it's deserved, of course,' she said, obviously struggling to keep a straight face. Her lovely brown eyes were alight with laughter. 'And a reprimand where it's not. I'm sure, as the new director, you'd agree, Luke.'

'I do agree.' Luke smiled, sending a promise of private retribution in his gaze.

Her answering smirk had his overworked pulse leaping about in anticipation.

His father's expression eased into a relieved grin. 'As long as the two of you are working it out.'

Luke could see Terri's teasing had been a thousand times more effective than all his attempts to soothe his father's concerns.

'Now, can I show Terri the garden?' said Allie in long-suffering tones.

'Sure,' said Luke. 'Don't be too long, though. Dinner's nearly ready.'

'Come on, Terri.' Allie took Terri's hand and tugged her along the path.

As they disappeared round the side of the house, his father said, 'Perhaps I should go, too. Terri might appreciate my tips for growing roses.'

'Perhaps another time, Dad.' With only the smallest trace of guilt Luke handed the wine bottle to his father. 'Terri brought this. Would you mind putting it on ice?'

He set off down the path after Terri and Allie, leaving his father to draw his own conclusions.

* * *

'Oh, this is gorgeous,' said Terri, when she saw the neatly laid-out garden.

'Dad put up the arch and we both planted the rose. See, it'll grow up all over the trellis.' Allie waved her hands expansively to demonstrate. 'I put in the little plants where Granddad said. And we have this bench. Come and try it.' Allie sat on the concrete seat and patted the area beside her. 'There's thyme on the ground underneath. It grows flat so when you stand on it, it smells nice.'

'You've all done a fabulous job.' The fresh clean aroma of the herb rose to greet Terri as she sat on the bench.

'Yes.' Allie's face held deep satisfaction. 'Dad said Mummy would like it.'

'I'm sure he's right,' Terri said, a lump in her throat. Sue-Ellen had been a much-loved wife and mother. What a wonderful epitaph to have earned.

'Yes.' Allie leaned sideways and rested her head on Terri's upper arm.

The simplicity of the moment was a gift that had Terri's heart stuttering. A snug, warm band tightened around her chest as she looked down on the dark head.

'And how are *you* now, Allie?' she asked softly.

'I'm good. Daddy said you and him might go out sometimes.'

'Did he?' Terri swallowed. 'Well, we might. Is that okay with you?'

'I think it'd be cool and I'd be able to come, too, sometimes, wouldn't I? Like today with the plants.'

'Of course. I'd like that.'

Terri looked up and saw Luke. He'd propped one shoulder against the smooth trunk of a gum, hands in the pockets of his jeans. He'd obviously showered and changed not long before she'd arrived because his hair was still dark and spiky with dampness.

His face, as he looked at Allie, glowed with love and pride. But when he moved his eyes to her, Terri read something different altogether. Dangerous. Seductive. Irresistible.

Her heart jolted, her defences crumbling. In that moment she realised she had little hope of protecting herself against this man and his daughter. By sharing themselves so unconditionally, they'd made a serious chink in her armour.

It was more than she'd ever thought she'd have in her life. More than she deserved.

A shadow passed over her spirits. Would she end up letting them down, failing them in some way she couldn't predict?

She would have to make sure she didn't.

Terri worked her magic effortlessly on his whole family, Luke realised as he looked around the table a couple of hours later.

He took a sip of wine as he watched his mother. Her face was alight with laughter at something Terri had said as the two of them stacked the dishes from the meal.

His mother obviously adored Terri…and this from the woman who'd given him and Kevin such a hard time about their motorcycles.

Carrying a pile of plates, Terri set off towards the house. Luke ran his fingers absent-mindedly over the rounded belly of his wineglass and down the stem to the base as his eyes followed her slender figure. She moved gracefully with effortless elegance. Womanly curves, nicely proportioned. Long, long legs. He suppressed the urge to gulp. Altogether a *very* nice package.

'Earth to Luke?' He started slightly and glanced up to find

his sister standing beside him, a grin on her face. 'Have you finished with your glass?'

He handed it over silently and Megan walked after his mother and Terri.

His sister. Another member of his family under Terri's spell. It was Megan who had sensed that Terri might help Allie. By taking her down to visit at the beach cottage, a link had been established between his daughter and the woman who had saved her life only a matter of days later. That link had set up the trust that had enabled Allie to confide her agonising guilt and set her on the road to recovery.

His father had thawed completely after Terri's banter. Anxiety that she felt displaced by the hospital board's decision was understandable. At least now, with concern eased, Luke would be able to get a better idea of how the man was coping psychologically after the heart attack. It was a relief because the faint ongoing hostility hadn't been good for any of them.

They were all putty in Terri's hands—including himself. Any way she wanted to handle him was just fine with him. Any way at all. The sooner the better for his sanity…

'Nice girl.' His father broke into his thoughts. 'Something special.'

Luke swallowed and hoped the rush of heat warming his face wasn't visible in the dusk. He yanked his thoughts back into line and looked across at the older man.

'Terri,' his father clarified, arching one eyebrow at him.

Luke cleared his throat. 'Yes, she is.'

'Allie likes her.'

'She does.'

'So does your mother.'

'Mmm.' Luke looked into his father's interested gaze. 'What are you getting at, Dad?'

'Nothing. Just making an observation.' Will brushed the leg of his shorts. 'Your mother would like to do some travelling.'

'Would she?' It was a curious segue. Luke wondered what was coming next.

'She's been at me again to retire.'

'Has she? How do you feel about that?'

'I used to think it was a ridiculous idea.' He sighed then continued after a moment, 'But since the heart attack...'

'You're thinking about it seriously, then?'

'Today, anyway.' A wry smile curled his father's mouth. 'Maybe tomorrow I'll change my mind. Anyway, I thought I'd float the idea at you, just in case. I'm sure the board would look favourably on you taking the director's job permanently. If you wanted it.'

'Okay. Thanks for the heads up.'

'Would you want it?'

'I'm not sure, Dad. I'd have to think about it. Sound Allie out. I promised her we'd only be here for a year.'

'She seems to have settled in.'

'She has now.' *Thanks to Terri.*

There was a companionable silence for a few minutes and then his father said, 'Well, it's something for you to think about.'

'Yes, it is.'

The back door opened and Terri came out with a coffee pot in hand. Allie, her faithful shadow, was beside her, holding the sugar bowl. His mother followed a few steps behind with the mugs.

Conversation meandered through various topics for another half an hour and then Terri stood.

'I should make tracks,' she said, turning to his mother. 'Thank you for a wonderful evening, Vivienne.'

'You know you are always welcome, Terri. Don't be a stranger.'

Luke rose, too. 'I'll walk you home.'

'Oh, no need.' Terri tucked a curl behind her ear. 'I can practically see my place from here.'

'That's a good idea, Luke,' said his mother. Luke blessed her and her fondness for observing the niceties. Never mind that Terri wandered backwards and forwards between the hospital and the cottage at all hours of the night when she was on call.

Good manners would be observed. And in this case, it definitely worked to his advantage.

He smiled at Terri, who made a small grimace at him.

'I'll be back shortly, Allie,' he said.

'No worries, Dad.' Allie beamed at him. 'Don't hurry. I'll go up to bed.' She gave a theatrical yawn. 'You can kiss me goodnight when you come back.'

'Er, right.' He stared at her as she kissed her grandparents.

Confident of her welcome, Allie walked over and put her arms around Terri's waist for a quick hug. 'Thanks for coming shopping with us today.'

'Thank you for asking me, Allie. I enjoyed it.' Terri smiled, her face soft with affection as she looked at his daughter.

'Goodnight.' With one last fierce look at him, Allie set off towards the house.

As he crossed the grounds with Terri, Luke was aware of everything about her. The way her slim arms swung slightly at her sides, the way her hair slipped forward when she bent her head.

'This is so silly, you walking me home.' Her voice was light and quick.

He detected the tiniest tell-tale catch. Wicked anticipation curled through his gut. 'It's what a well-mannered boy does at the end of a date.'

She rolled her eyes at him. 'This wasn't a date. It was an invitation from your mother, I seem to recall.'

'Ah, good point. That makes it even more significant than any ordinary date.' He nodded sagely. Out of the corner of his eye, he saw her misstep and reached out to steady her.

'Sorry?'

'You've had your feet under my parents' dining table.' He left his fingers curled around her arm as he expanded on his theory. 'In dating traditions, that's an important milestone.'

There was a small silence and then she teased, 'Does it count when it's outdoor furniture? Surely it's much too casual.'

'A table is a table. Tradition isn't fussy.'

'It certainly isn't when you're making up the rules.' She laughed as they approached the narrow line of trees that separated the house from the lower yard.

'Tsk. I'm starting to wonder if you're going to renege on that other time-honoured end-of-date tradition.' Her cottage was just ahead. Too close.

'It depends *which* tradition you're thinking of,' she said, not backing down an inch. '*Some* traditions might earn you a slap for your trouble.'

Heat sizzled along his nerve endings as his imagination conjured a scenario that would definitely earn him a slap. He swallowed the groan that crept up his throat. Being with her like this made him want to throw caution to the winds and find out.

'That's not what you said the other night.' He followed her up the front steps.

'That was then. This is now. Besides, a gentleman wouldn't remind a lady of her moment of weakness.' At the door, she turned to face him.

He braced his hand on the frame and looked down at her. Her light fragrance teased his senses. He resisted the urge to lean forward and breathe deeper. 'I'm not feeling much like a gentleman tonight.'

'Aren't you?'

'Nope. Invite me in.'

'And find out? I don't think so.' She flicked her hair back in a quick nervous gesture that made his pulse leap. 'You're in a peculiar mood.'

'Yeah, I am,' he murmured, reaching out to run his fingers along her jaw. 'So how are my chances for a kiss goodnight, then?'

'If we're taking things slow and sensible, they should be zero.' Her voice was ragged as he curved his fingers around the back of her neck and tilted her chin up with his thumb.

'Should be?' He bent and brushed his mouth across hers. Once, twice. She resisted him. On the third brush, her mouth softened, moved. Heaven. Sensitive nerve endings in his lips revelled in the warmth and sweetness. His muscles quivered as he ruthlessly suppressed the need to take more, take it deeper.

Take it all.

He caught her lower lip between his and sucked gently before moving his mouth across her cheek to the column of her throat just below her ear. When she arched her neck slightly to give him better access, he nibbled his way down to the nape.

'Oh. You are too good at this,' she moaned as a shudder ran through her. 'W-we should s-stop now. Please.'

He took a deep breath, inhaling her scent as he reached for control. He closed his eyes and rested his forehead in the curve of her shoulder. Her skin felt warm and alive beneath his brow.

'This is a bad idea.'

'Right this minute, it feels pretty good to me.'

'Yes,' she breathed. 'Me, too.'

He pressed his lips to her throat, felt the frenzied beat of her carotid pulse, felt her muscles move in a swallow. His heart leapt with the confirmation that she was as affected as he was.

'But that's in *this* moment.' Her voice was more determined. She shifted, inching away.

He let her. She was going to make him go. He moved back, his hand still braced on the doorjamb. His eyes moved over her face, taking in each fine feature. 'You don't think we should seize the moment, explore the possibilities.'

'It's not necessarily a bad thing. To leave possibilities unexplored.'

'Only if we're faint-hearted. Are we going to be faint-hearted, Terri?'

'Tonight? I... Yes. Yes, I believe we are. Goodnight, Luke.' She groped behind her back and the door swung open. He saw a gleam of white as she smiled then backed inside. 'Thank you for the escort home. See you on Monday.'

He smiled back. 'Monday.'

The door closed gently. He lifted his hand, spread his fingers on the wood and after a moment said softly, 'Lock your door, Terri.'

'I will.' Her voice came from just the other side of the door.

The latch clicked into place. In spite of his frustration there was some small comfort in the thought that she'd loitered there. Was she as torn as he was? He'd like to think so.

Terri pressed her hand to her sternum, feeling her wild thump of her heartbeat begin to settle as she listened to Luke's footsteps.

She felt so much, wanted so much when she was near him.

He made her wonder just how truly deep and beautiful a

relationship between a man and a woman could be. Made her wonder what it could be like between *them*.

How foolish she'd been to think they could agree on slow and sensible and keep things under control. Her hunger was unnerving and she sensed Luke's matched it. They were both too eager to take the next step.

It had taken all her willpower to resist inviting him inside.

Regardless of how tempting it was to throw caution to the winds, there was too much at stake for both of them. Professionally, personally and emotionally.

CHAPTER TWELVE

Two weeks later, Luke shrugged into his grey suit jacket and straightened his red tie.

Red for confidence, red for determination.

Red for passion and daring.

Excitement spiralled through his lower abdomen. He hadn't been this wound up about a date since he'd been a teenager.

An evening with Terri. Alone. Just the two of them… He chuckled softly. And a restaurant full of people, of course.

He picked up his car keys and wallet from the end of the bed then walked along the hall to his daughter's bedroom.

'Allie, let's go.' He tapped at her door. There was no reply. 'Allie?'

The door was slightly ajar so he pushed it open to see his daughter sitting on the edge of her bed, looking glum.

He frowned. 'Honey, what's wrong?'

'Nothing.' She studied the tips of her new sandals, refusing to meet his eyes.

She'd been fine half an hour ago when he'd gone to have his shower and get dressed for tonight. What had happened between then and now?

'Are you sick?'

A shake of her head.

He crossed to sit beside her, his hand automatically moving to her forehead. Her skin was cool to his touch and she wasn't having any obvious trouble with her breathing.

Silent alarm bells went off. Was it a return to the troubled days where Allie had been sullen and uncommunicative? His earlier excitement fizzled out abruptly. He wasn't going to leave it this time. He wasn't going to let her shut him out.

Maybe Allie didn't like the idea of him dating Terri after all. They'd discussed it but perhaps she'd changed her mind now that it was about to happen.

'Come on, Allie. What's going on?'

Her bottom lip wobbled.

'I'm staying right here until you tell me.'

'You can't.'

He took a slow deep breath in and let it out as he strove for patience. He couldn't believe it. Over the last couple of weeks he and Allie and Terri had spent a lot of time together. It'd been fantastic. But now it looked as though Allie's morose mood *was* to do with Terri.

'I can. You and I are getting to the bottom of this even if it means I have to cancel tonight. Terri will understand.'

'Oh, no!' Allie's gaze flew to his, wide with dismay. 'You can't do that.'

Her vehemence made him raise his eyebrows. 'So talk to me.'

She looked back at her shoes. He clenched his jaw and set himself to wait for as long as it took. After a moment, she mumbled, 'I don't see why I can't come, too. I'll be good and I can help.'

'Help?' He heard the strangled note in his voice.

The relief was so overwhelming, he had to work to suppress a great shout of laughter. Allie was happy for him to go out with Terri—she just objected to being left behind.

'Yes.' She looked at him, her face suddenly alight with enthusiasm. 'You know. With ideas and stuff. We had heaps of
fun at the movies, didn't we? And Terri likes me.'

'We did have fun and I appreciate that you want to suggest things to do,' he said carefully. 'But I'd like some time
with Terri so we can talk about things that would be boring
for you.'

'You mean like work things and that.'

'Like that.' He nodded.

'Will Terri want to do that, too?' Allie looked doubtful

'Yes,' he said firmly. 'She will.'

'Oh. All right, then, I guess.' She plucked the hem of her
shorts. 'Will you kiss her?'

Definitely.

Absolutely.

One hundred percent guaranteed.

But was Allie ready to hear that yet? She was used to
seeing him and Terri holding hands but was more going to be
difficult for her to handle yet?

A split second later, she said, 'I think you should.
Otherwise she won't know that you like her.'

He swallowed. 'Okay, then I'll make sure that I do. Are you
ready to go over to Nana and Granddad's?'

'Yep.' A small resigned sigh escaped as she stood and
picked up her backpack.

'Got your pyjamas? Toothbrush?' He reeled off the items
as they walked through to his parents' wing.

'Yes, Dad.'

'Inhalers? Drawing book?'

'Yes, Dad,' she said with a roll of her eyes.

'Pencils, Rubbers? A kiss goodnight for your father?'

She giggled. 'Probably.'

After he'd dropped Allie off with his mother, Luke jogged down the steps to his car.

It was his birthday.

He knew what he'd like from Terri as a present. Perhaps she'd let him put his order in.

He grinned. Or perhaps not.

Whatever happened, he was looking forward to having a great time. Slow and sensible might be agonising for him on one level but it was worth it. Terri was letting down her defences, relaxing with him. That was worth every bit of physical suffering.

Terri's heart lurched when she heard the knock at her door.

Luke.

Fortifying herself with a deep breath, she smoothed her hands down the heavy silk of her cheongsam and walked through the hall.

She'd shared wonderful family outings with Luke and Allie recently but this was different. This was their first real date.

The man waiting for her at the front door was starting to mean more to her than was sensible.

She turned the handle and opened the door, her pulse tripping crazily. He looked formal and so handsome dressed in a charcoal-grey suit.

'Hi.' Her grin felt wobbly.

'Hi, yourself.' His voice was husky. The broad smile on his face faltered as he ran his gaze down her length and slowly back up. 'You look fabulous.'

His eyes were dark and intense when they focussed on hers again, his mouth moving in a small enigmatic smile that had her catching her breath.

'Thank you,' she managed. 'You, too.'

He stared at her a moment longer. 'Ready to go?'

'Yes. I just need to get my purse from the kitchen.' She should have brought it with her to the door, she thought as he followed her down the hall.

She grabbed it off the table and turned to find him right in front her. Her eyes were level with his mouth.

He leaned forward, still not touching her. Her fingers tightened on her purse. The tiny beads pressing into her skin as her breath caught in her chest.

All she had to do was step back.

She didn't move.

His head tilted, moved closer, lips hovering over hers.

Closing her eyes, she waited. Sensations bombarded her, the musky scent of his aftershave, his breath feathering across her cheek.

And finally the delicious touch of his mouth on hers. Light and sweet and lingering with a hint of leashed passion. Her system quaked as she recognised a deep feminine desire to surrender.

He pulled back and she opened her eyes slowly.

'Mmm…nice.' His blue eyes were slumberous and inviting. 'I have it on good authority that's how I can let you know I like you.'

Laughter gurgled up her throat, catching her unawares, relieving the heavy sensual tension. 'Allie's been giving you dating advice again?'

'She has.' He grinned. 'Miss ten-going-on-twenty.'

His hooded gaze slid down to her lips. 'Though I think she's onto something with this idea. I should tell you…I like you.' He waited a beat before adding, 'A lot.'

She laughed again as he waggled his eyebrows at her. 'I'll consider myself duly warned.'

'I was afraid you'd say that.' He smiled wryly and held out his elbow. 'Shall we go? Your chariot awaits, my lady.'

She braced her jelly-filled knees and took his arm, feeling the strength there, allowing herself to be swept along by his old-fashioned chivalry.

Terri followed the waiter through to their secluded table by the large window. Luke's hand was spread over her spine, just below the small of her back. The contact felt intimate, made her acutely aware of her body, her movements. The sway of her hips, the tiny brush of her stocking-clad thighs against each other, the way her buttocks moved with each step she took in her high heels. Did he realise how astonishingly seductive it felt? She wanted to wiggle, just a little, to see if he would slide his hand even lower.

Heat raced across her skin, radiating out from his hand and spreading deep into her abdomen. She took a quick gulp of air and huffed it out. She didn't have to worry about Luke behaving tonight—she was doing a fine job of seducing herself.

Regret and relief vied for the upper hand when the wicked, tempting hand was removed so Luke could pull out her chair.

'Thank you,' she murmured. She looked around as Luke took his seat. The restaurant was in an old converted warehouse adjacent to the wharf. The seafaring theme was tastefully done with gleaming brass fixtures and dark wood panels. Strategically placed fishing nets had been draped across the upper walls with glass floats dotted here and there.

Candles in thick glass bowls graced each table and cast a romantic light.

'I'd heard this place had been done up,' she said, meeting Luke's gaze across the table. 'I've been meaning to come here for a meal.'

'I brought Sue-Ellen—' He stopped, his mouth twisting in a grimace. 'Sorry, I didn't mean... It's not a good way to impress my date for the evening, is it?'

'Don't apologise. Why wouldn't you mention her? She was a big part of your life. Yours and Allie's. It's good for Allie that you talk about her mother.'

'Thank you.' His voice was gravelly. 'You're a very special woman, Terri.'

She grinned, making light of the comment. 'I'm glad you think so.'

The waiter returned with the menus and wine list.

'Any preferences for wine?' Luke asked.

'White as we're having seafood but other than that I'm leaving it entirely up to you.' She looked over the delicious selection of dishes on her menu.

The waiter took their orders and returned a few minutes later with the bottle of wine. He filled their glasses and snuggled the bottle into the ice bucket. When the man had gone, Luke lifted his glass.

'To us. To slow and sensible.'

To slow and not so sensible. Terri bit her tongue to prevent the amended toast from escaping. She quickly tapped her glass to Luke's and concentrated on the wine. The cool rich liquid left a delicious lingering taste of oak. 'Mmm, lovely. Good choice.'

She met his eyes across the table. 'Allie's spending tonight with Vivienne and Will?'

All night?

No, no, no. She *wasn't* going to ask that. She didn't need to know.

'Reluctantly, yes.' Luke gave her a wry smile. 'She wanted to come with us to make sure we had fun. She's worried about whether I'll be able manage on my own.'

'Ah, more dating advice?'

'Yes. We…' He cleared his throat and she wondered what he'd been going to say. After a moment, he continued, 'I must remember to remind her about this in a few years when she starts dating.'

Terri chuckled. 'She'll be mortified.'

'I'm counting on it.' His quick laugh made her pulse skip.

He put down his glass and reached across the table to cover her hand with his. His voice was soft and husky as he asked, 'So, how am I doing? Are you having fun?'

'Oh, definitely.' With an effort she managed to keep her tone light. 'I promise to send you home with a glowing report card, lots of gold stars.'

His eyes sparkled with a dark, sensual invitation. 'In that case, I promise to do my best to earn every single one.'

Her heart did a slow, painful somersault into her throat, completely blocking her ability to reply.

When his hand slid away from hers a moment later in a smooth caress, she nearly protested. It wasn't until his gaze released hers that she realised the waiter was standing beside them, holding their meals.

She let out a slow breath and looked at her wineglass. Only one tiny sip and good sense had deserted her. She felt sinfully frivolous, intoxicated. *Luke*. She was tipsy with the heady influence of his company.

'Thank you,' she murmured to the waiter as she smoothed the napkin on her knee. She'd ordered pan-fried fillets and they looked delicious with their crispy, golden-brown coating and side order of thick roasted-potato wedges. A bowl of tossed salad sat in the middle of the table for them to share.

'Everything all right?'

She looked up to see Luke watching her. Her world seemed to tilt even further off its axis.

'Yes, perfect.' She forced her mouth into what she hoped was a reassuring smile and picked up her knife and fork. 'This looks wonderful.'

Now all she had to do was eat it. Laughing and flirting with Luke had wiped out her appetite for food completely.

'Did I tell you Dad's talking about retiring?' he said.

Thank goodness. A *safe* topic. Something to take her fertile mind off her overwhelming sensual awareness of the man opposite her.

'Is he?' She cut off a small forkful of fish, relieved when it melted in her mouth and slid easily down her throat.

'Mmm.'

'I know your mum would like him to take things a bit easier but I got the impression that he was adamant that it wasn't going to happen any time soon.' A second mouthful. She was getting the hang of this.

'He's mentioned it twice now with no prompting so I think he's seriously considering it.'

'Viv would be pleased, even if he only scaled back his hours.'

'Yes, she would.' Luke rested his knife and fork on the edge of his plate and reached for his wineglass.

There was a small silence during which Terri managed another couple of mouthfuls.

'Dad asked if I'd be interested in staying on in the director's position.'

The potato seemed to congeal into an unswallowable lump in her throat.

Luke.

Staying here.

Not going home to England. She couldn't make up her

mind if it was excitement or dread fizzing along her nerve endings.

She grabbed her glass and took a mouthful, using it to push the potato down her throat. 'Did he?' She put her glass back on the table. 'What do you think you'll do?'

He shrugged slightly. 'I'm not sure. There's no hurry to decide right now, but it's something to think about.' His gaze captured hers. 'It's been good to come home.'

Her chest tightened. She looked down at her plate, went through the motions of taking another forkful of food. 'How do you think Allie would feel about it?'

'I'd have to talk to her, of course.' He swirled the liquid left in his glass. 'But again, it's not something I need to do immediately. She's made great progress since you got us talking. I don't want to throw anything disruptive into the mix yet.'

'Yes. Although I think she's quite resilient now that burden of guilt has gone. She's really blossoming.'

'She is, isn't she? Maybe I'll sound her out to see if her ideas about Port Cavill are more open now.' His smile was filled with affection. 'What about you?'

'Me?' Her eyes flew to his. 'You have to make the best decision for you and Allie.'

'That's true.' His eyes narrowed and she had the feeling his attention was suddenly scalpel sharp. 'But what I was really asking was, what is your vision for *your* future?'

'Oh.' She pushed half a wedge of potato aside then carefully laid her knife and fork together in the space she'd created. Her fingers returned to adjust the position of the utensils before she moved the plate. 'When I came here, I— I didn't have a vision beyond putting myself back together after…'

'After Peter's death?'

'Yes.' She touched the base of her glass, twisting it slightly with her fingertips. 'After Peter's death.'

'What about now?'

'Now?'

'Now that things have changed.' With his elbows on the table, he steepled his fingers and looked at her intently. 'Now that you're in a relationship. How do Allie and I factor in your life?'

'Oh. I'm—I'm not sure I want to look too far ahead.' If she did, she'd have to face the fact that she hadn't been scrupulously open with him. She'd have to face the things she'd baulked at telling him.

His expression fell for the tiniest instant before he covered his reaction. She'd disappointed him, hurt him. Shame cramped deep in her chest. She looked through the window at the lights reflected on the glass-smooth water of the sheltered port. In a way, Luke had offered her a safe place in the haven of his family and all she could do was selfishly protect herself. He deserved better. She wanted to give him something…

'Luke…you and Allie are the most beautiful things that have happened in my life for the longest time.' Her voice choked with emotion. 'You're both very dear to me. More than I can say.'

'Thank you,' he said softly, his fingers curling around hers. His smile was so sweet that the tears gathering at the back of her eyes pressed for release. 'I'm glad. You're very dear to me, to us.'

There was a small silence. Part of her wanted to hide from the power of her feelings. The other part revelled that she could feel so intensely.

'Excuse me, sir, would you like to order dessert now?'

'No, thank you,' Luke said, still not taking his eyes off her. 'I think what we'd like to do now is have a dance.'

'Yes,' she whispered. 'That would be lovely.'

As the waiter cleared their plates away, Luke took her hand and threaded his way through the tables to the dance floor.

Dreamy notes from the string quartet had lured many other dancers to the floor already. He stopped at the edge of the floor and took Terri's other hand, guiding her into his arms. She came to him smoothly, fitted perfectly, as he'd known she would. Her lithe body swayed to the rhythm in easy, seductive movements.

He held her right hand, cradling it close to his chest. With his right hand splayed across her back, he felt the deep inhalation expanding her rib cage, then her exhalation whispered on the skin above his collar. A groan lodged in his throat. It was heaven and hell to hold her like this. He smiled slightly. He was going to enjoy every torturous, delicious moment of it.

He tucked her closer. 'This is nice.'

'Yes, it is.'

He could feel her fingers stroke along his collar. God, did she know what she was doing to him? He held his needs on a tight leash. They were making progress. Sure, it was slow but they were working towards something special, something lasting. A grab for quick gratification would ruin that.

He felt another inhalation, a tiny shiver through her slender frame.

'Luke?'

'Mmm?'

Her footsteps slowed to a halt and she leaned back in his arms. Wide and dark eyes looked into his.

'I—I want to stop being sensible.'

A hot streak of electricity jolted through him and his hand tightened on hers. He couldn't have spoken to save himself.

'Take me home, Luke. Please.'

'Hold that thought.' He steered her back to their table where the waiter met them with the dessert menu. 'I'm sorry but we're going to have to go. Would you mind organising the bill for me, please? I'll pay at the front register.'

'Of course, sir.'

Luke helped Terri with her lightweight shawl, his hands lingering on her shoulders before he tucked her hand into the crook of his arm. He was almost afraid to stop touching her in case the loss of contact gave her time to reconsider.

Foolish. If she changed her mind, he would find a way for that to be okay.

He brought her hand up to his mouth, kissed the delicate knuckles then let her go so he could sign the bill.

In the car, he drove feeling the weight of her silence. Was she even now thinking she'd made a mistake? He'd hurried her out of the restaurant with indecent haste.

He glanced across at her when he stopped to give-way to traffic at a roundabout. She was watching him, a small smile playing around her lips. She looked unexpectedly serene while he felt like a bundle of nervous energy.

At the beach cottage, she unlocked the door. He followed her inside, waited while she gracefully slid her shawl from her shoulders and draped it over a hook on the hall-stand.

She turned to face him then stepped close, her hands reaching for his tie.

He laid his hands over hers, stilling the fingers loosening the knot.

'Are you sure?' His voice was husky. How strange, he'd

been so worried she'd change her mind but now it was him giving her the opportunity to reconsider.

She sighed, her hands flattening on his ribs. 'Yes. And no.'

'No?' He made an effort to disguise the need that was thick in his voice. Was it possible to die of self-control? 'I don't want you to do anything you don't want to, darling.'

'I want to make love with you, Luke, but I'm afraid I'll disappoint you. I couldn't bear it.'

'You won't. You couldn't.' He gathered her into his arms, feeling his own nerves subside as he searched for the words to reassure her. 'This is us, Terri. Not a competition, not a race. We'll take it slow, we might have some hiccups, but it doesn't matter. We'll get there in the end, darling. Together.'

'Together. I—I'd like that.' Her lips pressed softly to his jaw, sending a thrill dancing through his body. 'Thank you.'

He turned his head, captured her mouth, felt the last tiny moment of hesitation evaporate as her lips opened for him and she kissed him back. She reached up to wind her arms around his neck, her body pressed to his, her breasts flattened on his chest, her belly aligned with his. They stood hip to hip and his heart nearly burst with huge, solid beats.

She pulled away and reached for his hand. 'Come with me.'

He followed willingly and found himself standing in her bedroom. Moonlight shone through net curtains, spilling across the double bed.

'I heard it's your birthday.'

'Yes,' he murmured.

'I—I wondered if you like the wrapping on your present.' She took his hand and laid it on the line of toggles along her collarbone.

'I love it.' He swallowed. 'Am I allowed to unwrap it now?'

'Yes, please.'

His eyes on hers, he released the first fastener. Moved to the second.

Terri ran her hands up the smooth thin fabric of his shirt, feeling the heat of his body on her palms. She released the buttons, impatient now to feel his skin on hers.

This man made her feel so special, so cherished. At this moment she wanted him more than she'd have ever believed possible. She wanted it all. Something to remember, something to hold dear in the future. He treated her with such care and affection that she wanted to weep.

They seemed to fit as though made for each other. No fumbling, no clumsiness. She revelled in his touch, her skin coming alive beneath his clever hands. It was special, satisfying, overwhelming. Enriching. She felt exotic and wicked and daring and courageous. He gave her all of that and more.

Much later, Luke propped himself up on one elbow and looked down at her.

'My head's spinning,' he said, as he leaned forward to kiss her lips.

She looped her arms around his back and smiled, not caring if her heart was in her eyes. 'Mine, too.'

He spread her hair over the pillow, slowly, as though he was enjoying running his fingers through the strands. 'I've been having fantasies about doing this.'

'Really?'

'Oh, yeah.' He smiled broadly. 'Remember that day at the nursery? Allie had to yell to get my attention.'

She laughed softly. 'She did have to call you a couple of times. You looked so guilty when you finally answered.'

His smile slowly faded. 'You know it's too soon for me to spend all night here with you.'

'I know.'

'I'd like to.'

'You've got a daughter who needs to be your first priority and that's the way it should be.'

'As long as you know I want to stay. Maybe, soon—'

'Hush, let's not try to make any time lines, Luke.' She put her fingers to his lips to stop the words. It was too soon and she wanted to revel in this moment. Bask in what they'd created here, together in the cocoon of her room, her bed. She didn't want to think about the outside world, the things she still needed to tell him. 'Let's enjoy what we have. Right now.'

He growled deep in his throat and gathered her close. 'I don't have to leave quite yet.'

'Mmm. Good.' She ran her hands up his back, loving the feel of his hard muscles tensing as he moved over her.

Later, she rolled on her side as he slipped out of bed. With her hand splayed over the sheet still warm from his body, she watched him dress.

'I'm not going because I want to,' he repeated as he shrugged into his shirt. 'Promise me you're not going to read anything into me leaving you like this, darling.'

'I promise,' she said obediently.

He fastened his trousers. 'Why do I get the feeling you're just saying that?'

She laughed at him. 'Now who's reading too much into things?'

'As long as I'm the only one,' he said with a sigh. 'I'll give you a ring tomorrow. We'll do something, a barbecue.'

'Okay.'

'Okay.' He stood juggling his keys in one hand, obviously still reluctant to go. 'Well…goodnight.'

'Goodnight, Luke.'

At the door, he turned. 'Promise me—'

'I do. Now, go home, darling.' She laughed.

'You called me darling.' He came back to the bed and leaned over to press another lingering kiss to her mouth. 'God, I wish I didn't have to go.'

'But you do. Now shoo.'

He sighed. 'Okay. I'll lock the door after me.'

After he'd gone, she flopped back on the pillow and stretched luxuriously. Luke was amazing, he made her feel like the most beautiful woman alive.

She laughed out loud at the happiness that fizzed along her veins.

Love. She was in love. How could she not love the man who made her feel so whole and normal?

A tiny doubt tried to creep in but she refused to let it, refused to listen to the malevolent voice that wanted to remind her about the things she hadn't told him about herself.

She'd faced so much in the last few years…surely she wasn't so bad for wanting to clasp *this* moment for herself, to hold tight to the present, not worry about the past and the future. Just for now.

CHAPTER THIRTEEN

'No REST for the wicked, you two.'

Terri looked around to see Dianne grinning at them from the doorway of the staff lounge.

'What's up?' Luke said.

'Three victims of a minor MVA on the way in. Details are sketchy but nothing serious by the sound of it. They've been scooped up by a Good Samaritan. ETA about five minutes.'

'Thanks, Dianne.' Luke picked up his mug and took a quick swallow as he rose to his feet. 'I'm on my way.'

'No worries.' The nurse gave them a quick indulgent smile and disappeared.

Terri's heart squeezed as Luke winked at her. He leaned down, his breath whispering over her ear as he murmured, 'I wonder how she knows we've been wicked, darling.'

She inhaled sharply then sputtered when her mouthful of coffee went down the wrong way. As she coughed, Luke helpfully patted her a couple of times between the shoulder blades.

'It might have something to do with being seen all over Port Cavill for the last two weeks holding hands,' she gasped between small coughs.

'Good point. Still, nice to have something true circulating on a hospital grapevine for a change.'

He looked so pleased with himself that she couldn't help laughing. Her own insouciance surprised her. The magic of her relationship with Luke had infected her with a carefree spirit that she hadn't felt for years.

Her gaze followed him to the sink, enjoying a quick feast on the lean length of him. She loved the way he moved, confident and full of masculine grace.

He turned, catching her eye, and his smile filled with mischievous intimacy. 'Relax and finish your coffee.'

'Thanks.' Her cheeks flooded with warmth as she grinned. 'I won't be long.'

A tiny shadow marred her happiness as she watched him leave the room. She still hadn't told him everything. Surely it wasn't so bad if she left it a little longer. Everyday was bringing her a greater sense of belonging, an easiness which meant the words, the courage would come soon.

She sighed as she got up and crossed to the sink. The little pact she was making with herself had disaster written all over it. This weekend. She would talk to Luke this weekend. That gave her just over three days to find the right way to broach the subject.

As she walked down the corridor, she saw Luke and Dianne heading towards the front door. The MVA victims must have arrived. She picked up her pace.

She turned into the main emergency foyer and the scene in front of her exploded into her senses.

A woman. Pregnant. Her groin and legs covered in red. Screams tore at Terri's ears.

'My baby. I don't want to lose my baby. Please, help me. I've hurt my baby.'

The air around Terri's legs turned to heavy syrup, dragging at her steps until she stopped. She felt disembodied. Time jerked past frame by frame.

'Pete! Where's Pete?' the woman sobbed. 'Our baby...'

Images flashed onto Terri's retinas, blotting out the scene before her.

Baby in peril.

Mother injured.

Blood everywhere.

Nausea swept up from her toes. She couldn't do this. Not again. She couldn't help them. She couldn't move.

Each pore on her skin iced over. She was failing.

Again.

Failing.

Luke flicked a glance at Terri.

Something was terribly, terribly wrong. She was rigid, face as white as a sheet, eyes fixed on the screaming woman.

'Terri!'

Oh, God. His voice wasn't reaching her.

He wanted to go to her, hold her, shield her from whatever nightmare was holding her in its thrall. He sensed Terri's crisis was the bigger emergency, but the patient in front of him was rapidly descending into hysteria.

'I've hurt my baby. Please, save my baby.' The woman clutched at his arm, dragging his attention back to her.

'We've got you now,' he said calmly. 'What's your name?'

'N-Nadia.'

'Nadia, we're looking after you and your baby. Are you in any pain?'

'N-no.' She hiccuped and looked at him in surprise. 'Not now.'

As he and Dianne settled Nadia on a gurney, Luke glanced across the foyer. Terri was gone.

It was paint, for God's sake. Nadia and her husband, Pete, had been travelling with an open can of paint—the pregnant woman had been holding it between her knees so she could stir it.

A contraction had caught them by surprise and Peter had driven into their front fence. With the impact, red paint had gone everywhere. A neighbour had piled the hapless pair into his car and brought them into hospital.

The contractions hadn't continued so no pattern has been established. Luke suspected it had been a set of Braxton-Hicks' contractions perhaps exacerbated by Nadia's fear. They'd keep her in hospital for a few hours and monitor her to make sure everything was as it should be. The baby's heart-beat was strong and regular.

He'd packed Nadia and her husband off to the showers to wash away the last of the paint and now he had to attend to the real emergency.

Terri.

'Anyone seen Terri?'

'I haven't seen her since…the call about Nadia and Pete,' Dianne answered, and the others looked around blankly.

'If you do, page me, stat. Please.' He ground his teeth. 'Same goes for any emergencies. I'm going to find her.'

Aware of the circle of concerned faces, he walked out of the department, leaving no words to soothe their fears. He had none.

Urgency drove his steps. He had to find Terri. She'd been shattered. Something about that case had pushed her into some private hell. He'd seen a glimpse of her terror before she'd disappeared. More than terror, she'd looked in danger of disintegrating.

He worked methodically, checking every room. Would she have gone all the way home? For some reason he didn't think she'd have been able to get that far.

She'd been like a wounded animal, looking for somewhere to tend her injuries, a private place.

He finally found her outside, behind the new gazebo. She was on her knees with her arms wrapped around her body. He could see her knuckles were white as though by gripping tightly she might hold herself together. But even that self-hug wasn't enough comfort for her. She rocked in a small rhythmic movement that broke his heart.

Weak sun shone on the chocolate of her hair, picking out bright threads of red and chestnut in the thick mane.

He crouched beside her, touched her lightly on the shoulder.

She jerked, her reflex beyond a normal fright response. He could feel the fine tremors that raced through her chilled flesh.

'Terri.'

The rocking started again.

'Talk to me, darling. Please.'

'No p-point. There's no point. It won't help. You can't help me. No-one can. G-go away. Please. Just…go away.'

He sat on the ground beside her, not caring about grass stains, and gathered her rigid body close.

'Tell me anyway,' he said as he rubbed her back.

For the longest silence, he just held her, rocked with her. Hoped that his body heat would help to thaw her.

'S-so much blood.'

'It was red paint.' But she didn't hear him.

'So much blood,' she whispered. 'She killed her husband, sh-she killed her baby.'

'No! No she didn't. Terri, listen to me. Her husband is fine. He's fine. She mightn't even be in labour.'

'But the blood…' She shuddered

He took her face between his hands.

'Terri. Look at me.' Her eyes slowly focussed on him. 'It wasn't blood.'

'N-not blood?' She sounded confused, as though he was speaking a foreign language.

'Paint. It was paint.'

'P-paint?' She tested the word as though trying to divine its meaning.

'Red paint. Nadia was in the car with an open can of red paint between her knees. She was stirring it.'

'I s-saw all the r-red.'

'I know, darling. I want you to come back now.'

'I c-can't. I mustn't. The b-baby…sh-she'll lose the -baby. You can't trust m-me.'

'What do you mean?'

'B-bad things happen. I killed my husband. I killed Peter.'

'The terrorists killed Peter.'

'And my b-baby. I killed my baby.'

'You lost your baby in the explosion?' Oh, God. How had he coped with that, alone, having just lost a husband as well? His heart ached for her. No wonder she was struggling.

'Yes. My fault. It was all my fault.'

'Why?' He needed to hear it all as much as she needed to tell him.

'I stayed too long. I stayed too long. I should have left as soon as I found out. But I didn't. I killed my baby.'

'Oh, darling, no. No, you didn't,' he said gently. 'You're a wonderful, brave woman who's carried a terrible burden all by herself.'

'My baby. My poor baby.' She made a strangled sound dee
in her chest and then the tears started in huge shuddering sob.
His heart broke for her. Just listening to her story was painf
beyond belief. He felt powerless in the face of her grief.

Her arms clung to him, desperation in their strength. A
he could do was hold her, be her rock. He was going to stan
by her, to help her heal. Hold her when she needed to cry, er
courage her when she was moving forward.

He would love her and protect her and support her unt
she was better.

And then, by God, she was going to marry him so he coul
love and cherish her as she deserved for the rest of her life.

Her sobs gradually quieted until the only sound was th
distant shushing of the waves.

Reluctantly, he broke the moment. 'Do you trust me
Terri?'

'Yes.' Her voice sounded raw from the weeping, still fu
of tears ready to be shed.

He was going to ask her to do more, to be braver. To d
something that he sensed she needed to do. A first minute ste
on the journey back to normality.

'I want you to come with me now. Come and see the youn;
couple who came in earlier. Nadia and Pete.'

'Nadia and P-Pete?'

'Yes.'

'I can't,' she said. With the storm of weeping over she'
moved into a passive acceptance of hopelessness. 'There's n
point. It's over.'

'You can.' He felt like such a bastard asking anything o
her when she was so raw and vulnerable. Setting his jaw, h
continued, 'Nothing is over. There's every point to coming
back.'

It was important not to let her withdraw. He was afraid for her, afraid for himself that he would lose her, if he let her retreat now.

'Come on. Wash your face, powder your nose, whatever it is that you need to do to face the world again today. Just for a few minutes.'

'I can't d-do anything for them. I ran away.' She looked at him through a welling veil of tears. 'I f-failed.'

He steeled himself against weakening. 'You ran away because you're traumatised. You haven't failed. I don't want you to do anything for them, I just want you to come and meet them. Not for long, just to see that they are okay. Come on, Terri. You can do it.'

She looked at him and then finally, she took a deep breath and said, 'I'll try.'

The bravery in those tiny, barely audible words brought a painful lump to his throat. 'That's all I'm asking, darling.'

Anxiety pinched at him as he helped her to her feet. She felt so shaky and frail. The last of her strength and vitality had leached away with her tears, leaving this frighteningly fragile husk.

He clenched his teeth. He needed to find out as much as he could about post-traumatic stress disorder. Stat.

Cuddling her close to his body, he walked her back to the building. Outside the women's bathroom he stopped and opened the door, ushering her inside. 'I'll wait outside. Yell if you need me.'

She nodded.

'I'll check on you in five if you're not out.'

She gave him a wan smile. 'I'll be out.'

'Okay.'

He shut the door behind him and braced one hand on the

wall. Terri needed his help and she was going to get it. Whether she wanted it or not. He was in awe of the fact that she'd come this far carrying the weight of her grief alone. But she didn't have to do it on her own from now on. She had him to help. He wasn't going to let her go. She would not shut him out, he wouldn't let her.

He felt a touch on his arm and turned to see Dianne looking up at him, her face creased with worry. 'Is Terri all right?'

'She's had a shock, Dianne. She'll be shaky for a while but she'll be all right. I'll make sure of it,' he said grimly.

'Good. If there's anything any of us can do, just say the word.'

'Thanks, Dianne.'

Luke kept the visit to the now-sheepish young couple short and upbeat before ushering Terri out of their room.

In the privacy of the staff lounge, he ran the backs of his fingers over her pale cheek. 'Go home, darling.'

'Luke, I think…' She took a deep breath in. 'I think I'd rather keep busy. Please?'

'Terri…love…you've had a hell of a shock. Cut yourself some slack and take the rest of the shift off. It's only an hour.'

She gave him a haunted look.

He stifled a sigh. 'Tell me honestly, do you feel up to being here?'

Her mouth opened then slowly closed, her shoulders slumping. 'No,' she whispered. 'No. You're right. There's no point being here.'

'Darling, go home. Rest, walk along the beach.'

She nodded.

'I'll come and see you as soon as I can.'

Another nod before she turned and walked away. He

watched her go. Had he done the right thing? But what else could he do?

She looked so crushed and utterly defeated that he almost called her back.

Just over an hour later, Luke took some correspondence back to his office. A single piece of paper lay in the middle of his desk. Cold inevitability gripped him as he leaned across and picked it up.

A resignation. Neatly typed. Terri must have gone straight home to write the damned letter.

No way was he going to let her run away like this. He couldn't. She needed help and support from people who loved her. Specifically, she needed *his* help, *his* support. He loved her.

He practised the persuasive words he'd use as he walked down to the beach cottage. When he got there the door was ajar but the place had an oddly deserted feel.

He knocked. Icy fear thrummed through him when there was no response. He yanked open the door then strode from room to room.

No sign of Terri but plenty of signs that she'd been here and been busy.

A suitcase lay open on the bed they'd made love in. Folded clothes sat in piles, waiting to be added to the case. As though she'd started packing but had been distracted from the task.

In the kitchen, pots and pans had been thrown haphazardly into a box on the bench. There was no chance that the lid could be fastened with the way handles bristled above the sides. At the other end of the bench was a stack of plates and a collection of glasses.

Without pausing, he opened the back door and stepped on to the verandah. A half-empty mug of coffee sat on the edge.

He could imagine her sitting here drinking it, staring towards the beach. Was that where she was now?

His pulse fluttered as he jogged off the verandah towards the trees. He didn't know what to expect, refused to think about what he might find.

She would be there.

She *would* be there…

And she was.

The tension in his body loosened abruptly, leaving his gut aching and his knees rubbery. She was sitting on the sand hunched over with her arms wrapped around her shins as she stared out to sea.

Jamming his hands into his pockets, he took a deep shuddering breath. Damp, briny sea air filled his lungs and he stood for a moment collecting his wits before he walked closer to his still oblivious target. When he was several feet from her, he stopped. Keeping his tone carefully neutral, he said, 'You've been busy since I saw you.'

She started as though he'd yelled at her.

'You know I'm not going to accept your resignation.' He stepped forward and lowered himself to the sand beside her, but not touching.

'You should.' She sounded so cold, so remote.

He had to connect with her so that she would listen to him. 'Why should I?'

Her head came around at his question and she looked at him. A frown slowly pleated her forehead as she thought about her answer. 'Because I can't be trusted. My judgement is flawed.' She shrugged and turned to face the water again. Her voice was too matter-of-fact for the agony behind the words she spoke. 'I'm so brittle I feel like I could fly apart.'

'Terri, you're suffering from post-traumatic stress disorder.'

She didn't acknowledge him.

He tried again. 'You need to get help so you can recover.'

Her gaze stayed on the horizon.

'You have so much courage. I'm asking you to use some now.' He watched her profile for any sign that he'd reached her. 'For me and for Allie. We need you. *I* need you.'

'Allie.' She shook her head and her chin trembled for a tiny fraction of a second. 'I don't know if I can be whatever it is that you need, whatever it is that she needs. You can't trust me to make good decisions.'

'I *can* trust you. I *do* trust you. It's you who doesn't trust you. And you should. You have wonderful judgement. Your thinking is just a bit scrambled at the moment because of your experiences.'

'You make it sound easy.' She shook her head. 'But it's not. I'm empty. You and Allie deserve more than I can give you.'

'Not true, darling. We deserve you. You're the person who saw what my daughter and I needed. You're the person who brought us together after months of grief.' He felt as though he was fighting a battle with no weapons, nothing to hold onto, nothing to let him see if he was making headway. He was losing her. 'I know it's not easy. I hear your pain, I felt your heartbreak when you cried in my arms.'

'Stop. Luke—'

'I know I can't understand what you're going through. But I know this, I'm here for you' He swallowed, feeling the crushing pain in his chest. 'I love you, Terri.'

Her hands came up to cover her face and her shoulders began to shake. *He'd reached her* but in doing so he'd given her more pain.

He pulled her into his arms and laid his cheek on her hair as he absorbed the tremors that shook her.

'It's okay, darling, it's okay.' He murmured the words ove
and over, knowing how very far from the truth they were.

At last, her sobs quietened.

'I feel broken.' Her voice was still thick with tears.

'You're in pain, darling, but the bits of you are all there
We'll find help and you can put them all back together again

'I feel so bad.' She took a deep shaky breath. 'What if
can't be fixed? What if this is me? What if…I can't be
doctor any more?'

'Then you can be anything you like.' He stroked her hai
'Be my wife.'

He felt shock ripple through her. He hadn't meant to sa
the words, not yet. But it was what he wanted. After
moment, she tipped her head back and looked at him.

'Marry me,' he said.

'Oh, Luke.' Her face screwed up in pain. 'I w-want to accep
your proposal s-so badly. But I c-can't. It wouldn't be fair.'

Pain squeezed his chest. 'To whom?' he asked softly.

'To you, to Allie.' She looked into the distance. 'Mayb
even to me.'

'Can you tell me why not?' He smothered the fear tha
clawed at him and held onto one tiny skerrick of hope. Sh
hadn't refused him outright.

'Because I don't think I know who I am any more. I nee
help to find out.' Her eyes came back to his holding a plea fo
understanding. 'What if I've changed? I'm not sure I ca
handle the weight of your disappointment.'

His spirits swooped but he made himself give her a nod o
reassurance. 'Then let's find you some help and see where i
takes you. I want to marry you, Terri. The offer is there, n
expiry or use-by date. And no pressure.'

'Thank you.' Her face was sombre.

He tightened his arms around her in a quick hug. 'In the meantime, I have more news,' he said dragging up the first change of subject that occurred to him. 'Ah, make that I have *lots of news* since I haven't told you what led up to it. Allie and I have been talking about staying in Port Cavill. We'll be house-hunting at the weekend. We want you to come.'

'You're staying? And you've talked to Allie about it?'

'Yes and yes. Um, I've been meaning to tell you,' he teased gently. 'But when I'm with you, I get sidetracked with other things.'

'Luke, that's wonderful.'

'I thought so.' He grinned at her. 'So how about it? Will you come with us? You'll know about workable room layouts and Allie tells me you have better decorating ideas than I do— you know, colours and that sort of thing.' He dragged out his best hopeless male look.

'I—I think I could manage that.' A relieved smile lifted the exhausted lines on her face.

His heart swelled with love. More than anything, he wished he could take away her sorrow and self-doubt. All he could do was wait, be there for support and encouragement.

And hope that when it was all over, he had a place in her life, her future.

Her heart.

CHAPTER FOURTEEN

Two months later.

'NOT there, Dad.'

Luke looked up from the bucketful of damp sand he'd just deposited at the intersecting corners of castle wall. 'What's wrong with here? I like it here.'

Allie giggled—a lovely warm happy sound. 'It's all wrong. It needs to be back further. We'll ask Terri.' She looked around to see if her consultant was back yet. 'She'll know how it should be.'

Luke suppressed a smile. Allie was right, Terri would know.

She'd been involved in every step of the house-hunting and under her inspired guidance the house had been decorated to suit a family. A perfect home for his family. Him-self, his daughter...

All it needed was a wife. And the perfect candidate for the post was coming through the tree line at the top of the beach, carrying a picnic basket.

'Okay, time for a break, workers,' Terri called. 'Come on. I've got sandwiches, watermelon, fruit juice and biscuits and fresh coffee.'

'Now you're talking.' He loped over to shake out the mat they'd brought down earlier. As soon as he'd laid it Terri and Allie lowered themselves into neat cross-legged positions. He sat beside Terri, his arm resting on his raised knee.

'Dad's put the corner thing in the wrong place, Terri.' Allie accepted a thick salad sandwich.

'Has he?' She looked at him under her lashes. 'Tsk. It's hard to get reliable serfs these days. So perhaps you can have two walls. You'll just have to get your dad to cart more sand.'

'Cool. That's what we can do, Dad.'

'Mmm, why didn't *I* think of that?' He sent a smouldering look Terri's way as she passed the plate of food to him.

She grinned and helped herself to a sandwich. 'Well, if you'd put the turret where you should have in the first place…'

He tugged the hair in the centre of his forehead. 'I'll try to do better, mistress.'

'Glad to hear it.' She exchanged a laughing look with him and his heart turned over. She was beautiful.

He was very proud of her. He wondered if he realised how far she'd come in the past two months. A spiral of excitement corkscrewed through him.

Day by day, she was relaxing a little more, gaining resilience, losing the haunted, frail look.

At the hospital, she was doing marvellous things. They'd discussed her hours and he'd pressed for her to come off the shift roster. But she'd been more than pulling her weight with running health clinics, reaching out to disadvantaged members of the community, organising preventative health initiatives.

In his life… He hadn't been pushing for intimacy in their relationship, knowing that he had to leave the pace up to Terri. Last night they'd made love. A thrilling heat ran through him at the memory of pleasure beyond anything he'd known.

If he spent the rest of his life worshipping her with his body he would be a very happy man.

After lunch, he cradled his coffee mug and watched Allie at the sandcastle. She had been joined by another couple of children and the three of them were working diligently.

'She's doing well,' Terri said.

'Very.' He swallowed the last of his drink and put the mug aside. 'Those breath exercises you taught her have been terrific. She's chasing me to make sure she does them.'

'Good for her. She's been one of my best pupils.' Terri laughed self-deprecatingly. 'But, then, I might be a little biased.'

The words gave him a warm glow. Terri cared, wanted the best for Allie and for him.

God, he loved her so much. He…

'Marry me.' He heard the words leaving his mouth, saw the twist of anguish flash across Terri's face.

In that one spontaneous moment he'd ruined everything. Why couldn't he have waited? Too late, he wished he could call the words back. He felt sick. She was going to say no.

'Luke…' She stopped, closing her eyes, gathering herself.

He should help her, say it was all right, say it didn't matter…that they'd still be friends.

But he couldn't do it—not even to spare the woman he loved from the agony of having to refuse him. His face felt numb as he waited for the sentence that would rip his heart out.

'You've been wonderful and I wouldn't have got this far so quickly without your support.' Her throat worked and he could see she was struggling to say the words. 'There's something that I have to tell you, something I've been hiding…even from myself.'

She looked at him and the sadness shadowing her eyes clawed at his gut. 'When I lost my baby…the placenta was

ipped from the wall of the uterus… Luke, I don't know if I'll
be able to have children.'

A family with him.

She wanted to have a family.

With him.

She looked at him solemnly. 'I can't marry you unless you
know that. I don't want it to come between us down the track.'

'I don't care.' He caught her by the upper arms and pulled
her into his embrace. 'I don't care. It's you I want. Only you.
If we had children together that would be wonderful, too. But
it's you I want.'

With his face buried in the crook of her neck and his eyes
squeezed shut, he took a deep breath. 'I'll sorry if it turns out
that you can't have children, but for you, darling, not for me.
You'd be a wonderful mother.'

He pulled back and looked at her. 'I love you. Marry me.'

Her eyes sparkled with unshed tears. 'Yes. I love you and
I'd love to marry you.'

'Yes!' He leapt to his feet, tugging her then scooping her
up to twirl her around.

'What are you guys doing?'

'Allie.' He laughed then sobered. He'd started preparing his
daughter for this possibility but had he done enough? 'Allie,
sweetheart, we're going to get married.'

'It's about time,' she said and her face split in a huge
smile. 'I suppose this means you're too busy to come and
carry sand.'

MEDICAL™ 2-in-1

Coming next month
THE SURGEON'S MIRACLE
by Caroline Anderson

Nurse Libby Tate had very good reasons for thinking that a high-society ball and an unexpected night of passion with paediatric surgeon the Hon. Andrew Langham-Jones couldn't possibly end with a pregnancy! But now that it has, Libby has a secret that could put their miracle baby and new-found happiness at risk…

DR DI ANGELO'S BABY BOMBSHELL
by Janice Lynn

Dr Darby Phillips needed a temporary date fast, and delicious doctor Blake Di Angelo seemed the perfect choice. But their little charade turned into romance for real – and now Darby must tell Blake he'll soon be hearing the pitter-patter of tiny feet!

NEWBORN NEEDS A DAD
by Dianne Drake

Brooding doctor Neil Ranard steers clear of relationships, but new (and pregnant) colleague Gabrielle Evans has somehow thawed Neil's guarded heart. And when he delivers her little son, Neil wants more than anything for them all to be a family!

HIS MOTHERLESS LITTLE TWINS
by Dianne Drake

Nurse Dinah Corday has received a warm welcome from everyone at White Elk – except from pediatrician Eric Ramsey! Yet this brooding doctor and his twin girls soon get under Dinah's skin…

On sale 7th May 2010

Available at WHSmith, Tesco, ASDA, Eason and all good bookshops.
For full Mills & Boon range including eBooks visit
www.millsandboon.co.uk

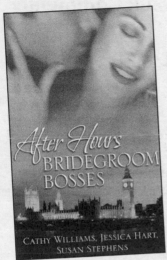

millsandboon.co.uk Community

Join Us!

The Community is the perfect place to meet and chat to kindred spirits who love books and reading as much as you do, but it's also the place to:

- **Get the inside scoop from authors about their latest books**
- **Learn how to write a romance book with advice from our editor**
- **Help us to continue publishing the best in women's fiction**
- **Share your thoughts on the books we publish**
- **Befriend other users**

Forums: Interact with each other as well as authors, editors and a whole host of other users worldwide.

Blogs: Every registered community member has their own blog to tell the world what they're up to and what's on their mind.

Book Challenge: We're aiming to read 5,000 books and have joined forces with The Reading Agency in our inaugural Book Challenge.

Profile Page: Showcase yourself and keep a record of your recent community activity.

Social Networking: We've added buttons at the end of every post to share via digg, Facebook, Google, Yahoo, technorati and de.licio.us.

www.millsandboon.co.uk

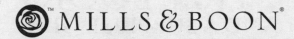

2 FREE BOOKS
AND A SURPRISE GIFT

We would like to take this opportunity to thank you for reading this Mills & Boon® book by offering you the chance to take TWO more specially selected books from the Medical™ series absolutely FREE! We're also making this offer to introduce you to the benefits of the Mills & Boon® Book Club™—

- **FREE home delivery**
- **FREE gifts and competitions**
- **FREE monthly Newsletter**
- **Exclusive Mills & Boon Book Club offers**
- **Books available before they're in the shops**

Accepting these FREE books and gift places you under no obligation to buy, you may cancel at any time, even after receiving your free books. Simply complete your details below and return the entire page to the address below. You don't even need a stamp!

YES Please send me 2 free Medical books and a surprise gift. I understand that unless you hear from me, I will receive 5 superb new stories every month including two 2-in-1 books priced at £4.99 each and a single book priced at £3.19, postage and packing free. I am under no obligation to purchase any books and may cancel my subscription at any time. The free books and gift will be mine to keep in any case.

Ms/Mrs/Miss/Mr _____ Initials _____

Surname _____

Address _____

_____ Postcode _____

E-mail _____

Send this whole page to: Mills & Boon Book Club, Free Book Offer, FREEPOST NAT 10298, Richmond, TW9 1BR